OUT OF THE FRYING PAN

C. David Cooper
PhD, PE, QEP
Professor Emeritus of Environmental Engineering

Independently Published

ISBN 9781973590446

Cover Art by Kelly Cooper Kwoka

Dedication

This book is dedicated to all my past students.

Foreword

This book is fiction – as is any book that portrays a vision of the future. Any resemblance to actual persons, living or dead, is purely coincidental. However, this book deals with a very real, present-day problem – one that is global in scope, potentially catastrophic in consequences, and politically beyond the power of any one nation to control. I am speaking, of course, of Global Climate Change (GCC) often called the Greenhouse Effect.

GCC refers to the far-reaching effects that the emissions of certain gases into the atmosphere are having on our weather and ecosystems. It is scientific fact that there have been steady increases of emissions of carbon dioxide, methane, and other greenhouse gases into our atmosphere during the past two hundred years. It is scientific fact that these gases absorb infrared radiation (heat) very effectively. It is scientific fact that the concentrations of these gases in our atmosphere have been increasing rapidly since the industrial revolution, and are now way above anything seen before. Emitted in enormous quantities from (mainly) the processing and burning of fossil fuels, these gases are causing our world to retain more heat energy. Ultimately, climate patterns will change on a global scale.

As I said earlier, this book is fiction, and any resemblance of its characters to real people, living or dead is unintentional. The story does contain many, many facts about GCC, but I have used literary license to exaggerate some effects and to compress the time scale of the warming in order to enhance the story. Nevertheless, the message is real. I hope someone out there is listening.

CHAPTER 1

Boston, December 8, 2017

C ome in.

Dr. Pitkowski looked up from his cluttered desk at the heavy wooden door, waiting for whoever had just knocked. He was in the middle of writing a paper on the chemistry of flames and was mildly annoyed that someone had interrupted his thoughts.

"Come in!" Pitkowski repeated, raising his voice to make it penetrate the thick door.

"Oh hi, Dr. P. I wasn't sure if I heard you say 'come in' or 'just a minute'."

"Zack - good to see you," Pitkowski said half-heartedly, glancing back at his desk. "Vot can I do for you today?" His heavy German accent made the "What" sound like "Vot."

"Did you see the news last night, Professor? Look what's going on in southern California – all those fires! Santa Ana winds of 70 mph, and so dry! Feeding all those fires in Ventura and Brentwood and Bel-Air. The national news said its summer-like conditions out there. They said more than 200,000 people have been evacuated, and when they showed people driving on the 405 freeway, it was like a scene from hell – the hills on both sides of the highway were nothing but huge flames. And just two months ago, they had those huge fires in northern California – entire neighborhoods burned to the ground – and no rain in sight! Very fitting for the Senate hearings on the Greenhouse Effect, don't you think? They're saying that 2017 is shaping up to be the hottest year ever, at least since they've been keeping weather records."

Zack continued enthusiastically, "Look who they've got testifying - Tim Ransen of NASA, Syuturo Wanashi of the Geophysical Fluid Dynamics Lab at Princeton, and Michelle Oberstein of the Environmental Defense Fund. And look at this quote from Senator John Bennett of Texas." Zack held up the paper and read aloud:

'We have only one planet. If we screw it up, we have no place else to go.'

"I mean, is that a great quote or what?" Zack was clearly excited, and eager for a response.

"Zachary, vot am I going to do vit you?" asked Pitkowski, in his heavy accent. "You are spending too much of your time on this greenhouse thing. What about all the snow they are having in the deep South right now? It is very unusual for Houston and southern Mississippi and north Florida to be getting snow, yes? So, I conclude that this is just normal variations of the veather."

"Professor, how can you say that? Climate Change is real, it's here! With more energy in the atmosphere, comes intense atmospheric circulation. Large masses of cold air can come ripping out of the polar region and reach all the way down into the south. The atmosphere is a lot more unstable – that's what causes these wild variations."

Zack was starting to get warmed up. He began gesturing more with his hands, and swinging his long arms back and forth as he spoke.

"Think about some of the other things that have been happening this year. Chickens were dying from the summer heat in the South; in the West there's still a major drought in progress. They're already comparing it to the great dust bowl days of the 1930's. Also, remember when President Trump had his picture in the paper in that cornfield in Illinois? Remember? The corn should have been above his head, but it was only up to his waist. He declared Illinois, Iowa, Kansas, and Nebraska disaster areas."

Zack was really windmilling his arms now. Pitkowski started to get worried that something would get knocked over.

Zack continued excitedly, "And not only are the fires destroying thousands of homes, the drought is destroying crops and cropland. Farmers are losing not just crops but also their soil. Millions of tons of rich, black topsoil have blown away in the last six months. The fires have burned nearly a million acres in Yellowstone - almost half the park! Between the fires and the soil dust, the air pollution blowing all the way into this part of the country is the worst it's been in thirty years."

Pitkowski eyed his graduate student with some alarm. Zack was now pacing and gesturing with abandon inside the small office. But along with his worry, the Professor felt a growing annoyance. He and Zack had had this kind of conversation more than a few times. And as he became more annoyed, his accent got more and more pronounced.

"Zachary, I've told you before, you cannot claim zat all zis is happening because of greenhouse effect. And I tell you again, zis is just natural variation of veather. People are getting too excited over zis. Yes, I know carbon dioxide level is rising, but earth has many, many feedback loops to help control temperature. Besides, I have my own research to do. I cannot try to be expert in all fields.

"Zack, you need to focus more on your own research. You are behind schedule, and I need your results. There are others who know far more than you or I about climate change. Let them vorry about the veather."

Zack's green eyes flashed momentarily as a surge of anger rose in him and was quelled. "But, Professor," he protested, "I'm really interested in the environment – I want to do <u>something</u> to contribute."

"No," said Pitkowski sternly, "you need to concentrate on your laboratory work. Zat is vot is funding my research, and zat is vot is paying your salary. And zat is vot you must do! Now do you understand me?"

"Yes, professor."

"Now, go back to your lab and get back to your work."

Zack left the office and walked slowly back to the lab. His shoulders were slumped, making his tall, thin body appear shorter than his six-foot four-inch height. He appeared dejected and beaten, but the appearance was not reality.

His eyes looked down at the floor as he walked, but his mind smoldered. He would not let Pitkowski beat his passion out of him; he would not give up his ideals! Yes, he would do the work Pitkowski required. He would do whatever it took to finish his PhD degree. He needed the degree to be able to get where he wanted to go – a professor at a respected university. Not necessarily a great research institution, but one where he could teach environmental engineering. And once he got there, he would damn well work on the things that were important to <u>him</u>, and not to someone else.

CHAPTER 2

New Orleans, January 3, 2023

G ood morning - and welcome to '*ENV 3704 - People and the Environment.*' I'm Dr. Zachary Taylor and I'll be your instructor this semester."

Zack surveyed the group of kids in front of him as the few stragglers quickly found seats, and the class began to settle down. A smile crossed his lips as he looked around; the room was nearly full, and there seemed to be a good mix of students both in age and in sex.

This class was one of the more popular introductory technical courses. At least to most of the students it was. The electrical engineering students didn't see much use in it, but of course they still needed it to graduate. So that meant they would have to come to class regardless. And if they were in his class, Taylor was confident that he would be able to get a few of them turned on.

"Good morning," Zack repeated after the room had quieted down. "And welcome to the first day of classes in this brand new year."

"As I said, I'm Dr. Zachary Taylor and I'll be your instructor this semester. I have prepared a syllabus for the course, and I'd like to pass out these copies. Then we'll review the course outline and see what kinds of things we'll be learning during the next four and a half months."

Taylor continued to speak while the syllabi were being distributed. He knew that it was important to gain their attention from the very start, and to establish himself as the focus of that attention.

"You know," he said, with a slight grin, "maybe I shouldn't have used that combination of words so soon after New Year's."

After he saw a half-dozen or so puzzled looks, he continued. "It really wasn't very considerate of me to say 'pass out' the copies of the syllabus. Here we are, at 8:00 in the morning on January 3, only two days after some wild New Year's Eve parties were just winding down here in the Big Easy, and I carelessly use the words 'pass out.' I'm glad that some of you didn't oblige me right here in the classroom."

That got a few laughs along with as many groans and Zack felt better. He had started the bonding process with this class and knew that it would be another good semester.

Zack finished his review of the course syllabus for the semester. He unconsciously raised his hand to his head and quickly ran his fingers through his thick brown hair. Then he finished his introduction with a friendly "Anybody got any questions?"

This same type of question, asked by someone else, using a different tone of voice and body language, had the often desired effect of intimidating the students and preventing those questions it purported to seek. Zack knew this from experience, and always tried to make his request sound and feel genuine. To reinforce the casual atmosphere he was trying to generate, he stepped in front of the lectern and sat on the corner of the instructor's table. He let one of his long legs dangle, the other maintained contact with the floor.

Just then, the door opened, and in walked two more students obviously embarrassed at being more than fifteen minutes late to their first day of class.

"Don't tell me," smiled Zack, "I've heard all the excuses! Let me give you one that always works around here for the first week or so: 'The parking lots were, like, totally full, sir'!"

The class laughed a bit as the latecomers started to shuffle towards the back of the room.

"Wait a minute," called Taylor. "Come up here." The two looked slightly panicked for a second then started up towards the front of the room. "I just wanted to make sure that you had your copy of the syllabus," he said giving them each a copy. Their eyes betrayed their relief that they weren't going to be made an example of in front of the class.

But then Zack continued with more authority in his voice, "Also, I want you to know that I expect everyone" -and here he looked at the rest of the class - "to be here on time every day. One of the reasons I like 8:00 classes is that you can beat the parking crunch. If you have to get up twenty minutes earlier than normal to ensure that you are here on time, then do it. I think this class is one of the most important in the University, and I sure don't want you missing any of it!"

"While we're on this topic, I'll take a moment to read something from the catalog." Zack looked just a bit disgusted as he pulled out his copy of the current catalog. He clearly did not like what he was about to do.

In a flat tone he said "I am required by the administration to read this to ensure that there are no misunderstandings." He read:

5

The faculty and administrators of the University of Southern Louisiana will not tolerate academic dishonesty in any form. Students seeking or giving aid on an exam will be warned by the faculty and may receive a failing grade on the exam in question. A second infraction will result in counseling by the Dean. Repeat offenders may be subject to dismissal. Of course, students have the right to appeal as explained in this catalog on pages 110-112.

After Zack finished reading, he thought to himself: Why couldn't they just have stopped after the first sentence? Probably written by some lawyer. Maybe a lawyer who was now a university administrator! Why couldn't they say what they meant? No, they were always covering their butts. Never willing to take a stand.

Taylor spoke to the class, "Now, for those of you who might be confused by this double-talk, I'll say it a little more plainly. I don't like cheating in any form. I don't usually have any cheaters in my classes. The reason is simple. I will respect you as students until you give me cause not to; students usually accord me enough respect not to try that sort of thing. But if I catch someone cheating, he or she will damn well wish that they hadn't tried it. And we won't have to go before some committee either."

Zack did not like having to talk to his kids like this. His feeling of uneasiness made him think of the strange phone call he had received just yesterday. "Is this Professor Zachary Taylor?" the caller had begun even after Zack had answered with his name, as usual. "Professor, we don't like what you've been saying in the press lately."

"What do you mean? Who is this?" Zack had asked immediately.

The voice was neither hurried nor loud, which made the next words sound all the more ominous. "We're giving you fair warning - your attitude against big oil and your attacks on industry are bad for this City. You're making some powerful people mad. It ain't smart for you to make enemies like that. If you was smart, you'd stop making all these public appearances. You could have an accident. Know what I mean?"

Then the caller had hung up. Zack thought maybe it had been a prank call but he had not been able to shake the sound of the caller's voice from his mind. For the past two years, Zack had been speaking out strongly against burning oil and coal; and he had been advocating for raising taxes on fuel use. Maybe he was starting to get some attention - but from whom?

Well, it was just a scare tactic - he was sure of that. Nobody would really <u>do</u> anything to him just to keep him from expressing his opinion. This was America!

Zack paused in his thinking, coming back to the present. He smiled at the class. "Now that we have that unpleasant stuff out of the way, let's get to work."

Taylor went to the blackboard and picked up a new piece of chalk. It looked small in his large hands. Starting at the far left, he drew a long straight line that extended across both boards, almost to the right hand side of the room. He walked quickly back to the left side and drew a vertical line. Now he had a large axis for some sort of graph. Next, he drew another horizontal line just above the first one, but at the far right side, he curved the end of the second line upwards dramatically. Pencils and pens dutifully scribbled a similar line in notebooks.

"Can anyone tell me what this is?" he asked the class. There were a few murmurs but no one chanced a statement.

"This" said Taylor "is the end of the world as we know it."

CHAPTER 3

In the Environmental Engineering departmental office, things were as hectic as always at the start of a new semester. Freshmen wandered in looking bewildered, not sure of where to go, and trying to ask questions of anyone who stood still for more than ten seconds. Several professors converged at the same time on Cheryl Lee, the departmental secretary, with basically the same request. They each wanted her help <u>now</u>.

"Cheryl Lee, I need this typed before 10:00, please!"
"Cheryl Lee, I need 85 copies of this for my 9:00 class."
"Cheryl Lee do you know if the Chair is in yet?"
"Cheryl Lee, what happened to the copy of my class roll? It's not in my box."

Cheryl Lee March stopped typing and silently incanted her 'start of the semester' prayer for patience. Then somehow she took the requests in order.

"Dr. Lin," Cheryl Lee began, "if you would just take this to Jennie, our new student assistant over there, she'll type that for you, no problem. Dr. Nelson, I'll have Soo Mi copy those for you as soon as she gets back from the mail room. Just leave them right here. Dr. Stern, Professor Maxwell hasn't come in yet, but I can ask him to call you when he does."

"No, don't bother!" Elizabeth Stern retorted. "I should have known he wouldn't be in yet. I'll have to catch him later." She whirled and strode out of the office.

A tiny glimmer of anger shown momentarily in Cheryl Lee's eyes, but then she continued smoothly, "Dr. Fayez we haven't received the new class rolls from Admin yet. It looks like they are going to be late again this semester."

Cheryl Lee smiled pleasantly at Dr. Fayez, her favorite, and resumed her typing. Dr. Fayez smiled back and just shook his head in awe at her efficiency. In these days of budget cuts and low salaries for the staff, the Environmental Engineering department was very lucky to have Cheryl Lee. He was sure she could make twice as much money working for industry. He thanked her and walked towards the coffee room carrying his cup.

At that same moment, a serious conversation was in progress in the office of Dr. Alan King, Dean of Engineering.

"Henry, you're going to have to get tough with Taylor," said King. "He's not publishing enough and he's not bringing in money."

Professor Henry Maxwell, Chair of the Environmental Engineering Department, had in fact come in earlier than usual today at the Dean's request. Right now, though, Maxwell was wishing he were somewhere else, anywhere else. King's eyes bore into him relentlessly. He didn't like this kind of conversation. It could easily end with King giving him some more work to do, perhaps something unpleasant.

"But, Alan," Maxwell began then stopped to gather his thoughts. Out of habit, he rubbed his bald head with the palm of his left hand, starting at his forehead and sweeping up and back and down again until he reached the remaining fuzz low on the back of his head. Reassured, he continued talking. "He's really a good teacher; all the students rave about him. And he's been pretty active in speaking to local civic organizations."

"No buts, Henry, you know that when I became Dean last year, I said I was going to increase research funding at this place. And I intend to do just that."

Maxwell looked out the window. It was a pretty January morning, warmer than usual for New Orleans at this time of year. His eyes wandered, looking for a way out of this box into which he felt he was being forced. They came back to rest momentarily on King's penetrating gaze. No help there!

King continued, "Taylor couldn't get tenure at the last place he was teaching, and he won't get it here unless he gets his act together. And you've got to tell him that!"

Maxwell almost shivered. There it was, he thought. I've got to confront Zachary. It was no use arguing anymore. He nodded, mumbling as he rose to leave, "OK, I'll speak to him."

As he got to the door King called out, "Henry, do more than speak to him; fire him up about research, get him motivated! Help him to make some progress."

After the door had closed, King shook his head. He thought the chances of Maxwell doing that were damn small.

CHAPTER 4

Back in classroom 203, Assistant Professor Zachory Taylor paused. He knew he had them and he was enjoying the moment. "The *end of the world* – now that's a pretty dramatic statement, especially in an engineering class. What do I mean by that?"

Silence.

"Well let me explain," Zack continued. He pointed to the board. "This long horizontal axis represents time since civilization began; let's say it spans roughly 10,000 years. This vertical axis, as we shall see during the next few days, can represent a number of very important environmental parameters. And this long flat line that curves up so sharply at the end is what I call an 'explosion' curve. For a long time it does nothing, then, all of a sudden, it explodes upwards. As I said it can represent any one of a number of trends. For now, let it represent two trends of grave importance to the world.

"The first trend is world population. Thus, this curve depicts the population explosion. For nearly ten thousand years, the population of the world stayed well below 1 billion people."

Zack gestured at the smooth flat part of the curve. "This smoothness is deceptive," he said. "It depends on the scale on the vertical axis. Or to put it simply, on how far away you are when you are looking at it.

"Sort of like the earth's surface. Viewed from space, the earth looks very smooth. But up close, we can see it is filled with mountains and valleys.

"For example, Mt. Everest, tallest on earth, is about 5 miles high. But the earth itself is about 8,000 miles in diameter. As a fraction, 5 divided by 8,000 is only 0.000625. It's nothing; it's less than one tenth of one percent. So, from space you wouldn't even notice Mt Everest.

"Same thing with world population. Over the course of the last 10,000 years, population would grow slowly as long as there were plentiful food supplies, but then would drop suddenly during wars, or famines, or the plague, for example. But even if 20 million people died, it was just a small blip on this curve, because the scale is in billions. And the world still had less than 1 billion people only 200 years ago."

Zack glanced around the room. Most of the kids were still with him. He went on, "Keep in mind that 200 years looks very small on this 10,000 year scale; it's only this last four inches of the board here. Yet here is where all the action is, so to speak. Here is where the explosion starts.

"Global population hit 1 billion in 1804, and 2 billion in 1927, but then thanks to modern food production, transportation, medicine, and so forth, it really took off. It was 4 billion in 1974, and passed 7 billion in 2011. Now we number 9 billion people on the globe, and despite efforts all over the world to slow population growth, projections are that we will grow to over 12 billion by 2060, a year in which most of you will be in your prime working years."

"Dr. Taylor?" A hand went up in the back.

"Yes?"

"How will the world manage to support all those people?" asked a boy with black curly hair. He was wearing jeans and an open collar shirt, and was sitting back in his seat. Zack couldn't decide whether the question was sincere or not.

"We are not really supporting even 9 billion now!" shot back Taylor. "And the more people we try to support, the lower, on average, will be everyone's quality of life."

"But," he went on, "the urge to reproduce is one of the strongest forces on earth. Even when parents are living in horrible conditions, and even when they see children dying all around them every day, as in countries like Bangladesh, or many of the African nations, they continue to have children. So even though everyone, including the leaders of those poor countries, knows that they need to get their population growth under control, I am certain that this trend will continue.

"Unless there is a major world famine, which is a very real possibility considering the droughts we've had in various parts of the world these past 5 years, there will be 120 million **more** people alive on earth next year than there are now. Every ten years the world adds another China! And we just don't seem to be able to stop. This population growth is the root cause of many if not all of our environmental problems. We **must** do more with population control! However, I'm just not optimistic that we can accomplish much in that arena in the next two to three decades."

Taylor went back to the board and drew another long flat curve that tailed up sharply at the end. It looked similar to the first curve, but didn't rise so sharply at the end.

He turned and spoke to the class. "This is the other trend line that I mentioned, and it is almost as significant. Furthermore, this one is something that we may be able to do something about! I'm talking about the concentration of carbon dioxide in the atmosphere. Over the last 10,000 years, a period of relatively stable climate and temperatures by planetary standards, carbon dioxide has remained very steady in the very narrow range of 260 to 290 ppm. Even on the bigger scale of the last half million years, carbon dioxide, which I'll just write as CO_2, has stayed between 180 and 290 ppm. This has been verified by ice core sampling. Based on the Vostok ice core samples, CO_2 in our planet's atmosphere is now much, much higher than it has been in the last 420,000 years! And CO_2 levels are highly correlated to average global temperature (AGT)." Zack showed another graph on the screen.

Zack gazed at the graph on the screen. "This graph was first published many years ago. In 1988, the World Meteorological Society formed the Intergovernmental Panel on climate Change (IPCC) as part of the United Nations effort to address climate change. The top climate scientists in the world got together and reviewed research from all around the world on this topic. This is one of the graphs they produced. Based on numerous surrogates for temperature, and analysis of gas bubbles trapped in deep ice cores, they showed that CO_2 and temperature have tracked each other very closely for more than 400,000 years.

"If you read some of its history, the IPCC was a highly respected scientific body in the 1990s, and published reports to the United Nations that influenced the actions of many countries. But there were many climate change deniers – people who for one reason or other did not believe that GCC was occurring, or that if it was occurring, that it was natural and not man-made. The IPCC had always tried to show the truth of the matter, but got itself into political hot water in 2009. Their email server was hacked, and it was shown that a few of its leading members had traded emails that called into question their motives, and the way they wrote their summary reports. Even their science was questioned by some politicians, but the science was overwhelmingly defended by many independent scientists around the world.

"The result was that in the United States, the political will necessary to take the expensive steps to start controlling emissions disappeared. In the time period from 2009 to 2017, the U.S. did not lead the world on this issue, nor did it even participate on a national level. But in 2017, we had 3 major hurricanes that hit the U.S. right in a row. And California experienced the worst wildfires in its history. That was the year that started to really convince people.

"Hurricane Harvey dropped between 40 and 60 inches of rain over 10,000 square miles of east Texas, causing major flood damage in Houston and the surrounding areas."

Here Zack paused for a moment, and shook his head. "That's a ridiculous amount of rain! Do you have any idea how much water 60 inches of rain is? And how much energy it takes to evaporate that much water and carry it around in the skies?" he asked the class rhetorically.

"The very next hurricane, Irma, had 185 mph winds while at sea, but fortunately, it weakened before it made landfall in Florida. It hit the keys, and then turned and ran right up the spine of Florida; the storm surge on the Atlantic coastal cities was huge. Downtown areas in cities from Miami, FL to Jacksonville, FL, to Charleston, SC, were flooded badly. High water persisted for weeks in some areas.

"Hurricane Maria destroyed Puerto Rico – literally destroyed it. People were without power and water for months. It was more than a year before the electric grid was repaired and power was restored to 100% of the island. By that time, more than 1.5 million people had moved to the mainland."

Zack was speaking quietly, and there was not a sound in the room; he had everyone's attention.

"During October, 2017, Northern California had more than a dozen different fires going at once. More than 100 people were trapped and died in the fast moving blazes. The fires covered more than 250,000 acres, and burned to the ground more than 10,000 homes. I still remember pictures of the burnt-out homes – row after row of them – on the nightly news. Nothing left but the brick chimneys. It was unbelievable."

"In November of 2017, the United States government published a report on climate that had some very interesting facts:

- CO_2 levels had topped 400 ppm, a level not seen since about 3 million years ago, when temperatures and sea levels were much higher,
- Tidal flooding – people in south Florida called them King Tides – were occurring almost once a week in 25 Atlantic and Gulf Coast cities,
- Since 1900, AGT had gone up 1.8 °F and sea level had risen 8 inches
- Sixteen of the seventeen hottest years in human recorded history occurred between the years 2000 and 2017.

Zack shook his head, and repeated his earlier statement. "Anyway, that was the year that turned things around in the fight against global climate change.

"Residents of California, Texas, and Florida led the public outcry for the government to do more to address GCC. The rest of the country joined in, and politicians had to listen if they wanted to get re-elected. By 2020, enough evidence had been accumulated that proved that Climate Change was the root cause of the extreme weather. The IPCC was vindicated, and most of the long-time climate change deniers had to admit defeat. The U.S. took on the role of world leader in this important fight. BUT," and here Zack hesitated.

"But," he repeated, "there are still climate deniers, and Big Oil and the Military recently have joined forces again to try to dismiss these concerns so we can continue to use fossil fuels."

Zack realized that he had been on his soap box far too long, so he stopped and smiled and looked at the class. He said "Sorry for my tirade – I get really passionate about this.... Let's get back to the topic of CO_2 in our atmosphere, which we measure in ppm."

"First, let's recall what ppm means. As you learned in freshman chemistry, ppm means parts per million which is a convenient way to report measurements of very small fractions."

Zack wrote on the board as he spoke. "For example, 275 ppm if written as a decimal fraction is 0.000275. To use our previous example, in term of height or distance, we could loosely say Mt. Everest is only 625 ppm of the earth's diameter."

Zack continued, "But what about this term: 'temperature anomaly'? Simply put, it is the difference between the actual temperature and some average or expected temperature at a particular place. It is a better statistical measure of global temperature changes because you are not trying to combine temperatures from all over the world. That is, you are not averaging actual temperatures in south Florida with those in Canada, or those in the forests in Oregon with those in the deserts in Mexico. You are computing the differences at thousands of places around the world, and then you average those thousands of anomalies to get one global temperature anomaly."

He showed his next Powerpoint graph on the screen, and then turned to face the class, and said, "Now, back to carbon dioxide. The concentration of CO_2 in our atmosphere started growing in the late 1700's when the world began burning more and more fossil fuels, coal, oil and gas due to the industrial revolution. And the growth really accelerated in the 20th century industrial boom."

Zack was starting to get more animated. He was pacing in front of the room, gesturing freely with his hands and arms. He fairly ran back to the computer to show his next graph.

"Let's take a closer look at recent carbon dioxide concentrations," he said as the next slide popped up on the screen.

"In 1958 when we first started measuring atmospheric CO_2 with great accuracy, the level had reached 315 ppm. By 1998 it had risen to 360 ppm. That's an amazing 14% change in just 40 years! Fourteen percent increase in the concentration of CO_2 in the world's atmosphere in just 40 years. And you can see on this graph how fast CO_2 concentrations have grown in the last 60 years!

"That is sort of the same thing as if Mt. Everest grew 4,000 feet taller in 40 years. When there's that much change going on in such a massive system as the earth's atmosphere, something has got to give. And when the change involves CO_2, that something may well be life as we know it on earth.

Zack continued, "Now CO_2 growth didn't stop in 1998 – oh no. By 2009, the level was about 390 ppm or 100 ppm higher than it had been in the last 450,000 years. It first surpassed 400 ppm in 2013, and now stands at 430 ppm. That's another 7.5% in the last 11 years – so the increase is accelerating.

"This gas, carbon dioxide, which is still a tiny fraction of the content of our air is absolutely essential to all forms of life.

"All of you know about green plants and photosynthesis. With sunlight, water, and that little bit of CO_2, green plants make all the food there is on this planet."

Here, Zack paused to really focus their attention on him. He lowered his voice and raised both his arms to emphasize his next words. "But carbon dioxide does something just as important to life on earth - it keeps us warm at night!"

A girl in the front of class blurted out, "But that sounds crazy! How can you say staying warm at night is crucial to life on earth?" She had blond hair that was short and straight as nails, and she was wearing shorts and sneakers. Zack thought she looked like the athletic type. He watched her face as she spoke and knew she was thoroughly engrossed in this topic.

Zack smiled. "I used those words to see if I could get some kind of response," he admitted. "But," he continued, "that statement is not as outrageous as it sounds.

"You all learned as children that it gets hot during the day and cooler at night. It gets hot because the sun is shining and a tiny fraction of that solar energy hits the earth."

Zack drew a simple sketch on the board - a childish picture of the sun on one end of the board. The 'sun' had straight line 'rays' coming from it, and the 'earth' was on the other end of the board.

"That solar energy is absorbed by the ground, the ocean, roads, buildings, everything! When the ground absorbs energy, it gets warmer. As the ground warms up, the air above it warms up too, but by heat conduction not by absorbing sunlight.

"That's a key point, the gases in the air let sunlight pass through, they do not absorb solar energy directly.

"Now, at night, the earth radiates infrared energy - <u>heat</u> - to space. This is how it gets rid of the heat it absorbed during the day." Zack now added squiggly lines coming from the earth, each with an arrow head pointing outwards.

"This is the earth's <u>energy balance</u>, a dynamic that has been going on for ten thousand years, without much change. That's why the earth's temperature has been pretty stable since the last ice age. If the earth hadn't been able to get rid of as much energy as it took in over the years, it would have gotten hotter; conversely, if the planet lost more energy than came in, we would have gotten colder.

"Most of you know that. But what you may not know is this. Carbon dioxide in the air absorbs infrared radiation - that is, it catches some of that heat - and prevents it from escaping to space."

Here he made a wide sweep with his arms, and completed the diagram by drawing a big circle around the earth trapping the squiggly arrows.

"So carbon dioxide keeps us warm. In fact without the small amount of CO_2 that we do have in our atmosphere, our planet would be a whole lot colder than it is now, probably too cold to support life. On the other hand if we had a lot more CO_2 in our air, then we would be a lot hotter than most living things could stand."

A hand from the back. "Professor, can you give us some numbers; how much colder or hotter?"

"I'll do better than giving you some theoretical calculations; I'll give you two real life examples!" retorted Zack, holding up two fingers.

"Consider, for a moment, Venus and Mars, our nearest neighbors in space. Venus is an inferno – the average temperature there is about 860 degrees (Fahrenheit), day and night, from the equator to the poles. Mars, on the other hand, has an average temperature of about 70 °F below zero!

"Now, it's true that the three planets are different distances from the sun, but that would only explain a small part of the temperature differences. The big difference lies in their atmospheres. Mars has a very thin atmosphere, and can retain essentially no heat, while on Venus, the air is very thick, and over 90% of its atmosphere is carbon dioxide! Venus suffers from a runaway Greenhouse Effect. In fact, because of its super Greenhouse, Venus is a lot hotter than Mercury, which of course is considerably closer to the sun. If Earth had the atmosphere of either Venus or Mars, life as we know it would not exist on this planet."

The athletic blond raised her hand again. "Professor, surely you're not suggesting that Earth is going to become like Venus?"

Zack paused before he continued, "No, I'm not. No scientist believes that we are headed towards becoming another Venus.

"Although, in truth, no one knows for sure how or when Venus oxidized all its carbon to create such a CO_2-rich atmosphere. It is conceivable that Venus once had a biosphere like Earth's, but something happened to essentially burn it up. That is, maybe all the life on Venus, got consumed by massive fires, turning all its carbon into carbon dioxide, and releasing all that CO_2 into the air."

Zack grinned. "Who knows? Venus has been called our twin planet. Maybe they evolved an advanced civilization like ours, but it was 10,000 years ahead of us. Maybe they went through a similar industrial period and started their own Greenhouse Effect. Only with them being closer to the sun, theirs got out of control.

"This sounds like science fiction, and it is - I'm just making this up. So don't worry, we are in no danger of heating the earth to the ignition point!"

"However, the analogy does work to a certain extent. With increasing CO_2 we will certainly get warmer. In fact, we've already gotten an average of 1.3 degrees (Centigrade) warmer in the last 50 years, and predictions are for another 4 to 8 °C within the next 50 years. People, the clock is ticking!

"You might think that 1.3 degrees or 4 or even 8 degrees is not very much. Keep in mind though, that this is the average temperature of the entire earth. A rise of even a few degrees represents an accumulation of a tremendous amount - an enormous amount - of heat energy for the planet. That much extra energy in the atmosphere and the upper layers of the oceans causes enormous instabilities in our weather patterns, and is causing some of these wild hurricanes we've been having the past few years.

"That much excess heat will cause major climate changes in all parts of the world. Of this, I am absolutely, positively..." Zack was emphasizing his words with sharp jabs of the chalk onto the blackboard. "... certain!" The loud snap of the chalk punctuated the silence that followed his words.

Zack glanced at his watch. He was out of time, but he needed to finish the point he was making.

"To show you what a few degrees can do, let's consider the last great ice age. At its peak, during the coldest part of the ice age, some 20,000 years ago, the average temperature of the world was only 9 °C lower than it is now! And with only that 9 degrees difference, there was ice on the ground a half-mile thick, stretching from New York to Seattle. And with all that water tied up in ice around the globe, sea levels were some two hundred feet lower than they are today - why, you could walk from Alaska to Russia!"

Zack looked around at the faces in his class. He was satisfied with today's lecture and the way this class was starting out. He figured it was about time to let them go back to getting their heads pounded with Calculus or Physics or something similar.

He announced, "We're about out of time for today; be sure to read Chapter 1 of your text before the next class. Anybody got any questions?" He looked around the room; they looked overwhelmed. "No? OK, see you on Friday."

CHAPTER 5

Tweeeet! Arthur Grant, the new head basketball coach at USL, blew his whistle and looked at the player with the ball.

"Billy, what do you think you're doing?!" he yelled. "Man, you just had a perfect opening to drive the lane. And you turn your back to the basket!"

Hey, sorry Coach - but I didn't see no opening."

"It was a small one, and those don't stay open for long. Let me show you what I want you to do. Williams, get back over there where you were; Wilson you move back here. Now Billy, you watch this!"

Grant dribbled the ball as Billy Jackson had done, but when the opening came Grant drove the lane hard and went in for the lay-up. "OK, Billy, now you do it," he said as he flipped the ball to Jackson.

Grant watched as his brightest hope for this year's team repeated Grant's moves with success. "Again!" he called, even though he sensed that Jackson had already learned the new move.

Grant was hot and sweaty, the players were hot and sweaty, the gym itself seemed hot and sweaty. Grant felt as tired as the players looked. Man, he thought, I ate way too much over the holidays. It seems like summertime in here.

"Do it again, guys, and look like you mean it out there!" It was hot in here, and Grant was ready to call it a day, but he didn't want to let the players off just yet.

Arthur Grant had become USL's new head basketball coach last September when the old head coach had been killed in a traffic accident. In spite of the tragic nature of the circumstances, Grant recognized his opportunity, and was determined to make the best of it. A 28-year old, black assistant coach did not often get the chance to lead a college basketball team. Just because he was the youngest coach in the league, and the new kid on the block, didn't mean that the other schools were going to beat up on USL. He would see to that.

At the same time, Grant knew the dangers of pushing too hard. Not physical dangers, although since the university grounds and buildings crew hadn't turned on the air conditioning system yet, those might be real enough.

No, the dangers he worried about were pushing so hard at basketball that he gave the players the impression that their studies were unimportant. He didn't want any of his kids flunking out. There was life after college basketball. Arthur Grant had gotten to college because of his basketball abilities, but to him basketball was the vehicle not the journey's end. He owed it to his players to make sure they understood that.

"Hey, Coach, can't we call it a day? I'm gettin' a little thin out here, man." Jackson, a natural team leader, was the only one with enough confidence to admit to the coach that he was getting tired.

"One last time, Billy, then all of you hit the showers." Grant could see relief in several other faces. After he watched his players heading to the locker room, he left the gym, got in his car, and headed home.

Thirty minutes later, Grant walked into his modest two-bedroom apartment announcing "I'm home," as he closed the door.

"Hi sweetheart!" Peggy Grant greeted him with a kiss. "How was the first day back to practice?"

"Rough," Grant acknowledged, "but I've still got some energy left!" He smiled as he grabbed her around the waist and pulled her closer.

Peggy put her hand up between their lips and shook her head. "We have company," she said.

Grant turned to look into the living room. "Zack!" he exclaimed. "How the hell are you? We haven't seen you since before Christmas."

Taylor smiled. "Well if you guys had come skiing with me and Susan instead of going back home to visit your Mom, we'd have seen each other."

Grant laughed, "Sure, we can join the jet set, and fly off to go skiing with you and your latest fling - Susan What's-her-Name."

"Susan di Georgio," said Taylor matter-of-factly, adding "and, just for the record, I've been dating her for almost five months now."

"Yes, you're right; that just might be a record for you," retorted Grant.

"Hey, never mind about my affairs of heart," said Taylor. "Let's go over to City Park and shoot some hoops. Maybe we can get into a game."

"Not today," pleaded Grant. "I just finished a long practice and we've got a game coming up this weekend."

"But what was this I just heard about all that energy you had left!" Zack turned to look at Peggy. "Peggy, does he often lie about things like that?"

Peggy gave Zack an innocent look and said "I'm sure I don't know what you're talking about."

Grant smiled defensively. "Hey, that's not what I meant. I mean I only want to map out some strategy for the game Friday night."

19

Zack gave him a sideways look and said "I doubt that was what was on your mind a few minutes ago! But if you're afraid you can't keep up with me, even though I am 6 years older than you, well I can understand...."

"That'll be the day," replied Grant. "But I really can't do it tonight, Zack. Next week we'll get back into a routine."

Zack rose to leave. "OK, Art, I won't twist your arm."

He looked at Peggy, saying "Goodbye, Peggy. Make sure the only thing he does tonight is to sit and plan game strategy. You heard him say that's what he wants to do!"

"Bye, Zack, drive carefully," she said.

They all laughed as Zack went through the door and began the "long" journey home - down the hall, down the stairs, and across the parking lot to the adjacent building to his apartment in the Oakwood Village complex.

Zack unlocked the door to his apartment, not paying much attention to anything other than the handful of mail he had just taken from his mailbox down the hall. He opened the door and walked through, his conscious mind preoccupied with the mail. But somewhere inside his brain, a sixth sense told him to watch out! Then he saw it, a large blurred shape hurtling through the air at him from the right. Too late to duck, he tried to brace himself for the impact.

Knocked to the floor by the charge of the 90-pound German shepherd, Zack rolled over and over to avoid its large mouth. But his efforts were futile; he quickly found himself on his back and straddled by the powerful animal. That same animal was now in the process of licking him on any and all exposed parts of his face and neck!

"Sam, you crazy dog, stop it! Sam, I mean it, stop now!" Zack's words had no effect except perhaps to intensify Sam's efforts to lick her master's features right off his face.

Zack finally succeeded in getting to a sitting position. "O.K., Samantha, O.K.!" he exclaimed. "You win. You really got me that time," he said, laughing. "I was lost in thought and forgot all about you."

The dog, who had stopped licking by now, sat back and cocked her head as if to say "Forget about me? - how could you!" Then she ran over to her toys corner, barked once, and picked up the frisbee. She looked back over her shoulder, frisbee in mouth, and waited.

Zack looked at Sam for a moment, then he glanced over to the clock on the kitchen wall. He noticed his sink - still mounded with dirty dishes, some dating from New Year's Day. Looking back at Sam, he grinned and said "Why not? I was thinking about going to City Park anyway. We can pick up some burgers on the way back. Come on girl, let's go!"

In the parking lot, Zack opened the door of his red Jeep Cherokee, and Sam bounded in, still carrying the frisbee. She jumped across the driver's seat and took her rightful place on the passenger side, dropping the frisbee on the floor in front of her. Zack leaned over to roll down the window before he started the engine.

Taylor lived in Metairie, in an area popularly known as Fat City. It was convenient to the University as well as to many parts of New Orleans. He wheeled out of the parking lot and quickly got on Veterans Boulevard heading towards the park. He drove fast but skillfully through the traffic, which was actually fairly light in his direction. It was jammed, of course, going the other way.

He crossed the 17th St. canal, one of the main drainage canals in New Orleans. It was, in fact, the one that had breached after Hurricane Katrina in 2005. Zack's engineering brain couldn't help but think about the City's continuing drainage problems as he drove across the large canal.

Most of New Orleans lies between 2 to 5 feet below sea level, and these drainage canals always have water in them. They serve the critical function of draining rainwater from the city streets. Of course, large pumps are required because the water cannot flow naturally out of the low city.

Pump Station 6, serving a large part of Orleans Parish as well as some of Jefferson Parish, discharged into the 17th St. Canal and eventually into Lake Pontchartrain. Pump Station 6 was centrally located near Orpheum Street, and had a capacity of more than 9,380 cubic feet per second. That is, it could pump over 17,500 tons of water each minute. It was the largest pumping facility of its kind in the world. And it was only one of several such stations that made up the water removal system for New Orleans.

Nevertheless, heavy rains often dumped more water than the pumps could handle, and local street flooding occurred frequently. The City covers about 60,000 acres. A heavy storm might drop 3 to 4 inches of rain in two hours. Three inches of rain over 60,000 acres amounted to an incredible 650 million cubic feet (4.8 billion gallons) of water that had to be handled. Heaven help the city if a hurricane stalled here, raining for 2 or 3 days!

In addition to the very real threat of flooding from heavy rains, the people of New Orleans lived with the unlikely, but implied, threat of inundation from the surrounding water. The city sits crowded in between two massive bodies of water - Lake Pontchartrain on the north (which connects to Lake Borgne on the east and eventually to the Gulf of Mexico to the south), and the Mississippi River on the west and south. Lake Pontchartrain is easily 5 times larger than the City, and the River is a mile wide as it passes through downtown New Orleans, having drained a sizeable part of the United States by the time it gets to the City. In fact, the Mississippi carries an amazing 500,000 cubic feet (3.7 million gallons) of water every second through the City and on to the Gulf of Mexico. That is enough water to completely fill the Superdome in 38 seconds!

So New Orleans is like a shallow bowl, surrounded on almost all sides by huge bodies of water. The water lies poised just below the lip of the bowl, but at a much higher level than the City, which lies at the bottom of the bowl. The only thing that prevents the water from pouring in to drown the City is the system of massive earthen and concrete dikes that line the Lake shore and the River. The River dikes are built to a much higher level than the Lake dikes, so all the drainage is pumped north, over the 10 foot sea-wall and into Lake Pontchartrain.

After crossing the canal, Taylor took Polk St. for six blocks then turned right on Canal Blvd. He was now headed towards the River and away from the Lake. In New Orleans, most people do not think of directions in terms of north or south, but rather in terms of 'towards the river' or 'towards the lake.' Actually, the Mississippi winds through the City like a massive boa constrictor, sometimes flowing east, sometimes south, and even due north on one stretch. The result is the most confusing street system in the world. The streets curve, converge and diverge, sometimes changing names and sometimes not, all bent to the will of the mighty Mississippi.

Zack turned left on Navarre Street, and drove into City Park, the largest open green area left in New Orleans. He parked his car, and told Sam to stay. Then he walked around to let the dog out on the passenger side.

Sam leaped out, obviously happy to be in the park. She barked excitedly and ran a few strides towards the grass. She stopped suddenly, turning to watch her master.

Zack said "Sam, you forgot your frisbee."

At the word frisbee, the dog raced back to the car, reached in and brought the frisbee out in her big jaws. Zack closed the car door and took the frisbee from her mouth. He flung the toy as far as he could, sailing it towards the large open area, with Sam in hot pursuit.

After about 40 minutes of frisbee play, Zack was feeling winded and Sam was panting heavily.

"Well, girl, looks like you could use a breather!"

Sam barked as if to say "Hey, come on, I can go some more," making Zack laugh.

"No," he said, "time to go to work," as he sat on a nearby bench. "Sam, Come," commanded Zack.

Sam's ears stood straight up and pointed forward. She trotted over.

"Sit.... Shake Hands..... Roll Over....."

Each time, Sam performed perfectly. Zack continued through several other simple maneuvers, and then some more complicated ones. He was satisfied that Sam was as sharp and alert as ever. He called her to him and caressed the dog's large head roughly. Sam growled gently with pleasure.

Zack looked up and noticed two women sitting and talking several benches away. They looked to be in their twenties and were dressed for jogging. One looked very attractive.

Zack smiled to himself. "Sam," he said softly, "just one more job. This is one of your toughest, but if you can pull it off, you'll eat steak tonight instead of hamburger!"

Still holding Sam's head, Zack turned the dog so she could see the girls. "Sam," he said, "go Make Friends!"

Zack watched as Sam trotted over to the pair on the bench, but looked away as she got there. Sam sat directly in front of the women and looked at them alertly, waiting patiently. The two looked around for the owner, but saw no obvious candidate. They hesitated; Sam was a big dog. But she was so well behaved. And she was so attractive; her black and tan coat glistened in the sunlight. Finally, one of the women reached out to pet the dog.

Sam went into her act. She wagged her tail furiously, and then "sat" and "begged." In rapid succession, she "lay down," "rolled over," and "spoke," much to the delight of the two girls. Then, when she was finished, Sam gently put her big head in the lap of the lady who had first petted her, looking up at her with soulful brown eyes.

Zack watched, waiting for just the right moment to go over and ask if his dog was 'bothering' the two. He smiled as he thought about the friendly greeting he would get, and how easy it would be to launch into a conversation now that Sam had broken the ice for him. Man's best friend - it was certainly true in this case!

CHAPTER 6

Somewhere in Iraq, January

Mustafa Babazadeh shook his head; he did not understand it. He turned to his brother Nabil, who was, like Mustafa, standing there stupidly in the rain with a big grin on his face.

"Nabil, it is amazing!" said Mustafa. "Allah is smiling on us for certain."

"Indeed, Mustafa, we are truly blessed this year!"

"This is the third year in a row that we have had plentiful rains. Our crops will grow even bigger this year."

"Even the desert flowers are blooming all around us. What do you make of this, Mustafa?"

"Nabil, it is the will of Allah. The Koran says that we are the favored people. My friend, Ghazan, you know him? Ghazan's father told him that he heard from an educated man that once, many centuries ago, this land was fertile, and received much rain. At that time the Tigris and Euphrates flowed full all the time and farmers like us grew much food, for everyone. Ghazan's father heard this with his own ears."

Mustafa's black eyes gleamed with excitement. He continued, "Who knows - perhaps Allah has willed the rains to come to us again, after staying away for so, so long."

He lifted his face to the sky. The rain continued to fall steadily, the drops landing gently on his face and running down towards the waiting earth in small rivulets.

Indeed, Iraq was blooming. In the past three years, Iraq, Iran and a large part of eastern Saudi Arabia had received more rain than in the previous ten years combined. It was a phenomenon that worried many strategic analysts around the western world, but one that delighted farmers and nomads throughout the eastern part of the Middle East.

However, delight was certainly not the word that described the feelings in many eastern African nations, including Egypt, the Sudan, and Ethiopia. The shifting rainfall patterns that were now rewarding Iraq and Iran, were devastating eastern Africa. A 3-year drought was in progress and showed no signs of relenting. The news reports and the graphic videos of starving Ethiopian children that had become common in the 1980's were back on TV almost every night. Only now it was worse.

Even with Western aid (and the aid was smaller and slower in coming now due to dry, parched lands in the grain producing areas of the U.S. and Europe), hundreds of thousands of people in northeast Africa were dying each year.

Egypt was particularly hard hit. Although Egypt had never received much rain, it had <u>always</u> had the Nile River to rely upon. Now, though, the wonderful rains that fed the Nile in Sudan, Ethiopia, Uganda and Kenya had all but disappeared. In addition, the upstream countries, desperate for water, had begun to divert more and more of that water for their own consumption.

For centuries, the clear waters of the Blue Nile, flowing down from the mountains of Ethiopia, had met the grayish waters of the White Nile in Khartoum, the only major city in the Sudan. Throughout the Golden Age of Egypt, billions of tons of water, laden with rich sediments and nutrients, had flowed daily through the Sudan and Egypt towards the Mediterranean Sea, carving out a narrow green band from the great deserts in those countries. Throughout the last millennium, farmers had scratched out a meager existence using the life giving annual floods of the Nile. In the twentieth century, technology created a series of dams to help regulate the water for irrigation. Lately, the dams had little water to regulate.

Now, Khartoum needed water. They were desperate for it, and there was less water available than anyone could ever remember. So they deepened their intake pipes and took what they needed, leaving even less for poor Egypt. Of course, with the small amount of water left to continue its journey downstream, the industrial pollution and sewage injected at Khartoum and other cities was even more offensive and dangerous to the farmers and fishermen of Egypt.

With the reduced flow rate in the Nile, fewer sediments and nutrients than ever made it into the Mediterranean. From Alexandria to Port Said, the fishing business slowly disappeared. Sardines, long an export item for Egypt, one of the few things that brought cash into the country, could no longer be caught in commercial quantities. Furthermore, what fish that were still available were often laced with pollutants, and were not being bought by outsiders. Of course, people still needed to eat, so the local fishermen sold to the local residents, without regard to the slow and silent poisoning of the people due to the toxic metals contained in the innocent looking fish.

Thus, while Mustafa and Nabil rejoiced in Iraq, millions suffered in Egypt. These long-suffering people did not complain, though. Even if they did, who would listen?

* * *

Amsterdam, the Netherlands, January

Peter Haarhuis came home from work and slammed the door. His face was flushed with anger, the redness contrasting oddly with his light gray hair.

"Hilda, it's not right, it's just not right!" he exclaimed as soon as he saw his wife.

"What's not right, Peter?" she asked.

"The designs are being scaled down, and corners are being cut!" Peter Haarhuis was a civil engineer for a major construction firm in the Netherlands. He was Chief Project Engineer on the Oosterschelde Barrier Improvements Project. He was clearly upset at the moment.

"Peter, calm down, whose designs, what corners?" Hilda, ever the calming influence on her husband, often helped him work out his frustrations from his job.

"That new boss, that young fellow, he thinks he can just waltz in and tell me my designs are too big. 'We can save money,' he says. 'You are getting conservative in your old age.' he says. Hah! I was designing dikes before he was even born!"

"Is this on the Oosterschelde Project?" asked Hilda.

"Of course it is, what else have I been working on for the past sixteen months?!" snapped Haarhuis. He saw the look on Hilda's face, and quickly apologized.

"I'm sorry, dear," he said. "It's just that he makes me so mad. He said I needed to listen more to my junior designers, and to trust more in their computer programs. Hah! Their fancy programs could be wrong; I mean, after all, they were probably written by some kids just out of college."

Hilda now was becoming a little concerned. Peter usually did not carry on this much. "Are they doing something dangerous to the dikes?" she asked.

"Dangerous?" he mused. "I don't know. Foolish, yes, but I can't call it dangerous...yet. They are trying to save money. So they try to reduce the amount of reinforcing steel in the dike, and they want to cut the height of it by one-and-one-half meters."

Hilda said with genuine alarm, "But you have always told me how important it is for the dikes to be strong enough to withstand even the biggest of the North Sea storms. Remember way back in 2017, when hurricane Ophelia came all the way to Ireland, and caused so much damage. We had high waves but our dikes held."

"Exactly," said Peter. "But now, with sea level rising, how strong is strong enough? They are claiming that their computer analysis tells them that the North Sea has gotten calmer, on the average, during the last three decades. And that we can save millions of dollars by cutting just this little bit. Even though sea level has risen 20 centimeters in the last 40 years, they claim they have data to show that the dikes do not need to be built so high.

"Data, hah! My father was killed when I was just a boy because we didn't have good strong dikes. It was 1973, you might not recall it – you were just a child then. I don't remember the actual storm because Mother and I were visiting relatives in Amsterdam. But Father was working in the Delta region, in Dordrecht. It was a very strange time of year for a storm, too, the end of October. Not much warning was given.

"Mother says it was high tide when the storm came ashore, sweeping over the puny dikes that we thought back then would protect us. The sea raced up the Maas and the Waal Rivers, beating down everything in its path. Almost 1,800 people died from that storm - my father was one among them."

"You have often said that is why you studied civil engineering. So you could build them better and stronger." said Hilda softly.

"Yes, that is true," replied Haarhuis, softer now. But, maybe they're right, maybe I'm getting too old and conservative. What do you think, Hilda?"

"No!" she said fiercely. "You are not too old. You have so much good experience. You must make them listen. They must do what is right. My God, one-fourth of our country lies below sea level! We cannot take risks with that. You are right, I'm sure of that. I believe in you."

"Ah, Hilda, my sweet love. You are so good for me." Peter Haarhuis hugged his wife tenderly. "I will do battle with them again tomorrow," he said. But even as he held her, he knew they were wearing down his resistance. They were young and had the energy of youth; and he knew that time was not on his side.

CHAPTER 7

New Orleans, January

Today, Thursday, was an "off" day for Zack; he had no classes scheduled on Thursdays this semester, and only one lab section, in the afternoon. He had just gotten his coffee and was talking to Dr. Mohammed Fayez in the hall.

"How are your classes looking this term, Mo?" asked Zack.

"Getting bigger!" said Fayez, smiling.

"Yes, the Department is growing, and we're gaining students, aren't we?" said Zack rhetorically. It's good to see more kids in the program. Three years ago, when I first came here, we didn't look nearly so strong."

"Is more better?" grinned Fayez. "It depends on what you want - quantity or quality. Our students are <u>weaker</u> than they used to be."

Fayez emphasized the word 'weaker' with his accent. After 35 years in the States, he still had a mild middle-eastern accent. But that was understandable; even though Fayez had married an American woman and was proud that the U.S. was his country now, he still had many relatives and strong ties to his native Egypt.

He continued to speak. "We don't work them hard as when I was in school. I remember when I first came to United States; I went to graduate school at Georgia Tech."

Zack had heard this story more than once, but he liked and respected Mo Fayez so he did not interrupt.

"My first course in Master's program was a microbiology course. Me, a Civil Engineer, in with biology majors. I flunked the first test. I went to the professor and asked him what I should study. You know what he told me? He said, 'There is the library - go read books!' So I did. And I made '<u>A</u>' on his second test. And I worked <u>hard</u> and I got 'A' for the course. You see, from 'F' to 'A' in one course.

"Now, these students today, they don't want to work. They think they can learn everything just by watching their computerized video textbooks."

"Hold on, Mo, not all the students are like that."

"No, you're right, not all. But too many!"

"Well," replied Zack, "all we can do is try to give them some good work habits as we teach the technical material of the course. Listen, I've got to run. Maxwell wanted to see me this morning."

"O.K., take care, Zack."

Zack turned and headed for the Department Chair's office. Maxwell didn't often call him in for conferences; he wondered about the purpose of today's meeting.

"Come in, Zack," said Henry Maxwell when Zack stuck his head in the open door.

"Hope I'm not interrupting anything," Zack replied as he walked in and sat down.

"No, nothing at all," said Maxwell. He shuffled some papers from one side of his desk over to the other. He looked at Zack. Then he cleared his throat and glanced away.

"You wanted to see me..." began Zack, still wondering why he was here.

"Yes .... yes." Maxwell fidgeted in his chair. He ran his hand over his head, front to back, "How are your classes looking so far?" he began lamely.

"Just fine, Henry. But of course you know this is only the second day. Are you feeling O.K, Henry? You don't look so good."

"No, no, I'm fine," Maxwell lied. "Did you have a nice Christmas vacation?"

Zack couldn't wait any longer. "Henry, you called me in to talk about something; let's get on with it."

"Yes, of course." He cleared his throat again. "Well, actually I wanted to see if you were making any progress on the research front."

"What do you mean 'research front'? You know that I've only got one graduate student. Right now, he's working on analyzing rainfall trends in the Gulf area. We're trying to find a pattern that we can correlate with the rising CO_2 concentrations."

"Well, not that actually." Maxwell glanced out his window again. "You see, I was talking with the Dean yesterday...."

A light bulb turned on in Zack's mind. So this was the reason for the meeting!

Maxwell was still speaking. "...says you need to bring in some funded research. You know you're not making much progress towards your tenure, Zack."

"What do you want, Henry? Should I work on some trivial problem for two years, selling myself to some local chemical company, or should I be studying and spreading the word about the most serious problem ever to face mankind?!"

Zack continued, "You know, this Greenhouse problem has been building for more than two centuries now, and no one seems to realize that our time has just about run out. The potential for global disaster has been with us ever since we humans got numerous enough and powerful enough so that things we did started to affect the world instead of the other way around.

29

"I happen to think it's a lot more important for me to work on this, rather than some meaningless research on some obscure industrial chemical reaction."

"Zack," said Maxwell, "I'm not saying what you're doing is not important. It's just that Alan...and I...think you need to be more productive."

"But," protested Zack "I am a productive teacher. I teach a lot more students than most of the other faculty."

"That's because they're doing research," replied Maxwell. "You know, if you got funding, you could cut down on your teaching load, too."

"Henry, I like teaching. That's why I got into this profession." Zack paused to think. This argument was going nowhere. "O.K., I understand what you're saying. I saw an interesting Call for Proposals from a group I never heard of before - International Defenders of the Environment. Maybe I'll pursue that."

"Good!" said Maxwell, obviously relieved. Then almost as an afterthought, he added: "What is the subject of the Call?"

"Well, it's a little unusual. They don't really want basic research. They are looking for innovative ideas to physically demonstrate the potential consequences of large scale actions that are harming the environment - such as deforestation, filling wetlands, and so forth. It looks like they're specifically interested in the Greenhouse Effect. They want a dramatic demonstration, but something based in reality. It seems they think this is the only way to really communicate with the public and the politicians. Actually, it's kind of a neat idea, and one I think I could do well, considering my interest in Greenhouse."

Maxwell smiled. "That sounds perfect for you, Zack. You should definitely pursue it."

Zack smiled back and stood up to leave. But his smile was ironic. As he left the office of the Chair of the Department, he thought to himself that Maxwell would have told him it 'sounded perfect' no matter what idea Zack had described.

Taylor walked back to his office and sat down at his desk. He looked at the stack of paper and just shook his head. 'One of these days,' he promised himself, 'one of these days I'm going to get organized.' Of course, he realized even as he said it that he had made that same promise many times before.

Just then he was startled by the loud ring of the telephone. It sat next to a recently relocated stack of papers on the left side of the desk. Zack picked it up quickly to avoid a second assault on his ears.

"Zack Taylor," he answered. He then cradled the phone between his left ear and shoulder, and continued to search for that Call for Proposals he knew was on his desk somewhere.

"Hello, Dr. Taylor." Cheryl Lee greeted him, her voice as cheerful as always. "How are you this morning?"

"Fine, Cheryl Lee, thanks. You doing OK?"

"Yes, Dr. Taylor, only I need some help advising a student who is registering late. Do you have some time now?"

"Yes, I do, Cheryl Lee. Send him down." Taylor hung up as he found the document he had been looking for.

Zack was still holding the Call in his hands thinking about what he had just read when he heard the knock on the door. "Come in," he called, swiveling his chair to face the door.

"Dr. Taylor? Cheryl Lee sent me down for advisement."

Zack mentally fell out of his chair! It was as if someone had dropped a bookcase on his head! For a long moment he could do nothing but stare. My God, he thought to himself, this has to be the most beautiful woman in the world, and she has just walked into my office!

"Are you the student Cheryl Lee sent down here?" he stammered stupidly, immediately realizing that he was asking her the same thing she had just told him.

She smiled. He nearly fell out of the chair for real this time. It was magnificent, that smile! It was the kind of smile that men die for.

"Of course you are!" he said. "You just told me that." Zack struggled to regain his composure. This wasn't the way a meeting between a student and faculty should start.

"What's your name?" he asked, trying to get his pounding heart back under control.

"Jordan," she answered. "Jacqueline Jordan. I just moved down here from New York last month. I got my application in late, and I missed registration. I know this is a bother for you, but I could use some help getting into some classes."

Zack replied quickly, "No, it's not a bother, Miss Jordan, none at all. Let me see that paperwork you're carrying. Oh, and have a seat here, please."

He tried very hard to look at the file she handed him, but his eyes kept moving off the page to her face. She had tan skin, her smooth complexion highlighted by her luxuriously thick black hair. The hair was done up in a bun, but it was not tight or severe. A few strands of black dangled down here and there, accenting her face. Her lips were thin, yet well-defined with just a touch of red lipstick. Her perfectly shaped nose supported large round glasses that accentuated her clear blue eyes and made them even more striking. Those blue eyes were resting on Zack at the moment. He had to say something.

"Well, there's not much here," he ventured.

"I know," Jordan replied. "I didn't have time to have all my records sent before I applied here. I've written off to my previous school and requested official transcripts."

"Good..." Zack began.

Just then, she crossed her legs, and Zack's brain shut down again momentarily. She was tall; he had seen that when she walked in. A lot of her height was in her legs, which were shapely and extraordinarily smooth. She was wearing a red blouse with white polka dots, and white shorts. The white shorts fit her extremely well, showing off her tan legs to good advantage.

Zack hurried on, "Those are very good, uh, I mean, that's very good... the transcripts, that is. Uh, we'll need those to see exactly how far along you are in your courses. You are majoring in Environmental, aren't you?" He prayed that she was.

"Yes, I am," came the blessed reply. "And I'm really eager to get started into some of the major courses," she added hopefully. "In fact, I've been told that I should try to get into your course - the 'People and Environment' class. I've heard you're a really good teacher, and I'd really like to have you."

This was too good to be true! Zack almost said 'I'd like to have you, too,' but then caught himself.

"Yes, of course. I mean, of course you should get into that class first. I think there's room; let me check my class roster."

He opened his lower right desk drawer and pulled out a yellow-colored computer print-out of a class roster. He looked at the class roll without really seeing it, and said, "Well, I do believe you're in luck! We can add you to the roll right now and you can officially add the class during Add/Drop, later today."

"Oh, super! How can I thank you, Dr. Taylor?"

'Thank me?' thought Taylor. 'No, thank you for moving here. Thank Cheryl Lee for sending you down to me. Thank my lucky stars I was in the office. Thank anyone but me!'

Zack continued out loud. "Let me give you a copy of the syllabus, Jackie. You don't mind if I call you Jackie do you?"

"Actually, I do. I prefer Jacqueline."

"That's fine; Jacqueline it is. Here's a copy of the syllabus. By the way, class meets tomorrow morning at 8:00 am, and I always start on time."

"Great, I'm an early riser, too. Do you want me to take my file back to Cheryl Lee?"

"No thanks. I'll bring it back later. I...want to look this over more carefully."

"I'll look forward to seeing you in the morning then," she said as she rose to leave.

"Uh, right, see you tomorrow," was all he could manage to say as she opened the door and was gone.

Zack sat for a long moment staring at the back of his closed door. His mind was a whirlwind of conflicting thoughts and emotions. In one sense, he felt very lucky to have met such a woman and to know he would be seeing her many more times. But at the same time, he felt almost distressed that they were in the roles of instructor and student, a relationship that he had always honored. He shook his head; he was not going to resolve his confusion right now.

Zack looked at the class roll he still held in his hand, only this time he looked at it more carefully. It was from a class he had taught two years ago! He put the yellow sheet of paper back in the drawer, shaking his head for the second time in two minutes.

Taylor shoved some of the papers in front of him towards the back of the desk until he had cleared a small area in front of him. Then he began to study the thin file left behind by Jacqueline Jordan. There wasn't much to see. There were no official transcripts, but she did have some photocopies. She also had a brief resume. She had attended City College in New York for three years, quitting in 2016. So that would make her about 27 or 28 years old, thought Zack. While in college, she worked for a modeling agency part time. More recently, she had been employed as a buyer for an import/export business.

The file also contained a home address - 2517 Leontine. So she lived over in the Uptown area, Zack realized. Probably in a garage apartment or a converted old house near St. Charles Avenue. It was an historic area, made beautiful again during the last 20 years as younger people had moved in and started restoring old houses. And it was convenient, too; near buses and the more romantic street cars. But it did have its drawbacks - it was fairly close to a pretty rough part of town, and it had a tendency to flood during heavy rains. Zack noticed that there was no phone number listed.

Just then there was a knock on the door. Zack put the file down hastily, and swiveled to face the door. Somehow he felt a vague sense of guilt for having been holding it.

"Come in," he called.

"Hi, Dr. Taylor," came the disembodied voice of Jeff Mitchell followed a moment later by the person.

"Hi, Jeff," replied Zack. "What's happening with my favorite graduate student?"

"Well, we finally set the date, that's what!" Jeff blurted out. "It's going to be a June wedding."

"Congratulations," laughed Zack "or should I say condolences, now that you're leaving bachelorhood."

Jeff, who was serious to a fault, did not smile at the intended joke. He simply ignored the comment. He lowered his backpack to the floor and sat down. He took off his round wire-rimmed glasses and cleaned them methodically on his tee shirt. He then put them back on, slipping the loops around his ears, tight against his close-cropped blond hair. Only after the ritual of cleaning his glasses was done, did he look up at Taylor to speak.

"Anna and I would like you to come to the wedding, if you can make it."

"Wild horses couldn't keep me away," declared Taylor. "Where is it going to be?"

"Boise, Idaho. Both Anna's family and mine are all there. We went back over Christmas to tell our Moms. They're real excited. They've already started planning a huge party. You probably didn't know it, but Anna has roots in the Basque culture.

There is a very large Basque community in Boise, so it might turn out to be a big wedding."

"How was Boise? Have they been suffering the effects of the drought?" asked Taylor.

"Not as bad as some other areas. Boise always has been dry, but the Boise River runs right through the city, you know. They irrigate everything. On the other hand, I don't know if drought affects temperature, but Boise sure seemed colder than I remember it being."

Zack laughed. "I think you're getting acclimated to the South. A couple more years here and you'll never want to move back."

Mitchell said earnestly, "Oh, no, Dr. Taylor, you're wrong. I love the West. I grew up in Pocatello, you know. I used to go hiking, fishing and camping all the time. The scenery is fabulous. It's so clean and fresh out there in the mountains, especially compared with New Orleans. The people out there really care about the land."

"But if you love the mountains so much, how did you end up here?"

"You know I was in the Navy; I'm still not sure why I joined. I do know that I was getting really burned out in school, though. We had just moved from Pocatello to Boise two years before. I was in Geophysical Engineering at Boise State, and felt like I was getting nowhere. Everyone was giving me advice. I just had to break away."

Zack nodded. "OK, and somehow you decided to come back to school and finish your degree, and to stay on for graduate school. But why here?"

"Yes," replied Jeff. "Well, actually the Navy had something to do with that, too. I hate to admit it now, but I had never heard of USL before coming to New Orleans. If it hadn't been for the Navy base here, I probably would not be at USL now."

"Well, I'm glad you're here," said Taylor. "Say, did you manage to find all those references I wanted?"

"All but two; here are copies of the ones I think are really good."

"OK, thanks," said Taylor, taking the packet of material from Mitchell. "Listen, I have something else for you to work on. With your mechanical interests and skills, this may prove to be a lot of fun."

"Great, what is it?"

Taylor handed Jeff the Call for Proposals. "Jeff, take a look at this. Ever hear of this group - International Defenders of the Environment?"

Mitchell shook his head as he looked at the document.

"Neither have I, but this sounds like a neat approach. I've never seen anything quite like it before. I've got an idea that would really make them sit up and take notice. But before we write up a proposal, we've got to do our homework. I have a feeling my idea could get to be pretty intricate and expensive. That group is going to want to see some details before they give us any money."

"You can count on me to help; what's the idea?"

"OK, listen carefully. This may sound crazy, but I think we could pull it off if we can get Tulane to cooperate. And Jeff, don't breathe a word of this to anyone until I clear it."

Zack looked straight at Jeff and asked, "Have you ever heard of the Ross Ice Shelf?"

"I think so. Isn't that a big iceberg in Antarctica?"

"Close. But actually it's a hell of a lot bigger than an iceberg. A couple of years ago, a very small piece of it broke off and floated free into the sea as an iceberg - glaciologists call that 'calving.' Only this calf was as big as the state of Delaware!"

Jeff whistled. "Amazing!" he whispered.

Zack went on. "Well a lot of people heard about the Ross Shelf for the first time back in the early 1980's when somehow the press got the story that the Greenhouse effect would soon melt all the polar ice. At first, people thought that sea level would rise dramatically, but later realized that a lot of polar ice is floating, so the sea level is already equalized.

"Just like a glass of water with ice cubes in it. When the ice cubes melt, the glass doesn't overflow - the level remains the same because the ice was already displacing water.

"Later though, people discovered that the Ross Ice Shelf is <u>not</u> floating. Rather it's like a long, wide sheet of thick glass. It's connected on one end to the continental rock of Antarctica and supported on the other end only by three or four small islands. It's thousands of feet thick. It extends 500 miles out to sea from the solid rock of Antarctica, and almost all of the ice is <u>above</u> sea level, not displacing water so sea level is not equalized. And it's all supported by just a few small, strategically located islands.

Jeff nodded, too absorbed in what Taylor was saying to interrupt.

"Furthermore, the Ross Shelf is not the only ice shelf in Antarctica. Ross is the biggest, but the Larsen, Ronne, and Filchner Ice Shelves are all quite sizeable. And they're all anchored to the Continent - not free floating.

"When ice that is <u>not</u> floating melts, the meltwater is a net addition to the oceans, and sea level does rise. Recent predictions for sea level rise in the next 50 years are 4 to 8 feet, about twice as much as the government was predicting just ten years ago.

"Now 4 feet does not sound like much, and it isn't much if you live on the White Cliffs of Dover. But if you live in Holland or Bangladesh or even here in New Orleans, you've really got a problem. Two feet of vertical rise results in tons of extra water pressure on dikes and seawalls. If you have no seawalls, and live on low flat land, your shoreline moves hundreds or even thousands of feet inland. And if you live on a low flat island nation, like the Maldives, you might just lose your entire country!

"However, don't worry about the Ross ice melting. That is not the real concern. It would take centuries of extreme warmth to melt all that ice. The real concern is this: what happens if the shelf cracks and slips into the sea?"

35

Zack didn't wait for an answer. "I'll tell you what happens if the Ross Ice Shelf collapses - a gigantic chunk of ice falls into the ocean, displacing an equal weight of water. Instant sea level rise, and not by a puny few feet either. It's like taking a full glass of water and dropping in another big ice cube.

"How much does the level of water rise? It depends on how big the ice cube is and how big the glass is. I've heard estimates of sea level rise of between 10 and 40 feet. And that's what I want you to find out, Jeff!"

Mitchell, who had been following Taylor's monologue pretty well, seemed perplexed. "I don't know what you're asking me," said Jeff.

"I need to find out exactly how much ice is perched there in Antarctica, mainly in the Ross Shelf, but also included in the others. And I need to know how much water there is in the oceans.

"Jeff, I want you to get on your computer, and/or just go to the library, and browse the shelves. See what you can find. Then do the calculations and tell me your most precise estimate of the resulting sea level rise. Assume the worst; assume that the whole thing breaks free and slides off those islands into the ocean!"

"But why do you need this information?" asked Jeff, still puzzled by this odd request.

Dr. Zachary Taylor chuckled at the thought of it. He said, "Remember, I said we'll need Tulane's cooperation? I recall seeing in the paper just last week where Tulane is going to completely renovate their football stadium. It's going to be out of use for a year or two."

"Well, I want to build a model, a big one, say the size of a football field - maybe we can rent Tulane's. I want to model the eastern seaboard of the United States of America, complete with major shoreline cities. And I want to dig a scale model, at least with respect to total volume, of the Atlantic Ocean. Then I want to drop a scale model of the Ross Ice Shelf into our model ocean. I want to show those fatheads in Washington what will happen to our country if they keep ignoring Greenhouse!"

CHAPTER 8

Steve Resnick was mad. He sat in his big, new, flashy, chrome-covered pick-up truck going nowhere fast. He was stuck in some kind of major traffic jam on Carondelet Street. He could just see his lunch hour evaporating right before his eyes. He was going to meet Julie at a place on Bourbon Street and didn't want to be late.

"C'mon move it!" he shouted in frustration.

Steve's right hand gripped the steering wheel tightly while his left kept busy bringing the cigarette to his mouth for short nervous puffs. He was somewhat overweight, and had a rough, pockmarked face - nature had not been kind to Resnick in his teen years. He had reddish-brown, curly hair and a ruddy complexion. His face was somewhat redder than usual today, and his shirt was sticking to his sweaty back. He had the air conditioner on but still had his left side window rolled down. He tossed his cigarette butt out the window onto the street and lit another.

He thought about the meeting his boss had scheduled for 1:30 to discuss pricing strategies for their 'new, improved' regular unleaded gasoline. He knew he had to be at that meeting. But he didn't want to miss talking with Julie either.

He muttered to himself, "If I can just make it to the next corner, maybe I can cut over to Magazine St." He looked in his right side mirror. He saw a late model Ford driven by a middle aged woman. She didn't look the type to react very quickly. He saw the traffic inch forward; there was his opening! He pressed the accelerator and wrenched the wheel to the right.

Horns blared as he squeezed between the two cars. His right tires went up on the curb eliciting angry shouts from some pedestrians. 'Who cares about them,' he thought.

At the corner, he turned right on red, nosing his truck in front of a more timid driver of a four-door sedan, and sped down the street swerving into the left lane near the light. Again he ignored the horns behind him. He had won! He turned left onto Magazine St. and into relatively clear traffic.

Resnick knew he would never be able to park in the French Quarter so he found a parking garage near Canal Street and walked the remaining few blocks. In spite of the sweat dribbling down from his armpits, his mood picked up as he neared his destination. He hadn't seen Julie in a week, and he was looking forward to this. He crossed Iberville, then Bienville, headed for the depths of the French Quarter, the historic and often romanticized heart of old New Orleans.

Steve Resnick unconsciously wrinkled his nose at the smells of urine and decaying garbage nearby, but the smells did not register in his conscious brain. He did not bother to look at the peeling paint on many of the historic buildings. His eyes were looking only for the sign outside the place where in just a few minutes he would see Julie again. Then he saw it and turned into the door. The sign on the outside said 'Talk to a Naked Lady - $3.00 per minute - credit cards accepted.'

After his "lunch," Resnick was returning to his office and bumped into his boss in the hallway. He was still 15 minutes away from his 1:30 meeting time, but the chance encounter accelerated the schedule.

"Resnick, I need to see you in my office for a few minutes." Steve Resnick's boss, Joseph Del Gado, was the Assistant Vice President of Marketing of Global Oil. When he requested (commanded) your presence, you went - no questions asked.

"Of course, Joe," Steve answered, hoping his boss wouldn't smell the beer on his breath. Steve wondered what this was about. Del Gado had had his weekly staff briefing yesterday, and usually he doled out the new work assignments then and there.

"Come in, Resnick. Sit down."

Resnick did as he was told.

Del Gado opened with, "We've got a problem and we need to deal with it. Ever hear of Zachary Taylor?"

Resnick paused to consider this off-the-wall question. Was Del Gado testing him? "Wasn't he a President or something in the 1800's?" he replied.

"Very good, Resnick, go to the head of the class," said Del Gado sarcastically. "Not Taylor the President, Resnick, I mean Taylor the Professor, the one at USL. Haven't you been reading the paper? That guy has been bad-mouthing us for two years at least."

"Oh, yeah, he's the one with a bug up his ass about oil companies. He thinks we're making it too cheap and easy for people to get gasoline, and other fuels for all their energy needs. He says we're putting the alternative energy companies out of business. He says we should be investing in wind energy, or producing cheap solar power, or making hydrogen. Shit, he doesn't know anything. We're doing the American public a great service, getting them quality energy products at prices they can afford."

"I don't need any speeches from you, Resnick. What I need is information on this Taylor guy. There must be something we can use to pressure him. He's started to get too much media attention, and that kind of publicity is bad for us. I want you to dig into this, come up with a plan to quiet this guy down. You understand?"

"Sure, Joe, you can count on me," Resnick replied.

Later that day, as Resnick drove home, he drove slower than usual. He didn't cut people off or try to bully the other drivers with his big pick-up. He was thinking about his new assignment. He pulled up in his driveway and slowly lowered his frame out of the truck. He looked at his yard and decided that it could wait another day or two.

"Hi, Steve, how was work today?" Molly Resnick greeted her husband without much enthusiasm, but at least with the attempt at civility.

"It was fine," replied Steve, thinking mainly of his lunch break. But then he remembered his new assignment. "Del Gado gave me something new to do today, I'm going to have to get started on it right away. It might be fun for a change."

"Oh, no," Molly wailed. "You promised you'd help me pick out a new sofa today. You're not going to start working the minute you get home are you?"

"Look, this has got to be done. Can't you understand that?"

"All I understand is that you spend all your time at work or on work. We never seem to do anything together anymore. Not that we did all that much before!"

Resnick snarled his reply. "What's your problem, Molly? I provide you a good home, don't I? You got money to spend, don't you? I paid to get Gerald through college, didn't I? What else d'you want from me?"

He turned his back on her, and stomped into their family room. He went to the bookcase and pulled out the fake trilogy by Poe, revealing a hidden control panel with a numeric keypad. He flipped a switch and punched in the code that only he knew.

A panel in the wall slid open revealing a secret room behind the wall. Steve Resnick walked into his haven from the rest of the world, trying to make himself feel better. He looked around, satisfied with what he saw. He had done a marvelous job on this room, outfitting it with stereo, wet bar, television, even an oversize vibrating recliner. He had done everything himself too, from the rough-out carpentry, to the electrical and plumbing, to the finishing work. His skills with tools and his eye for design were especially evident in the fine cabinet work throughout.

The problem, he thought, was that he had no one to share it with. Molly disdained working with her hands, and didn't appreciate his talents. It had taken him quite a while to build this room, and Molly had bugged him constantly during the project. Consequently, he had excluded her from using it. He loved to show it off, though, whenever they had company, which seemed to be a lot less frequently these last couple of years.

He pressed the remote switch for the TV and absently flipped through the stations. Then he switched it off. He felt irritated. He couldn't seem to relax. He opened the secret panel leading back out to the rest of the house.

He walked back through the kitchen where Molly was starting to fix supper.

"I'm going out to the shop," he announced.

"Haven't you finished that set of chairs, yet?" asked Molly.

"No, I haven't." Steve mimicked her whining tone. "You ought to know by now these things take time. If I'm going to have them ready for Gerald and Betty in time for the wedding, I need to work on them, regular."

"If you weren't such a perfectionist about your woodwork, you'd have more time for the yard and other things around the house. And for me."

Resnick thought to himself that was one bonus of his woodworking, but didn't say anything.

He entered his well-stocked shop and sighed. He looked around. Everything was in place, just as he had left it. He walked over to the area where a fine mahogany chair was nearing completion and another was starting to take shape. He picked up a new sheet of black, extra fine sandpaper, number 600, and gently started rubbing the curves of the back of the chair.

Slowly, Resnick could feel his tensions easing. Soon, his conscious mind was soothed by the comforting motions of his hands rubbing the fine grained wood. He became occupied solely by the details of what he was doing. Steve Resnick was no longer troubled by any of his problems at work or at home, at least for the time being.

CHAPTER 9

Zack, we have a problem....' The computer voice gently informed Zack that it did not understand what Zack wanted it to do. The older models would simply have stopped, printing out some useless message such as 'illegal format, error code 1354,' but this one spoke to him and told him precisely where the communications between man and machine had gone astray. Zack re-typed his instructions, his fingers flying around the keyboard, this time hitting all the right keys.

'Thank you - processing has begun,' came the reply from a machine with so much artificial intelligence built into its microchips that sometimes Zack was convinced it could actually think.

"You're welcome," muttered Taylor, as he leaned back in his chair. He knew this version of the global climate model program would take several hours to run, even on his new PC with its AI-986 chip. He thought about what else he could be doing. He picked up the phone and dialed Arthur Grant's extension.

"Art? This is Zack - how about playing a little one-on-one this afternoon?"

"Hi, Zack. Hey, I'd like to, but I really can't this afternoon. I've got a steering committee meeting for the Black Educator's Society in about 30 minutes, and usually those meetings last for a couple of hours."

"Hey, man, you have to learn how to say no," said Zack. "Before long, you're going to be on every damn committee at this University. Believe me, there's a lot of them - I was on 12 different committees last year!

"Besides, what do you do on those committees? None of mine actually accomplished anything. You know what they say about a committee, Art - it's a group of people who keep minutes and lose hours. You know, if the Administration of this school would ever realize how much faculty time they throw away on all these do-nothing committees, they would be sick. If the state university system was a business, we'd be out of business!"

"Zack, I agree with you as regards most of them. But you know how I feel about making sure our black students get every chance for success. If we black educators won't donate a little extra time to the process, who will?"

"Arthur, Arthur." Zack paused; this was a point he had been meaning to discuss with Grant for some time. But he wanted to tread lightly. "I know it's important to you for your students and players to graduate. But I also know you believe in the value of hard work and self-reliance. I've heard you tell that to your kids many times. What I don't understand is why you turn around and push for special considerations for your black students?"

Grant replied, "Not special considerations, but just more sensitivity. You don't really understand the situation that many of these kids grow up in. You can't unless you were there, like I was. I was lucky. Basketball got me out of the slums, but it was education that kept me out. Education is the key. That and developing a strong work ethic. But we have to do it gently in many cases."

"OK," said Zack. "I'm not going to argue with you, I know how you feel, and I can see your point. If your meeting gets done early, give me a call."

"Will do, Zack, thanks. Bye."

Zack hung up the phone and looked at his watch. It was too early to leave work, but too late to start something new. He looked at his desk. No, he definitely was not in the mood to straighten up. He picked up the Call for Proposals and looked at it thoughtfully. He grabbed a pad of paper from his right side, middle desk drawer and began to make some notes.

* * *

At home, after eating a microwaved "dinner," Zack was just putting his dinner plate and glass into the uncharacteristically empty sink when the phone rang. Sam's ears picked up and she watched Zack move around the counter to answer it. "Hello."

"Hi, lover," crooned Susan di Georgio on the other end. "What 'cha up to?" Her 'Charmer' accent was thick.

"Nothing much," returned Zack. For some reason he did not fully understand, he was not anxious to talk with Susan tonight.

"Well, how's 'bout I come over for a li'l visit. Like an angel of mercy, so ta speak."

"Susan, I don't think so, not tonight. I've got some papers to grade," he lied.

"Las' time you had papers ta grade, we did that together, remembah? You said it was the mos' fun you evah had gradin' papers."

Zack paused, thinking back to that night. Susan was making him a tempting offer.

"No, thanks Susan. I just don't feel like it tonight."

"Zachary, what's going on? You haven't called me ever since we got back from skiing, and that's been more than a week, now."

"I don't know, Susan, maybe we were together too much on that trip. Maybe we just ought to cool it for a while."

"You, cool it yourself, bustah!" she exclaimed, as she slammed down the phone.

Zack stared at the phone for a minute. He wondered about her words: 'what's going on here.' To be honest, he did not know himself. Certainly, Susan was attractive, with her black hair and flashing black eyes. And, despite the fact that she was almost a foot shorter than Zack, they had a great physical relationship together. But something was missing. What was it? He couldn't put his finger on it.

Sam trotted over, sensing her master's distress. She licked his hand and then nosed her muzzle under his arm so that his arm encircled her head.

Zack caressed her big head. He roughly massaged the base of her skull behind her ears. Sam growled low with pleasure. Zack smiled. No questions here, no complicated feelings to sort out. The love between dog and man was pure and unconditional. He wondered if human love could ever be this simple or beautiful.

CHAPTER 10

Swoosh! The crow zoomed past Zack's head and landed a mere ten feet away, near the other ever-present urban pests.

Zack was walking from his office over to the building that housed his classroom this semester. The morning was cloudy and cool, more normal weather for the City this time of year. The squirrels were out in force this morning, hopping around with the ever-present crows, searching for scraps. They were all scouring the ground near the permanent 'portable' hot dog stand that serviced passing students, and sometimes faculty. Zack frowned as he walked; 'these squirrels are getting pretty aggressive,' he thought, as one hopped right up to him looking for a handout.

He walked into the classroom at 7:58, glad to see that most of the students were already seated and waiting for him. He looked for and found Jacqueline Jordan; she was sitting near the center of the room.

Most of the male students were looking at her. Even as he watched them watching her, one good-looking guy leaned over to her to introduce himself. Zack could not hear her reply, but apparently it was very effective. The boy pulled back almost as if he had been slapped, his face reddening.

"OK, class, good morning. Let's get started, shall we," said Zack. He reached over and picked up an old piece of chalk. He looked at it, half lost in his large hands, turning it over between thumb and fingers, then put it down. He replaced it with a longer piece.

By this time the class had settled down, so he started his lecture. "Today we're going to look a little closer at that CO_2 curve I put on the board last time and talk about why it started growing so fast in the last two centuries."

Zack turned to the board and re-drew the long flat line followed by the explosive upwards curve at the end.

"Recall this curve represents the last 10,000 years of atmospheric CO_2 content," he said as he drew. Only this time he drew it on only one board. Instead of taking up the entire front of the classroom, he used only half. He had plans for the other half of the board.

"What has happened during the last two hundred years - remember this last couple of inches of the board, where all this growth is occurring, represents only about 200 years out of 10,000 years of recorded history - what has happened to cause this exponential surge, this explosion of carbon dioxide?"

Zack paused. He preferred to ask questions like that, and to let them think for a moment or two before he answered them. He felt this was much more effective than straight lecturing.

Several hands shot up. This was even better thought Zack; if some students started to answer his questions, others would soon join in. The class would become infinitely more interesting.

"Yes," said Zack, pointing to a lanky boy in the back.

"Burning of oil and gas for energy," came the answer.

"Right," said Zack. "Only let's not limit it to oil and gas, just because we're in Louisiana. World-wide, coal is the biggest source of energy for electricity, and is the biggest contributor to carbon emissions. Let's lump all the fossil fuels together and write that on the board." Zack wrote 'FOSSIL FUELS.'

"This idea - that burning fossil fuels will put more CO_2 into the air which in turn will warm the earth - is not a new idea. It was first proposed by a Swedish chemist, Svante Arrhenius, back in.... Well, first let me tell you what he observed and what he said, exactly."

Zack pulled a small note card from his pocket and looked at it as he spoke.

"Arrhenius noticed that people of his day were burning more and more wood and coal, and he put two and two together. He summed it all up by saying:

'We are evaporating our coal mines into the air....[which must eventually cause]... a change in the transparency of the atmosphere.'

Zack continued, "Now, when did he reach this startling conclusion? The year that he first published those words in a scientific magazine was 1896, about 130 years ago.

"People, I cannot emphasize this enough. The burning of fossil fuels is the major contributor to the increase in carbon dioxide in our air. Our society continues to transform yesterday's carbon into today's pollution. And today's pollution is tomorrow's air. Over the past two centuries, the world has shifted from mostly agricultural to mostly industrial economies. Transportation, manufacturing, even agriculture itself now all depend almost entirely on using cheap energy. We are addicted to it.

"Transportation is a perfect example of how things have changed, just in the last 130 years. You see, 130 years ago, horses were the standard mode of in-city travel; the gasoline engine car had just been invented. Now, there are over 250 million of them – cars and trucks, that is - in this country alone. There are probably 800 million more in the rest of the world. <u>And each one spits out its own weight in carbon dioxide each year!</u> That's about 300 million tons of carbon dioxide each year just from on-road motor vehicles in the U.S., and maybe a billion tons of it worldwide – each year! And that CO_2 will stay in the air that we will be breathing for the next five hundred years.

"Consider too all the fuel used by boats, trains, airplanes, farm tractors, lawn mowers, jet skis, leaf blowers, snowmobiles, and all the other non-road vehicles, not just in the U.S. but all around the world.

"Now throw in the oil, gas and coal used to generate electricity, to heat homes, and to fuel industrial boilers around the world, all of it burning to the end product of CO_2, and you have got a monumental amount of the stuff. About 7 billion tons <u>per year</u> of carbon emissions which equals about 25 billion tons per year of carbon dioxide.

"Now I have trouble visualizing 25 <u>billion</u> tons of anything, so I thought of an example for you. Picture this: a wall made of 25 billion tons of empty aluminum cans - say Coke and Pepsi cans."

Here Zack paused and smiled at the class. He said, "Or you can picture beer cans if that makes it easier." A couple of fraternity boys in the left corner of the room laughed and exchanged knowing glances.

Zack continued, "Anyway, this wall is made of aluminum cans standing side by side, all stacked on top of each other. The wall is big, very big. Let's say it is a hundred feet high and forty feet wide. My question is: How long is it?"

No one answered; everyone was trying to picture this aluminum wall, 100 feet high and 40 feet wide.

Zack went on. "I have an advantage on you; I've already done this calculation." Again, he paused and looked around the class. As he spoke his next words, his long arms swept around in a great circle. "The wall is more than 750,000 miles long - it would circle the world 31 times!"

The lanky fellow in the back spoke up. "But Dr. Taylor, that's impossible! There aren't that many aluminum cans in the world."

"That's right," replied Taylor. "I purposely picked aluminum cans because they take up a lot of space and they don't weigh very much. So I knew that much weight - 25 billion tons - would calculate out to a tremendous number of cans. More cans than have ever been manufactured."

Zack continued, "But everyone is familiar with aluminum soft drink cans; they know what they look like, they've held them. So cans help me to make my point. Twenty-five billion tons of something is a tremendous lot of that something. And that's how much CO_2 is going into our air every year."

He addressed the class, and asked the next logical question. "But the burning of fossil fuels is not the only source of carbon dioxide. What are some others?"

"Decomposition of solid waste," answered the athletic blond, who was sitting in the front again.

"Right," said Zack, "all that garbage and paper and plastic we throw away produces a lot of carbon dioxide as it decomposes. In fact, not only do our landfills warm the earth with CO_2, they also contribute to global warming by generating methane - but then that's another lecture!" He turned and wrote 'SOLID WASTE' on the board.

"Deforestation," called out another voice.

"Right again," returned Zack, and wrote 'DEFORESTATION' on the board.

"Billions of cans of soft drinks!" said someone while Zack was writing. Everyone laughed.

Taylor turned to face the class. He was smiling too. "Actually, you're right!" he said. "Many industries burn natural gas just to get clean CO_2. Soft drink companies use it to put carbonation in their drinks. Of course, when you drink those products, you simply let most of that CO_2 back out into the air, hopefully as burps rather than the other exit pathway." The class laughed again.

"But let's get back to deforestation. That's a double-edged sword, and it gives us some serious cuts. As to carbon dioxide, it cuts in two major ways. First, when large tracts of forest lands are cleared - and, by the way, they are being cleared at an incredible rate - a lot of tree-stored carbon gets put back into the atmosphere when the trees are burned.

"I said the forests are being cleared at an incredible rate. I'm talking about developing countries here, not the United States. In fact, in the U.S., we now plant more trees each year than we cut. But that shouldn't make us too complacent; on a global scale, the picture is bleak, particularly for the tropical rain forests. An article I read recently documents just how bad it has been during the last 20 years. In 2010, the area of tropical rain forests cleared for agriculture and wood products was the size of South Carolina, and in 2025, it was the size of Louisiana and South Carolina put together.

"Now this is not just Brazil I'm talking about, but also in Thailand, Indonesia, Burma, Colombia, Venezuela, Ivory Coast, Zambia, Gabon, Cameroon, and most of the other less developed countries in the world."

Zack knew he was getting a little off track. He figured the students knew it too. So he did the logical thing - he told them that he knew.

"I know I'm wandering a little here, but bear with me. This subject is so complex and so intertwined that a lot of paths you start out on end up crossing each other many times. We will eventually get back to carbon dioxide and we'll try to simplify the big picture when we do."

Zack then shifted back into his lecture.

"Anyway, the clear cutting of large expanses of forests destroys whole ecosystems and drives many plants, insects and mammals to extinction. So why do these countries do this? The answer is easy: for food, for survival of their ever growing populations. Back in the 1970's, in order to survive, they began selling the only resources they had. They were selling their birthright back then, and they still are today.

"But this should not surprise you. After all, both Europe and the United States set the example. We each did the same thing - much more slowly of course - in our pioneering days. The reason deforestation happened so much slower 250 years ago is that we didn't have the 'help' of the industrialized world and huge mechanized equipment back then.

"Now, after you cut down all these trees, what do you do with them? Mostly, you just burn them, because you really just wanted the cleared land to plant crops. All that stored tree-carbon goes up in smoke and the carbon dioxide spreads around the globe. During the last 20 years, deforestation has added about half as much carbon dioxide to the world's atmosphere as has the burning of fossil fuels. So make that another 3 billion tons of carbon or 12 billion tons per year of carbon dioxide being created today and being emitted directly into our future."

"Dr. Taylor?" It was Jacqueline Jordan with her hand up.

"Yes, Miss Jordan?"

"That's the second or third time you've used that phrase - emissions into our future. What do you mean by that?"

"You're right, that is one of my favorite expressions. It means that our pollution today will have its major impacts on the citizens of tomorrow.

He went on to explain, "During the 1970's, 80's, and 90's, we had to deal with a lot of hazardous waste dump sites that were created by industries in the late 1800's and early 1900's. In a similar vein, the people who live on this planet 50 to 100 years from now are going to have to deal with the carbon dioxide problem that we are leaving them. Only the carbon dioxide problem is going to be much harder to deal with than simple hazardous wastes. It may well be impossible. Carbon dioxide lingers in the atmosphere for centuries, it spreads all around the globe, and the amount of it is enormous.

"But, again, I digress. Let's get back to deforestation. The second way deforestation hurts the world's carbon dioxide equation is on the subtraction side. The carbon dioxide balance of the world can be written as a very simple equation. Even though all the pieces of it may be hard to identify, the whole equation is very simple. Let me write it for you."

Zack wrote on the board:

ACCUMULATION = INPUT - OUTPUT

"This equation says that as long as carbon dioxide is put into the air faster than it is taken out, the atmosphere will accumulate CO_2. I mean, where else can it go? And this results in increases in the carbon dioxide concentration in the air.

"Now what takes CO_2 out of the air? Why, green plants of course, including trees. Trees and other plants breathe out CO_2 too, but they breathe in more than they breathe out. They store a big part of that carbon as plant fiber. Trees are especially good at storing it and keeping it out of the air for years and years.

"When we cut down forests, there are fewer and fewer trees left to remove CO_2, and so it accumulates even faster in the air. Before the industrial revolution when we started burning coal, and before the pioneering clearing of lands, the equation was balanced. Now it's out of balance; that's why the carbon dioxide concentration in the atmosphere is increasing.

"Other processes remove carbon dioxide from the air besides trees. The oceans are a major, perhaps the major, sink for CO_2. The oceans, in fact, hold far more CO_2 than the atmosphere. Plankton and other plants in the water remove CO_2 through photosynthesis like plants on land. Also, CO_2 dissolves directly from the air into the water. But the oceans also release CO_2 back into the air, and right now the oceans and the atmosphere are pretty much in balance.

"So the scary fact remains that we continue to add roughly 9 billion tons of carbon or 32 billion tons of carbon dioxide to our air every year by burning fossil fuels, by deforestation, and by several other pathways. All the while turning up the thermostat on our children's future home, a thermostat that is neither quick nor easy to readjust."

Zack finished his lecture and released the class. A couple of students walked up to the front, wanting to speak to him. One of them was the athletic blond.

"Dr. Taylor, I thought your lecture was very interesting today," she said.

"Well, thanks, but does that mean it wasn't interesting two days ago?" Zack laughed. "Just kidding," he said. "Say, what's your name? I always try to get to know most of my students each semester."

"I'm Bailey Phillips. I'm a Psychology major, and I'm on the soccer team," she volunteered.

"Well, good for you. I think college athletics are great for students."

"Dr. Taylor, you said something in your lecture that I wanted to ask about."

"OK, shoot, what is it?"

"You said that clear cutting our rain forests and replacing them with food crops, led to serious reductions in species diversity. That we were taking great risks with the world's gene pool. What kind of risks? I mean, most of those jungle plants we never knew existed anyway. How can their extinction really cause us any serious harm?"

"So, Bailey, what you're saying is that if you don't have something useful to you now, you don't mind losing it and its potential forever. Is that it?"

"Well, yes, I guess so."

"OK, let me give you a prime example of why that thinking is dead wrong. Last year, I remember seeing an article in the paper about medical researchers at Johns Hopkins. They had found a cure for AIDS! It still needed testing, but it looked like a sure winner.

"The key ingredient in the AIDS cure comes from a previously unknown vine that grows only on certain trees and only in one small area of Africa, in northern Ghana. It seems that vine just won't grow anywhere else in the world. No one knows what all the conditions are that make that vine grow in just that spot, but if those conditions change, the vine may go extinct.

"And guess what, Bailey? Last year, Ghana cut down 20 percent of the forest area in which the vine is found."

"My God," whispered Phillips. "What are they going to do? Will they stop cutting those trees?"

"I don't know," said Zack somberly. "Last I heard was some drug company was trying to buy the rights from the Ghana government, but since the cure is not proven yet, they don't want to pay too much money. Meanwhile, Ghana needs cash and they know they can get it by selling to timber companies."

CHAPTER 11

Cairo, Egypt, February

An urgent meeting was in progress in the office of Anwar Abdelal, president of Egypt.

"But, President, I am doing everything I know how to do!" complained Gamel Haddad, Minister of Irrigation. He looked pleadingly at Abdelal.

The president of Egypt was a handsome man. His dark eyes, and brown skin were offset by very white teeth. He had a full head of black hair, streaked with just the right amount of gray, and with patches of pure gray at the temples. At the moment a vein just in front of the gray patch at his right temple was pulsing, reflecting his agitation.

"You must do more!" barked Abdelal. "The flower of Egypt is wilting, the body of Egypt is dying from this drought!"

Haddad tried again. "It is those cursed Sudanese - they are stealing our water. For 10,000 years, the River Nile brings life-giving waters to our people. We do not waste this precious gift; we preserve it. We are using the water management techniques I learned in the U.S., and even newer water conservation measures that I learned from our friends, the Israelis. I was educated in the U.S., but I was born here. I know the true value of water."

Abdelal lowered his voice, but his tone remained serious. "Gamel, old friend, I know you are smart, and I know you are a very hard worker. Most of all, I know you love our country. But this problem may well be the end of us. We are losing people faster than ever this year. Those that do not die from thirst or starvation simply flee the country. Already, the European Union has filed an official protest with me about all the Egyptian refugees. And the U.S. - hah! - they just closed their borders to Egyptians. We <u>must</u> find more and better ways to use what little water we have left!"

Haddad replied, "The River Nile is Egypt; it is our history, it is our destiny. Yet now, these upstart Sudanese claim it is their river. They take water carelessly. They pollute what is left and expect us to lap it up like dogs! If we had the River Nile back like it was when we were children, all our water problems would be solved. We must take back what is ours!"

Abdelal was somewhat surprised by Haddad's statement. He said slowly, "Gamel, you are beginning to sound like General Badi-Sadr. Would you have us go to war?"

"If the leopard must fight the pack of jackals or die from thirst, then it will fight!"

"Tell me, is our drought somehow related to the good fortune of those Iraqi dogs these last three years?"

"Anwar, in truth, I do not know. But it is most unfair if it is. When that madman Hussein burnt all those oil wells in Kuwait 40 years ago, it was like burning five percent more oil in the world that year. For almost a year those fires raged. The smoke polluted the whole Middle East; some say that smoke went all around the world. I remember my father said that his stupidity would change our region forever."

Abdelal muttered, "I have heard it said that all that pollution helped change our rainfall – and to their benefit! It is most unfair!"

"Indeed it is. To see those stupid Iraqis with so much water now is maddening."

Abdelal shifted in his chair. "Listen, old friend, I need you to work more of your magic with our tired old River Nile. Squeeze a few more drops from it to give our people a chance. One day our River will come back to us. Until then, we must do the best we can."

"Yes, Anwar, I will try. But I am not a miracle worker."

Gamel Haddad, the tired old Minister of Irrigation, left the room. A few minutes later, the President of Egypt picked up the phone and spoke to his secretary.

"You may send in General Bani-Sadr, now."

* * *

Caracas, Venezuela, February

The airport in Caracas, Venezuela, was hot and humid, but that was not unusual, even in February. After all, Caracas is only 10 degrees north of the equator. The airport workers all wore open collar, light colored shirts. Most of the rest of the people were tourists, and they, too, were dressed down. There were, however, a few unfortunate souls who had flown in on business from northern climate cities, and were dressed in suits. Doug Cunningham was one of those few.

Doug Cunningham was a sweater; that is, he sweated easily. He always had, ever since puberty. Standing there in line, in the heat, his jacket in one hand, his handkerchief in the other, he thought about his sweating.

Sweating had always caused him a problem. The first time his sweat glands had let him down big time was the night of the senior prom. For weeks he had worried about asking Janice, but he had finally worked up the courage to do it. Then the big night came, and he was dripping almost before they had gotten to the dance. Then at the dance - Jesus, it still embarrassed him to think about how the other kids had pointed out his soggy shirt and pants. It had been unusually warm that night, hadn't it?

Cunningham's attention was drawn to a man waiting nearby. The man looked patrician; he was dressed in a finely tailored wool suit. He was tall and dark, very dark. In fact his skin was almost black. He looked African, except for his facial features. He had a thin nose and thin lips. But there was something else. What was it?

Cunningham saw the man's eyes light up with recognition. Then the tall gentleman moved gracefully away to join two other people who looked and were dressed a lot like he was. Cunningham replaced his damp handkerchief with a dry one and mopped his face again. Suddenly he knew what had drawn his attention to the mysterious man. He had not been sweating! Cunningham glanced back over his shoulder but the trio was gone.

The three tall black men entered the airport meeting room. There were three women and one man already seated at the table. Each was dressed impeccably, each was tall and dark, and no one was sweating.

"Ah, Simon, I see you have found the others," said the woman at the head of the table.

"Yes, Marguerite, we are all here now. We can begin."

When Marguerite stood up, the group grew quiet.

"The Council of Seven is assembled," she said. "The Council shall come to order. First we shall have our status reports. Rodrigo, you start."

"Emissions are still growing. New discoveries of oil and gas reserves have kept prices down, so more gas is being burned now than at any time in history. Fracking and other technologies are keeping energy prices so low that there has been little progress on solar or wind energy.

Marguerite turned to the man on her right. "Emilio, what of the climate predictions?"

"As long as emissions keep growing, carbon dioxide will keep rising. The best climate modelers in the U.S. and Japan agree that the average temperature is up 1.9 to 2.5 degrees now and that it will rise another 7 to 10 degrees by 2065.

"Their specific forecasts are not in agreement. The Japanese models show the U.S. grain belt becoming arid by 2035, but the U.S. models do not show that. It appears that certain U.S. politicians have influenced their EPA to show less severe consequences. They appear to be trying to hide the truth from their public."

"Aranxta," said Marguerite, "speaking of politics, how goes the battle at the United Nations?"

The woman seated to Marguerite's left spoke. "The scientists on the Intergovernmental Panel on Climate Change made a report to the Multi-government Negotiating Committee in Nairobi, Kenya, last month. In it, they censured the United States in the strongest language I have yet seen from them. The IPCC said that the U.S. must stop dragging its feet on this issue. Most of the countries in the world are willing to take mandatory cuts in carbon emissions - but not the U.S. Furthermore, China, India and Europe do not want to hurt their own economies if the U.S. is not willing to take the proportional cuts that they should. These big 4 are the world's biggest consumers of fossil fuels, and the world's biggest emitters of carbon dioxide. Unless the U.S. agrees to the mandatory cuts, no one else will do so."

Marguerite interrupted angrily. "The U.S. has been stalling since the early meetings in the 1990s!"

"Yes," agreed Aranxta, "even though their public started demanding actions six or seven years ago, there are still some powerful holdovers in the denial camp. With the new satellite network, each country is able to monitor CO_2 emissions from all the others, yet those politicians simply refuse to go along. They say there is still no solid proof!"

"Unbelievable!" exclaimed Marguerite. "Must we be forced to reveal our history? To explain what can happen to an entire planet, to make them believe and take action?"

Simon stood up. "Marguerite, wait, let me report on the research front."

"Yes, Simon, I'm sorry. I should have called on you."

Simon began his report. "The research committee, as you know, has been quietly funding work all over the globe for decades. We have been backing alternative energy research, mainly. But last year we decided that it might be better to apply our funds to proving the depth of the crisis to the world leaders, especially in the U.S.

"So we have begun a new research initiative under the name of 'International Defenders of the Environment'. We hope to get some remarkable demonstrations of the potential devastation that can be caused by Greenhouse. As Aranxta said, the problem is not with the scientists, it is with the politicians."

Ricardo spoke. "May I address the Council?" Rather than wait for a reply, he stood and began speaking. "I know I'm new to the Council, but I really don't see the urgency for action here. Our own models have shown that earth can heat up another 25 or 30 degrees with no danger to the existence of the planet itself. Of course, many species would not survive the enormous changes this would bring about. There would be a major die-back in the human population as well. But human beings are very resilient. They would cope, they would adapt.

"And, personally, I would welcome that extra warmth. I see most of you dressed warmly for this trip, as did I. We all might find the earth a little more pleasant after the warming."

Marguerite stood up. Her height at 6'2" was impressive though not that unusual by standards in the room today, but her face at that moment demanded immediate silence and attention.

"Do not ever bring your personal likes or dislikes into this Council again," she said. Her controlled voice was betrayed by her clenched jaw muscles and the tendons visible in her neck. "We are here to try to help civilization deal with their biggest challenge ever. We must remain impartial! And, as I said before, we may have to reveal ourselves and our long history to finally get their attention."

An old gray-haired man at the other end of the table spoke for the first time. He did not stand as the others had done, but all eyes turned to him the moment he cleared his throat.

"I was leader of this Council in the 1970's and 80's, and I must tell you that you are talking grave danger here. You all know the history of the Council. For hundreds of years we have operated secretly, yet we have been effective at influencing world events. No one knows of us, and no one should. We must not reveal our true nature."

Others chimed in now, not waiting to be recognized. Some agreed and some disagreed; all wanted to be heard.

Many voices sounded. "But, sir, if we do not act soon, it may be too late, even for us! We must take action while we can."

"No, it is too dangerous."

"Perhaps we can do something to spur the world to act."

"That hasn't worked before; why should it work now?"

"Quiet, please! We must vote," said Marguerite. The room quieted down as each person thought about what he or she was about to do.

"All in favor of acting openly and revealing ourselves to the humans, raise your hands."

Marguerite looked around the room slowly; only two hands were raised. She said "The vote is 2 for and 5 against. It appears we will wait another year at least." She paused and then said firmly, "This Council meeting is adjourned. Everyone please leave separately. I don't have to remind you to be careful."

CHAPTER 12

New Orleans, February

Knock. Knock. Zack rapped his big knuckles on the old wooden door. Sam stood patiently by his side, watching the door expectantly.

Knock. Knock. Knock.

"Gator, it's me, Zack. Open up, I know you're in there."

Zack was impatient to get inside. The car trip from New Orleans to Gator's shack had seemed tiresome today. The route followed decent roads most of the way, staying on pavement through Chalmette, St. Bernard, and finally Delacroix. After that, it was tough going, even for Zack's Jeep. You could actually drive to within 250 feet of Gator's cabin, on dirt and shell roads. After that, you walked on tree stumps and rocks the rest of the way.

But the trip was always well worth it. Zack had been making it five or six times a year for the last two years, ever since he had met Gator on an otherwise boring guided tour of 'Cajun Country' - the bayous of very far south Louisiana.

Finally, the door creaked open on its rusty hinges, giving way to the sun-browned, wind-beaten face of Jerome 'Gator' Boudreaux. A two-day growth of beard revealed more white whiskers than black. Gator's thinning hair told the story of more than fifty years of living. But Gator's enthusiastic greeting belied his age.

"Zack boy! Comment ca vas, my good frien'? You got Sam wit' you? 'Course you do! Hello, Sam, you ol' wolf!"

Gator's heavy Cajun accent was full of life; his face was creased with a large smile, carelessly revealing a few brown teeth and some gaps where teeth used to be. He gave Sam a rough pat on the head and a scratch behind the ears.

"Gator, I would have called to let you know we were coming, but you don't have a phone," said Zack jokingly.

"Don't want one, no how" replied Gator, seriously. "Dem phone be trouble, for sure. Any time people calls you up, it be trouble. I don't need to get myself no calls.

If I need to call somebody, which I don't, I take myself to that pay phone down in town."

It was a long speech for Gator, and it settled the issue, so Zack changed the subject.

"Gator, it's Saturday, I'm off work, and I was hoping we could go out in your airboat, maybe catch a few fish."

"Maybe, but first you bring yourself and your wolf inside here and set yourself down for a spell."

Zack entered the small cabin, and looked around for something new since his last visit, but of course he knew he wouldn't find anything. The cabin was very sparsely decorated. No, decorated was not the right word. It was stocked with essentials, and ornamented with trivia from Gator's past. There was a shotgun and a rifle mounted on one wall, three fishing poles and a cast net on another. The largest bass Zack had ever seen was mounted and hanging near the fishing poles. Two kerosene lanterns and an ancient Coleman stove hung from the ceiling in one corner.

But the dominant feature of the room hung from the fourth wall. A collection of knives, various sizes and shapes, were displayed there. Although many were obviously old, they were all shiny and well oiled, protected from the damp sulfur air of the nearby swamps. The huge hunting knife in the center of the collection fairly gleamed in the sunlight coming through the opposite window. Off to the left side of the knife collection, was mounted the gape-mouthed head of a large water moccasin. The photograph of a plain, almost homely woman was hung on the wall just to the other side of the knives.

Sam sniffed around and, as usual, growled when she came to the large alligator skull sitting in the corner.

"Sam, she still don't like Big'un," commented Gator. "Can't blame her none; I don't really like Big'un either. Just keep him around to remind me to be careful huntin' dem gator in dem bayou. Big'un almost got me; he give me this scar here, don't you know." Gator pointed to a long double scar running from his left shoulder to his left elbow.

Zack shook his head. "I can't believe you still go out and hunt alligators with nothing but a rope and a knife. One of these days, another 'Big'un' will come along and take you down to the bottom of the swamp."

"Not if I be careful!" declared Boudreaux. "And don't you be sayin' swamp - it be a bayou not a swamp. Only two things you got to watch out for in dem bayou - dem gators and dem mocs. One of dem gators, he almos' got me. And 'bout three year ago, one of dem mocs, he got Effie. I be missin' her, still."

Boudreaux paused and looked over at the photograph on the wall, his only physical reminder of his departed wife.

"But I got that moc, don't you know. There he be, too," he declared, looking at the stuffed head of the water moccasin. "He won't be making no more sorrow for people, with him hangin' up there on my wall like dat."

Both men were quiet for a moment. Sam came up and lay down near Zack's feet. Boudreaux broke the silence first, his nostalgic mood gone.

"So you want to go catch dem fish, eh?"

"Sure do, Gator. You reckon you can still find where the big ones are?"

"Boy, the day come when ol' Gator can't find no fish, dat be the day when they ain't no more fish 'round these here parts!"

After getting the poles and equipment together, the two men walked around the shack to where the airboat was tied up. The shack was in the middle of a large swamp, in the Mississippi River delta region, south of New Orleans. The water came right up to the back porch, and the two men stepped off the porch and into the boat.

The airboat ride was short and pleasant. Gator knew some good fishing holes not far from his house. Zack's face was filled with the pleasure of being out in the bayous today. As the boat slowed and stopped, he turned back to face Gator and help him make ready for the fishing.

"Zack boy, you be looking mighty happy today. What be de reason?"

"No reason, Gator, just glad to be out here in the 'Glades."

"The what?"

"What did I say?"

"You said the 'Glades - what be dem?"

"I'm sorry, I was thinking of when I was a boy. The 'Glades are the Everglades - it's a huge swamp, uh, bayou, in Florida, where I grew up. In high school, I had a favorite teacher. He was my chemistry teacher, and I owe him a lot. Probably more than I even know.

"He was short and had a mustache and slicked back gray hair, and to look at him you wouldn't think he ever got outside his lab. But all the kids respected him. I remember once when a football player, nearly twice his size, was cutting up in the lab. Dr. Brackett wouldn't put up with that. He grabbed the boy by the shirt collar and literally dragged him out into the hall. I don't know what he said to him, but there was never a problem in the lab again.

"Dr. Brackett was a good chemist, and an excellent teacher. But he was also a naturalist."

"Say what?" questioned Gator.

"He loved nature, and he especially loved the Everglades. He used to take me out there on weekends. I really learned to love the 'Glades with him. We would go canoeing for hours through the ... bayous, and watch for birds, turtles, even alligators. There's plenty of them in Florida you know."

"Well, then, I might have to bring myself down to Florida one day," said Gator.

Zack replied, "If you do, I'll be sure to take you out to the 'Glades where you can catch a Florida alligator. They're even bigger there than they are here."

"Impossee-blay," declared Gator Boudreaux, "they ain't no gator anywhere, any bigger or meaner than dem that's livin' rite cheer in Loosianne!"

Zack laughed. He said, "Well, I don't care about big gators, but I do care about catching some big fish. So let's get started, OK!"

CHAPTER 13

Washington, D.C., February

W ell, J.R., what do you want me to do about that rogue commander, kill him?"
Tssscht.
J.R. Hunter leaned back in his chair and sucked air in through the small gap in between his top front teeth. It was a harsh, grating sound. His upper lip curled up to allow the air to rush inwards. His tongue blocked all entrances except for the small opening between his two front teeth. The result was a loud, irritating, squeaky sucking sound.

Tssscht.

It was a habit he was almost unaware of, especially when, as now, he was contemplating an important decision. The habit was particularly annoying to those who didn't know J.R. well enough to be afraid of him.

Tssscht.

"No, not yet. Let's wait and see if his own people will do that for us."

"OK, it's your call. I'm headed back to Colombia tonight, on the 8:05 flight out of National. Call me if you change your mind. You know where I'm staying."

"I know. Leave by the back way."

"Of course."

"And, Carlos..."

Tssscht.

"Yes?"

"Don't do anything stupid."

After Carlos had gone, J.R. Hunter, Lt. Col, US Army (retired), now Chief of Covert Operations – Caribbean Basin, Defense Intelligence Agency, stood up and paced around the windowless office. Talking with Carlos about the operation in Colombia had made him feel antsy. He wished he could go to the field with Carlos on this one. It would be like the old days, exciting. He hated being cooped up in this office.

But, he had to admit, he liked the power. As a field agent, he had gotten to enjoy the hands-on stuff, especially the wet work. But he could only do one deal at a time, and then only if he got permission. Now he was the one who gave permission. He was in control, at least in control of Caribbean Basin operations.

As a member of the DIA, Hunter had to be careful not to let his operations people get crosswise with CIA people. He had to 'deconflict' all their operations. He smiled. Of course, sometimes that meant he couldn't tell anyone in the CIA about what he was doing; they were always so quick to claim 'conflict.' The pansies. They were almost as bad as the FBI. Hunter knew better than to try to work with the FBI. They had legal authority and congressional mandates to be the sole operator inside the continental USA. That sometimes could get in the way of a good operation.

Hunter went back to his desk. He pulled out a file, glanced at it to get the right code name. He punched the name into his computer and read what showed on the screen.

Tssscht.

He picked up the phone, the one with the scrambler device permanently attached. He dialed the area code (504) and the rest of the number.

Tssscht.

The 504 area code was for New Orleans. Hunter knew he was crossing over the boundaries here, but what the hell, New Orleans was on the Caribbean basin, wasn't it? Also, he figured if he could score on this one, then he might get that old fart boss of his, Chief of Covert Ops - Eastern Hemisphere, kicked upstairs. Then J. R. Hunter could move up. He would have a lot more power, and a lot more pawns to push around the board.

Tssscht.

"Hello," said the voice on the other end.

"Mockingbird, this is Hawk. Turn on your scrambler."

There was a pause, a button was pressed.

"OK, J.R., it's on."

"Don't use my name on the phone - even on scrambler!"

"OK, OK, sorry."

"I want an update on the target. Can you come to Washington?"

"I guess so. When?"

"This weekend. I'll meet you at the usual place."

"Oh, that place seems so sleazy."

Tssscht.

"Can't we meet somewhere else? Please?"

"No."

"Oh, all right."

"One more thing, Mockingbird...."

"Yes?"

Tsssscht.

"Find out if he's planning to make any trips in the near future."

"I'll try."

"I know you will. Hawk out."

J.R. hung up the phone. His agent in New Orleans was well placed. Even his own staff didn't know about this operation. Just as well, thought Hunter, just as well.

* * *

Amsterdam, February

Peter, just listen to reason." Haarhuis' boss, Nils Lindgeren, was practically pleading with him.

Haarhuis was being pressed, but was not going to budge. "No, you listen. If we build a weak dike, it may take ten years or twenty years to fail but it will fail. And when it does, how many hundreds or thousands of innocent people will pay for our mistake, pay with their lives?"

Henry, one of the junior engineers, said "Mr. Haarhuis, we have done computer simulations. The results show that the new design is still within the safety criteria. It has a 98.5 percent probability of lasting its design lifetime."

"What is your data base?" asked Haarhuis. Before Henry could answer, Haarhuis said "It really doesn't matter, whatever it is I know it is not sufficient."

Nils said, "Peter, that doesn't sound like an engineer talking. You always are saying 'show me data, show me proof.' Yet when we bring you new cost saving ideas, new designs, you reject them out of hand."

"I am not rejecting them out of hand. I am rejecting them because they are unsafe!"

"But Henry and George are using the latest computer techniques. They have access to the latest government data bases on North Sea activity for the last thirty years."

"What about 76 years ago? Hmmm? What about the biggest storm to ever hit our homeland? Why isn't that in the data base?"

"Peter, I am told that our new designs are well within all government codes and will withstand anything the North Sea can throw at them. Henry, isn't that so?"

Henry nodded.

Lindgeren continued, "And the new designs will save the company over nine million dollars. We cannot ignore that."

"And saving that much money will make you look good before the president. How fortunate," said Haarhuis, sarcastically.

"The new designs will work, Mr. Haarhuis," said George. "We learned this new matrix technique in school."

Haarhuis stated flatly, "They are weaker than my designs."

"I agree with that statement," said Nils, quickly, seeing an opportunity. "I understand. But your designs utilize the old methods, and you are designing for an unrealistic risk. So your dikes are bigger and stronger than they need to be. It is just like an old man to want more insurance than he can afford."

Haarhuis spoke slowly. "You are right about one thing Nils; I am an old man. Thank God I am, because I don't want to be around when your wonderful new dike, built with the new design, crumbles, and the sea swallows one-fourth of our homeland!"

"You are being melodramatic. Now please sign the document."

"No, I have not yet been convinced. As an engineer I must listen to facts and I will believe in the numbers when I see them for myself. But you must extend the database back to 1953. Nothing less will do.

Peter Haarhuis stood up. "I am still Chief Engineer on this project. You need my signature to proceed. I have made a reasonable request for more data, and I will not sign until I have seen the new analysis."

"You know I can get you removed as Chief Engineer," threatened Lindgeren.

"Not for what I am asking. Not without a lot of publicity, and that you do not want, I know. No, let us dance a while more, Nils. You may still win. After all, I am an engineer - I will listen to the facts and the data. But right now, I am still in command of the design team. So for now, we do it my way."

CHAPTER 14

New Orleans, February

"Mom, this is Zack." Taylor was speaking into the phone. "I'm coming to visit you in three weeks. I have a convention in Orlando, and I'll come by afterwards on Saturday the 28th to see you. Try not to schedule a golf game that day, will you? Thanks. Good-bye. Oh, yes, please call me at home tonight to let me know that you got the message. Bye, now."

Zack hung up the phone. He didn't especially like talking to voice mail, but in his mother's case it was an absolute necessity. She was never in. Where she got her energy, Zack didn't know, but hoped that it would be hereditary.

Knock. Knock.

"Come in," called Taylor.

"Hello, Dr. Taylor," said Jacqueline Jordan, "I was hoping to catch you. Are you busy?"

Zack resisted the impulse to stand up and usher her into the office. He said simply, "No, not really. Come on in, Jacqueline. How can I help?"

"I was just wondering...." Then she noticed Taylor's plane ticket on his desk.

"Going on a vacation so soon after class has started?" She smiled a playful half-smile, her eyes twinkling a bit. "What's the matter - did the students get to you already?"

Taylor loved the way her eyes sparkled, the way she inclined her head. He wanted to reach out and touch her, to take her in his arms, to press his lips against hers. Instead, he forced his mind to come back to reality, and to continue the conversation.

"Just got finished making some plans to go to Florida. Big conference there on Greenhouse, Science vs. Politics."

"You're really into this Greenhouse Effect thing, aren't you? I saw you the other night on the 6:00 news. Do the TV people talk with you a lot?"

"A fair bit. I have a friend at WNOT, plus I guess I come across well on the tube. I'll use whatever means I can to get the word out to as many people as I can. Sooner or later, it might start to sink in."

"What you were saying about the oil companies encouraging Americans to use so much oil was pretty blunt, and you weren't very complimentary to the American military. In fact, you sounded downright hostile."

"Jacqueline, when you come to know me better..." Zack paused, thinking about his choice of words. "...then you will realize I can be pretty blunt sometimes.

"And I am hostile to the military. They burn fuel like crazy, for no good reason. The Russian threat ended nine years ago, and the Chinese three. Still, our military go on these massive training exercises, transporting men and equipment all over the world. They build millions of tons of bombs, store them for thirty years and then burn them up or blow them up when they become obsolete. They take an extraordinary part of the national research budget that could be used for alternative fuels, or environmental restoration."

Jacqueline was looking directly at him, her clear blue eyes met his. She said, "You sound like you're committed to do battle with them."

"I feel like I'm fighting a war on this - one battle after another. My father died from respiratory failure during the heat wave of 2015. He had lung problems - caused by air pollution, I'm sure of it. His old lungs just couldn't handle the hot polluted air that summer.

"These extremely hot summers are being caused by excess carbon dioxide which is directly tied to burning all these fossil fuels. Unless people get involved, unless we try to change things, it will only get worse."

"But don't you feel kind of like Don Quixote, fighting the oil giants and the military all by yourself?"

"I was named after Zachary Taylor, our 12th president. He was a real battler, Old Rough and Ready. A hero of the Mexican and Seminole Indian wars - the General Schwarzenegger of his day."

"You mean General Schwarzkopf!" interrupted Jordan.

"Oh, yes, you're right. The Army general from years and years ago - he was famous briefly. How did you know about him?"

"Oh, it's not important. Go on, you were saying?"

"Anyway, my Dad was convinced we were related to Old Zachary Taylor, but could never prove it. Didn't matter, he named me after him anyway. And he taught me to be a battler. 'Don't look for a fight, son,' he would say, 'but always be ready for one. And always, always fight for what you believe in.'

"Beliefs, convictions, principles - you know, Jacqueline, when it comes right down to it, those are the only things worth fighting for."

Zack stopped, then smiled, mildly surprised at how he was opening up so freely to a student. He said, "But I've gotten way off track. What was it you were wondering?"

"Wondering?"

"Yes, that's what you said when you first came in, just before I went riding off on my white horse."

"Oh, yes. I was wondering if you could give me some advice on buying a computer. I guess I'll be needing one for my classes here."

"Yes, you will. And I'd be happy to give you some advice. How much do you want to spend?"

"I have a fair amount of money saved up; I'd like to get a good one. What's this model you have?"

"Oh, I don't think you'd need one this powerful. I use this to run some pretty sophisticated climate models. I know of some good computers more suited for students...."

Jordan stopped him with one of her smiles. Her smile radiated warmth, and filled Zack with a desire to shut up and just bask in that warmth for a while.

"Oh, Dr. Taylor, thank you but I think I'd rather buy the best and just sort of grow into it. Now tell me more about this one and what kind of climate models you're running."

Zack could tell she had a genuine desire to learn. In her eyes he could see the innocent pleasure of the anticipation of a student eager to learn something new. Yet, Zack thought he detected a hint of something else in those blue depths as well.

CHAPTER 15

Orlando, FL, March

T he conference looked like it was going to be everything Zack had hoped for and more. The Sheraton Twin Towers were filled to capacity and the exhibit hall was overflowing with vendors and consulting firms hawking their wares and/or services. Zack had already met an old friend during registration and had made some plans to go to Disney World later in the week. Right now he was headed to the Grand Ballroom for the opening keynote address. Having arrived late last night, he had overslept and now he was hurrying to avoid missing any of the speech.

The moderator was just finishing his introduction, "...give you our chief proponent in the Congress, the Environmental Senator from Wyoming, the Honorable Lane Stillwater."

After the applause died down, Senator Stillwater began to speak.

"Thank you. I'm honored to be asked to open this 34th International Conference on the Intersection of Science and Policy Regarding on Global Climate Change. The issues we will discuss over the next 3 days are of major importance to all governments, both here and around the world.

"I'd like to open my speech today with something I borrowed from my old friend Greg Woodward, director of the International Global Warming Institute, and a recognized authority on global warming." Senator Stillwater read:

> *In every international forum over the past two years*
> *where the United States has had an opportunity to*
> *offer political leadership to a world hungry for*
> *constructive insights on the warming of the earth,*
> *it has squandered that opportunity. The result has*
> *been a significant, unnecessary, and costly delay in*
> *taking steps internationally to control the warming*

of the earth....

Stillwater paused and looked up from his notes. "Now, my friends," he said, "unfortunately, this quote is not new. It was first uttered back in 1991. Even more unfortunately, that quote is as true today as it was way back then.

"There will be no winners in global warming. As the earth gets warmer, climates will become more unstable, and we will encounter greater difficulties with such basics as agriculture, water supply, forestry, sea level rise, more frequent and more severe storms, and new and more exotic diseases.

"The few apparent advantages, such as the warming of Siberia, or Canada, or even Wyoming,..." Stillwater paused while the audience laughed politely. "...are only superficial, and do not outweigh the many disadvantages, including the possible submergence of entire island nations!"

The contingent from the Maldives stood up and led the group in applause for recognition of their most urgent problem.

"I don't have to tell this group about all the dangers. But I will relate one story that I think bears on this problem. As it gets warmer, bacteria in the environment work faster. Actually, all life processes speed up, but bacteria speed up more because they're so tiny and so numerous. Well, as these little critters live faster, they speed up the decay processes in forests and swamps and ocean sediments, and they release even more carbon dioxide. Which in turn warms the earth even more.

"You scientists call this a positive feedback loop, but I call it a vicious cycle. I'm told that there are quite a few of these vicious cycles around. Like the melting of the polar ice caps. White ice <u>reflects</u> sunlight energy directly back out to space <u>as light energy</u> - it never turns into heat. But when ice melts, it exposes dark water or tundra, which <u>absorbs</u> sunlight energy and retains it as <u>heat</u>. This of course accelerates the melting of more ice.

"Now my point is this: if you strike a match, it will burn with a small flame. You can easily blow it out any time you want. If you let that match ignite a piece of newspaper, then you have a bigger flame, somewhat harder to manage, but you can still control it. If that newspaper ignites a forest, forget it, you've lost control. The fire just has to burn itself out.

"My friends, I'm afraid we've just about lost control. Unless we take some drastic and rather painful steps now, we are going to be faced with a 'forest fire' the likes of which has never been seen before."

Senator Stillwater continued to speak, but Zack's attention started to wander. He began to browse through the program of today's events. It seemed only moments later that the audience was applauding and the Senator was done. Stillwater wished the conferees good luck and pleaded other pressing engagements as he left the podium. Zack stood up also. He wanted to try to catch Stillwater before he left.

Outside the ballroom, Zack saw the Senator walking briskly towards the door with two aides, both talking at the same time. Zack hurried over.

"Senator! Senator! Excuse me," Zack called.

Stillwater turned around. "Yes?" he said.

Geez, he looks <u>old</u> thought Zack, when he got closer.

"Senator, I wanted to tell you how much I liked your opening remarks this morning. And I wanted to introduce myself. I'm Professor Zachary Taylor from the University of Southern Louisiana, in New Orleans."

As soon as Stillwater heard where Zack was from, that he was not a constituent, he looked a bit less enthusiastic. He said, "Nice to meet you, son," then glanced at the aide on his left. The aide moved to step between them and hustle the Senator off.

Zack hurried on. "Senator, I've been teaching students about the Greenhouse Effect for three years now. Most of the scientists and engineers at this conference have been working at this a lot longer than I have. As a group, we've been researching the Greenhouse Effect for maybe half a century. But I don't see any results, Senator - there haven't been any changes in our national policy. What I wanted to ask you is this: What else do we need to do, Senator? What else do we need to do?"

Stillwater looked weary when he answered. "Son," he said, "you're worried about the wrong color house."

"Excuse me? What do you mean by that?"

"You and all the rest of you science and engineering folks are working hard on the <u>Greenhouse</u> problem. But where you should be putting more of your efforts is the <u>White House</u> problem. Convince the Administration, Son, that's what you need to do. Focus on a different color 'House.'

* * *

That evening Zack was sitting at the hotel lobby bar. He was waiting for his friend; they were going out to dinner. The bar was practically empty, so he had started talking with the bartender. He ordered a martini, not really sure why.

"Here you go, sir. You here for the conference?"

"Yes, I'm a professor from New Orleans."

"New Orleans, huh. Man, that's a wild and crazy town. I never worked there, but I been there once. A real party town."

"I guess so, but I'm not into parties too much. Tell me about some of the things to do here in Orlando."

"Well, Professor, if you're not into partying, then you'd better be into tourist attractions. We got them by the ton here. Disney World, EPCOT Center, Universal Studios, Sea World, Magic World, you name it."

"And the prices are real good, too. They're not as crowded anymore. Used to be you had to stand in line, and pay through the nose for most of those places. But for the last four years or so, the industry's been in a major slump.

"Everyone says it's too damn hot here now - the heat wave of '21 killed a bunch of people in Florida. So the summer trade has really dried up. Mosquitoes have gotten real bad too. They're bigger and meaner than ever. You know, Orange County used to be called Mosquito County 150 years ago."

"No," said Zack, "I'd never heard that before."

The bartender went on. "Be sure to spray yourself if you're going out tonight. Wasn't cold enough this winter to kill them all. We've had some encephalitis around here this year. Seventy-five people have died so far from encephalitis in Florida this winter, most of them old folks. And that Zika is still popping up every now and then.

"Between the heat and the mosquitoes, most of the tourists just got driven away. Rumor is that Disney is going to build a new park in Canada. If that happens, this area will dry up for sure. Hotels are hurting real bad, too. Ever wonder how come you guys got such a good deal on this hotel for the convention? No more tourists."

Zack said, "You know, all this is related to something I've been working on for years now. You ever heard of the Greenhouse Effect?"

"Sure, and I believe in it too. I didn't used to, but I do now. But what can we do about it? Nothing."

"Zack! Hey, Zack!"

Taylor turned to see his friend waving at him from the lobby. He waved then turned back to the bartender.

"Yes there is; you can stop driving your car so much! Better yet, drive it into the ocean and don't replace it! And convince others to do the same," said Zack. The bartender smiled and shook his head. Zack wanted to say more but he felt the pull of his waiting friend.

"Listen, I gotta go. Thanks for the info," he said. "And don't give up hope." He paid for his drink, leaving a modest tip, and headed towards his friend. He wondered if they sold 'Off' in the hotel gift shop.

"Hey, barkeep." The short but powerfully built man at the corner of the bar was holding up his glass.

"Yes, sir, another?"

Tssscht.

"You got it, barkeep, and keep them coming until I tell you to stop."

CHAPTER 16

U.S. Air Flight 626 from Orlando to Miami is a short and scenic flight, especially if you like coastlines. The plane rises to about 12,000 feet and then flies southeast towards the coast, intersecting the Atlantic Ocean in the vicinity of West Palm Beach. From there on, the plane follows the beaches south until it gets to Miami Beach, where it turns inland towards Miami International Airport, some eight miles away.

Zack had a window seat and was enjoying the gorgeous view of Bal Harbour and Miami Beach. The sky was clear in all directions today, a welcome relief from all the rain they had been getting. The ocean was a deep blue-black away from the shore, but turned to a rich translucent green as it met the yellow-white sand of the beach. The zone in between the blue-black and the shimmering green was various shades of blue-green and was topped with tiny white ribbons of foam as the waves began to break and make their run up to the shore.

The narrow strip of sand that was the famous Miami Beach seemed so tiny from the plane. It seemed that only a few feet of sand separated the vast Atlantic Ocean from the elegant hotels and condominiums that walled Miami Beach from the rest of the state.

As the plane descended smoothly from 12,000 feet to 6,000 feet, Zack could easily see the entire width of the long skinny island that is Miami Beach. It was only six blocks wide at its widest and narrowed to a mere two blocks at some points. The Intracoastal Waterway broadened out into Biscayne Bay and bordered Miami Beach along the west just as the Atlantic confined it on the east. He stared at the hundreds of fancy homes along the Bay, with their many canals and channel cuts, fingering their way another thousand feet inland. The canals had been dug in one of the early development boom periods in order to provide those rich few that could afford it a house that had access to the bay and ultimately to the ocean.

The plane began the slow turn towards the airport. Zack was impressed with how clearly he could see the common houses now, row upon row, a sea of roofs, marching inland. Away from the expensive waterfront areas, the houses were smaller and closer packed. They were separated at regular intervals by streets that were straight as sticks, having had to avoid no hills during construction. Zack was struck, once again, with how flat everything was around here.

As they got closer to the airport, he saw numerous square or rectangular ponds, colored like green and blue jewels, glistening in the sun. He knew these were construction 'borrow pits.' Holes in the ground where people had mined limerock and coquina in order to make the concrete blocks that were used to build the millions of homes necessary to house the nearly eight million people who now lived in South Florida. Of course with ground elevation only a few feet above sea level, all those holes had filled with water soon after they had been dug.

Then he saw the Everglades - the River of Grass, so-named by that grand old lady of Florida, Marjory Stoneman Douglas. The Glades extended for miles westward, both to the north and the south of Miami. Coral Gables, Miami, Hollywood, Ft. Lauderdale, all were cities crowded in between two oceans - one of saltwater, the other of sawgrass and freshwater swamps. 'How did this ever come to be?' he asked himself.

Zack had many fond memories of the Everglades, but none would come to mind just now. As he looked down from the plane, too high to see any of the individual parts of the Glades, all he saw was a mass of humanity. They were crowding westward, pushing the limits, nibbling away at the last frontier of Florida. As the plane banked to begin its approach, Taylor turned his head away from the window.

* * *

As he walked with the other passengers past the ever-present security guards, Zack saw his mother before she saw him. Her tanned faced showed the effects of too many days in the sun. Her gray hair was cut shorter than Zack remembered, and was done in tight curls, a style more for convenience than anything else. She was dressed casually as he knew she would, wearing shorts and sneakers.

"Mom! Hi, you didn't have to meet the plane, you know."

Her face lit up at the sound of his voice. She turned and her smile beamed at him. It made Zack feel good to see that beaming face. She hugged him tightly.

"Zachary! How good to see you! Now, what's this about the plane? Silly boy, of course I had to meet your plane."

She loosened her grip on him a bit and leaned back to look at him. "You don't come visit your Mother very much anymore."

"Mom, you know how busy I get at work."

"My son, the Professor. Yes of course I know; I'm just so happy to see you." She hugged him again.

Mary Taylor released her hug at last, and stood back to get a good look at him. "I hope you're eating well," she said.

"Not as good as when you used to cook for me," laughed Zack. "But probably more than I should." He patted the small roll on his stomach.

Just then, Zack noticed an old man standing nearby, watching them and looking somewhat uncomfortable. Mary noticed Zack's look and said, "Oh, forgive me. Joe this is my son, Zachary. Zachary, this is my friend, Joseph Rosenthal."

Rosenthal had very thin gray hair, combed in long strands over to one side. He was short, perhaps about five and a half feet. He was not exactly fat, but he was not very trim either. He stepped forward with his hand extended.

The two men shook hands and exchanged greetings, then Rosenthal turned to Mary. He gently grasped her upper arm and said, "Mary, we really must be getting back to the car." Then he turned back to Zack and said "Zachary, do you have any other bags?"

"No, just this," said Zack, taking a dislike to the man for no particular reason.

They rode in the car, Rosenthal driving and Mary talking, leaning over from the front seat. They drove south from the airport towards Coral Gables. Zack sat in the back of the car, half listening to his mother's chit-chat. He was absorbed in seeing the areas he remembered from his childhood. Things looked smaller and less grand than he remembered. All of greater Miami was in the sunset of its history, trying to hang to former glories.

"....does that sound good, Zachary?"

"Umm, sorry, Mom what was that you were saying?"

"Zachary, have you been listening to anything I've been telling you?" teased his mother.

"Of course, Mom, it's just that I was kind of thinking of the old times."

"And how wonderful they were, too," said Mary. "When you were in school and your father was still able to get out and do things. Coral Gables is a great place to live. Why don't you apply for a job at the University of Miami?"

That was the last thing Zack wanted to do, but he couldn't say that to his mother.

"Mom, I'm real happy right where I am. But you know, it's getting awful crowded down here. And it's so hot nowadays. Plus you've always got to worry about hurricanes. Miami's way over due for one you know. Why don't you consider moving to North Carolina? You could be near Margaret."

"Margaret and her family are doing just fine on their own. And she at least visits her mother more than once every three years, like some people I know."

"Besides I like it down here," Mary continued. "The heat suits me. Where else could I play golf every single day of the week? I've even taken up water aerobics at the Club now."

"Mom, I just don't know where you get your energy!" exclaimed Zack. "You continue to amaze me."

Rosenthal broke into the conversation. "Zachary, your mother and I play golf together twice a week. We met at a golf mixed scramble at the Club just about a year ago. In fact, we're playing in that same scramble again next week, this time as partners." He reached over to pat Mary on the leg.

"Is that so?" said Zack, coolly. Then he added "Are you a good golfer?"

Mary said "Joe can't hit them too far, but he's real good with his putter. He knows how to score." Then she patted him on his leg and giggled. Rosenthal threw her a quick glance. Zack clenched his hands in the back seat and said nothing.

When they got to Mary's house, Rosenthal said good-bye from the car. "See you around 7:30," he called before he drove off.

"What's going on at 7:30?" asked Zack.

"Joe's going back to his condo - he lives right there on the Beach, just off Collins Avenue - to rest up a bit. Then he's coming back here and we're all going out to dinner."

They walked up the driveway and around to the side door. Once inside the house, Zack couldn't stand it any longer.

"Mom, what's with you and this Rosenthal guy?"

"Zachary, that's a very rude question! Just what do you mean by that? And his name is Joe, not 'Rosenthal guy'!"

"I mean, are you seeing him? Who is he? I've never heard you talk about him before? You're almost 64 for goodness sake, and he looks like he's 75."

"Zachary, whoa, slow down, it's OK. I'm a grown woman, I have a life of my own, you know."

"Mom, I know that," said Zack slowly. "It's just that the thought of you with that old guy..."

Mary's jaw tightened, and her voice got very firm. "Zachary Taylor, you listen to me. You are my son whom I love very much. I loved your father totally for more than 30 years. Joe Rosenthal isn't going to take the place of either one of you. But, now I find that I want some male companionship. I like Joe. We enjoy golf together, we have fun together. I think he is a dear, dear man. I need you to understand that, Zachary. And, I want you to be nice to him."

Zack looked at his mother for a long moment. For the first time in a long time, he was seeing her as she was and not as he wanted her to be. He said, "OK, Mom, I think I can understand that." But he was not sure he truly felt that way.

Mary beamed at her son. "That's good, Zachary, now come sit down. I have to tell you all the news about your sister. The big news is that Margaret and Bill just had another boy, little Andrew. Two little boys now; I have some pictures." She dug into her purse. "Look, aren't they cute!" Mary looked up from the pictures to Zack. "Of course, it <u>would</u> be nice to have a granddaughter, too.

"By the way, Zachary, when are you going to settle down with some nice girl in New Orleans? It's high time I had some grandchildren from you!"

CHAPTER 17

New Orleans, March

Zack looked at the pink telephone message sheet that he had just removed from his departmental mailbox. It was dated Friday and said: 'Call Steve Resnick, 646-3131.'

He looked at the back of the sheet but it was blank. He flipped it over again and re-read the front: 'Call Steve Resnick, 646-3131.' That was it - no company, no other message. 'This doesn't make sense' thought Zack. 'Cheryl Lee's better than this.' He walked over to her desk.

"Did one of our new student assistants take this message?" asked Zack.

Cheryl Lee looked unhappy.

"No, sir. I took that message on Friday."

"Why doesn't it say more?"

"Dr. Taylor, I tried, I really did. But he just wouldn't give me any information except his name and phone number. I can't explain it."

"O.K., Cheryl Lee, don't worry about it. There's an easy way to find out what this is about. I'll just call this guy."

Zack smiled and turned to go.

"Oh, Dr. Taylor, I almost forgot. The Dean called earlier this morning, and left word that he wants to speak with you today."

Zack grimaced and said, "Thanks, I guess. I bet I know what he wants to talk about."

Zack checked his watch. He had about thirty minutes before class started. He walked back to his office, got his lecture notes, and then walked down three flights of stairs to the Dean's office. He entered the office suite and stopped at the receptionist's desk.

"Hi, Peggy Sue, is Dr. King available?"

Peggy Sue Miller looked up from her typing. She smiled and said, "I don't know if he is, Zachary, but I am."

Zack had dated Peggy Sue when he first came to USL. They had gone out a few times, but the relationship hadn't gone anywhere. After they stopped dating, they had remained friendly. They still kidded each other good naturedly, but every now and then, her familiarity made Zack feel a little uncomfortable.

She saw that this wasn't the right time for a joke. "Oh, never mind, Zack," she said. "I'll see if Dr. King can see you now."

"Thanks," said Taylor gratefully.

Peggy Sue picked up the phone and dialed King's extension. "Dr. Taylor is here to see you.... Yes sir....Yes sir, I'll send him in."

"You can go on in now," she said to Zack.

He smiled his thanks and walked around her desk and back to the large corner office in the suite.

"Zachary, glad you could stop in on short notice," said King when he saw Zack. He waved him inside.

"Of course, Alan, no problem. What's up?"

Dr. Alan King sat back down in his chair, and gazed out the window. He steepled his fingers in front of his chin, deciding how to begin.

"Zachary, I got an interesting call last Thursday. From a group called 'Friends of the Earth.' Seems they have recently acquired some money they want to give us."

"Well, that should make you a little happier," said Zack.

King shot Taylor a quick glance before he continued talking.

"The money is an anonymous gift, but it has stipulations. First, it must be used to map the extent of toxic trace gases in the air in New Orleans. Second, it's a long term project, with several years of guaranteed funding. Last, and most important, it seems that the donors want you - and only you - to work on this project."

"Me, why me?"

"Well, you are an Atmospheric Chemist. Who else is better trained in your department?"

"Why did they call us? Why not open it up to Tulane and UNO? They've got people who are more research oriented than me."

"I admit it sounds a little strange, but let's not look a gift horse in the mouth, shall we? This is a great opportunity for you. From what I've been told, this is a lot of money. You could use this to start an extensive line of research and get a lot of publications. Frankly, Zachary, you haven't been doing so well in the research area. This could be a big break for you."

Zack was thoughtful. He wanted to succeed at USL, but he knew how much work would be involved with jumping into a major project like this.

"Well, I'm not sure. I've got my classes I'm teaching this semester, and I'm working on a real interesting proposal right now. It's due in two weeks."

King sat forward in his chair. His eyes narrowed a bit and met Zack's. "Dr. Taylor, I don't think you fully understand what I'm saying. I've already told them that we're interested, that you're interested. I want you to jump on this, Zachary. This could mean a lot of money, and some good publicity for the College of Engineering. I don't have to tell how important this could be for your career."

Zack stiffened. "No sir, you don't," he said. He got up to leave, saying "Excuse me Dr. King, but I have class in a few minutes."

King held up his hand. "One more thing. They said they would have their representative get in touch with you to give you more details. A man named Resnick."

Taylor made his exit from the Dean's office and walked hurriedly towards the classroom building. He kicked at an acorn lying on the sidewalk. He swore under his breath. "Damn! This just isn't right!"

He slowed his walk as he neared the classroom. He was upset and he wanted to be calmer and more focused before he walked through the door to start teaching. He stopped at the door and took a couple of deep breaths. He walked in and put his notebook on the table in front of him, then looked around at the students.

"Good morning, everyone! I see a lot of bleary eyes out there - it must have been quite a weekend." Zack was still trying to forget his run-in with the Dean before jumping into his lecture this Monday morning. His gaze settled on David Chase, who he knew was on the tennis team.

"David, how'd the team do against Clemson, Saturday?"

"Not too great, Dr. Taylor. They have some awesome players."

"Well, how'd you do? Did you play well?"

"Actually, I did. I won 6-4 in the third, but then my partner and I got creamed in doubles."

"Too bad, maybe you'll get them next time."

"Yeah, we can hope. Thanks for asking, Dr. Taylor."

Zack looked around. It was after 8:00 and there were still a few people missing. Well, he had to start.

"OK, class, let's get started. For the last several lectures, we've been discussing water pollution and ocean acidification, along with some of the ways the water environment is tied in with the other environments, such as the atmosphere and the land. Today, we return to my pet topic – Global Climate Change."

Taylor turned on the projector and as it warmed up he said, "Before we get into the nuts and bolts of today's lecture, I thought you might like to see some visual reminders of the Greenhouse Effect. Most people can't notice changes that happen slowly relative to their own lifetime. But those changes occur none-the-less. Consider, for example, glaciers. Glacier National Park, which is in northern Montana, was created in 1910. At the time, it was estimated to contain 150 glaciers. By 2010, that number had dropped to 25, and now there are less than 10 left. Take a look at these side-by-side photos of glaciers taken decades apart. See how much these huge glaciers have shrunk in just 60 to 100 years." Then he showed a few photos on the screen. Everyone in class stopped their small conversations and just stared. Some of the photos were remarkable in their contrast.

Zack continued, "OK – that's the reminder. Now, let's move on to the nuts and bolts of today's lecture. It is well known that gases other than carbon dioxide contribute significantly to the global warming problem. The United States EPA in cooperation with the National Center for Atmospheric Research has recently published their latest findings on the contributions of various gases to increases in the Greenhouse Effect during the last decade.

"Today we're going to identify some of the other gases that contribute to global warming, and see what their trendlines have been doing for the past 50 years or so. There are three other gases we want to discuss - methane, nitrous oxide, and fluorinated gases, mainly chlorofluorocarbons. The two main ones in this last group are the freons that we use in home and auto air conditioners."

Taylor turned and wrote on the board:

$$CH_4 \qquad N_2O \qquad CFC's.$$

"As you know by now, global warming results because gases absorb infrared energy - heat - which the earth emits at night to cool itself down. Carbon dioxide, the main greenhouse culprit, absorbs energy at wavelengths of 13 to 15 micrometers. The earth radiates at between 7 and 15 micrometers, so that still leaves a fairly wide window for heat to escape.

"However, methane and nitrous oxide absorb strongly between 7 and 8.5 micrometers, so they close the window a little bit. The CFC's - and there are a bunch of different ones, the most common being freon - close the window pretty much completely. They absorb in wavelengths from 8 to 14 micrometers. Not only that, but freon, because it is a bigger molecule than CO_2, absorbs a lot more energy per molecule. So one CFC molecule is anywhere from five to five hundred times more 'powerful' as a greenhouse gas than carbon dioxide."

Zack turned and drew a big circle on the board. He divided the circle in one very large, and three small pie slices, and wrote CO_2-80%, in the large slice. He wrote CH_4-10%, N_2O-6%, and CFC's-4%, in the other three slices.

"Let's take these gases in order. Methane is the main constituent of natural gas, and gas leaks and purposeful venting from the production, transport, and use of natural gas releases millions of tons of methane each year around the world."

Zack continued his lecturing. "Methane is also produced by the wagonload by anaerobic bacteria. Anaerobic - that means without air. Oxygen is toxic to these bacteria, but they thrive in places where air is excluded.

"These bacteria decompose organic materials in the absence of air. They abound in fresh water wetlands, in estuaries, and anywhere else that has no oxygen. As part of their life processes they give off methane. Let's identify these bacteria by their scientific name."

Zack turned and wrote on the board:

METHANE FORMERS

He turned back to the class, smiling, but there was no reaction. He tried again, saying "I never did like those Latin names." There was still almost no reaction; only two students, David Chase and Bailey Phillips, smiled weakly.

Zack shrugged and said "I guess it's still too early on Monday." A couple of heads nodded agreement. Zack went back into lecture mode.

"So if methane forming is a part of nature, what's the problem then?"

"Well, it's just like with CO_2; people have overloaded nature's cycle. Humans have increased methane production way above historic natural levels, and the balance equation is now out of balance." He wrote the balance equation on the board:

ACCUMULATION = INPUT - OUTPUT

"The input term of the equation has increased, and methane is accumulating in our atmosphere. Indeed, it is building at a rate far faster than atmospheric chemists thought possible a decade ago."

He turned and drew the now familiar-looking 'explosion curve' on the board - long and flat for most of the board, then exploding upwards at the end.

"The concentration in our air today is about 2.0 parts per million. Back in 1970, the concentration was 1.5 ppm, and way back in the 1600's, in the pre-industrial era, methane was only 0.8 ppm. And, like CFC's, methane is a more powerful greenhouse gas than carbon dioxide.

"People are increasing methane production in a number of ways. First, there's solid waste."

Zack wrote 'METHANE' on the board and drew a line under it. Then underneath the line he wrote '1. SOLID WASTE.'

"Remember, I said several weeks ago that in a landfill when bacteria decompose solid waste they generate carbon dioxide. These are those same anaerobic bacteria and they also generate as much or more methane as carbon dioxide. The U.S. EPA estimates that from landfills in the United States alone, some 12 million megagrams of methane are released into the air each year. A megagram equals a thousand kilograms or 1 metric ton.

"Second, there are agricultural crops, mainly rice."

He turned and added the word rice under solid waste.

1. SOLID WASTE
2. RICE

"Trying to feed the hordes in Asia, farmers there are covering more and more land with water to grow rice. Of course, rice fields that are underwater are perfect for excluding air, and the little methane forming bacteria get right to work decomposing muck to make methane.

"Again, there are the good ol' boys at the oil companies. They drill holes in the earth looking for oil, discover natural gas, and promptly vent it to the air. Only if it's a commercial find do they try to capture it and bring it to market. And fracking has opened up a lot more places to find natural gas."

Zack turned and added '3. NATURAL GAS' to the list.

"On top of that, once they get all that methane to market, they lose some of it. In the older cities in Europe, they're still using hundred-year old wooden gas lines. One estimate is that one-fourth of all the methane sold in London simply leaks out to the air.

"And last but not least we have..."

Zack turned and wrote on the board, but shielded the word from view by his body. When he turned around, he finished the sentence verbally and visually: '4. CATTLE.'

"Actually, it is more correct to say RUMINANTS. These are certain hoofed mammals that chew the cud and have complex three or four chambered stomachs. Ruminants include cattle, camels, sheep, and goats, but not horses. These animals harbor anaerobic bacteria in their complex stomachs which help them digest grass and hay and such. In that process, these little bacteria are quite happily protected from oxygen down there in the gut of the animal.

"Now, don't laugh but in early 1990's, EPA gave several hundred thousand dollars to a couple of universities to try to define just how much methane cattle produce. Picture this."

Zack raised both hands to chest level and stretched out his arms to their full length, holding an invisible instrument of some sort. He partially turned his head to one side and tilted it back. He had a pained look on his face.

"Picture this," he repeated. "Some poor graduate student out there in a cow pasture with a gas analyzer standing at the south end of a north-bound cow, waiting for you know what!"

This time, the class laughed as Zack had known they would. He smiled and then continued talking.

"Actually it wasn't that bad. It turns out that most of the methane is emitted from the <u>front</u> end of the cow. Cows belch about a hundred times an hour and release a gram or two of methane with each good belch. How about this for the title of your master's thesis - 'Methane Production From Burping Bossies,' or 'Environmental Impact of Bovine Belches'?"

The class was really enjoying this now. Most of the kids were sitting up and were laughing or smiling with Zack.

"The only tricky part to measuring that methane was to figure out how to put an air sampler close to the mouth, but not so close that the cow would try to eat it. Cows are really dumb.

"Well two grams of methane per belch add up when you belch 100 times an hour. Each cow or steer can emit 100 pounds of methane per week. Herds of cattle emit tons of methane per week. And we have thousands of big herds of cattle in this country alone. In fact - and I'll have you know that I looked this up in the Statistical Abstract just for this lecture - there are over 11,000,000 milk cows, and over 96,000,000 beef cattle in the United States!

The herds of cattle are getting larger every year. Why? Because you and I and several hundred million other people on earth all want to eat a hamburger for lunch. Here, it's a Big Mac; in Russia, it's a Bolshoy Mackorsky.

"The EPA estimates that cattle and other ruminants produce about 15% of all the methane released each year to the atmosphere. And now that McDonald's has opened many more stores in China, it won't be too long before the world demand for beef really takes off.

"Methane could be involved in a nasty positive feedback loop, as well."

At that, Bailey Phillips raised her hand.

"What do you mean by a positive feedback loop?" she asked.

Zack thought for a moment, then said, "It means an action which causes a reaction that reinforces or builds on the original action. It's like when you're at a sports awards banquet and the microphone starts to squeal.

"I was at a conference two weeks ago, and heard that term 'positive feedback loop' called a 'vicious cycle.' This particular methane loop could be especially vicious.

"Under the Arctic Ocean, and extending all the way down to the southern United States, there are cold ocean sediments all along the Continental Shelf. In that mud on the ocean floor, methane is trapped in an unusual form. Under conditions of cold temperature and extreme high pressure, in the presence of water, methane gas freezes solid. It forms methane ice. Apparently, there's a lot of this methane ice around; published estimates are about 20,000 <u>gigatons</u>. There is also plenty of methane trapped in frozen tundra or permafrost in Alaska and Canada and Siberia. As the earth warms, the polar latitudes warm faster than the equatorial regions. And as the permafrost begins to melt, methane is released to the air in vast amounts.

"A gigaton is one billion tons. The atmosphere contains about 2 parts per million of methane which translates into about 5 gigatons of methane in our whole atmosphere. So right now, there is about 4,000 times more methane trapped in ocean sediments and permafrost than is in the atmosphere."

There were murmurs of disbelief from several students.

"Now here is the vicious cycle I mentioned earlier. If the ocean temperature rises a little bit, then some of that methane will unfreeze and will bubble out of the mud there on the ocean floor. It will contribute to more global warming, which will raise the temperature some more, which will cause more methane to escape, which will accelerate the warming even more, and so on. The end result is that, once started, global warming might well happen a hell of a lot faster than anyone now imagines."

Zack paused and surveyed the room. Everyone seemed to be paying attention to him now, the Monday morning blahs had been scared away.

"The second gas I mentioned is nitrous oxide (N_2O), but we should really look at all the nitrogen oxides (NO_x). NO_x are emitted from every combustion process known. We in the United States made good progress in controlling NO_x in the early 2000's, but for the last few years their recent trendline is up. They are formed when the nitrogen in the air combines with the oxygen in the air which only happens at very high temperatures. One major source is the hot flames of burning oil or coal in electric power plants, another is the internal combustion engine – cars and trucks.

"Also, many coals and some wood fuels contain organic nitrogen. That can be oxidized to NO_x as well. In addition to their role in Global Climate Change, nitrogen oxides are a large part of the problem of acid rain. Also, they are a major part of urban smog.

"The actual greenhouse form of nitrogen oxides is nitrous oxide, N_2O. This gas is produced by soil bacteria acting on the nitrogen fertilizers that we use to help grow more crops. Also, it is emitted directly as N_2O from some unlikely sources. A major one is the manufacturing process for nylon. Another is the automobile catalytic converter, which substantially reduces NO emissions but produces small amounts of N_2O."

Zack stopped and looked around. "Does anyone have any questions, so far?"

A hand went up from the left front side of the room. "If nitrous oxide, this N_2O, is the greenhouse gas, why are we so worried about emissions of NO and NO_2? Besides their contribution to acid rain and urban smog, I mean."

"A logical question," said Zack, "for which there is a logical answer. NO and NO_2 are emitted into the air where they eventually form nitrates or nitric acid and come back to earth. That's acid rain. But that increases the supply of nitrates available to certain soil bacteria that happily convert some of those nitrates to N_2O gas which goes back into the air. As I've said many times in this course, you can't throw anything away on this planet. It's all interconnected.

"Anyone else have a question?"

"OK, let's move on. The third and final topic for today is chlorofluorocarbons, or CFC's. Back in 1930, when CFC's were first invented, they were a chemist's dream come true. They are non-toxic, non-flammable, odorless, non-corrosive, and very, very stable. Their use grew dramatically, especially after it was discovered that they made excellent refrigerants.

"Freon is a common name for these refrigerants, but actually there are several molecular forms in commercial use. Some freons are used in automobile air conditioners, others in homes and commercial buildings, and others in refrigerators. CFC's also were used for decades as propellants in aerosol cans to spray out everything from hair spray to deodorant to paint. Other CFC's were widely used in industry as cleaning solvents, and fire extinguisher chemicals.

"The bad news about CFC's started coming in 1974, when two chemists theorized that they were contributing to the destruction of the ozone layer. In a remarkably quick effort, that theory was soon proven, and since 1978 the use of freons in aerosol cans has been banned in the U.S., Canada, and several other countries.

"But unlike bad news, which travels quickly, the CFC's move very slowly in the atmosphere. They are very stable so they hang around in the environment for 50 to 100 years. The CFC's that were released in the 1940's and 50's continued to waft their way up into the stratosphere where they worked their damage on the ozone layer in the 1990's. And they are still doing their thing today. In the 1985, a major hole in the ozone was discovered over Antarctica, and ozone layer thinning was documented all around the world.

"Keep in mind that all the while that the CFC's are destroying ozone, they are also absorbing heat and contributing to Greenhouse.

David Chase held up his hand. "Dr. Taylor, I think I remember reading something on that in our text. Some treaty or something about ozone protection and CFC's. What was that about?"

"You probably saw a discussion about the Montreal Protocol of 1987. Back in '87, the U.S. and 46 other nations signed a treaty to cut production of CFC's back to 1975 levels by the year 2000. That was the year they were to do the final accounting as to which countries have met their goals. But even today no country has made provisions to retrieve the CFC's that are out there in old air conditioners and refrigerators.

"This is a tough problem. What happens to a 20-year-old refrigerator? In the U.S. it gets junked. In less developed countries, maybe it gets repaired and sold. Either way, the old freon gets released to the air by some low-tech junkman or repairman.

"And there's plenty of demand for refrigerators out there. China has recently announced its most recent ten year plan for economic prosperity. Part of that plan calls for a refrigerator in every household by 2040. Right now they have them in about 20% of the households. Imagine! China is going to try to add about 500 million refrigerators - each with a full charge of freon - to the world by 2040. And by 2060, half of them will be leaking."

"Dr. Taylor?" Without waiting for acknowledgment, Bailey spoke up. "Why doesn't China do something about this <u>before</u> it happens?"

Zack paused before he answered. "China still can't afford to develop new refrigeration technology. Even though they are a major world economy, they are still way behind us in many areas. I believe it's up to the developed world to help the developing world improve their standard of living without making the major environmental mistakes that the western world did during its development.

"Actually, China is being somewhat responsible about Greenhouse. They're controlling their population growth better than most countries, and they're participating in world conferences on Greenhouse solutions. China and the most populated country in the world now, India, will be impacted more severely than western nations by the expected climate rifts caused by Global Warming.

"Now, the Russian Commonwealth - that's another story! They're not real anxious to stop Greenhouse. A recent article I saw said they loved the idea of having an ocean port that remained open year round. Now that Siberia has become a major wheat producer, and Russia has become a world grain exporter, their economic growth potential looks better and better to them. And they owe it all to Greenhouse!

Twenty years ago, even though they had several climate summits and lots of discussion, the world just could not work together to reduce carbon emissions. There were too many ways to cheat. But in 2016, NASA launched OCO-2, the Orbiting Carbon Observatory, and now there are several more in orbit. So now, the world can reliably measure the CO_2 emissions from every country, and there is no longer a good excuse for the countries not to work together to control CO_2 emissions.

Zack checked his watch. It was still well before class change time. But he had reached a good stopping point. He said "That's about all I have for you; I'm guess I'm going to have to let you go early, today. Anybody got any questions?" He waited. There were none. 'Mondays,' he sighed mentally. "OK, class dismissed."

Zack watched as the students shuffled past. Usually, one or two would linger to ask him something one-on-one that they hadn't wanted to ask in front of the whole class. But no one seemed so inclined today. He noticed that Jacqueline Jordan wasn't getting up to leave. She was just sitting there watching him. Zack waited until the last student left the room, then said,

"Hi, Jacqueline, did you want to talk with me?"

"Well, yes, actually. Umm, I don't know quite how to ask this, but I was wondering if maybe you could help me again with a computer problem?"

"Of course, Jacqueline, what is it?"

She hesitated. "Well, I've bought a new system, and I.... I can't seem to get it hooked up right. I was wondering... if you wouldn't mind...would you please come over to my apartment this afternoon and help me set it up?"

CHAPTER 18

Miami, March

Deborah Jones was worried. As the Plant Manager of the Eagle Point nuclear power plant, she worried a lot. Her plant, as she liked to think of it, supplied a large part of the electric power to the grid in the greater Miami area. It was crucial that Eagle Point remain in service all the time. It was usually taken off-line only during the scheduled Spring or Fall turnarounds when demands for electricity weren't as high as the peak periods in summer and winter. It was Spring now, but it was still a month away from the scheduled down-time, and right now she was worried about making it another month.

"Tell me again about this structural defect," she said, not really wanting to hear it again but not willing to believe what she had just heard.

"I'm afraid I can't make it sound any better," said Earl Wilson, maintenance superintendent. "Our X-ray inspection team caught it on a routine check. The bracings on the number 4 and number 5 stanchions are internally cracked. Just wore out over the years, I guess."

"We'll have to replace them at the turnaround."

"If they last that long, Deb. I wouldn't want to guarantee them."

Jones fixed her top maintenance chief with a hard look. "Earl, are you telling me that they <u>are</u> going to fail, or that they <u>could</u> fail? I need to know what you're saying."

Wilson backed down under the pressure of her cold gray eyes. "No, I'm not saying they are definitely going to fail tomorrow. They've probably been like this for the last two years. As long as we don't have any big storms or heavy winds, they could last another six months or so."

"What happens if they do fail?"

"The other stanchions might hold, and then nothing happens. But if the others don't hold we could lose the main cooling water lines to the reactor core!"

"OK, that's the worst case. What's the condition of our backup cooling water lines and the stanchions that support them?"

"Excellent, they were refurbished during last year's turnaround. They'll withstand wind loadings up to 250 miles per hour."

"Very well, then. Log this in with the NRC and put it on the turnaround list. Post operating instructions to watch the weather forecasts, and to call me day or night if high winds are forecast. We'll try to live with this another month."

* * *

Coral Gables, March

At the same time that Jones was worrying about what to do at Eagle Point just a few miles away, Bill Phillips, Director and Chief Meteorologist of the National Hurricane Center, was doing the same thing at his office in Coral Gables.

"Millie," he called through the open door. "Please find Rafael and ask him to come see me."

"Yes sir, Colonel," called back Millie. She had worked for Phillips before he retired from the Air Force to take this job and just couldn't break herself from calling him Colonel.

A few minutes later, Rafael Munoz appeared at the door.

"You wanted to see me, Bill?"

"Yes, Rafee, good morning. Please come in. Want some coffee?"

"Already on my second cup, thank you."

"Let me just refill mine then."

Phillips thrived on coffee. It was known throughout the Center that Phillips would consume 12 to 15 cups a day. And that was during normal days. When a hurricane was coming, it might go up to 25 or 30. All that coffee didn't seem to affect him, at least not that anyone could tell. What did affect him, though, was if they ever ran out of coffee. It had happened once three years ago when Millie had been on vacation. The staff at the National Hurricane Center had vowed never to let it happen again.

Phillips walked over to the Mr. Coffee on the table under the big tracking chart that was covered with clear plastic, and poured more of the hot black liquid into his well-used cup. There were ugly brown stains all along the outer and inner rims. No one knew what the bottom looked like; no one had ever seen it.

"Rafee, you know that West Africa is getting more rain this year."

"Yes, I've been following that. It is not going to be good for us, I think."

"I know. It's got me worried. Last year we were lucky. For some reason or other, all the big storms missed us. Several hit the outer islands then sailed out to sea.

Mexico got clobbered twice and Galveston got hit hard. Charleston got the shit scared out of them by Loretta - they still remember Hugo - before she changed her mind and moved on up to do a number on the Northeast. Long Island still hasn't cleaned all the broken up houses on the south shore, and Coney Island got leveled. They haven't completely rebuilt the park yet."

"Yes, Bill, but we gave them enough warning. They were able to get most everyone out of there. We can pick these storms up earlier than ever with our new satellite."

"I know, that's not what has me worried."

"Well, what is it then?"

"Remember the two small ones last year that came before Loretta - Jill and Kevin?"

"Of course I remember - I still have family in Puerto Rico. Fortunately, they were small storms, and no one was killed. After they hit Puerto Rico and Haiti, they turned north and finally went back out to die in the north Atlantic."

Phillips took another sip of his coffee. He stood up and walked over to the large chart that covered one entire wall. With his right forefinger he absently traced the track of an imaginary hurricane.

"Those storms last year seemed to me to have more erratic tracks than usual, didn't you think? It was harder for us to predict their paths. Remember? We had to revise our computer forecasts significantly several times."

"Yes, so?"

"Well, remember how we agonized over whether to call for an evacuation of Miami? Both Jill and Kevin gave us fits. For a time there, while they were still pretty far out, we thought for sure each was going to hit Miami.

"Miami hasn't had a big one in over fifty years, and there are so many people here now. That's the real problem, Rafee, all those people who don't know a damn thing about how to get ready for a hurricane, and who don't want to leave their homes until the last minute.

"I was talking to Alvarez at Civil Defense last week about this. There are six and a half million people living in South Florida now, and over two million of them live within two miles of the ocean. He says we'll need at least 48 hours to pull off a full evacuation, and that's if everything goes perfect. If there are any major accidents on I-95, forget it."

Rafael's eyes widened. "Bill! Forty-eight hours? We can't be sure that far in advance!"

"Right! So that's our dilemma. If we call for the evacuation too soon, and the hurricane misses, then people will think we've just cried 'wolf.' They'll be a lot less cooperative the next time. If we wait until we're certain, they won't have enough time, and not everyone will get out.

"We've got to get even better at predicting these storms. We need to be right, and we need to give the people all the time we can. Rafee, my old friend, something in my gut tells me this might be the year. This might just be the year for Miamians to renew their experience with hurricanes."

CHAPTER 19

New Orleans, March

Zack couldn't believe his ears. He had just been invited to come over to Jacqueline's apartment. Unbelievable! Wonderful! But, wait, he couldn't do that, could he? A million conflicting thoughts began racing through his mind.

"Dr. Taylor?" said Jacqueline.

"What?"

"Well..., do you think you could come over today?"

"I...uh...what about the computer store where you bought your new system?"

"I ordered it through a catalog to save money."

"Oh...yes...well, don't you know any students who might be able to help you?"

"No, I haven't made too many friends, yet. Listen, Dr. Taylor, you don't need to worry about anything. I just need help with my computer, that's all. But if you don't have the time, or if you feel uncomfortable...."

"No," Zack said hastily, "it's ... well, I guess you're right. It's just to help with your computer. And I do have some time this afternoon."

"Oh, super! Thank you so much." She reached into her purse. "Here's my address and phone number. Is 4:00 OK?"

"Yes....I....I'll see you then."

She flashed him her 10,000-watt smile, and simply said, "Great, see you then."

Two students, arriving early for the next class, came in the door. Jacqueline stood up to leave. Zack, his mind still racing, walked absently out the door and back towards his office.

His brain was conjuring up hundreds of different scenarios, some tantalizing, others acutely embarrassing. He tried to picture himself in her apartment. How would he react if she....? What if he....?

Zack shook his head to clear the images away. He should not have said yes. Why did he do that? He felt confused, unsure of what he should do. Should he call her and cancel? Maybe he was making too big a deal out of this. She was a student of his who needed some help, that's all. After all, hadn't he gone over to Jeff Mitchell's to help him set up his first computer? What was the big deal?

But Jacqueline Jordan wasn't Jeff Mitchell, was she? That was the crux of it. So what was he going to do? By the time Zack arrived back in his office, he still didn't know the answer to that question.

Zack was still engaged in playing out imaginary scenes in his head when there was a knock on the door. He turned in his chair and called "Come in." It was Mo Fayez.

"Hello, Zack, how are you this morning?"

"Hi Mo - doing well, and you?"

"Fine, fine. I just wanted to ask you something. I'm heading up the Curriculum committee, you know."

"Better you than me," grinned Zack.

"I know, I know. We spend 20% of our time working on things we get paid for and 80% working on things like this. These committees are getting worse every year. But, listen, I am here to get your enlightening opinion. What do you think about this set of courses for the Core?" Fayez handed him a sheet of paper with a list of suggested required courses on it.

Zack barely glanced at it. "It looks O.K. to me," he said.

Fayez peered at Zack over his bifocals. "Something on your mind, Zack?" he asked.

Zack shot him a quick glance, momentarily caught off-guard by the question.

"No....well, yes, there is."

Zack was still bothered by his conversation with the Dean. This was a good chance to talk with a trusted friend about it. He told Fayez about the meeting and what King had said.

"Zack, you know I like you," began Fayez. "You do a good job teaching, and you're out here pitching in with student activities a lot. But teaching is only one part of our job. You need to increase your efforts on research. That is important if our department is to become well known."

"Are you saying I have to take this project even if I don't like it?"

"I have often said the best job in a university is a tenured full professor. Much better than a Chairman or a Dean or a President. Especially a President. When you are a full professor, you can do what you want. But before then, you must sometimes do things you may not like. And when the Dean speaks you must listen! You want my advice. I advise you to take the project and work hard on it."

"But what if I just can't right now?"

"No one can force you to do it. But if you don't get tenure, you could be asked to leave next year."

Zack remained quiet for a moment. It was not what he had wanted to hear. "OK, thanks for the advice, Mo. I'll give it some thought."

Fayez stood up to leave. "Give it some serious thought, Zack, some serious thought."

No sooner had Fayez left when the phone rang. It was Art Grant.

"Mornin', Zack."

"What's good about it," replied Taylor.

"Whoa, my man. Sounds like you've experienced Monday all day already."

"I guess you could say that, Art. I've got a lot of things on my mind right now. What's up?"

"Just calling to see if you wanted to work out with the team this afternoon. They could use a look at some different playing styles."

"Sure...oh, wait, no I can't. I've...got a meeting this afternoon."

"OK, but you ought to take advantage of these opportunities to keep your skills sharp. At your age, they start to go quickly." Grant chuckled at the other end of the line.

"Thanks a lot, buddy. I'll remind you of those words next time I run you into the ground. See you later."

Zack hung up the phone. He reached up into the bookshelves to pull down a copy of the textbook for the course he was teaching. But before he could even open it, the phone rang again.

"Must be my lucky day," he muttered as he reached over and picked it up.

"Zack Taylor," he answered.

"Dr. Taylor, this is Steve Resnick. I called last week." The words and the tone of voice accused Zack of not returning the call right away last week.

"Oh, yes, Mr. Resnick. I'm sorry; I was tied up last week. I was going to call you this morning," Zack lied.

"Listen, Dr. Taylor, can we meet somewhere today? I'd like to talk with you about this project you'll be working on."

"Uh, Mr. Resnick, I'll be happy to meet with you, but I must tell you that I haven't made up my mind yet about working on this project. I want to know more about it."

"But I talked with your boss, Dr. King. He said you'd be the one working on it."

"Yes, I'm sure it sounds a little confusing. Why don't we just meet and discuss it."

"OK, how about down here at my office. It's just behind the Superdome, near the corner of Simon Bolivar and Josephine - 2918 Josephine."

"OK, I have to be down in that area this afternoon anyway. How about 3:00?"

"Fine, see you then."

"Goodbye, Mr. Res...," Zack was saying when he heard a click at the other end of the line. Resnick had ended the conversation and had hung up. Zack wondered what kind of man he would be dealing with.

Zack slid his chair back and stood up. He wanted another cup of coffee. But before he could take a step towards the door, he heard a knock on it.

"Must be one of those days, for sure," he muttered, as he sat back down. "Come in," he called.

A smile crossed his face when he saw who it was.

"Hi, Dr. Taylor," said Jeff Mitchell.

"Hi, Jeff, come in. It sure is good to see you. The day's been kind of rough so far. Hope you were able to find that information I wanted?"

Jeff nodded and adjusted his wire rimmed glasses before he spoke. His demeanor was serious as usual. "You were right about one thing, Dr. Taylor, that Ice Shelf is enormous."

Jeff was here to discuss their proposal to the International Defenders of the Environment. Zack wanted some basic facts. The more he thought about it, the more he realized that his idea might be totally off the wall.

To build a scale model of the east coast of the United States in a football stadium, and then to drop a scale model of the Ross Ice Shelf into a scale model Atlantic Ocean, and watch the massive flooding that would result! It was absurd. He needed the data that Jeff was researching to see if there was any chance at all that it would work.

Jeff said, "I found this really good book on Antarctica by Sir Roger Thurlow, published in 1986 by the Royal Society of Natural Science in London. They were very thorough in documenting the geography of the ice sheets there."

"The British usually are thorough," commented Zack. "Let me see that please."

Jeff gave a running commentary as Zack thumbed through the book to the pages that Jeff had paper-clipped.

"The world oceans have a surface area of 360 million square kilometers, and a volume of 1.38 billion cubic kilometers. That would give an average depth of 3.8 kilometers or a little under 2.5 miles.

"Now this page documents the total amount of ice in Antarctica. The area of ice is 11.5 million square kilometers and the volume is 29 million cubic kilometers. Therefore, average height of ice is 2.5 kilometers.

"The book says that sea level will rise one meter for each 31 meters of ice in Antarctica that melts. I've calculated that if all that ice were to melt, the oceans would rise 81 meters or 263 feet! Dr. Taylor, is that possible?!"

"Certainly it is. In past geologic ages, the oceans were much higher than they are today. In fact, at one time all of Florida and most of Louisiana were under water.

"But, remember, I said that we shouldn't worry about the ice melting. Even if the earth got warm enough tomorrow, it would take a thousand years or more to melt all that ice. You should calculate sea level rise based only on displacement of water by the Ice Shelves sliding into the sea."

"OK, in that case look at this page here." Jeff flipped the pages to the right one.

"This page gives information about the ice sheets. The Ross Ice Shelf is the biggest, but the Ronne Shelf is almost the same size, and there are several others. In fact, they think the one called Larsen B is about to crack and fall into the ocean sometime real soon. Larsen C broke off in 2017 and created an iceberg the size of Delaware! This one is much bigger! Should we do our calculations assuming they all fall into the ocean at the same time?"

"Hmm," Taylor slowly rubbed his jaw with his left hand. "First of all, we only want to consider ice that is supported by land. Larsen is already floating so if it cracks off, it won't affect sea level – it is already at equilibrium with the water level. Ice that is supported on land and that falls into the ocean will create an immediate rise. So just consider the land-based ice shelves only.

He continued, "And I don't think we should assume they all fall off at the same time. That would be too much of a coincidence. Just base it on Ross alone. That way, the height of sea level rise is less, but the probability of it is greater."

"OK, just a minute." Jeff pulled out his pocket calculator and began punching numbers. He spoke softly as he worked, partly to allow Zack to follow what he was doing and to correct him if necessary.

"Ross is 830,000 square kilometers...average height above sea level is about 600 meters...gives a volume of....Assuming area of oceans remain same...rise is 3.8 meters or 12.5 feet."

Zack rubbed his jaw again. "Twelve and a half feet," he repeated. "Enough to submerge this city forever. And all of South Florida."

"And hundreds of other cities all around the world," added Jeff. "It couldn't really happen, could it, Dr. Taylor?"

Zack looked out the window. It was class change time and he could see hundreds of walking students, some on the sidewalks but more cutting new footpaths across the green grass, in their never-ending battle against the grounds crew. The blue sky and trees helped frame this perfect picture of a little slice of life. He turned back to Jeff.

"I hope to God it won't," he said slowly.

Then with more energy in his voice, he spoke again. "Jeff, we're going to need to re-double our efforts on this proposal. I want to create a realistic looking East Coast. I want people to see for themselves how much they will lose if a 12-foot wave comes rolling in from the sea and doesn't roll back out.

"I want you to do the design, that is, you do the basic scaling calculations. Start with the dimensions of a football field, that's all we have to work with. I want answers to some basic questions. Like, where to put the coastline - down the sideline or in the endzone? How deep will we need to make the ocean? And what vertical scale should we use on the land? It's probably going to have to be significantly different from the horizontal scale to make the landmarks visible.

Jeff interrupted. "Do you want to show the whole Gulf Coast, too? I mean, we are living in New Orleans."

"If we can fit it all in, yes, the whole thing. I've thought of something else we can do too. While the flood plays out before them in miniature on the field below, we can show news clips of major floods from the past on the big scoreboard screen. At the same time they watch 1,500 miles of our Nation's coastline disappear, they'll see close-ups of men, women, and children being swept away and drowned, all on a 40-foot screen."

Jeff said, "It'd be neat if we could show at least one coastal city in larger scale."

"That's a great idea, Jeff! Visual effects like that are always the strongest. I know; let's make it Washington D.C. That would make those politicians sit up and take notice. Find out how much above sea level Washington is.

"If it can't be Washington, we'll make it some other big Northeastern city. If I'm right, when the right people see this, they'll scream bloody murder, and then the politicians will have to take some action."

✳ ✳ ✳

Later that day, Zack walked up to the door that had 'Friends of the Earth' stenciled across the dark glass. Like other glass doors in this neighborhood, it was accompanied by an outer door made of heavy iron bars. Zack was glad this meeting was happening during the daytime.

He walked in the door and told the receptionist who he was then sat down on the small sofa. Zack looked around. The office was small and looked...'sterile' was the word that came to his mind. The furniture all looked new and there were just the two most recent issues of <u>Time</u> on the end table. The few posters on the wall were all of whales or dolphins and had trite expressions printed in the white space at the bottoms. It was extremely quiet inside, there seemed to be no one here except himself and the blond at the desk.

Suddenly there was a third person in the front room. Zack had not seen or heard him come in from the inner office, but there he stood, watching Zack.

Zack got to his feet just as the girl was saying "Mr. Resnick will see you now."

Extending his hand, Zack said, "Steve? I'm Zachary Taylor. Pleased to meet you."

"Likewise. Come in, Dr. Taylor."

They walked back into Resnick's office. Again Zack had a feeling of unease. The office seemed so...barren. There were no family pictures, no trinkets of any sort. A neat package of papers lay on Resnick's desk.

Resnick motioned for Zack to sit in the small chair in front of the desk, while he walked behind the desk to a larger, more comfortable looking chair.

"Dr. Taylor, let me tell you about our project." Resnick handed Zack the top paper from the stack. "You can look at this outline while we talk.

"As you can see, the scope of our project is considerable. We want to try to pinpoint the air quality in detail in the entire city of New Orleans. We know there are many sources of air pollution. Some of them are big petrochemical plants, but there are many, many others as well. We want to find out about those. The study, as we envision it, is huge. It would involve numerous air measurements at different points throughout the city and would provide funds for at least two or three graduate students for the next three to five years. Plus, there is a very considerable budget for yourself of course. It should keep you busy for several years at least."

It was a researcher's dream - long term funding, a big budget. Zack held up his hand. "Wait a minute. Who's funding this project?"

"Can't tell you. The donor wishes to remain anonymous."

"Well then, how long has your group been in business? I've never heard of you guys."

Resnick fidgeted in his chair. He took out a pack of cigarettes and lit one. Zack now saw the full ashtray on the little table beside Resnick's chair. He said, "Friends of the Earth has been in business about three years. We were founded mainly to distribute the money of our anonymous donor."

Zack thought to himself that there was no way this office could have been open for three years. Things weren't even dusty.

"What other projects has your group funded?"

Zack's attention was drawn to Resnick's hands. They were always doing something. Either playing with his cigarette, or drumming the desk, or picking at something on his suit coat or pants.

"Well, a couple of others, in other cities. It doesn't concern you. This project is the one we want you to work on."

"That's another thing," said Zack. "Why is it that you don't want someone from Tulane or UNO or LSU to bid on this project? I'm not that proficient at air sampling. Someone else would likely do a better job for you."

Resnick's voice rose a little in pitch. "Dr. Taylor, our benefactor specified that it must be you. Now, I've already talked with your Dean and he assured me that you would become involved in this project. I'm sure you don't want me to report back to him that you're not cooperating."

"Mr. Resnick," said Zack, "I've had a bad feeling about this project since I walked in here. And now I'm getting a bad feeling about you. I don't want anything to do with this project or with your money. And frankly, I don't give a damn what you report to my Dean!"

Resnick's facade started to crumble. His bullying tone of a moment ago became one that now was almost pleading.

"Wait a minute, Dr. Taylor, don't be hasty. Please, we can work something out here. How about if..."

Zack cut him off. "No, Mr. Resnick, I don't want to hear anymore. I don't know why exactly you were trying to buy me, but I'm not for sale! You can go back to your bosses and let them know you failed."

Zack stood up and turned his back on Resnick. He strode out of the room. Resnick puffed nervously on his cigarette, as his fingers wound around each other, and then unwound, time and time again.

CHAPTER 20

Zack pulled up and stopped in front of the house where Jacqueline Jordan lived. For a long moment he just sat there with both hands gripping the wheel. He had driven around awhile to cool off after his meeting with Resnick. The anger he had felt thirty minutes ago was now replaced by nervousness. His palms were sweaty as they hung on to the steering wheel.

For the hundredth time today, he wondered if he should be here. He leaned to the right to look at himself in the rear view mirror. His left hand relinquished its grip on the wheel to let Zack run his fingers quickly through his hair. Having his left hand free of the wheel seemed to allow Zack to reach a decision.

"This is stupid," he muttered. He wiped both his hands on his pants legs, then reached over to open the car door.

Jacqueline answered the door dressed in a light weight, very soft looking pink sweater and faded blue-jeans. The jeans were form fitting, and had the little zippers down low on the legs that made it possible for a person to put them on. Her long black hair was down today, and was brushed till it shone. Zack thought she looked fabulous.

"Hi," she said. "Please come in."

"Hi, Jacqueline. You look great in that outfit," said Zack. Then, to himself, 'I didn't mean it to sound like that!'

"Thank you," she said simply, acknowledging the compliment. "Did you have any trouble finding the place?"

"A little bit. Even with Google Maps, I took two wrong turns. This City!"

Jacqueline led Zack into her living room and sat down on one end of her big sofa. Zack naturally sat down on the other end.

"I could have drawn you a map; it's a skill I picked up from my father. He was Army."

"Oh, so you were an Army brat?"

Jacqueline looked directly into Zack's eyes. "I really dislike that term - it sounds so impersonal. Like you're grouping me in with ten thousand other people, none of whom you like very much."

"Sorry - I didn't mean that of course."

Her face softened. "That's OK," she said. "Most people don't realize that the words they use can shade a relationship right from the start. I hope you don't mind that I told you how I felt. I believe it's better to be up front with someone on things like that. I hope I didn't sound too harsh."

"No, you didn't. Don't worry about it."

Zack took a moment to look around the room. Jacqueline lived in an old house that had been subdivided into three, maybe four apartments. There was a large fireplace on one wall with a big carved wooden mantle around it. The wooden floors were dark and needed refinishing. She had a rich looking Persian rug in front of the sofa. It was old and looked authentic.

Zack was sitting on one end of an old sofa. He noticed now that there really weren't any other places he could have sat. The room was decorated in Modern Student - there weren't many pieces of furniture. There was, however, a nice looking stereo system with a new Compact Disc player alongside the digital VCR and laser TV.

Jacqueline re-started the conversation.

"Anyway, Dad always was trying to give me skills that he thought would make me more self-reliant. He taught me how to read a map, how to use a compass, and how to find my way out of the woods when I was a little girl. He enrolled me in a karate self-defense course when I was ten, and made me stick with it until I was eighteen. He didn't have to teach me world geography; I learned that as we traveled from one Army base to another.

"On weekends, we used to go camping, when he could get two days away from his duties. When he couldn't, then he'd find a little slice of time, somehow, so we could go jogging or bike riding or just go for a walk."

"Your Dad sounds great - is he retired now? Do you get to see him much?"

Jacqueline paused momentarily before she answered.

"No," she said, "Dad died eight years ago. He was wounded in that stupid war in Afghanistan, and the wounds never healed properly – it eventually killed him. You know, it seemed so right for us to go in there when we did. We all supported it. But then Dad was hurt so badly. And it just seemed so pointless when our government wouldn't let our troops finish the job."

Jacqueline stopped again, gazing past him. Zack didn't know what to say, but he felt he had to say something.

"Well, what about your Mom? Sometimes a death in the family will bring the survivors a little closer. I lost my Dad twelve years ago. Since then, I think Mom and I understand each other better."

"Mother died when I was very little. Caught some kind of rare disease in one of those out-of-the way places. Dad was the only family I knew. Anyway, I've been on my own for eight years now."

"Jacqueline, I'm really sorry. That must have been really rough for you when your Dad died."

"I was pretty shook up," she said. "I was young and in college and enjoying myself. Life was decent. Then one day it wasn't."

"So you didn't have anyone to turn to?"

"There was one person who helped me get my head together back then, eight years ago. An old Army buddy of Dad's. I think they were in Afghanistan together. Dad didn't talk about him a lot, but he did tell me once that if I ever got into anything really bad, something I just couldn't handle, and he wasn't around, then I should contact..." She hesitated, then continued, "...John...Robertson. I think Dad saved... John's...life once, and John saved Dad's life another time. For some reason, Dad always felt that he owed John something big. I would have thought they were even, but Dad kept saying that he owed John a debt that he could never repay. But, you know, it was strange, they weren't friendly after Afghanistan; they rarely saw each other in the last few years before Dad died."

"But somehow you got in touch with John after your father died?"

"Actually, it was John who contacted me shortly after the funeral. I had lost direction in my life completely. He helped give me some new insights, he helped me ... find work."

"That was when you dropped out of college and took up modeling, right?"

Now it was Jacqueline's turn to look surprised.

"How did you know that?" she asked.

"It was in your resume that you handed me on your first day at USL," replied Zack.

Jacqueline smiled, her lips parting slightly to reveal her straight white teeth. "Oh, yes, my 'resume'. It wasn't much of one, was it?"

"You really do have a beautiful smile," said Zack, almost without thinking.

Jacqueline's smile grew slightly bigger. "Thank you," she said. "I think your smile is nice, too. And I really like your style in the classroom. You make everything so...understandable. It's easy once you explain it. And you really seem to care about your students. You know, you're different from what I expected. You're really a nice person."

Zack was puzzled but just laughed. "Are you saying that you expected me to be mean?"

Jacqueline laughed in reply. "No...that's not it. I guess I don't know what I expected, exactly."

They both sat there for a moment, looking at each other. Zack had been enjoying this conversation and had gotten quite at ease, talking with Jacqueline. Now, he suddenly remembered where he was and who he was with. He found himself thinking of her not as a student, but as an attractive, articulate, interesting woman. He thought she might be attracted to him as well. His brain started flashing 'danger ahead' - he needed to get back on safer ground.

"Uh, Jacqueline, you said you wanted some help with your computer?" Zack surveyed the room again. "Well, where do you have it hidden?"

"Oh, yes. I'm sorry for taking so much of your time. You probably have lots of other things you'd rather be doing right now."

Zack thought to himself, 'Not true, at all. There is nowhere else I'd rather be right now.'

Jacqueline continued, "It was good of you to come over here to help me. Let me show you where I want to set up the system. I've already taken all the components out of the boxes. It's all back here in my bedroom."

Zack got up slowly from the sofa. He followed Jacqueline towards the bedroom door. He could feel his heart beating faster; his mind was racing. Next thing he knew, she was opening the door and leading Zack into her bedroom.

* * *

At that very moment in another part of the city, a telephone rang noisily. The telephone shook Henry Maxwell out of his daydream, and brought him from his favorite fishing spot back to his office and his desk.

'Damn phone,' he thought. 'And just when I was getting ready to leave, too.' He swiveled away from his scenic window view and reached over to pick up the phone.

"Henry? This is Alan," said the voice at the other end.

"Oh, hello, Alan," replied Maxwell, coming alert.

"Listen, I just wanted to tell you that I spoke to Zachary this morning about a new research opportunity for him. It's in his field and carries a lot of money with it. It's a little odd how this came to us, but it looks like a sure thing. I want you to follow up with him on this, OK?"

Maxwell could tell it wasn't a request, but a command.

"Sure, Alan, be glad to. Want to tell me a little bit about the project?"

"I don't really have time right now. Tell you what, I'll have a copy made of my file, and have it carried up to your office today. You are going to be there a while more, aren't you?"

Maxwell gave a small sigh. "Of course, Alan. That'll be fine," he said.

* * *

Jacqueline's bedroom was big and bright. Light streamed in from the row of small windows high up along the entire length of one wall. A set of French doors on another wall overlooked a private patio and garden. She had her dresser positioned on the first wall, the one with the row of small windows. On the dresser was an eight-by-ten framed photo of a proud looking man in an Army uniform. Above the dresser, in a glass-covered thin wooden box hung on the wall, were a number of ribbons and medals.

Jacqueline's bed was on the third wall. From that wall a closed door indicated another room, presumably the bathroom. The bed was large with heavy wooden posters. It was neatly made, but right now, the bed was covered with operating manuals and instruction booklets.

"Excuse the mess," she said easily. She waved her arm towards a pile of equipment and a new-looking desk sitting against the fourth wall. "Here it is."

Zack's first fleeting feelings were those of disappointment. But they were quickly replaced with relief.

"You really <u>do</u> have a new computer system," he said.

Jacqueline looked puzzled. "Yes, of course. What did you think?" she said, giving him a curious look.

Zack was flustered, but recovered quickly. "I mean, it's really <u>new</u>, state of the art," he said hurriedly.

"Oh," she said, still looking at him. Then she gave him a tiny smile and said, "You can see why I wanted to set it up in here. As dark as the living room is, this bedroom is bright. I really love this room."

"Yes, I can see why. It' beautiful; it suits you. And it has that great view of the garden."

"Mmm-hmm," she nodded.

Then she pointed and said, "I'd like to have the computer set up over here. That way, it can be close enough to the outlet so I can plug in the router too."

"Oh, you bought a router, good. I didn't realize that you knew enough about computers to need a router."

Jacqueline looked a tiny bit embarrassed. "Well," she said, "it came with everything else. I got that powerful computer you recommended, and most of this other stuff just came with it."

"OK," said Zack, as he eyeballed the computer equipment. "Well, you got yourself one hell of a good system. Let's get started putting this together. I think you should come over here so you can watch as I connect it all up. That way, you'll be able to do it in the future if you get tired of having it here."

Zack started by plugging the printer cable to the back of the computer. When Jacqueline came closer, he became aware of the perfume she was wearing. He looked over to say something. Their faces were only inches apart. He turned his eyes back to the computer. 'Lord, give me strength!' he thought.

"That's a great smelling perfume," he said, trying to keep his voice under control.

"Thanks," she said, "it's called Poison. What are you doing now?"

She leaned over to get a better look, her hair brushing against Zack's forearm. He could barely speak.

He thought, 'She's got to know what she's doing to me! But I'm not going to do anything foolish!'

"I...I'm... hooking up the router cable to the computer," he said. "I'm pretty sure this is right."

They continued to work together until the system was all hooked up. Zack felt satisfied that he had done a good job. He turned to Jacqueline and said, "Go ahead; turn it on."

She reached over to turn on the big red switch on the side of the computer.

Zack stopped her. "No, not that one," he said. I've set it up so that all the components - the computer, the screen, the printer, and the router - can be turned on from this one switch here on the master surge protector."

Jacqueline turned on the master switch and the system sprang to life. The computer booted up and began checking itself for proper internal switch settings.

"It came pre-loaded with all the software," said Zack. "It looks like it's ready to go."

"Thank you so much," said Jacqueline. "I would have been lost without your help."

"No trouble," said Zack. "Now, all you need are some major programs to run on it. Using this baby just to do your homework is sort of like using a nuclear can opener to open a can of tuna fish!"

"Speaking of that," said Jacqueline, "it's almost dinner time. Can I fix you something to eat?"

Zack thought for a moment. "No thanks," he said. "I really ought to be going. Samantha's waiting for me at my place, and she's probably getting hungry herself."

Jacqueline flushed at Zack's statement. Zack thought he detected a glimmer of jealousy in Jacqueline's eyes. He knew exactly what the next question would be. After the many times she had flustered him today, he found himself enjoying this moment.

Jacqueline tried to keep her voice conversational, but failed. "Who is Samantha?" she asked.

"She and I have been living together for some time. I call her Sam," said Zack, and paused a beat. He continued with "and she's very obedient; she always comes when I call her."

He laughed. "Actually, Sam's a German Shepherd, and the best dog anyone could ever want."

Jacqueline laughed too, then said, "You did that on purpose!" Her blue eyes were sparkling.

"Did what?" said Zack, with feigned innocence.

"Teased me like that. What you said about Samantha! You know! You said it that way just to get to me."

"Well, maybe I did. But it serves you right. You've done a few things today to get to me, too."

"I'm sure I don't know what you're talking about," she said with a playful tone in her voice.

"Oh, I think you do." Zack smiled. "It's been a lot of fun, Jacqueline. I really like talking with you, and I feel very much at ease around you. I do have to go now, though."

"OK, I know you do. I just want to say that I like talking with you, too. You're a whole lot different from what I thought you'd be."

Zack was puzzled once more by her choice of words, but didn't say anything. He made his way back out to the front door. At the door he turned. "Good-bye, Jacqueline. Let me know if anything doesn't work right with your computer."

Jacqueline had followed him to the door so she was right there when he turned around. She reached her right hand out and took his left. She gave it a slight squeeze. "Thank you, again," she said, then dropped her hand.

Zack didn't remember walking down the walkway to his car, nor getting in, nor starting the engine. As he drove home in the evening traffic, he kept recalling different images of Jacqueline Jordan and this afternoon's events. He was not sure what to think. His brain and his heart were sending two entirely different messages. He was sure of one thing, though. Jacqueline Jordan was definitely not your everyday student. She was a mystery, a beautiful mystery. He was happily looking forward to getting to know her better. But at the same time, he was keenly and unhappily aware that she was a student, and he was her professor.

Jacqueline watched from her front window as Zack got into his car and pulled away. After he was gone, Jacqueline went back into her bedroom, walked over to her dresser and took a small screwdriver from the top drawer. She then walked to the computer, and slid it away from the wall. She quickly and expertly unhooked the router, and then, reversing the wires, hooked it back up again, this time correctly.

Then she sat down at the keyboard and started typing instructions, quickly and efficiently. The system came to life in response to her typed commands. A connection was made. She typed in a password, and soon Jacqueline Jordan began receiving screen after screen of information from a very large computer in Washington, D.C.

* * *

Zack arrived home still in a great mood. He was greeted by a frantic Sam.

"Sam, what is it, girl? What's the trouble?"

Sam whined, then barked and looked anxiously at her master. She wasn't in her playful mood. It was definitely a mood of anxiety.

"Sam, what are you trying to tell me?" Sam barked again, loud in his small apartment. "OK, OK, let's look around the place." He walked into the bedroom. It was a huge mess - clothes were strewn around the floor, draped over the backs of chairs, and piled in one corner. Zack muttered, "Don't see anything wrong in here." He started to walk out and almost tripped over Sam. Then he saw the problem.

"Sam, I'm sorry!" he exclaimed. He strode over to the sliding glass door that led to his private patio, and opened it quickly. "I forgot and left that shut this morning, didn't I, Sam?" he said.

Sam was already out the door sniffing the small grassy plot enclosed by the redwood stained fence.

After Sam was finished, she came back in and walked over to Zack. She stopped by his knees and looked up at him. Zack could almost read her mind. "I'm sorry, girl, I must have not had my head screwed on right this morning when I left. Speaking of today, this was a real doozy. But it ended fine, Sam, just fine.

"Still, I've got some real problems, girl. The Dean... and this guy Resnick. I know I'm not going to work with him, but how do I tell that to the Dean? And what in the world am I going to do about Jacqueline, Sam? Hmm, what am I going to do about her?"

Sam, who had already forgiven her master for his forgetting about the door, put her big paw up on his knee. Zack reached down to scratch her behind the ears, the way she loved. They sat there for a full minute, both enjoying that simple pleasure. Then Zack said, "Enough of this couch potato stuff, Sam, let's go for a run!"

CHAPTER 21

Cairo, March

G eneral Bani-Sadr looks so calm,' thought President Abdelal. 'Even as we discuss war, he remains so calm. Remarkable!' The President voiced his concern. "But, General, how can we be sure that the Libyans will not join with Sudan once we attack?"

"Mr. President, we do not know for sure, of course, but our intelligence people think they are too weak to do much even if they did join the Sudanese."

General Abu Bani-Sadr was the supreme commander of the Egyptian armed forces. He was widely known for his courage and military skills. He was not known for his mercy.

He continued, "The key to our success, if we are to succeed, is twofold. First, we must have total commitment to action. There can be no turning back once we start. That means that you, Mr. President, must be secure in your decision.

"Second, we must achieve total surprise. Again, sir, this responsibility lies with you. If you consult too many people, rumors of our plans will leak out. Then we will be compromised. You must make the decision yourself. Surprise is of utmost importance."

Abdelal again raised a concern. "But how is it possible to achieve surprise? With all the surveillance satellites the Americans have, they will know each of our moves as soon as we make it. And the Americans will shout it from rooftops, no doubt."

"I am aware of the American capabilities and their weaknesses," said Bani-Sadr quietly. "But their military can keep secrets for a while. That is why you, Mr. President, must convince the United States not to say or do anything!"

"But that is ridiculous!" exclaimed Abdelal. "The United States is such a busybody. And with their huge dependence on oil, they are watching and worrying about this region all the time."

"Of course," said Bani-Sadr. "That is well known. That is why we must approach them with a detailed plan that supports their ultimate interests. And we must convince them that if they do not support us, they will hurt themselves in the long run." Bani-Sadr paused for effect; he looked straight into Abdelal's eyes. "The only way to do this is to enlist the aid of the Israelis!"

"Israel?! How can you suggest....?"

Bani-Sadr cut him off. "I know, I know. It sounds preposterous. But Israel will benefit from a free-flowing River Nile, too. Do you remember last year, when those two Israeli hydrologists sharply criticized the Sudanese for taking so much water from the Nile? They claimed to have proof that diverting so much water was ruining the fishing industry in the entire Eastern Mediterranean Sea. We have known this for some time ourselves with regard to Egyptian fishermen.

"Well, just last week those scientists were in the paper again. This time they are saying that these massive changes to the Nile are actually reducing the rainfall along the whole coastal area."

Bani-Sadr smiled viciously. His white teeth gleamed in contrast with his dark skin as he continued.

"So you see, when Sudan takes water from our River Nile, they are not only stealing from us, they are literally stealing rainwater from Israeli farmers as well. Yes, I think we can persuade Israel to help. Furthermore, if Israel supports us, and if they tell the U.S. in advance that they intend to support us, then the United States will not interfere with our actions."

General Bani-Sadr sat back in his chair, looking confident and sure of himself.

President Abdelal was swayed by Bani-Sadr's logic, but was still unsure of taking such a gamble. He asked, "Do you think it might actually work? We might actually be able to restore the River Nile?"

Bani-Sadr replied, "Well, I don't think it is the same River Nile as in the olden days. Haddad says that even if the Sudanese dams were not there, the banks of River Nile would not be flowing full. But we can re-take what is left, what is rightfully ours!"

"But how would you do it? I mean, what targets would we hit first? I will not be a killer of women and children!"

"You will not have to be," said the old general. "We have the technology, now. We have the same technology that the Americans used to pin-point and destroy targets in Iraq thirty years ago. If we can make a decisive strike on their dams and water factories, then we might not even have to invade with ground troops."

Bani-Sadr's wolfish smile flashed again. "Of course, after our strikes, we must expect that they would strike back. So, in addition, we must strike their air force and major troop installations."

"So, it would involve our troops then?"

"Yes, eventually. That is why it would be better to conduct a massive invasion right from the start. We must commit ourselves totally, Mr. President. There can be no hesitation!"

The president of Egypt looked pained as he said, "I must have time to think."

"Anwar, your time is running out; Egypt's time is running out. I don't think our country can survive another summer like last year."

"I must have time to think! This is not a decision to be made in haste. I will talk to Haddad again. I must know precisely the consequences of not getting the River Nile flowing again this year.

"Meanwhile, General," concluded Abdelal, "continue to make your plans. Go over them again and again. If we decide to go to war, we must be successful. Egypt lives or dies with us, with our success or failure."

CHAPTER 22

New Orleans, March

Clarence 'Bud' Bennett came home from work and kissed his wife, Janet, briefly on the lips. Then he went back towards their bedroom to remove his oil stained coveralls. When he came back to the kitchen, he opened the refrigerator and peered in. "Jan, are we out of beer?" he called.

"No, Sugar, look in the back, on the bottom shelf."

"Oh, yeah, here's some."

He popped the top and carried the cold beer to his favorite chair in the den. He sat down heavily, giving out a big sigh at the same time.

"Rough day at work, Sugar?"

"You better believe it!" said Bud.

"Tell me about it," said Janet, not skipping a beat in cutting the tops off the green beans.

"This city - I jus' don't understand where our taxes go! Our streets is all tore up. Sidewalks is all cracked. Over in Garbage, the trucks is always breakin' down.

"That's OK, though, I can put up wit' that. But tell me, hon, can you think of anything stupider than to put off takin' good care of the big pumps? I mean, if them pumps go out, the whole city gets shut down by a big storm. I been workin' on keepin' the pumps runnin' pretty near 30 years now. Never before have I seen them puttin' off maintenance like they are now.

Bud said "Know what my boss told me today?" He looked over at his wife, waiting for her reply.

"No, Sugar," she said dutifully. She had finished cutting the green beans and was transferring them into a pot.

"He told me I couldn't order any new parts until the end of this quarter. They been pinchin' back now for two years. 'Keep on patchin' them old pumps,' they says. 'Jus' keep puttin' oil in 'em,' they says. 'Keep 'em runnin' for another month or two, 'till we get some money to replace 'em.' they says! I tell you, hon, this can't go on forever. Sooner or later we gonna get a big rain, I mean a really big rain, and them pumps jus' goin' to quit workin'. When the water gets five or six feet deep in the whole city, that's when them bosses will have to explain to the people of this here city how come they didn't take good care of them pumps!"

* * *

"This is Smitty Smith, live on WNOR talk radio. We're back with our special guest tonight, Dr. Zachary Taylor, a professor at the University of Southern Louisiana, right here in New Orleans. He's been telling us some of the dangers of the Greenhouse Effect. Don't forget, listeners, you can call in with your questions any time during the show. Just dial 228-WNOR. OK, let's get on to the next question. Go ahead, you're on."

An old lady's voice came over the speaker. "Hello...my question for Dr. Taylor is this: if this problem is so bad and so urgent as you say it is, why haven't we heard more about this from our government?"

Zack leaned forward to speak into the microphone. "The politicians in Washington are trying to hide from this problem. They are being pressured by two pretty powerful forces - Big Oil, who wants you to keep buying all the gasoline they can make, and the military, who equate national defense with having and using a lot of fuel.

"So the politicians don't want to face this problem, and they hide the truth from the people. The reason they think they can get away with it is that the consequences of the Greenhouse Effect are always 'tomorrow.' By that I mean that many politicians think any serious problems are still 30 to 60 years away. Of course, since those politicians are only worried about their next election, they don't think they have to try to solve the problem. They just put it off, and cover themselves by saying more study is needed.

"But, I don't agree with that at all. I think the Greenhouse Effect is already well underway, that it has been proven, and we are in for some very tough years ahead of us here in New Orleans."

The phone line light flashed on, indicating another call. Smitty broke in, "Here comes another question. Go ahead, you're on the air."

A man's voice came out of the speaker. "Dr. Taylor, what kinds of solutions are you recommending?"

"The most basic kind. We have to stop emitting so much carbon dioxide into the air. We need a nation-wide policy to switch away from fossil fuels, starting tomorrow. Last year, the White House published yet another National Energy Plan. The document was 214 pages long, and only 11 pages of it were devoted to solar power, wind power, and other alternative energy sources. You know, it's shameful. It was way back in 1974 when the first Arab oil embargo demonstrated how vulnerable the United States is to foreign oil. We greatly reduced our dependence on foreign oil when the oil industry invented fracking, but we still import oil from foreign sources. And our efforts in wind and solar, which looked so promising just a decade ago, have stalled. This is due, in part, to the artificially low prices for oil products and natural gas.

"That is to say, we haven't done near enough to develop those non-polluting, renewable energy sources. Our government should be spearheading this. Now, if a U.S. consumer wants to buy a solar powered home heat pump, he has to buy it from Mitsubishi. Our government should mandate an energy plan strong on renewables and short on fossil fuels!

"Now what can ordinary people do? Other than pressuring our elected representatives, of course. First, people need to stop driving their big cars and trucks so much, or at least buy more electric vehicles. As long as we demand so much gasoline and diesel, it will be hard to move away from oil dependence. We need to conserve energy every chance we get. We need higher taxes on oil, gas, and coal, especially. We need to develop and use solar power in so-called 'low tech' applications, like home water heating and heat pumps. We need large fields of wind turbines. We need to plant more trees, trees by the millions. And we need to push our elected officials to cut our military dramatically, and use that money to fund alternative fuels."

The man was still on the phone. "But those things you're saying about higher taxes and so forth, those cost money. I don't particularly want to pay higher prices for gasoline or for electricity."

Taylor replied, "You're right - these actions will bring higher prices for energy. But not that much higher if we make simultaneous cuts in the military budget. Also, if we don't do that, we might see higher prices in other basic commodities, like food, for instance. Climate change could completely change our crop growing regions, and wreak havoc on our nation's agricultural system.

"It is a difficult choice. Pay more today to avoid even bigger costs in the future. But you've got to realize that our costs, and the costs to our children and grandchildren, will be enormously higher if we do nothing.

"Let me give you just one example. I'm sure you're aware of the massive droughts out west for the past three years. I'm convinced these droughts are effects of Global Climate Change. This year they broke the record for the worst drought in California's history.

"'So what?,' you say, 'that's just California.' Zack smile ruefully. "OK," he said, "Let's forget about the lost revenues to hotels and restaurants in their cities. Forget about the parched lawns and dead landscaping of all the homeowners in southern

California. Forget about the deadly fires in northern and southern California. Those are all just California problems, right?

"Wrong! The State Water Board had to ration water so severely that they slashed water deliveries by 75% to more than 20,000 farmers, most of them in the San Joaquin Valley. California has a 25 billion dollar agricultural industry that uses 85% of the state's water in non-drought years. And it supplies fruits and vegetables and meat throughout the United States. Well, what's happened over the last 2-3 years to your grocery bills? I'll tell you what's happened to mine: they've just about doubled. And that's a cost that we might have to live with from now on.

"If we don't make some hard decisions now, there may come a time in the future when even bigger cuts and costlier actions may not help us."

Smitty broke in. "Here comes another call. Go ahead, please, you're on the air."

A low, ominous voice filled the studio. Zack had heard that voice before, but this time it made his blood run cold. "Professor Taylor, if you keep making trouble, something's gonna' happen to you. Something real bad. You're gonna' wish you never opened your mouth about...."

Smitty cut off the speaker and broke in. "Who is this? This is a free forum, a free exchange of opinions. You can't make threats like that. WNOR is happy to present all sides of controversial topics." But the caller had hung up.

Smitty looked at Zack's pale face, and made a decision. He did something he hadn't done in years, ever since that pregnant lady had gone into labor on the air. He said, "That's the end of the program for tonight folks. We are going to switch you to "The Best of the Oldies" a little early tonight. This is Smitty Smith of WNOR signing off for tonight." He switched on a pre-recorded tape.

Smitty turned off the mike and looked at Zack. "What was that about?" he asked.

Zack said, "I'm not really sure. It appears there's at least one person out there who is not a fan of mine."

"That's putting it mildly," said Smith. "That guy sounded like he was for real."

"I know. It scared me, the way he said that. Plus, I've heard that voice before."

Smith was astonished; he asked "You have? Where? When?"

"A couple of months ago. He called me at my office and told me basically to keep my mouth shut. I just let it go. Thought it was a prank call."

"Well, this sounded like something more than a prank call. I think you better report it to the police."

"What can they do?"

Smith looked thoughtful. "I don't know. But at least it will be on record."

Zack smiled ruefully. "Hell, Smitty, you've already got it on record - or at least on tape."

"Hey, man, don't kid around with this. This guy sounded serious. Maybe you should stop doing so many interviews and appearances. Maybe you should cool it for a while."

"No way. You guys in the media are my only hope. I can't reach out and touch our politicians. I can't vote any stock in any oil companies. You guys are my only hope for reaching a lot of people."

"Well, OK. But, Zack, be careful out there."

"Zack laughed. "You're forgetting about Sam. If anyone comes around to mess with me, they're the ones that better be careful." He got up to go. "Thanks for airing this, Smitty."

"Hey, no problem, man. You always generate calls, and my ratings are high. Glad to have you on the show, again. See you later, pal. And be careful!"

Zack drove home slowly. He kept thinking about the threat he had just received. It sounded bad, but how real was it? Things could happen in this city, could happen anywhere for that matter, and you never knew who or why.

He got to the entrance of Oakwood Village Apartments and turned in. Instead of parking at his usual spot, he parked on the other side of the complex. He looked around twice before he got out of the car.

He walked slowly towards his apartment. He looked behind him every few steps. He tried to see into the shadows in front of him. He made it into his apartment without incident, and bolted the door behind him. Sam padded out to greet him. He reached down to pat the dog's big head. He thought, 'This is really dumb. I can't let this get to me.'

Zack jumped, however, when the phone rang. He walked slowly over towards it. He picked it up. "Hello," he said, his voice cautious.

"Zack, it's me," said Arthur Grant on the other end.

"Art! Good to hear your voice. I hate to admit it, but I was worried it might be someone else."

"Yeah, I was listening. Man, did that guy sound spooky, or what? What's this all about, Zack?

"Damned if I know. But it's the second call I've gotten from that same guy. I don't like it."

"I don't either. You want to sleep over here for a few days?"

Zack thought about it, then answered, "No, but thanks anyway, Art. I don't think it's that bad. Besides, I don't want to burden you guys."

"Hell, it's not a burden. You will have to supply your own dog food for Sam, though!"

Zack chuckled. "That's right. Don't forget about Sam. Actually, I feel very safe over here right now." He scratched Sam's head behind her ears. Sam licked her master's hand. "I'll be fine, Art. Thanks for calling."

Zack walked to the kitchen and opened the cupboard. He was hungry, but first he needed to feed Sam. He poured her a bowl of dry food, then looked at it for a minute. Deciding against it, he poured the chow back into the bag, and went to the refrigerator. Taking out a pound of hamburger meat, he grabbed about half of it and broke it into her bowl. "Here, Sam, this is for just being here," he said. Then he formed the other half into a large burger for himself and got out a frying pan. He found a can of green beans in the cupboard and opened that. Dinner was on its way.

Zack was feeling much better after supper. He was flipping through the TV Guide when the phone rang again.

The ring brought back some of the tension he was feeling before, but not as bad. He picked up the receiver.

"Professor Taylor?" said the voice.

"Yes, this is he."

"This is Buck Mullens calling." There was a pause on the other end; Zack tried but could not remember a Buck Mullens. The voice continued. "I'm the U.S. Congressman from the New Orleans district."

"Oh, yes," said Zack half-heartedly.

"I heard you on the radio tonight. You were very outspoken and pretty tough on us 'politicians.' Do you really believe all that stuff you were saying about the Greenhouse Effect?"

"Of course I believe it, Buck. I wouldn't have said it if I didn't."

Mullens chuckled. "In my business, we say a lot of things we don't believe, so I was just checking."

Zack said, "Based on that statement, I might like to get to know you. You don't sound like a typical politician."

"Well, there are some of us who aren't 'typical,' you know. Listen, Zachary. May I call you Zachary?"

"Call me Zack. Only my mother calls me Zachary."

Mullens chuckled again. "OK, Zack. Listen, I have a proposition for you. You may not believe this, but I happen to agree with you about the Greenhouse Effect. And I want to do something about it before it's too late. I'm especially concerned about sea level rise and what that might do to our district. Unfortunately, I don't have time to sort fact from fiction, and I could use a bit of tutoring. Would you be willing to help me get up to speed on this? In return, I may be able to get you in to see some pretty powerful people in Washington."

Zack couldn't believe his ears! Finally, a chance to talk to some people who could make things happen. "Sure," he said, "I'd love to spend some time with you if there's a chance we can do some good. When and where do you want to meet?"

"Any day this week is good for me. I'm on a visit back here in the home district to meet the folks. I do have a few appointments, but they're all at my office downtown.

Would you mind calling my secretary tomorrow and setting up an appointment? I'm really looking forward to meeting you."

"Thanks, I'm looking forward to meeting you, too. And I'll call for an appointment. Good-bye."

Zack hung up the phone, letting his hand remain on the receiver even after it was down. "Sam," he said, looking at but not seeing the phone. "Things might be looking up here, they just might."

Then he looked down at Sam and said "Let's see, it's been awhile since we did any tricks together." Zack walked over to the sofa and sat down. "Come here, Sam," he said. "Time for a pop quiz."

* * *

In class the next day, Zack was interrupted by a voice from the back of the room. "Dr. Taylor?" Zack looked up and saw the raised hand.

"Yes, Meagan?"

"What you're talking about today - conserving energy, doing more with solar and wind power, using renewable fuels, planting trees - these are all small potatoes. I mean, how much good can they do? What about the possibility of high tech solutions to this problem? I was reading in the Sunday supplement in the Times-Picayune about some scientist in California who wants to zap Greenhouse gases with laser beams."

"Yes, I saw that too. Actually, they were talking about shooting powerful laser beams through the sky that are tuned to just the right wavelengths to split apart CFC molecules. I think it's pretty ridiculous, myself, but it is being considered. Faced with technical problems, Americans love a 'technofix.'

"But actually, solar energy, wind power, and other renewables don't have to be just 'small potatoes'. The U.S. uses about 120 Quads of energy each year to run all the factories, homes, cars, stores, etc. in the entire country. Just 10 years ago we were using about 100 Quads. Now, one Quad is a quadrillion BTU's of energy or about as much energy as 170 million barrels of oil. Right now, renewable energy - mostly hydro power - accounts for only about 24 Quads or twenty percent of the total. This is much better than it was in the early 2000's when renewables were only about 8 percent of the total. If the government were to really push solar and wind energy, we could be up to say a realistic 35 percent of the total by 2040.

"But, we might as well mention some of the other technological fixes that have been proposed over the last few years. A workable, but expensive, proposition that is still being developed, is to scrub the power plant combustion gases with seawater. The oceans can absorb a lot of CO_2 and scrubbing the power plant gases transfers the carbon dioxide directly to the oceans, keeping it out of the atmosphere.

"There are other ideas – some that are really off the wall." Zack smiled, and not being able to resist the double pun, said "A bright idea that was floated around for a while in the early 1990's was reflective balloons.

"Yes, balloons. Someone proposed letting loose billions of highly reflective, aluminum-painted, hydrogen filled balloons that would float up into the stratosphere and reflect incoming sunlight before it ever reached the earth.

"Along the same lines, but even higher tech, it was once proposed that NASA launch into orbit 50,000 giant mirrors, each about 40 miles square, to reflect sunlight.

"A dirtier suggestion - literally - was to use our military to fire naval guns to shoot shells high into the stratosphere. Each shell would be filled with dust, and the dust would reflect sunlight. Other dirty ideas were to release dust by high flying B-52's, or even to release sulfuric acid up there. The sulfuric acid would form droplets that would reflect sunlight."

David Chase practically rose from his chair as he said, "You can't be serious! They were really considering those things?"

Zack smiled. "Some of these were ideas that came from reputable scientists and some from crackpots. Can you guess which ones came from which group? I can't!" Several people in the class laughed out loud.

Zack continued. "But one of the wildest ideas by far is one that is still being pursued actively by scientists at NASA. They want to shoot rockets to Mars and release tons of CFC's into the Martian atmosphere. Their hope is to start a greenhouse effect there which will warm the planet enough to melt some of their ice and to release some carbon dioxide from their soil. Green plants would be introduced in about two hundred years to start making oxygen. They believe that within a thousand years or so, Mars can become hospitable to human life. Some think it might be handy to have a spare planet hanging around."

The class seemed stunned, unwilling to come to grips with the idea. Bailey finally asked, "Dr. Taylor, is that possible, what you're saying?!"

"Believe me, it's all physically possible. I'm not saying it would be wise, and there are a lot of ethical questions that can be raised about 'terraforming' another planet. But it is possible. And it seems to fit our mentality - when this planet is trashed, just move on to another one!

"But hey, who knows, maybe that's how we got started here. Maybe some other civilization seeded our atmosphere with carbon dioxide and warmed up the Earth to the point where life could evolve. It sounds like science fiction, but ..."

"Dr. Taylor?"

"Yes?"

"Dr. Taylor, what's reality, here? You get off on these tangents and when it comes to test time, we don't know what to study from our notes. Can you just tell us what the important points are?"

Zack struggled to maintain his self-control. There were always a few students who never seemed to get into the course, who only wanted to pass the tests and move on.

"As I've been trying to tell you guys for the past two months, this whole thing is complicated with a lot of moving parts. Plus, all the parts are inter-related. There aren't any easy answers. I suggest you spend a little more time studying the big picture, and let the tests take care of themselves.

"The Greenhouse problem lies squarely on our shoulders, therefore the solution to it is in our hands. Number one, we must take a much stronger stand to control world population growth. That's the single most important step. But there are other steps we can take simultaneously. We've got to stop using so much fossil energy, and start using more solar- and wind-generated electricity. We must cooperate more internationally. We've got to find a way to stop clear-cutting the rain forests. We should stop consuming so much beef and dairy products - that will reduce methane and help prevent more forests from being turned into pastures. These are all things we know how to do; we just need to make up our minds to do them."

"But, Dr. Taylor..." It was Meagan again. "These things are nice but they won't reverse the trends. From what we've learned so far this semester, this Greenhouse Effect is like a huge freight train. We might slow it down, maybe, with these actions you're talking about, but we won't stop it. I think we need something dramatic."

Zack stopped. 'Out of the mouths of babes', he thought. "Yes," he said slowly, "you're probably right, Meagan. Dramatic is the operative word. Dramatic and immensely effective on a large scale. But the problem is, nobody knows what that is."

CHAPTER 23

Dr. King, this is Steve Resnick," said the voice on the phone. Alan King, who had answered the phone while reading a memo, put the papers down and sat back in his chair. He turned to look out his window at the beautiful spring scene before him. "Hello, Mr. Resnick. What can I do for you today?"

"I just thought I'd call to tell you that your school is in danger of losing out on some mighty good money here. It seems that your uppity professor, Taylor, thinks he's too good to take on this research project."

"Yes, I know. Dr. Taylor told me about his meeting with you the other day."

"Well, I talked with our people, and I've been authorized to sweeten the pot, so to speak. We really want this project done, so we are willing to donate an extra $50,000 to the College. Plus, we can create three $20,000 scholarships for students of your choice."

"That's very generous of you Mr. Resnick. Let me ask you this: how about if I assign another professor, one who is even better known than Dr. Taylor, to this project? Or, better yet, how about two professors?"

"No, we can't do that," said Resnick quickly.

King paused a long moment, then said "That's too bad. I kind of thought you might say that."

As he had been talking, King had been watching a group of students discussing something on the walkway outside. One pulled out a book and flipped through it, apparently trying to find an answer to settle the argument. A few partially completed thoughts crossed King's mind: free and open discourse, academic excellence, pursuit of knowledge. There were a lot of good things about a university.

Dr. Alan King swiveled back around to face his desk. His voice hard, he spoke slowly into the phone. "Mr. Resnick, don't bother me again with your calls. We don't need nor do we want the kind of money you're offering. Furthermore, we never will. Good-bye."

King hung up the phone and returned to his memo. According to the provost, the legislature had again failed to adequately fund education. Somehow, he had to cut another $70,000 from the operating budget.

* * *

Looks like it's a beautiful afternoon for a run, Sam," said Zack as he drove into City Park through the west entrance. He had had a long day and was looking forward to a relaxing run through the back trails.

At almost the same moment, Jacqueline Jordan arrived at City Park on the south side. She leisurely got out of her car and did some stretching exercises. She was dressed in her usual jogging clothes - black shorts and a pink tee shirt. Her hair was tied into a pony tail in the back, and a pink sweat band encircled her head coming across high on the forehead.

She jogged across the grassy area near the parking lot over towards the wooded paths. She often jogged the back trails, preferring them to the open country runs. She started jogging down one of the sunlight-streaked trails that looked particularly pleasant.

At that very moment, Zack also was enjoying his run. He had entered the trees and sandy trails in the less traveled area on the west side of City Park. Sam was loping easily beside him. They ran quietly and efficiently.

Jacqueline was about five minutes into her run. She came to an area where the path narrowed and passed through a thickly overgrown area of trees and vines. She knew that a clearing lay just beyond the sharp curve in the trail just ahead. But, when she rounded the curve, she had to stop abruptly to avoid running over a heavy-set man lying in the path in front of her.

"Oh, excuse me!" she said, trying to catch her breath. "I didn't see you there. Are you OK?"

Then Jacqueline noticed two other men about four feet behind her, sitting on the ground with their backs to trees and holding beer cans. She had run right between them, but hadn't seen them because of the shadows and her attention being focused on the man lying on the ground.

The man on the ground stood up slowly and faced Jacqueline. He was not only heavy but also fairly tall. He had a scraggly brown beard and dark beady eyes, and was holding a beer can. The two guys behind her stood up also, their expressions blank. Jacqueline realized suddenly that she now could go neither forward nor backward; she was trapped between these three men in the woods.

The heavy-set guy spoke first. "Yeah, babe," he said, "I'm OK, especially now that you're here." He winked at the other two guys, who laughed nervously.

Zack had just passed the one mile mark and was not feeling at all tired. He was approaching a clearing when he noticed a small group of people on the other side of it. Something about the scene made him stop before he ran into the clearing.

There were three men standing and talking to one woman. Zack couldn't get a clear view of any of the faces, but even from this distance, Zack could tell that it was not a friendly meeting. He decided to skirt around the clearing, staying in the trees until he got closer.

He moved quietly with Sam around to his left, being careful to keep trees and bushes between him and the group. He finally got close enough to hear the voices. A man's voice said "Come on, baby, just go along and you won't get hurt." Another voice chimed in "You know it's gonna happen - it's just a matter of time." The third voice sounded angry: "Watch her, man, the bitch can kick hard, dammit!"

Zack peered around the tree in front of him to get a look. He couldn't believe his eyes! Less than ten feet away stood Jacqueline Jordan. She was dressed for jogging, but right now she was standing with her back to a tree, her body tensed, her arms slightly in front of her.

She looked scared, but her voice was firm when she said, "Look, you guys just get out of here and I won't say anything to anyone. But you'd better leave now!"

The three men had their backs towards Zack. One man was rubbing his right forearm, but none of them gave any indication they were ready to leave.

Before he even thought about what he was doing, Zack squeezed out of the bushes behind them. "Freeze!" he said. "Nobody move!"

His voice froze them, but only momentarily. The biggest of the three turned his pock-marked face and saw Zack. He laughed. "Hey guys, look, it's only one skinny twerp. And he ain't got no gun, neither."

Trying to make his voice sound firm, Zack said, "You'd better leave like the lady said."

"Oh yeah? You gonna make us, twerp?" the apparent leader of the group spoke again. All three men were facing him now. Jacqueline stooped and picked up a rock. The leader took a step forward towards Zack.

Zack held his ground. He said, "My friend and I will make you, if necessary. But you'll wish you had just gone away, nice and peaceful."

"What friend?" laughed the big guy. "You got an invisible friend?" He leaned forward and lowered his shoulders, getting ready to charge.

A low, deep growl started from nearby. Zack called, "Here, Sam!" Sam sprang from the bushes to stand beside Zack. Her ears were back, her teeth bared, her front legs spread apart and the hair on the back of her neck was bristling. Her growl increased in volume and menace. Zack put his hand on her back.

The three men turned pale. They started backing up. "Hey, listen mister, we don't want no trouble. Just hold onto that dog. We're leaving, OK?" They continued to back away until they were close to the edge of the clearing, then they turned and ran across the clearing and into the trees on the other side.

Only after they had disappeared from sight did Zack let out his breath. He turned to Jacqueline. "Are you OK?" he asked.

"Yes, I'm fine. Those creeps never touched me. But I'm sure glad you happened along! Thank you! And let me thank your friend here; this must be Samantha."

Jacqueline started to walk towards Zack and Sam, but took only two steps when her legs buckled and she fell to the ground.

Zack rushed to her and knelt beside her. He helped her sit up. "I'm sorry," she said, "I shouldn't feel so weak. Damn, those guys! They had me pretty scared, I guess."

"Hey, it's all right to be scared. I know I was! Just sit here for a while, it's OK now. Do you want to talk about it?" Jacqueline shook her head. Zack said, "OK, let's just rest here a bit. You wanted to meet Sam. Well, let me introduce you properly."

Zack turned to his right and put his hands on either side of Sam's big head. He gently shook her from side to side. She licked his face in return. Satisfied that Sam was calmed down, Zack faced her towards Jacqueline, and said "Sam, Make Friends."

Sam went through her routine for Jacqueline, ending by lying just in front of where she was sitting and putting her muzzle across Jacqueline's lap.

Jacqueline laughed with delight. She reached down and hugged Sam around the neck, burying her face in Sam's thick fur. She murmured, "Thank you, Sam, thank you so much. Today you were a girl's best friend!"

For a while, the three of them just sat there, making no sounds. Then Zack asked "How are you feeling now? Do you feel like walking back to your car?"

"I'm fine now. But I'd appreciate it if you'd walk back with me."

"Of course – I wouldn't dream of not walking you back."

They started back towards the main part of the park, heading in a direction opposite to that taken by the three men. As they walked slowly along the jogging trail, Zack made conversation to keep Jacqueline's mind off the incident. He told her several stories about his days as a college basketball player. Most of the stories were of adventures he had had with his teammates, usually on the road trips, many of which ended up with Zack in some kind of jam. He told her of his times as a graduate student. He talked about his efforts now to stay in shape. Soon they had reached the parking lot.

"Thank you again, you and Sam, for helping me." She unlocked her car and got in.

"Drive carefully, and remember, next time you come here, don't jog those back trails!"

"I will," she said, "remember, that is." She flashed him one of those wonderful smiles, then backed her car out and was gone.

Zack watched her go until the car was out of sight. He sighed. Then turning to Sam, he said "Come on, girl, I've got some excess energy I need to burn up." They jogged back into the park, being careful to keep to the large open fields on their run.

CHAPTER 24

New Orleans, April

We got it! We got it!"
Zack was practically yelling into the phone to Jeff Mitchell. "We got that grant to demonstrate the effects of the Ross Ice Shelf disaster. I just received the notification this morning. ... Yes, it is wonderful news.... Yes, we'll be able to get started immediately; they said the funds would be transferred to USL within the week. We need to get together right away to discuss our next move. Can you come to my office this morning?" ... OK, see you in about an hour. Bye."

Zack was happy and excited, but he was also worried. There was so much to do! He had to finalize the designs, he had to sign the contract with Tulane. He had to find a swimming pool contractor, maybe several. He had to hire someone - he still didn't know who - to do the scale model of the Eastern Seaboard. He had to find a model builder to construct the larger scale city. So much to do!

* * *

Washington, D.C., April

The tall, dark-haired woman walked into the hotel lobby, stopped and looked around for the man she was to meet. She was obviously out of place here, and attracted immediate attention because of it. Her face was grim as she surveyed the room. She finally spotted him at a table on the far side of the dingy room, and began to walk in that direction.

Heads turned to follow with sullen interest her progress across the worn carpeting. The hotel was in a poor section of the city; there were characters both inside the lobby and hanging out near the front entrance whose presence contributed to the woman's grim-faced look. She focused on her destination, and looked neither right nor left as she walked.

"Hello, Mockingbird." J. R. greeted her with a slight smile on his lips. "Good to see you again."

"Cut the code-name crap, J. R.," retorted the woman. "There's no one in here who would know or care about us."

Tssscht.

"OK, if that's what you want." J. R. was in a good mood. He could give a little on formalities, especially here, in one of his 'safe houses.'

"What was so urgent that you had to see me, Jackie?"

Hunter purposely used the nickname that he knew she despised, teasing her. It was fun. Jacqueline Jordan gave him a lethal look, but said nothing. She looked past J. R. out the window for a moment, then turned back to him.

"You got my last report. As I wrote, there's really nothing more to be gained by my being there. Zack Taylor's no threat to DIA. I've broken into his computer; there's nothing there that isn't public information. Actually, as it turns out, I think he's an OK guy."

Tssscht.

"So, it's 'Zack' now, and he's an 'OK guy.' What's going on, you getting the hots for him?"

Jacqueline looked disgusted. "As usual, J. R., your mind is in the gutter. You're always quick to jump to the wrong conclusions. No, it's not that at all. I just happen to think he's a nice, decent person. He believes strongly in what he's doing, but he's certainly no threat to you or your precious military establishment."

"You let me be the judge of that!" J. R. hissed. "You're being paid to be a field agent, not a strategic analyst."

Jacqueline's eyes narrowed momentarily, then she looked away. "That's something else I wanted to talk with you about," she said, looking back at J. R. "I...I'm tired of this type of work. I can't make any friends; I can't let anyone get to know me. I want to get on with my life; I want this to be my last job."

Tssscht.

"What would your father say, Jacqueline?" J. R.'s playful mood was gone; he became both more polite and more vicious at the same time. "What would your dear old Dad say? He and I were buddies, we always helped each other. I saved his life! He always said I could count on him. If I remember correctly, you promised him that you'd pay back his debts to me if ever he couldn't."

Jacqueline was silent. Her eyes grew moist and her voice quivered momentarily. "That's a dirty trick, J. R.," she whispered. "You know I've paid that debt already. I've done your spying for six years now. Enough is enough!"

"Not enough!" J.R. whispered back fiercely. "I'll tell you when you've repaid your father's debt. Until then, you do exactly what I say. And I say we're not finished yet. You go back to New Orleans and keep tabs on him. And do it right!"

Jacqueline lowered her eyes, saying nothing.

Hunter sat back in his chair and smiled. He knew he still had control. At the same time, though, he knew Jacqueline was right. Taylor just wasn't the threat that he had thought. But he couldn't let her know that. He had to show her who was in control of the situation. And he had! She was beaten. Her misguided loyalty and love for her old man still bound her. Maybe the time was right for him to try something else.

"You know, Jacqueline," he said, a smile that was almost a sneer, growing on his lips, "it's starting to get dark outside. In this part of town, it's not real smart to be on the streets after dark. I've got a room upstairs, if you'd care to ...."

Jacqueline looked up, her blue eyes flashing anger. "Dream on, you slimy bastard! I'd rather take my chances out there! Yes, I'll work for you, J. R., but don't ever think that it goes any further than that."

With that, Jacqueline stood up abruptly. J. R., conscious of the difference in their heights, remained seated. Jacqueline whirled and walked defiantly towards the door, not looking back. A dark haired man sitting at another table watched her go, then turned to look at Hunter. J. R. shook his head slightly, one time. The man did nothing. J. R. continued to sit watching the door. He had lost a little bit of his control, and he didn't like that.

Tssscht.

He would have to teach her a lesson.

* * *

Amsterdam, April

Peter Haarhuis walked into the executive conference room and looked around. The room was carpeted with a thick rich maroon carpet that accented the elegant old mahogany table. The walls were adorned with a few old design drawings and with many aerial photographs. Photographs of past projects, many of them his projects, representing thirty five years of loyal and valuable service to the company. Thirty five years of his life.

Normally he enjoyed being in this room, but right now he had a sick feeling in the pit of his stomach. From the piles of computer print-outs in front of George, the ambitious junior engineer had apparently done his homework well. From the look on Nils' face, he could tell that Nils was confident of victory. Haarhuis had done his best, he had delayed this day for months, but it had come at last.

"Peter, good of you to find the time from your busy schedule to meet with us," intoned Nils.

"You said you had finished some new simulations," said Haarhuis carefully.

"Yes, we have. With interesting results, I might add." Nils smiled, and Haarhuis almost could see him licking his lips. Nils turned and said "George, please show Chief Engineer Haarhuis the results of your study."

As George thumbed through his papers, Peter said, "By the way, George, what happened to your friend, Henry?"

Nils answered the question before George could. "Henry has been transferred," said Nils quickly. George gave Nils a funny look, then went back to finding the right pages.

"Oh? Why, and where did he go?" asked Haarhuis.

"He ... uh, wanted to spend some time in the Corporate long-range planning department. He's at the home office now." Nils changed the subject abruptly. "George, are you ready?"

Haarhuis thought the stated reason for Henry's move sounded suspicious; long-range planning was not a position that talented young engineers often desired. But he wasn't allowed to think about that for very long; George stood up and walked to the whiteboard at the front of the room.

"Spare me the lecture, please!" said Haarhuis sharply. "Just give me the data and your analysis."

George looked a little disappointed. He sat back down. "Very well, Mr. Haarhuis. We expanded the North Sea data base back to 1946 - that includes your 1953 hurricane, of course. We couldn't go back any further because all our records were lost in the War."

Haarhuis thought bitterly, 'He speaks of the War in such abstract terms! My father lost his father in the horrors of that war. Then to be killed thirty years later by ... ocean water!'

George was still talking, "...also take into account the very slight rise in general sea level over the last 20 years and project it at the same rate for the next 20 years. With all this data, our computer projections reveal that the new designs are even safer than we first thought - a 98.9% percent probability of not failing under the one-in-one-hundred-year storm."

Haarhuis shook his head. He must concentrate. He must find a flaw in their logic.

"What you are saying then is that there is a 1.1% chance that they will fail if we have the one-in-one-hundred-year storm?"

George looked puzzled. "Of course," he said.

"What about the one-in-five-hundred-year storm?"

Nils broke in. "Wait a minute, Peter. We have all agreed that the one-in-one-hundred year is the design storm. The whole country understands that."

"I'm not so sure the people understand that at all! I understand it, I'm pretty sure that George understands it. I sometimes wonder if you fully understand what that means."

Nils flushed at Haarhuis' reference to his non-technical degree. "Never mind that, Peter. What matters is the results of this analysis. We have done everything you requested. We have researched all the data. We have taken into account every objection you raised, and have overcome them. You have no choice but to approve these new designs." Nils smiled triumphantly as he looked at Haarhuis.

Peter looked at Nils for a long moment. He looked at George, searching his face for some sign of weakness. There was none; George was ambitious, and wanted to advance. Perhaps that was why he was here now instead of Henry.

Haarhuis knew he was beaten. But he still had one last resort, one last card he could play.

"That's where you are wrong, Nils. I do have a choice. Therefore, I tell you now that I still refuse to sign these plans."

"You must!" Nils lost his composure. He continued, "Old man, you have no choice. Otherwise, I will have you replaced, and transferred to a job that I guarantee you will not like!"

"Save yourself the trouble," Haarhuis said quietly. Something about his calm quiet voice caused Nils to stop blustering. The room was silent for a moment. "As of now, I resign."

"You will lose your pension," Nils said. It was not a threat, but an almost gentle reminder.

"It is better than losing my honor," said Haarhuis, looking hard at George. George flushed but said nothing. Peter slid his chair back slowly from the long conference table. He took a long last look at the old aerial photographs hanging on the walls. They are just photographs he told himself. Somehow, that thought did nothing to ease the tightness in his chest, nor to sweeten the bitterness in his mouth. Haarhuis turned slowly on his heel and walked out of the room.

CHAPTER 25

New Orleans, April

Zack called up his contacts and dialed Art Grant. "Art, hi, this is Zack....Yeah, it <u>has</u> been a while. I've been working pretty hard on the project.... Yup, it's really hectic, trying to get all the preliminary planning and coordination done. We want to try to do the big demo in July, during the summer break....That's right, it will give Tulane time to restore their field before their first home game in September. Listen, I'm really feeling stressed out - we <u>need</u> to go down to the park and play some ball. You got all your Saturday morning chores done around the estate?" Zack paused, waiting for a 'Yes' answer. "Good! Get dressed, I'll pick you up in ten minutes outside your building. Bye."

Zack threw his basketball in the back seat of the Jeep. Sam jumped into her usual spot in the front. Zack said, "No, Sam, get in back." Sam looked at Zack with her big brown eyes as if to say 'Do I have to?' Then she climbed down out of the car, and then climbed back into the back seat.

They swung around the apartment complex and picked up Grant outside his building. On their way to City Park, they drove across the 17th Street Canal.

"Look how full this baby is!" commented Art.

"Yeah, must be due to all the rain we've been having this spring. Sure wish we could direct some of it out west. The drought is really killing them in Oregon and northern California."

"Well, I know we've had a lot of rain, but this is ridiculous. This drainage canal is just about totally full. We're lucky we don't get any high water where we live."

Zack glanced in his rear-view mirror. The canal <u>was</u> full, almost to the point of overflowing. He said thoughtfully, "I wonder if they've been having pump problems again. Remember that article in the Times-Picayune a couple of Sundays ago? About the poor maintenance on the big drainage pumps?"

"Yeah, I do."

"Well, if those pumps can't pump the water out into the lake, then these drainage canals just fill up. That must be what's happening again. But you're right about us living where we do - it's one of the last places in the City to flood during a heavy rain. In fact, our complex is probably the highest elevation in the whole city. I looked it up once. We're on the Metarie-Gentilly ridge, a whole four feet above sea level!"

Grant laughed, "Gives you a real sense of security, huh!"

Both men grinned as they continued their drive towards City Park. Neither one noticed the brown four-door sedan behind them, the same one that had been following them since their departure from the apartment parking lot. Inside the sedan, a man picked up a cell phone and dialed a number from memory. He spoke briefly into the phone and hung up. He continued to follow the red Jeep keeping a discreet distance behind.

It was a pretty morning at the park, and the basketball courts were uncharacteristically deserted. One group of young teenage boys was noisily competing with another - shirts against skins - for the championship of the world. But aside from that, the courts were empty. Zack let Sam go off exploring; he knew she wouldn't get lost - she had been in this part of the park many times before.

The two friends alternated taking shots and warming up with lay-ups. After they had both started to sweat a little, Zack said, "Looks like I'm going to have to whip you all by myself today. Hope you don't get your feelings hurt easily."

"You keep talkin', man. Your feelings may not be the only thing that gets hurt today," retorted Grant. "First one to twenty; shooter calls fouls, OK?"

"OK! What shall we play for? How about a six-pack?"

"You're on! Here, I'll even give you the ball first."

The score was 16 to 14 and Zack had the ball in his hands. He was sweating profusely, and breathing in short gasps. "Time out!" he said.

Grant, who was not in any better condition at the moment, grinned weakly. In between his own labored breaths he said, "What's the matter, man, getting a little tired?"

"No way," panted Zack, "I just wanted a time out to discuss strategy, that's all."

The two walked over to the bench to sit down for a few minutes. They both sat with their heads hanging down, the sweat dripping from their noses and foreheads onto the ground in front of them. After a while their breathing returned to normal, but they remained seated, still not ready to resume their game.

Just then, Art noticed that there were two men at the other end of the court. They had their shirts off, and their skin glistened with sweat. Apparently, they had started playing while Zack and Art were in the midst of their game. What was unusual at the moment was that they were not playing, but were just watching Art and Zack.

As Art was about to point out the other people to Zack, one of the strangers called out "Hey, man, you guys want to play some two-on-two?"

Zack looked up at the voice and saw the two men. Then he turned to Art. "What d'you think?" he said.

"I don't know, man, those guys look more like weight lifters than basketball players."

"Sure they're in great shape, but neither one is as tall as you or I. I bet we can take them!"

"OK, old buddy, but don't say I didn't warn you." Then Grant turned to the two men who by now had walked over closer. "You guys are on!" he said, as he got up from the bench. "I'm Art and this is Zack."

"I'm Joe and this is Jimmy," said the one who had initiated the request for this game. "We'll take the ball first."

From the start, it was a strange game. The two new guys were silent and played without great skill, but with great intensity. And from the start it was a very physical game. The two musclemen seemed to single out Taylor especially for their fouls. He was getting worked over pretty good.

"Unngh!" Zack was thrown to the ground by the impact of a particularly violent collision with Jimmy. Art couldn't stand it anymore. "Hey, watch it, man! There's no need for that!"

"Your friend here was elbowing me!"

Zack got up from the hard surface of the court. "I was not!" he retorted.

"You calling me a liar, prick?" snarled Jimmy.

"No, dammit, I'm just saying I wasn't elbowing you!"

Without warning, Jimmy hurled himself at an unsuspecting Zack. Taylor crashed backwards, his head bouncing on the pavement. Jimmy began punching Zack's unprotected face.

Grant was stunned. This was all happening too fast! He launched himself at Jimmy and succeeded in knocking him off Zack. Zack rolled over and got to his knees. Just then, the other muscleman, Joe, ignoring Grant, aimed a mighty kick at Taylor's neck. Zack tried to dodge it and partially succeeded. The kick caught his left shoulder, dislocating it and spinning him over onto his back again.

Grant was pinned to the ground under Jimmy's bulk. For some reason he couldn't understand, Jimmy was not beating on him, merely holding him and preventing him from coming to Zack's aid. Grant struggled in vain to release himself from Jimmy's grip. He was powerless to help his friend. All he could do was watch the punishment Zack was taking.

Zack struggled up to a kneeling position. Joe kicked Taylor again, this time in the mid-section. All the air was expelled from Zack's lungs. He knelt briefly, then rolled over onto his side. He lay there, doubled up on the hot concrete, his one good arm clutching his stomach. His left arm was splayed out flat at a crazy angle.

Joe stood above him, not even breathing hard. He said calmly, "Taylor, you've made some people mad you shouldn't have. Maybe now you'll keep your mouth shut."

Joe stomped on Taylor's right ankle, smiling in satisfaction at Zack's scream of pain. He reached down to pull Taylor up, intent on continuing the beating.

Suddenly, Joe was thrown violently to the ground by the snarling fury of Sam! She had been across the field and too far away to prevent what had happened in the previous few moments, but had raced here with a vengeance. The normally gentle dog was now consumed with a primeval passion to defend her master and kill his attacker.

Joe screamed in pain and fright as Sam repeatedly bit and slashed at this arms. He was trying desperately to protect his throat and face, and Sam was trying just as hard to get to them.

Zack was in a semi-conscious state and could do nothing but watch. Art watched in awe and some fear himself as Sam's fury continued. He was not even conscious that Jimmy had gotten up and raced over to his athletic bag. Nor was he conscious of the police sirens, off in the distance.

Suddenly, a shot rang out, followed by another. Sam yelped in pain, and was spun around by the force of the bullets. Released from the onslaught of the dog, Joe scrambled to his feet and with his friend's help, ran to a waiting car, the brown sedan. The rear car door opened as the two men ran up; the sedan sped away as soon as the two were inside.

Blood was streaming from two holes in Sam's chest, but she was not dead. She inched towards her master. Each movement hurt her, and she whimpered as she crawled. Still, she crawled on.

Zack was bleeding from his nose and mouth, from the back of his head, and from somewhere inside his gut. He saw and heard Sam's ordeal. He tried to speak, to tell her to stay, but he couldn't get the words out. She continued her agonizing crawl towards Taylor. He couldn't crawl, so he rolled over towards her. They met nose to muzzle, both on their stomachs on the blistering concrete court.

"Sam," Zack's breath finally came back, "Sam," he whispered, "Sam, don't die. Please don't die, girl."

Sam whimpered again. She stretched both paws out in front of her, and slowly laid her muzzle down on them, inches from Zack's face. She licked his face, feebly.

Zack was pleading with her now. "Everything will be OK. Just don't die, Sam. Please!"

The sirens grew louder, Grant was kneeling somewhere beside him, on the hot asphalt, but Taylor was oblivious to all else but Sam. He reached out with his good hand to stroke Sam's muzzle. Sam sighed, a big, heavy, final sounding sigh. She coughed, and blood dribbled out from her mouth. Her big brown eyes gave Taylor one last, long, loving look; then Sam closed her eyes and died.

CHAPTER 26

Zack blinked his one good eye open to a fuzzy image of worn and yellowed flower-print curtains, partially blocking the light from a window to his right. He was in a bed in Mercy hospital, his right leg in a cast and his left arm tied down across his chest. He was groggy and disoriented. Why was he here? In fact, where was 'here'? Then he remembered! "Sam!" he called, trying to sit up.

"Easy, Zack. Lie down, man." Arthur Grant was sitting in a chair in the corner. He rose and walked over to the bedside. "You were beat up pretty bad, but the doc says you're going to be OK. Course, you won't be moving around very much, with your leg and arm like that. Doc says you got a broken ankle and a dislocated shoulder."

Zack made the effort to focus on Grant's face. "What about Sam? Will she be OK?" he asked.

Grant dropped his eyes. "You're pretty lucky, Zack. It could have been a lot worse. The doc says..."

"What about Sam!!" Taylor implored.

Grant looked around the room, trying to find anywhere else to look but at Zack's eyes. "Zack, you know she saved your life," he started.

"I know that! How is she?"

Grant sighed and looked at his friend. As gently as he could, he said "I'm sorry, man, she didn't make it."

As the words sunk in, Zack felt a tremendous sense of loss. It built up inside, greater and greater, until he felt he couldn't stand it anymore. His eyes began to burn; then the tears started to run down his cheeks. He turned his head away from Art.

"I'm sorry, man. I'm really sorry," Grant repeated. It was all he could think to say.

* * *

Back at USL, Jacqueline had searched out Jeff and stopped him in the hallway near Taylor's lab. She asked "How's he doing, do you know what actually happened?" She surprised herself when her voice betrayed more emotion than she had intended. Jacqueline had just heard the bare essentials from Cheryl Lee who hadn't known any of the details. Now she was staring intently at Jeff, waiting for more information about the beating that had occurred over the weekend.

Jeff Mitchell had only met Jacqueline once before, but of course remembered her. "He'll be all right," said Mitchell. "It was a brutal attack, without any apparent cause. They were just playing basketball at the park; I guess they got into a fight about the game and it turned nasty. He'll recover, but he was lucky that they stopped beating him when they did. His dog saved him, you know."

"Sam? She's a great dog. One time, she came to my rescue....." began Jacqueline.

Jeff interrupted. "You haven't heard the whole story," he said, even more solemn than usual.

"What are you saying?" Jacqueline looked worried again.

"They killed Sam, those two guys. When she attacked the man who was beating up Dr. Taylor, the other guy shot her."

Jacqueline's hand went to her mouth; her face drained of color. "I...I hadn't heard," she said. "Oh, God, poor Dr. Taylor, poor man. He loved Sam so much!"

Neither spoke for a moment, then Jacqueline asked, "What hospital is he in?"

"Mercy - Room 512. I went to see him earlier this morning." Jeff fidgeted, and looked towards the lab door. He said, "Listen, I've really got to go. This project that Dr. Taylor and I are working on is driving me crazy. Now that he's out of action for a while, I've really got my hands full. Plus, I'm getting married in thirty five days!"

Jacqueline looked thoughtful. "Jeff, maybe I can help you on this," she said. When Jeff gave her a funny look, she hurried on. "No, just listen to me for a minute. I'm not taking any courses during the summer, and I'm not working, so I've got a lot of extra time. I've got some experience coordinating things and I'm good at working with people. I could give you guys a lot of help. Plus, I want to do it - I feel like I owe it to Dr. Taylor, and to Sam."

Jeff rubbed his chin. "Well, I guess so. Sure, why not? You wouldn't have to do any of the design work; we've got most of that done. I could use someone just to make phone calls. I've been having a lot of trouble even getting these contractors to call me back."

"Have you gone to see any of them at their offices?"

"No. I didn't think that would be necessary."

"Sometimes it really helps to talk to these people face to face. Let me handle that part for you." She smiled briefly. "I think they'll let me in to talk with them."

Jeff nodded gravely, not catching the irony. "I'm sure they would, but I'll have to clear this with Dr. Taylor."

"Listen, Jeff, I know you're really busy right now. And I want to go visit him in the hospital, anyway. I'll just clear it with him this afternoon."

"OK. That'll be great. After that, come see me here in the lab, and I'll fill you in on the details of the project. Don't worry about finding me, I'm always here."

* * *

Jacqueline Jordan drove her black Tesla Photon through the crowded streets of New Orleans towards Mercy hospital. She drove fast, weaving in between cars whenever there was a slight opening. She ignored the horns behind her as she passed one car after another. Jacqueline felt an urgent need to be at Mercy Hospital right now, and every slow driver that delayed her became a personal enemy. She didn't quite know why she felt the way she did, but she knew that it was critical for her to be there.

She arrived at the hospital and pulled up to entrance to the staff parking lot. The understaffed hospital had long before eliminated a human guard at the gate. She drove partially up on the curb and around the metal arm barring the entrance and parked in a space that said 'Reserved for Physician.' She was out of the car and to the doors of the building within moments. She went straight to the nearest elevator, not stopping to ask anyone for directions.

Caught up in the act of trying to negotiate the unfamiliar hallways, she didn't think about actually being in Zack's room. So, almost before she realized it, she found herself standing in front of a door marked 512. Now she hesitated. 'Really,' she thought, 'what am I doing here?' She looked left and right but saw no nurses, nor anyone for that matter.

She knocked softly on the door. No response. She pushed gently on it and the door swung open.

Taylor was apparently asleep, the white bedsheet up to his chest. His bare right shoulder and arm were visible, but his left shoulder was heavily bandaged, and his left arm was hidden underneath the sheet. His right leg, in a cast, was strung up in a traction device. His face was cut and bruised in several places. One eye was a deep purple color and was swollen completely shut. The single small vase of flowers did little to lift the dreariness of the drab room. As she stood there for a full minute or more, Jacqueline felt her heart go out to him. She began to better understand why she had felt a sense of urgency to come see him.

She walked over to sit in the chair. Something, perhaps a noise she made, or perhaps the smell of her perfume, caused Zack to stir. He opened the one eye and blinked a couple of times, trying to focus. When he succeeded and saw who it was, he tried to grin, but it looked more like a grimace to Jacqueline.

"Jacqueline," he croaked, his voice still hoarse from sleep. "Hi. So this is what I have to do to get you to come see me?"

"Don't joke about this; it's not funny. Are you hurting much?"

"Only when I laugh," he grin/grimaced again.

"I told you - don't try to be funny! Do you have any idea why this happened?"

Zack was fully awake now and tried to sit up. He was too awkward with one arm taped to his body, and his leg in a heavy cast, so he just lay back down. "I've been thinking about that all day. It all happened so fast. One minute we were playing ball, and the next I was getting mugged. Maybe it's related to that call that came in during that radio talk show three weeks ago."

"Why do you say that?"

"Because of something one of them said. Something about the beating being a payback for my making waves, and a warning to keep my mouth shut. Plus, I remember that he called me by name. They knew who I was, Jacqueline, they knew who I was."

Jacqueline's eyes flashed. "You've got to go to the police!" she said.

"Oh, they've already been up here. Took my statement. And they've interviewed Art."

"Who?"

"Arthur Grant, the basketball coach. We're good friends. That's who I was with when this happened."

"What happened to him?"

"Nothing - that's how I know I was the target."

"But, once something like that starts, I would think that both of you would get beat up."

"I know - it seems strange to me too. Those guys must have had a lot of self-control."

"Or some very specific instructions," said Jacqueline quietly, her eyes narrowing.

Zack's voice got husky. "I guess you heard about Sam," he said.

Jacqueline looked straight at him. She scooted her chair over closer to the bed and took his good hand in her two. "Yes, she said, "I'm so sorry, Zachary. I'm sure you miss her so." The use of his first name came so naturally that Jacqueline didn't think twice about it. But even though it happened so easily, it marked a significant change in their relationship.

Taylor said nothing but his one good eye glistened with moisture.

"I'm so sorry," Jacqueline repeated. She intertwined her fingers with his and squeezed. With her free hand, she stroked the back of his hand. Despite his pains, both physical and mental, Taylor for the first time since Saturday began to feel somewhat comforted.

It was dark when Jacqueline left Zack's hospital room. Not that it was night, but rather the darkness was due to the heavy rain clouds that filled the sky. 'Not again!' she thought briefly. Just then the rain started; big massive droplets of water fell on her head and shoulders. She ran towards her car, but by the time she got there, she had already gotten soaked.

Jacqueline got into the low-slung sports car and started the engine. She turned on her wipers and lights, and gunned the car out of the parking lot exit. She paid little attention as she pulled out into traffic, and accelerated fast to get into the left lane to head back towards her house.

She was upset by what Zack had said. 'They knew who I was, Jacqueline.' His words kept echoing in her mind. How could they have known who he was, and what his schedule was unless.... No, she couldn't finish the thought; it was too grotesque. She could not accept her initial conclusion that the information she had gathered might have been used against him in this way.

Jacqueline's mind raced along with her car engine. She thought about the things that she had reported to J.R. over the past five months. Could she have been the source of the information they needed to plan and execute this attack on Taylor? She came to the sick realization that she could have been. She mentally cursed J.R., then as if to emphasize the depth of her feelings, she said in a solemn voice, "If J.R. had anything to do with this, I'll get even with him somehow, Zachary - I promise you that. I promise you that!"

She drove on in the rain, as fast as she dared. From recent experience, she knew the streets near her house flooded easily. Once they filled up, her little car was useless. She didn't want to wade home again tonight.

CHAPTER 27

Coral Gables, May

The sun was shining brightly in Coral Gables, and it was already hot this morning. In many parts of the country, May is a beautiful spring month. In Miami, however, May is definitely a summer month, and though certainly not as bad as July or August, May can have some scorching days. Mary Taylor was waiting in her driveway with her golf bag as she watched Joe Rosenthal's big Cadillac pull up.

"You're late!" she accused, as he lowered his power window.

"You're right," Joe replied. "It was another one of those King Tides. The usual streets were flooded, along with several others that are usually open. I had to detour quite a bit to get around them. Seems like these tides are coming more and more often."

"Yes," Mary agreed, "and it's just such a nuisance." She loaded her bag into the trunk, and said "all set. You ready for a good round, this morning?"

"Sure am, but I don't know about the heat today," said Joe, who had gotten out of the air-conditioned car too late to help Mary with her golf bag. He wiped off some beads of sweat that had immediately sprung to his brow.

"Oh, this is nothing!" exclaimed Mary. "Today's going to be gorgeous. You just be sure to wear your hat, though."

"Of course, I always do. I always put on sunscreen too, Mary." Joe looked at her pointedly, and held out the bottle towards her.

"Oh, I don't bother with that stuff. My old skin is so leathery, nothing can affect it anymore."

"That's not true. Just two weeks ago you went to the dermatologist and had another skin cancer removed. You and I both know what he told you! The ozone layer is thinner now than it ever used to be, and those ultraviolet rays are especially damaging down here in the South. You need to use sunscreen. Now, take it and put some on." When she still hesitated, he added, "Do it, or I won't take this car out of the driveway!"

"You sound more like my father than my boyfriend," teased Mary. But she took the bottle and dabbed a little on her forehead and nose.

"It's just that I care about you," said Joe with genuine concern in his voice.

Mary stopped dabbing and looked at Joe. He did care for her, she knew. "And I care about you, too." She stepped closer to him and gave him a strong hug. "Very much," she murmured.

She released her hug and said, "Look, I'm even putting some on my arms, today."

Joe smiled his satisfaction. "OK, Terror-of-the-golf course. I guess I'll go with you, now."

"You'd better go with me! I don't want you golfing with any of the other ladies at the Club!"

"No one but you - ever again. You know why, don't you? I wouldn't want to risk losing my mixed couples championship, and the parking space that goes with it!"

"Joe Rosenthal! Is that the only reason you like playing golf with me?!" Mary said, in mock indignation, hands on her hips.

"Well, I must admit, there may be another reason or two," teased Joe. They both laughed as they climbed into the car. As soon as he had backed out of the driveway, Joe said in a more serious tone. "You know, Mary, we've known each other for more than a year now. I really like you a lot, and I'm pretty sure that you like me."

Mary interrupted. "Now, Joe, don't go getting serious on me again. We're just out here to play golf today. I don't want to have to think about any serious relationship stuff." She laughed easily and then added, "It'll ruin my concentration and add ten strokes to my score!"

"Dammit, Mary, you have to get serious sooner or later. Have you even thought about what I suggested last week? About going with me on that Alaskan cruise later this summer?"

"Yes, I did think about it. That was very sweet of you, Joe, but I just don't think I want to do that."

"But it would be great fun. We'd see some beautiful scenery, and we'd be away from here for most of August."

"I know you really want to go, but I think I'd go crazy on a boat for three weeks. Just cruising along, not able to play golf or tennis. I just think I'd miss all my activities too much."

"But it's so hot here in August - the cruise would be perfect."

"No, all we'd do is eat, and I'd gain twenty pounds! I don't want that to happen. And you wouldn't want it either!"

"Enough, already," Joe gave in. "I can tell when your mind is made up. But sooner or later, I want to get you away from here, so we can spend some quality time together. I want the chance to have some serious discussions with you, without your activities distracting us every day."

Mary gazed at Joe as he drove. She did care for Joe, more than he suspected. But she was afraid that one day he was going to ask her to marry him. And she was not at all sure that she wanted that kind of commitment in her life again.

* * *

At the same time that Mary Taylor was wondering about commitment, not more than two miles away at the National Hurricane Center, Bill Phillips was wondering about commitment of another kind.

"Millie," he yelled, "Come in here please!"

"Coming, Colonel!" Millie, who had worked for Phillips a long time, could tell when he was angry. She didn't waste any time getting in to see him.

Phillips was sitting behind his desk, with his coffee cup in one hand as usual, but with an unusual deep scowl on his face. He was staring at a letter he held in his other hand.

"How long has this letter been in the office? What the hell's going on here?" he snapped.

Millie was not sure herself, and she told him so. "I'm not sure I know what you mean, Colonel. I put yesterday's mail in your in-box just like I always do. Have I done anything wrong?"

Phillips looked up at her quickly, and saw the hurt look in her face. He immediately felt guilty about his tone of voice. "Oh, I'm sorry, Millie. No, you haven't done a thing wrong. It's those idiots in Washington! Here, look at this."

He handed her the letter, and continued to talk as she read. "They're postponing the launch of the latest GOES satellite again! Another screw-up! NASA is blaming the contractor, and the contractor is claiming NASA changed the specs again. Can you believe it?"

Millie handed back the letter. She knew how important the Geostationary Operational Environmental Satellite, GOES, was to their weather forecasting abilities. She said, "This is terrible! We've been getting by with just one satellite for nine years now. And they've been promising to send up a newer model for the last four years."

"Right on, Millie." Phillips stood up and started to pace. "When I first got started in this business forty years ago, we had one polar satellite and three spotter planes. Then, when we put up GOES-1, we had a bird's eye view of the country from 22,000 miles up. Man, we thought we had it made! Next, they launched GOES-2 and repositioned GOES-1, and by God, I swear I thought we had died and gone to heaven. We got real good at spotting and tracking storms, and predicting their movements. Americans got used to seeing actual time-lapse photographs of clouds and storm systems right there on the six o'clock news.

"The problems started when the imager on GOES-6 failed in 1999. GOES-7 was left all alone, and it finally ran down in 2003. For a whole year it was like we were back in the 70's - just one polar satellite and spotter planes - until GOES-8 was launched in 2004. But there were a number of failures in the late 2000's, so we were quickly up to GOES-13. And, lately, the transmissions from it have been getting less frequent. If we don't get number 14 up there soon, we may go back to 1960's weather forecasting again!"

Millie looked thoughtful. "What about that European satellite, what was it called - Meteostat-9?"

Bill stopped in mid-sip, and slowly removed his cup from his mouth. He just stood there and stared at her for a moment as he held the cup poised in the air. "Millie, you never cease to amaze me. How did you know about that?"

She smiled, saying "I like to keep up with things other than just typing and getting the mail, you know."

Phillips shook his head and smiled. "Well of course you're right; we could request a hook-up with Meteostat-9. But, it would take 10 or 12 months, and would cost us 90 million dollars, give or take a few mill. Plus, there are a few technical problems. The European satellite would have to be moved to a new orbit to do us any good. But then it would be out of range of the European ground stations, so the raw data would have to come to our North Carolina station.

Phillips paused while he took another sip of coffee. Then he spoke again, "Also, we can't process the data in their format. So we have to bounce the raw data off another satellite back over to a weather office in Germany, where the Germans process it, and finally beam it back to us. A lot of opportunities for error.

"Besides," he added, "NASA keeps telling us they'll have GOES-14 up there by the time we could get hooked in to Meteostat! I doubt it myself, but then I'm not in charge of this crazy operation."

Phillips gave an exaggerated shrug, almost spilling his coffee. "Finally," he said, "if the truth be known, the GOES data are better. GOES gives us atmospheric temperature and humidity soundings - which can be critical in forecasting the ultimate strength and direction of a big storm. Plus, in weather conditions of imminent danger, GOES can update every 15 minutes."

Phillips rolled his eyes towards the ceiling. "That is," he said, "it's 15 minutes when everything's working right. Lately, with the old clunker we've got up there now, the best we seem to be able to do is once every two hours."

Phillips suddenly stopped pacing. His face lost some color and he quickly sat down in his chair.

"What is it?" asked Millie.

"Nothing," murmured Phillips, after a moment. "Just had another one of my little dizzy spells, but it's gone now."

Millie's former somewhat abstract concern for the satellite was instantly replaced by her very personal concern for her long-time boss. "Colonel Phillips," she said in a scolding tone of voice, "you shouldn't worry yourself so much. It's not good for you. When was the last time you went to see a doctor? You really need to get regular check-ups you know. And another thing, Colonel, you...."

Phillips finished the sentence for her, "... drink entirely too much coffee. I know, Millie. I've heard you tell me that once or twice before!"

"Well, it's true, and you know it!"

Phillips chuckled. "Look, I'm fine. Really. And if I don't have my coffee, you know how grumpy I get. As far as stress goes, I'm a lot better off with the black stuff than without it."

Millie gave him a stern look, but knew she wasn't going to win this argument. However, she needed to fire the last shot. "All I'm saying is that you ought to start cutting down on how much of it you drink, that's all. And you know I'm right!" She turned and walked back to the outer office without giving Phillips a chance to say anything else. He wouldn't have though. After so many years working with Millie, he knew better.

* * *

A few minutes later, Kelly Carter, Assistant Branch Chief, walked into the office without knocking. "Looks like we got another one, Bill," she said. Carter was in charge of the Tracking Branch while Rafael Munoz was away. "Bartholomew has just formed."

"Bartholomew - where's she coming from?" Over many years Phillips had come to accept male names for hurricanes, but had never quite gotten away from using the feminine pronoun to refer to them.

"Looks like <u>he</u> might be home brewed, right here in the Caribbean." Kelly emphasized the male pronoun in retaliation. "<u>He</u> popped up too close, and <u>he's</u> too small to be from Africa."

"It's not quite June yet; a little too early for those African giants, I think," said Phillips, taking the mild rebuke in stride. Then he added, "Have you heard from Rafee? Is he back from Puerto Rico yet?"

"Rafael called in yesterday while you were out. He says not to worry, his family are all well. Abigail did a lot of property damage all along the shorelines, but Rafael's parents live high up in the hills, and they made through the storm without much harm done. Fortunately, Abigail was nowhere near as bad as that monster Maria was back in 2017." Even seasoned hurricane experts still held Maria in awe for all the damage it had done to Puerto Rico.

Kelly shifted gears, and continued talking. "Fortunately for the U.S. mainland, Abigail turned northeast and headed into the North Atlantic. She's still holding together, but will probably start to dissipate before too much longer. No hurricane has ever remained intact long enough to make it all the way from the Caribbean to Europe before."

"That's true, but even if she doesn't, Europe's got a good fix on her. They'll have plenty of warning. By the way, did Rafee say when's he coming back?"

Kelly gave Bill a sour look. She said, "I can handle the Branch just fine while he's gone."

Phillips silently cursed, and sighed slightly. Out loud he said, "I didn't say you couldn't, Kelly. I just asked when he was coming back." He made a mental note: 'talk with Rafael about Kelly; this girl has a major chip on her shoulder.'

Kelly still didn't say anything so Phillips said, "You've been doing a fine job this last week. I'd just feel more comfortable with Rafee here, too, that's all."

"Well, OK, if you put it that way. Sorry." She stood there, still not volunteering the answer to Bill's question. Phillips began to lose patience, but he tried a different tack.

"How about filling me in on Bart?"

"Thought you'd never ask," she said, and then proceeded to give him a thorough and clear briefing on the latest hurricane. She ended by saying, "He already looks like he'll miss Puerto Rico, and might even miss the entire Southeast. No telling about the New Jersey/New York area."

In his friendliest voice, Bill said, "Still too early to make any forecasts about landfalls, you know."

"I know!" snapped Kelly. "I wasn't forecasting - I was just giving you an informal opinion." She turned to go.

"Kelly!" said Phillips sharply.

She stopped and turned to face him.

"You never did answer my question about when Rafael is coming back. I want an answer now."

Kelly returned Phillip's hard stare, and answered him in a defiant monotone. "Tomorrow," she said, with her lips tight and her eyes squinted. "He's due in tomorrow."

"Thank you," Phillips said coldly, as Kelly turned on her heel and vanished through the door.

CHAPTER 28

Washington, D.C., June

Senator, a Buck Mullens is here to see you."

"Who?"

"The Congressman from Louisiana - New Orleans area. He's on your calendar."

"Oh, yes! I remember. OK, just give me a minute or two more here, Theresa."

Senator Lane Stillwater, Democratic party hopeful for the Presidential nomination next year, turned back to face his Chief of Staff, James Cooper.

"Coop," he said, "I want the results of those polls as soon as they come in! Not a minute later. Can do?"

"Can do, Senator."

"Before you go, give me a ten-second run-down on this Mullens guy."

"Elected to his second term last year. Environmentalist. Good, down-to-earth guy, no big money behind him. Popular with the voters. Could help you in the South."

"Good summary, Coop, thanks. On your way out, tell Theresa to bring him in."

Stillwater brushed his fingers through his silvery hair and straightened his tie. He opened his top drawer and swept the small pile of newspaper clippings that were on top of his desk into the drawer. His walnut desk top gleamed. A knock sounded on the heavy wooden door. Stillwater swiveled his chair to face the door, his face assuming his 'friendly' look that he reserved for colleagues he did not know very well. "Come on in," he called cheerfully.

Buck Mullens walked into the office. He looked a little nervous, which was natural since this was his first time over in the Senate Office Complex.

"Hello, Senator. I'm Buck Mullens," he said as he extended his hand.

"Hello, Buck." Stillwater stood up and shook hands. "Call me Lane. Grab yourself a chair and sit down." Stillwater sat back down behind his desk, keeping it between

Mullens and himself, a minor but clear signal that he was in control. "What brings you over this way?"

"Lane, first let me say that I know that you're deeply concerned about the environment. I know you chair the Senate Committee on Global Climate Change. Also, I'm aware that you're on the Senate Armed Forces Committee, so I know that you are in a good position to have some meaningful influence on their budget requests. Finally, I've heard you speak before about how some of the military budget should be diverted to environmental causes."

"Well, Buck, I must say you've done your homework. But why? What's the reason for your sudden interest in me?"

"Because I think we can help each other. I'm also very supportive of environmental issues, you know. I recently had the most extraordinary discussions with someone in my district, someone that I think you will want to meet. He's a professor at the University of Southern Louisiana, in New Orleans, and he is as sharp as they come with regard to the Greenhouse Effect and what it can do to us."

"I've got some very sharp folks on my staff who are up on that issue, Buck. They're in touch constantly with top people at the Environmental Protection Agency."

Mullens looked at the Senator closely before he asked, "Sometimes, though, I wonder if you have access to contrarian opinions? After talking to Professor Taylor, I have to believe that EPA is deeply discounting some of the very real possibilities for disaster that might be facing this country. I wonder if the administration could be pressuring them to paint a rosy picture, if you get my meaning."

Stillwater sat forward in his chair. "Are you saying that you think the White House boys are trying to pull a cover-up? That they're trying to hide some bad news from us regarding the Greenouse Effect?"

"I don't know about any cover-ups, but I do know that Professor Taylor is convinced that things are a lot worse than the administration is saying. He has done some climate modeling on his own computer, and he believes we are on the verge of what he calls a 'positive feedback loop instability'."

Stillwater blinked twice in rapid succession.

"Run that by me again, Buck."

"A positive feedback loop instability. Taylor says it means an out-of-control event, where something - say temperature - changes so fast that it goes out of control and we can't do anything but watch it until it settles down at some new point of stability. You know that recent EPA report that says the average global temperature will rise another 1.5 degrees over the next twenty years? Taylor says they could be wrong by a factor of ten! He thinks it could be as much as fifteen degrees."

"Fifteen degrees! I've never heard anything like that! Is this guy a nut or something?"

"He's not a nut; in fact, he's very convincing. He's not claiming it <u>will</u> happen, just that it <u>could</u> happen. I think you ought to talk with him."

"Well, OK, bring him up here and he can meet with my staff. I guess I can find twenty or thirty minutes to see him myself after the staff meetings."

"I don't think I can do that, Lane."

Stillwater's face clouded over; he was not used to being told no. "Why not?" he demanded.

"Taylor's dedicated to stopping global warming, but he's got this one little problem about coming up here."

"And what is that?"

"He hates us!"

Stillwater looked genuinely surprised. "He hates us? You mean, 'us' as in you and me?"

"No, 'us' as in politicians - all of us."

Stillwater relaxed and sat back in his chair. He smiled, "Oh, that's OK, Buck, sometimes I hate 'us' too."

Now it was Mullens' turn to look surprised. After a moment's hesitation, though, he continued speaking. "But anyway, he can't come to Washington any time soon. He's working on a big demonstration project in New Orleans. He wants to dramatize the potential consequences of the Ross Ice Shelf falling into the ocean. He's building a scale model of the East and Gulf Coasts in Tulane's football stadium. He's going to model the Atlantic and the Gulf of Mexico, and demonstrate the flooding that could occur if the ice shelf detaches from Antarctica. It's going to be a big show, and it's scheduled for next month. I think you should try to be there. You could at least meet him then."

Stillwater was silent for a moment. Then he said, "Hell, I played in that stadium once, when I was in college. I was a defensive back for Arkansas, you know, way back when. It might be fun to see that place again. Say, will there be any press there?"

Mullens smiled. Stillwater was hooked. "You bet there will. That's my part of my deal with Taylor. In return for him bringing me up to speed on global warming issues, I've promised him a good turnout of people, and lots and lots of press."

Stillwater was practically salivating. "Will there be any speeches?" he asked.

"Not many - Taylor doesn't want this to be a political show. But he did agree to my making some opening remarks." Mullens paused and looked directly into Stillwater's eyes. "And he said I could invite one prominent speaker, if the talk could be kept to twenty minutes or less." Another pause. "Lane, I can't think of anyone I'd rather invite than you."

Stillwater had been unconsciously holding his breath and when he released it, his sigh of relief was audible. It almost embarrassed him. Almost, but not quite. "Buck, you've got yourself a speaker! If I can ever do anything for you,..."

"Well, Lane, here's one thing for sure: you can sit and visit with Dr. Taylor and me sometime shortly after the demonstration to discuss some specific action steps that can be taken by the United States to fight back against the Greenhouse Effect. We want your help to get access to all the military weather databases and all the EPA climate models - not just the ones they put out for public consumption.

Mullens continued, "You know, Lane, this'll be good for the environment, plus it might prove to be useful in your campaign."

Stillwater was back in control. He recognized the deal that was being made, and said simply. "You got yourself a deal, Buck. I'll be there for the big demonstration, and I'll look forward to seeing you later to talk specifics. Please, let Theresa know the trip details and dates. She knows my entire schedule. Now, if you'll excuse me, I've got another meeting, and I'm already running late."

CHAPTER 29

New Orleans, June

Jacqueline unlocked the door to Taylor's apartment and held it open. Zack hobbled in through the open door. His eyebrows arched in mild surprise; he was still not used to seeing his place look this clean and neat. Even his old basketball trophies in the bookcase had been dusted. Despite the fact that it had been looking like this for more than a week now, it still caught him off-guard when he first came in the door. He made his way to the sofa and eased into it. He put his leg up on the upholstered chair, and laid his crutch down on the floor. Jacqueline handed him back his keys and remained standing.

"I just can't get over it, Jacqueline. You've really transformed this place. It's neater than it's been in years. You've been a major help to me this past few weeks. I don't know what I'd have done without you. You really didn't have to straighten up like this, but thank you very much."

"You're welcome," she said easily. "I know I didn't have to, but you really needed the help. This place was a mess!"

"I know - I have this tendency to be a bit sloppy."

"A bit!" laughed Jacqueline. "That's an understatement."

Zack smiled too. "I'm guilty - I admit it. But I'm curious - how are you managing to do all this and keep up with your classes, too?"

Jacqueline paused uneasily, then changed the subject. "That's good news about your cast coming off next week."

"You bet - it's the best! I can't wait to get rid of it. Oh, and thanks again for taking me to the doctor today."

"You're welcome, again." She laughed. "Actually, I kind of enjoy taking care of you. Maybe I should have been a nurse."

"Instead of an Environmental Engineer?" asked Zack, looking at her.

Jacqueline didn't answer. She wondered why he was continuing to press her on this today. She looked away and walked over towards the kitchen counter.

Zack's eyes followed her. When she didn't respond, he resumed talking. "But I guess that's just another debt that I owe you. I'm getting worried that I won't be able to repay you for the good care you've given me."

"Don't worry about it one bit. Like I've told you before, I'm happy to do it. Just consider it a repayment for you and Sam saving me that day in the park."

At the mention of Sam's name, Zack's face fell momentarily. Jacqueline noticed it and mentally kicked herself for bringing it up. She needed to change the subject again. She decided that the project would be a good safe topic.

"You met with Jeff, yesterday. How's the Ross project coming along?"

"He says everything's going well, but that's another reason why I'm anxious to get this cast off. I really want to get out and look at the construction in person.

"By the way," Zack said, looking directly into her eyes, "Jeff told me yesterday that you were a tremendous help to him on getting that project started. I didn't know you were even working with him until he said something. He seemed surprised that I didn't know about it. Why didn't you tell me?"

"I didn't want to bother you with it, that's all."

"Well, I'm going to put you on the payroll. You need to get compensated for your time. The project has a good budget."

Jacqueline really felt uneasy now. She didn't like the way this conversation was going at all. "That's really not necessary," she said.

"Nonsense. A student, even one of apparently independent means," Zack smiled tightly, "can always use extra income."

Jacqueline didn't return the smile. Her stomach felt tied in knots, and her head was starting to ache. She felt caught in the middle of a major mess.

Jacqueline had stopped sending any more reports to J.R. the day she found out about the attack at the park. She had decided that she was going to quit working for him once and for all. But the problem was she had not yet told J.R. about her decision to quit.

Another problem was what to tell Zack, and when to tell him. So far, she had not told him anything. She desperately wanted to tell Zack about her real identity, but she didn't want to risk upsetting him while he was recovering. Also, she was afraid of what J.R. might do. She wasn't sure if J.R. had set up the beating at the park, but she knew he was capable of it.

There was also something else that Jacqueline was afraid of risking. She hadn't yet admitted it to herself consciously, but she had fallen in love with Taylor. She was afraid to tell him of her previous involvement; she didn't even know how to start. How was she ever going to be able to explain this all to Zachary? Would he ever trust her again?

Jacqueline became aware of Zack staring at her, waiting for a response. She forced a smile to her lips, then said simply, "OK, thanks." She glanced at the clock in the kitchen. "Are you hungry? I could fix you a sandwich."

Zack's eyes squinted in frustration, and his voice became abrupt when he said, "Jacqueline, will you please quit changing the subject? Come over here and sit down. We need to have a talk about something."

"About what?" she said guardedly, as she walked over to sit on the other chair near the sofa.

"I think you know what it's about, but I'll spell it out for you. I want to know why you've been avoiding any talk about yourself or about school. For the past two weeks, every time I've brought up anything remotely connected with your studies at USL, you've changed the subject. What's going on here? What are you hiding?"

Jacqueline looked around the room, desperately trying to figure out a way to avoid the very question that she had skillfully avoided so many times in the past fourteen days. She could find no help from the inanimate walls. She was tired of lying to Zack, but just couldn't bring herself to tell him the truth, at least not right now.

"Well, I'm not taking any classes this summer. That's why I have the time to do this."

"OK, I can understand that. But that still doesn't explain why you decided to not take classes this term."

"I guess I just got tired of sitting in the classroom."

Zack looked hard at her for a moment. "Now, wait just a minute, Jacqueline. I'm not buying that. You just started here this year. And you were in my class, so I know what a good student you are."

"No, you don't know. I...I'm not a good student. I'm not any kind of a student."

"What do you mean by that?"

"I...I can't tell you."

"Oh come off it!" Zack's voice sounded loud and harsh, reflecting his frustration and his growing anger. "I would hope that we know each other well enough by now so we don't have to play these little games! Now tell me the whole story, Jacqueline, please!"

"I'm not playing games with you, not any more. And you don't have to raise your voice," she retorted.

"Great!" Zack said, still with a raised voice. "What did that comment mean – 'not any more'?"

Despite her feelings of guilt, Jacqueline was now warming to some anger of her own. "Why don't you just accept the fact that I'm here and I'm trying to help you? Why do you have to dig into my past?"

"Look, Jacqueline, I appreciate what you've done for me. I really do. But I'm getting more than a little frustrated with you. I feel like you're hiding something from me, and I don't like it. Now tell me what it is! I need to know!"

Zack fairly yelled his last statement. Jacqueline's blue eyes flashed angrily; she stood up. "No, you look, mister! I don't have to account to you for everything I do or ever have done. You don't have any claims on me. And if you don't like me being around here, then maybe I'd just better leave!"

"Maybe you'd better!

Jacqueline got up quickly, grabbed her purse and stormed out the door, slamming it as she left. Zack was left sitting on the sofa, at a complete loss as to how to explain her behavior. Why had she refused to answer his simple questions? Why had she gotten so angry? Neither could he explain his own behavior. Why had he gotten so pushy? His feelings towards her were changing. Now that he had been around her awhile, he no longer felt overwhelmed by her physical beauty, although he was still very much aware of it. He was very grateful for her help, yet he resented that she remained so aloof. He felt more tenderness towards her, yet he had become less tolerant of her mysterious nature. Damn! Why wouldn't she answer his questions?

Just then the door flew open. There stood Jacqueline, her face still angry, but with tears in her eyes.

"I'm tired of lying to you," she cried. "I came back to tell you the truth!"

Zack was still angry. "Tell me then, dammit!" he replied.

Her face contorted as if in physical pain, Jacqueline forced the words out of her mouth, "I'm not a student at all; I'm a spy!"

"What the hell does that mean?" interrupted Zack.

"Shut up and listen, Zachary!" Jacqueline commanded. "Please," she added. "This is going to be hard enough for me without stopping to answer your questions every other sentence."

Taylor nodded, his anger being replaced with a growing curiosity.

"As I said, I'm a spy. I work for the DIA - that's the military equivalent of the CIA. They sent me here to keep an eye on you because your public criticism was starting to get them worried. I work for a man named J.R."

Jacqueline paused to catch her breath. She went on. "I said 'work'; actually that's wrong. I quit the day after you were attacked."

Zack's face went white with re-born anger as his mind leaped to the unbidden connection. "Do you mean," he said slowly, not wanting to believe his own words, "that you set me up for that beating?"

"No! Absolutely not! I would never do that." Jacqueline was crying freely now. "But...."

"But what?"

"I don't <u>know</u> that J.R. had anything to do with that attack on you, but I know that he <u>could</u> have."

"What exactly do you know, Jacqueline?"

At the tone in his voice, Jacqueline grew frightened. But she had come this far. She had to finish. "I know that with the information that I sent him, J.R. knew all about you. He had the knowledge, and he's the type of person who would use it. He could have arranged for that beating to take place. But, there was no <u>reason</u> for him to do that. So I just don't know for sure if he did or if he didn't. And there's no way to find out.

"But I'm through with him now," she declared. "I'm through with all of that business."

She now looked at Zack, expectantly. She had played this scene in her mind many times. She anticipated that he would now deliver a heated angry outburst, perhaps cursing her, perhaps yelling at her. She was ready to take her punishment. But Jacqueline had not anticipated correctly.

In a voice as cold and impersonal as ice, Zack said, "So you're the one to blame for Sam being killed."

His words stabbed her like knives. Jacqueline's eyes grew wide. "No!" she cried. "I told you I don't even know if J.R. did set it up. I was never told about any plans to do anything like that. I was just supposed to keep tabs on you. I would never hurt Sam!"

"Get out." The ice cold voice seemed to come from someone else. Zack's grim mouth seemed not to move at all, the words just hung there in the air.

"What? What did you say?" She could not believe her ears.

"Get out!" This time the words exploded into the apartment. "Get out, and don't come back! Ever!" Zack's body started to shake.

"How can you say that? I...I...love you!"

"Get out!!" Zack screamed. "I never want to see your face again!" Zack's shaking was uncontrollable now. Jacqueline's mind was spinning as she turned and ran blindly from the apartment.

CHAPTER 30

New Orleans, June

Z ack paced the floor inside his apartment. He had healed enough to want to start getting exercise again. He hated being cooped up like this, and he was angry at the weather. In addition, he felt a sense of malaise that he couldn't pass off on the rain, and was angry at himself, both for feeling it and for not knowing why he felt it.

It was a perfectly miserable day outside, raining steadily at a moderate rate, but punctuated with occasional hard cloudbursts. It was more than enough to prevent anyone from doing anything outside. Zack had been confined here by the rain since yesterday afternoon. The misery of the rain seemed even worse in contrast to where he had recently been.

Zack had arrived back in New Orleans three days ago from a terrific trip to Boise. As he stared out the window, Zack thought about how grand Jeff Mitchell's wedding had been. Jeff's relatives and friends had been extraordinarily nice to Zack. It seemed that in Boise, even strangers had gone out of their way to help him, especially as he had still been using crutches. Zack had been especially impressed with Anna's Basque relatives. They had a tremendous cultural unity, and a sense of family that wouldn't quit.

The weather out west had been as he expected, hot and dry, but the scenery had been magnificent. The brown hills, the rugged mountains, and the clear blue sky were all so different from what Zack was used to seeing in New Orleans. Then, after the wedding, a group of family and friends had gone up to McCall to help the newly-weds "enjoy their honeymoon." Zack had driven along the scenic Payette River, and had enjoyed seeing the white water rapids and the tall pine trees that grew in those mountains.

In spite of what some of the local folks had said, Zack thought the river looked fine. Jeff's mother had complained bitterly of the prolonged drought that had lowered the lake level twenty feet, and dried up some beautiful forest areas. She had proclaimed how grand the Payette had looked just seven or eight years ago, before the years of drought had started. Other Boise natives had not wanted to talk about it at all.

Drought out west and a deluge here! Right now, Zack longed for some dry weather. To make matters worse, Zack had just gotten off the phone with his prime contractor at the Tulane stadium. There would be more delays now because of this rain.

"Damn!" he muttered to himself, "damn, damn! Things were going so well before we left."

Now it was a coin toss as to whether the construction work would be done in time. What would he do if it wasn't finished? What could he do? A lot of advertising had been done. He didn't have many options.

Just then a knock on the door interrupted his thoughts. Zack turned towards the door, wondering out loud, "Who in the world would be crazy enough to go out in this rain?"

Zack checked that the chain was in place and peered through his recently acquired peephole, but when he saw who it was, he quickly undid the locks.

"Gator!" Zack said, the surprise evident in his voice, "What the hell are you doing out on a day like this?"

Gator grinned at him. "Well, for one damn thing, it wasn't no day like this when I started out this mornin'. I knowed she was goin' to rain today - I could smell it, me. But I didn't know she was goin' to rain like this here! One reason for my bein' here is on account of I must get myself into the city every now and then to buy dem supply."

Zack stood in the door smiling with genuine pleasure at seeing his friend. He had only come to Zack's twice in two years. Right now Gator looked as wet as Zack had ever seen him. Water dripped off his nose and chin as well as his rain hat and poncho, the various streams merging to form a pool beneath him on the hallway floor. His tall rubberized boots were covered with wet mud.

"Well, boy, you goin' to stand there gawkin' at me all day or you goin' to ax me to come inside your house?"

"Oh, of course! I'm sorry. Uh, let's see, what can we do with your boots?" Zack turned and looked back into his apartment. But while he was looking for a solution, Gator had already found one.

"Tell you what - I jus' be leavin' dem boots right here in the hallway. It be wet and muddy anyway," he said, looking back along the trail he had left. With that he sat down on the hall floor and unfastened the snaps to his boots, slipping his feet out of them a minute later. He laid his hat next to his boots and then slipped off his poncho. Finally he wiped his face on his sleeve. In remarkably short time, he looked no wetter than Zack.

As they walked into the apartment and sat down, Zack asked, "How'd you get here today?" He always liked to hear how Gator got around in the modern world without owning a car.

"Took my airboat over to Point a la Hache. Then I hitched a ride on a sulfur truck all the way into the city. From there, it be easy as catchin' dem crawfish. Dem bus still be runnin' - even in the rain. But you don't be axin' no more questions! I be axin' you questions now!

"Boy, the main reason I brought myself to see you was 'cause I ain't been seein' you in so long. I begin to get that worry bug. So, the first t'ing you must tell me is where you been keepin' yourself these past two months? But even more first, before you start tellin' your tale, you got any o' that Dixie beer in your icebox?"

"I do believe that I have a few Dixies left in the refrigerator," said Zack, as he walked over to the kitchen. He took out two bottles, and twisted off the tops. He walked back to the couch, and handed one to Gator. He then proceeded to bring Gator up to date on his life, starting with the attack on him at the park, to the progress on his Ross demonstration project, to his recent visit to Boise. He left nothing out, including his growing involvement with Jacqueline, involvement that had ended abruptly three weeks ago.

"I be real sorry to hear 'bout ol' Sam, but I do believe there's somethin' else besides that be givin' you the misery right now. It sound to this ol' Cajun that you be in love wit' that young lady friend of yours. That be right?"

Zack paused a long time before he said, "I guess I have to admit I still care for her. But how can I ever forgive her for what she did?"

"Boy, you be as dumb as a tick on a coon dog! From what you say that she say, she didn't know nothing 'bout that mess! You got to at least hear her story."

"But she spied on me for months! She lied to me as smooth as silk. I don't know if I could ever trust her again."

"Zack boy, you mus' give her a chance to explain. You owes that to yourself and to herself."

"Maybe....I don't know."

Zack looked out the plate glass door at the heavy rain that was still falling. Gator followed his glance.

"OK, I jus' leave that be. I mus' tell you 'bout somethin' else! This las' week I been seein' some mighty strange things happenin' 'round dem bayou." He paused and took a long swig of his beer.

"Well," said Zack, "don't leave me hanging. What strange things?"

"Dem animal - they all be movin' further inland, away from the Gulf. Dem possum, dem coon, dem bayou rat. Especially dem rat - they are smart. I saw one yesterday. It were big as a dog. I mean to tell you it were big! And it were movin' north with a purpose - not huntin' for food, no sir. Jus' a movin' straight on north, like a damn duck in spring."

Zack was intrigued; he had never heard Gator sound so serious before. He asked, "What does it all mean, Gator?"

"Zack boy," Gator pronounced, "It be a sign - a sign sure as I be sittin' here. We got us a big storm a comin'. I seen dem animal move like that twice before, and each time, 'bout a month later, a big mama hurricane, she come and blow away most everything down there. I think we got us another big mama hurricane a comin'!"

Zack was spellbound by Gator's story. All he could think of to say was, "When?"

"Don't rightly know for sure. Could be a week, could be a month. But you best be ready."

Zack seemed to rouse himself at that last comment. "Gator, listen, you should come here." Gator started to shake his head, but Zack pressed on. "Really, this apartment complex is on the highest spot of land in the City. This would be the best place to ride out the storm."

"Well, you may be right - if'n you can't get out of this here city. I think you should leave. That's what I would do if I had any family left to go to."

Zack shook his head. "I can't leave now. I'm working on that big project. We've got to finish it - a lot of important folks are coming to town in less than a month from now."

"If'n I be right, nobody be comin' here a month from now!"

"Well, I'm not going to leave. And I think you should plan on staying here with me. Meanwhile, I'll take your advice and stock up on some provisions."

"Make sure you got plenty of Dixie," Gator laughed. "That be a most important part of ridin' out dem hurricane." Then his face became more earnest looking. "Well, if you be serious 'bout this, then I accept your kind in-vite to stay wit' you."

"Great, but how would you get here?"

"If there be enough time, I will brought myself up here the usual way; I'll hitch. But if she come in too fast, then findin' a truck comin' up here might be a problem. Also, dem street in downtown go under water pretty easy." He stopped to think for a minute.

"Say, I got me an idea. You ain't far from the Lake marina. How be dem street in this part of town?"

"This part of town is the highest part of New Orleans. From here to the Lake, the streets stay pretty clear."

"OK, then here be the plan. If a storm be comin' in quick, I will get myself a good boat down there near where I live. Dem rich folk, they got a ree-zort marina not far from me and they won't be needin' no boat in a storm. I will just pick me out a good'un, an' brought myself right here, an' you can meet me at the marina."

Zack shook his head in disbelief. "You can't be serious!? Take a boat ride up here with a hurricane coming?"

Gator laughed. "I'm goin' do it, me!" he said. "You just wait an' see!"

CHAPTER 31

New Orleans, June

D r. Alan King, who operated at high stress levels as the hard-driving Dean of Engineering at USL, was quite the opposite in his garden. He was as relaxed and peaceful a gardener as you could ever find. This particular Saturday, he was weeding and fertilizing the extensive azalea garden in his back yard. He was joined in this labor of love by his wife, June. They worked quietly, neither one feeling the need to speak as they worked their way around bush after bush. Painstakingly, on hands and knees, they pulled the dandelions and other weeds, and cleared minor sticks and debris.

The sun was shining brightly and it would have been hot work, except for the shade of the three tall oak trees that they had planted some twenty-two years ago. Their branches merged into a beautiful canopy of leaves, high above their heads, creating a vast pool of shade on the ground. The shade helped the azaleas, but hurt the grass, and had turned the lawn patchy. As a consequence, the Kings had slowly added to the azalea garden over the years, nibbling away at their back yard grass.

Alan looked up from his weeding, and rocked back on his legs. He glanced up at the trees, surveying the branches above him. The big main laterals started about ten feet above ground level, but some reached as high as 35 or 40 feet. As he continued to gaze up through the filtered sunlight, he said, "You know, Dear, maybe we ought to get these branches thinned again this year. What do you think?"

June looked upwards too. "I don't know, Dear, I sure do like this shade."

"Yes, it is nice, but these trees are looking a bit crowded. A little more sun might do these azaleas some good, too."

"It's going to be expensive. Remember what they charged us four years ago."

"Yes, I know, but it should be done. With these branches this thick, if we have some high winds, one of those trees might just topple. If we thin them, there will be a lot less wind resistance."

"Well, whatever you think, Dear; you're the engineer."

"OK, I'll call a tree service next week." That settled, the Kings went back to their gardening.

* * *

Coral Gables, June

"The National Hurricane Center in Miami today upgraded tropical storm Bartholomew to hurricane status. Maximum sustained winds are now 83 miles per hour. Bart is still well out to sea and poses no threat at this time to the United States. His coordinates are 59 degrees west longitude and 19.5 degrees north latitude. He is moving slowly to the west-northwest at this time. Stay tuned to this station for further updates."

Bill Phillips turned off the TV. He wondered why they never said National Hurricane Center in Coral Gables, but rather always incorrectly put them in Miami. Another of life's little mysteries! It seemed strange to Phillips to listen to reports of Bart on the television that were hours out of date by his old standards. The problem was that now with the one remaining satellite malfunctioning, the TV reports weren't nearly as out of date as they should be.

Phillips felt sick. He paced the floor, coffee cup in hand, waiting for the next satellite update. For the hundredth time, he glanced at the last report - now nearly two hours old. Longitude - 71.8, latitude - 24.4. Winds sustained at 110 miles per hour. Barometric pressure - steady at 28.4 inches of mercury. Bart was a big hurricane, but they had had bigger. Thank God she had gone north of Puerto Rico. Coming so soon after Abigail, Bart would have dealt the island a heavy blow. But the problem now was that Bart appeared to be heading straight for South Florida.

Phillips did not want to think about it, but of course he knew he had to. Miami hadn't had a major hurricane in over fifty years. How would the people respond to an evacuation order? Phillips had to wait. He couldn't make the call too soon. The consequences of a false alarm, would be almost as bad as not providing enough warning. But there were so many people to move out of here! If the target was South Florida, he had to give them enough time.

"Millie," called Bill Phillips, "tell Rafael I need to see him right away please."

"Sure thing, Colonel."

Phillips walked over to the table to pour himself another cup of coffee. Just as he got there, he felt light-headed. He reached down to the table edge for support. The feeling passed a few seconds later. Phillips just finished pouring his coffee when Rafael appeared at his door.

"You wanted to see me, Bill?"

"Yes, Rafee, thanks. Sit down." He picked up the old wooden dowel he used for a pointer and waved it at the big tracking chart on his wall. He said, "Look at Bart's path so far. It's almost like a ruler-straight line towards Miami. It's uncanny; almost as if she knows her target."

"Now, Bill, it's too early to worry yet. Bart still may turn, you know. So far, he has only churned up a lot of water."

* * *

Washington, D.C., June

Senator Lane Stillwater was clearly shaken when he walked through the door of his office.

"Theresa, hold all my calls. Get Cooper over here as fast as you can."

He walked into his inner office and collapsed into his big chair behind his desk. He swiveled to look out the window towards the Capitol Building. He usually loved the view, but today it didn't do anything for him. He thought about the briefing he had just attended, still unwilling to accept the news. Egypt was on the verge of starting a war in the Middle East!

The briefing had been short and filled with guesses and opinions. As usual, Stillwater thought that the administration people weren't telling the Senate leaders everything they knew. But what the briefer had told them was bad enough: Egypt appeared more than willing to go to war! War in the Middle East again! Would this be the one to escalate out of control? Would the Israelis be drawn into it? Would the U.S. feel like it had to send troops over to stabilize the area?

And all because of water! Or more precisely, all because of the lack of water. After several thousand years, the weather patterns had finally shifted enough to drive Egypt to the breaking point, and it was probably due to Greenhouse. 'Who'll be next?' Stillwater wondered. Then a thought struck him. "My God," he said out loud, even though there was no one else in the room, "this could become a world war, and it's all because of the Greenhouse Effect!"

He flipped the intercom on. "Theresa, bring me in that file on Greenhouse-related weather events," he snapped.

In a minute, Theresa brought in two files - one filled with briefing papers, and another filled with newspaper articles clipped from the Washington Post over the last year or so. After Theresa left him, Stillwater began flipping through the newspaper articles. He read only the dates and headlines:

11/14/21 - 'Typhoon Mike Slams into Phillipines – 1,800 Die'
11/16/21 - 'Mudslides follow Mike in Phillipines – 4,300 more Dead'
12/30/21 - 'Egyptian Refugees Drown in Mediterranean Storm'
5/2/22 - 'Bangladesh Reeling after Typhoon Prateep - Death
Toll Climbs to 41,000'
5/23/23 - 'Heat Wave in South Carolina Kills 18,000,000
Chickens'
6/11/22 - 'Summer Sizzles - Corn Fizzles in Iowa'
6/12/22 - 'Drought Continues in California - New Dust Bowl?'
8/21/22 – 'Fires Rage in California – 200,000 homeless'
9/20/22 - 'Waves Pound Bar Harbor – President Narrowly Escapes'
3/5/23 – 'Water rationing in California worst in years'
6/19/23 - 'Abigail Strikes Holland - Major Damage to Dikes'

Just then, the door opened and James Cooper walked in. "You wanted to see me, Senator?" he said.

"Damn right I do, Coop! Listen, I've got a new angle for our campaign. We need to talk about this, then I want you to get with our campaign people and figure how to use this to our best advantage."

* * *

Coral Gables, June

Phillips awoke with first light the next morning on the old Army cot in his office. He swung his feet over the side and stretched his arms up and out. "Whoa," he mumbled, grabbing his lower back, and glancing down at the cot, "and to think I used to sleep like a baby on these things!" He stood up stiffly, massaging his back. Then he rubbed his hand across the mostly white stubble on his jaw.

Phillips walked over to the table and dumped the old grounds out of the coffee maker. He tore open a new package of filters, placed two in the holder, and scooped in more than the recommended amount of coffee. He walked out to the sink in the outer office and filled the carafe. Only after he had poured the water into the machine, and had touched the 'on' sensor, did he look at his printed messages.

As he read the messages from the office in Washington summarizing the data from the polar satellite, his heart sank. He glanced at the grease pencil trail on his wall chart, mentally extending the black line to the most recent reported position. Bart had turned directly west, and was now at 72.6 degrees west and 25.0 degrees north.

He activated his computer, and tried without success to access the GOES satellite. "Dammit to hell!" he cursed.

"That might be a good place to send it!" a voice behind him said. Phillips jumped. He turned to see Rafael standing in the doorway.

"Jesus, Rafee, don't sneak up on me like that! You scared the pee out of me."

"Sorry, Bill, I just now walked up, and I couldn't resist agreeing with your curse on this hurricane."

"It wasn't on the hurricane, it was aimed at that damn satellite! We can't get anything out of it except every two hours. It's so frustrating!"

By about 7:00 that afternoon Phillips was exhausted. It had been a long day. The information they had been getting had been encouraging at times, and discouraging at times. But the six o'clock pictures from GOES had just about sealed it. He was discussing options with Rafael, but Phillips knew in his heart that he had run out of options.

"What do you think, Rafee?"

Rafael looked unhappy. At first, he didn't answer; he just looked out the window. The sun was still fairly high in the sky, and the weather looked deceivingly good. He turned back to face Phillips.

"Only you can do it, Bill, but I think you don't have much choice. You must give them enough time to evacuate. If you wait until morning, it will be too late."

"You're right of course. If we wait even two more hours, too many people will want to stay put for the night. We've got to do it."

Phillips jaw was set, but his eyes revealed his lingering doubts. He continued to sit there.

"Bill," said Rafael gently, "you've got to do it."

"What if we're wrong, Rafee? What if that high pressure area moves in tonight and forces Bart back out to sea? God, I'd hate to cry wolf on this!"

"Bill," said Rafael, "what if you don't call for the evacuation and then Bart keeps moving in? You couldn't live with yourself then. We've waited as long as we can. You've got to do it now!"

"I guess you're right, Rafee. O.K., thanks, let me be alone for a minute, will you?"

After Rafael left, Phillips sat at his desk and stared at the wall chart. Once more he studied the most recent satellite photos. Then he made his decision; he picked up the phone, and made the call to order the evacuation of Miami.

Less than 24 hours later, Phillips was bitterly regretting his decision – Hurricane Bart had turned sharply north while the eye was still 100 miles from the Florida coastline, and had headed out to die in the north Atlantic. The costly and extremely inconvenient evacuation had not been necessary; William Phillips was the little boy who had cried wolf.

CHAPTER 32

New Orleans, July

Z ack walked into his apartment carrying his lunch in a Burger King bag. He had just come from the project site, at which place it seemed he was spending most of his waking hours lately. He checked his phone and noticed he had a message. He listened as he walked into the room.

"Zachary, this is Jacqueline. I assume that since you haven't called, you don't really care about me the way I care about you. I'll be leaving New Orleans soon, and I just wanted to tell you that I'm really sorry things didn't work out for us....Good luck with your project. I'll never forget you...I...I really did love you."

Zack sat there for an agonizing minute then made up his mind. He called back Jacqueline's number. Damn! Her voice mail was responding. At the tone, he said "Jacqueline - this is Zack. Don't leave the City! I...I do care for you; I want to talk with you. Please call me back." Zack hung up and stared at the phone. A moment later it rang, startling him.

"Jacqueline?" he blurted into the phone.

"No, this is Al down here at the field. We got another problem on this construction. Can you get down here right away?"

Zack sighed, and his shoulders slumped. He didn't want to go back there again, but what else could he do? "Yeah, sure, Al. I'll be right down."

Taylor grabbed his briefcase full of design notes, and headed back to his project, for what seemed like the hundredth time in the past week.

After an afternoon spent in the summer heat working with the contractor at the stadium, Taylor returned home. Hot and sticky, he needed a shower, but was eager to find out if Jacqueline had called. He checked for messages.

"Dr. Taylor, this is Jeff. I've got some bad news, and I need to talk with you right away. Please call me at once. It's about the project. Very urgent. Good-bye."

Taylor was in the process of dialing Jeff's number when he heard a knock on his front door. He walked quickly to the door and opened it to face a distraught looking Jeff Mitchell.

"Dr. Taylor? I've got some bad news, some really awful news! I just had to come right over here." Mitchell stood at the door, looking miserable. He had his notebook under his arm.

"What is it Jeff?" asked Zack, adding, "Wait, first, come in," as Jeff appeared to be ready to start speaking right where he stood in the hallway. Jeff walked in quickly and sat on the sofa. "Now tell me about this awful news," said Zack.

"Well, remember when I first calculated that information for you about the sea level rise due to the Ross Ice Shelf? When we were first preparing that proposal?"

Zack suddenly had a sick feeling in the pit of his stomach. He nodded and said "Yes, I remember. I checked you as you did it. What about it?"

"Well, I was just going over my calculations for the twentieth time. But this time I started way back at the beginning and did everything over. I wrote it all down, each step of the way. When I finished, I went through them again, this time backwards just so I would be sure."

"Jeff, what are you trying to tell me?"

Jeff gulped, and said quietly, "I'm trying to say that I made a mistake in the calculations. Right at the beginning. It's a subtle error and I don't think you caught it either."

"What kind of mistake? Tell me, please!"

"A bad one, I'm afraid. Instead of a dramatic sea level rise of twelve and half feet, it's only three and half!"

"What! Only three and half feet! Are you sure?"

Jeff nodded. Zack sat there thunderstruck. The whole basis for his big demonstration had just been ruined. He felt himself getting angry. "How could you have made such a mistake?! How do I know you didn't make one just now? Give me those papers!"

Zack grabbed the notebook from Jeff, who just sat there looking miserable. Zack reviewed Jeff's new calculations step by step. He snatched the calculator that Jeff silently offered him and punched the numbers himself. He was furious, more at himself for never checking Jeff's numbers thoroughly before now. But he took his anger out on Jeff.

"Why did you wait until now to tell me?! Are you trying to make me look like a fool?"

"No sir, Dr. Taylor. I ... I just...."

"Dammit, Jeff, what do you expect me to do now? The demonstration is less than two weeks away! We can't change anything now! What do want me to do?"

"I don't know. I just thought you needed to know so you could...."

"Could what?" demanded Taylor angrily.

"Could, you know, tell people. I mean, you've always told us in class about ethics and academic honesty. I just thought you needed to know about this."

Zack's mouth was open to continue berating Jeff, but that last statement stopped him in his tracks. When he next spoke, his tone was much gentler. "Jeff, I'm sorry I flew off the handle with you. I was acting like one of those ancient Romans who killed the messenger that brought bad news. Have you told anyone else about this?"

Mitchell shook his head.

"OK," Zack said thoughtfully. "Please don't tell anyone. I don't know what I'm going to do with this news, yet. But I'll think of something. Thanks for coming over, Jeff."

"I'm sorry, Dr. Taylor, I'm really sorry."

"Don't worry about it," said Zack absently, his mind already working on possible courses of action. He got up and walked Jeff to the door. "Remember, not a word to anyone else, OK? That's great, I'll be in touch."

CHAPTER 33

The killer was conceived approximately three months before she was born. The spring had been extremely wet in the Sahel region of western Africa for the third year in a row. But this year, the rains came earlier and stayed longer than ever before. The countries of Senegal, Guinea, Sierra Leone, Liberia, and Mali were getting more rain than they ever had. Even while Egypt, Sudan, Ethiopia and others in east Africa were dying of thirst, many western African nations were drowning.

The Gambia, the Rokel, and the Cestos Rivers had grown from large streams to large rivers, the Senegal and the Bandama from large rivers to major torrents. The Niger River, coursing through the bulge of western Africa, had overtaken the mighty Zaire (formerly the Congo) as the largest river in the Dark Continent. The weakening Nile had been surpassed easily four years ago. In fact, the Niger River was now the second most powerful river in the world, surpassed only by its mighty cousin in South America, the Amazon.

And every minute of every day, all these rivers in western Africa wasted billions of gallons of fresh drinkable water. They poured relentlessly into the warm salty waters of the Atlantic Ocean off the coast of equatorial Africa, changing ever so slightly the density of the water in that region, and the patterns of the swirling currents there. It was there that the killer was conceived, in the late spring of 2023.

In those tropical waters off the west coast of Africa, lie the Cape Verde Islands. The Cape Verde Islands lie smack in the path of the Atlantic Conveyor Current as it flows up alongside western Africa and turns west to round the huge bulge of that great continent. Were it not for the Cape Verdes, the current would have a smooth shot into the north Atlantic. Of course, these islands are really tops of undersea mountains, so they get in the way of the Atlantic Conveyor. They cause part of the undersea current to diverge and then converge after it flows through these underwater mountain passes. Even these magnificent underwater mountains, which we see as only small islands, don't really disrupt this mighty conveyor; they merely tickle it a little. They create some relatively minor disturbances, a few small counterclockwise eddies or swirls in the water. But sometimes a small eddy is all it takes.

The killer was born in mid-July, the same way they all are. In the warm blue waters off the Cape Verde Islands, a small circulating current of water that was just a bit warmer than its neighbors, met a wandering breeze of air. No more than a large puff, really, this breeze was warmed by the water and began to rise. As it did so, its initial counterclockwise motion was enhanced by the circulation of the water, and the puff stayed together rather than dissipating.

As the parcel of air rose, it left behind a region of ever-so-slightly lower pressure, and more air from outside the parcel moved in to fill the void. Over the next few hours, the warm circulating water worked together with the increasing mass of upwardly spiraling air. There were no wind shears or summer squalls or other disturbances to cause a premature death to the infant, and so was born Cleopatra, the third hurricane of the season. History would not mark this moment in time simply because no weatherman could pinpoint the exact moment of Cleopatra's birth. However, history would certainly mark Cleopatra, for she was destined to become the biggest, fiercest, deadliest hurricane since people started keeping track of such things.

* * *

Coral Gables, July 23

"Looks like we got another one, Bill. Pretty far out there, but already she's getting big."

Rafael Munoz was standing in Bill Phillips' office doorway. He was holding a sheet of paper between thumb and forefinger. It was July 23, and the National Hurricane Center had been experiencing an uncharacteristic lull after the frenzied activity of the previous month.

"What? Where?" snapped Phillips, his coffee cup in hand.

Rafael pointed to the area on the far right hand side of the big tracking chart on Phillips' wall, the area of open water east of the Caribbean. Then he said, "Looks like she might be coming in from the Cape Verde Islands."

Phillips took the paper that Rafael was holding out to him and viewed it critically. His experienced eye quickly gleaned the important information from the sheet. He whistled softly between his teeth. There was no doubt in his mind that this was going to be a major hurricane.

"Hello, Cleopatra," he said softly.

Rafael corrected him gently. "Technically, Bill, she's not Cleopatra yet."

"I know, Rafee. But we both know this 'tropical wave' is going to grow big enough to name before long. And I think you'll agree with me that this baby will grow a lot bigger than 'big enough.' I hope she stays well away from us."

* * *

Miami, July 25

"The National Hurricane Center in Miami today upgraded tropical storm Cleopatra to hurricane status. Maximum sustained winds are now 90 miles per hour. At the present time, Cleo is still well out to sea and poses no threat to the United States. Her coordinates are 58 degrees west longitude and 18.5 degrees north latitude. She is presently moving slowly to the west-northwest. Stay tuned to this station for further updates."

Deborah Jones turned off the set. It seemed odd in a way to get hurricane information from the national network news when the Hurricane Center was right here in town. She turned to her husband. "Did you hear that, Al? Another hurricane! I wonder if this one will come as close as that last one?"

"No way to tell, just yet," he said. "But I tell you what, those weather bureau guys better get it right this time. After that last evacuation fiasco, people aren't going to be very cooperative. How many people left their homes at night, five weeks ago, just to get snarled up on I-95 for ten hours in the dark? And after all that time sitting in traffic to hear on the radio that the storm had veered away and wouldn't hit Miami after all. Then to top it all off, they all had to try to get home along with everyone else, and go to work that day! I tell you what, Deb, I might just sit it out right here at home next time."

"Now, Al, don't close your mind like that. I'm sure those people have a tough job. They're doing the best they can."

"How hard can it be? You sit there with all the satellites and radars in the world tracking a storm. You have big computers calculating the Bermuda High, the position of the jet stream, and all that. Then you issue a statement that says the hurricane has a 50% chance of hitting land somewhere between Miami and Jacksonville. Gimme a break!"

Deborah knew better than to argue with him when he got like this so she remained silent. Her thoughts turned to her niece, her departed sister's grown daughter and their children. They lived in the next city up the road, Hollywood Beach, less than a quarter-mile from the ocean. Would they heed the warnings in time?

Then, unbidden, another worry sprang to her mind - Eagle Point. How would the nuclear power plant ride out the storm if it came? The plant was in good shape even though it was getting old. They had just passed a very thorough inspection, and replaced those stanchions that had caused her some anxiety back in the spring. Everything about it was strong, it had been designed to withstand 250 mile per hour winds. Surely that would be strong enough! It had to be - Eagle Point was vital to Miami. Jones thought of all the hospitals, the schools and other buildings that would serve as emergency shelters. They all needed electricity.

In any case, she knew where she would be if the storm did hit. She was needed at the plant. She hoped that Al would be able to take care of himself and would listen if the evacuation order came. She would be at Eagle Point for many hours, perhaps days before any hurricane arrived.

* * *

Coral Gables, July 27

"The National Hurricane Center in Miami today announced that Hurricane Cleopatra is now a Category 3 hurricane. She continues to move at about 10 miles per hour in a west-northwest direction. Maximum sustained winds are now over 135 miles per hour. Cleo is some 410 miles almost due east of Puerto Rico and more than 1,000 miles southeast of Florida. Cleo poses no threat at this time to the United States. Her coordinates are 66.4 degrees west longitude and 22.8 degrees north latitude. Stay tuned to this station for further updates."

Mary Taylor was watching the news as Joe Rosenthal prepared one of their favorite suppers - his homemade cabbage soup. He had been listening to the part about the hurricane, and started talking as soon as it was over.

"What do you think - is it coming our way?"

"Not to worry, Joe; it's a thousand miles away. We can still play golf tomorrow."

"Mary, at 10 miles per hour, a thousand miles is only four days away. And that's if it doesn't speed up. I think we ought to leave Miami tomorrow."

"Oh, don't be such an old worry-wart. First, tomorrow's way too early. Second, who says it's going to hit Miami? It may turn around and head out to sea tomorrow night. That last one, Bart, was headed this way but at the last minute, it went north and missed us. I think it must be something in the jet stream that steers them away."

"Don't be ridiculous. The jet stream doesn't affect hurricanes. It all high pressures and low pressures. I was reading about it in the Herald this morning. And Cleo has one hell of a low pressure already."

"You were out today. Didn't you notice the weather? It was gorgeous, and it's supposed to be the same for tomorrow. I'll worry about the weekend weather when it gets here. But tomorrow I'm going to enjoy my golf."

"You go ahead and play golf Ms. Know-it-all. But you'll play without me. I won't leave the city without you, Mary, but one of us has got to take some precautions. I'm going out to buy some canned food and other supplies."

"Old Mr. Worry-wart. Well, OK, I can get up a game with one of my friends at the Club." They were both silent for a while. Mary thought about Joe's concern for her. She thought about her feelings for Joe.

"Joe," she said softly, "if it comes, you shouldn't be here right on the beach. The storm surge is the killer part; the winds aren't so bad. Day after tomorrow, if it's still coming this way, come over to my house. We'll ride it out there, together. Please."

Joe gave her a long look. "You really aren't going to leave the city," he said. It was a statement rather than a question. "All right, I'll come over. Whatever happens, we'll be together."

* * *

Coral Gables, July 28

Bill Phillips' gut was knotted up with the tension. He took another sip of coffee as he looked at the last report - now nearly two hours old. Longitude - 71.3, latitude - 24.1. Winds sustained at 180 miles per hour. Barometric pressure - 27.2 inches of mercury and still dropping. God, she was still consolidating! Cleo was a killer storm, and she was still growing. Thank God she had gone north and missed Puerto Rico and Haiti. But it looked like the Bahamas were in for it. And after the Bahamas...could Florida be far behind?

Phillips shuddered to think about it. Just a few weeks ago, Bartholomew had made him do exactly what he had dreaded for years. Phillips had waited as long as he had dared, waited and watched while Bart had moved inexorably towards Miami. Finally, Phillips had pulled the whistle cord; he had given the evacuation signal for Miami. And it was not like in the old days, when they simply hung the hurricane warning flags, red with black centers, outside the office and strung them along the beach. The evacuation signal now involved police, firemen, civil defense, bus companies, thousands of people in authority, all trying to shepherd two million or more folks to safety. It was mass confusion, compounded by the darkness; he had issued the order at seven-thirty at night. It had taken a few hours for the word to spread, so the bulk of the exodus had started about ten o'clock at night.

Then, less than twelve hours after that, Bart had turned suddenly and decisively to the northwest. Its fringes merely brushed Miami with some heavy rains and that was it. But the panic that set in with the evacuation, now that was something else.

The traffic accidents, the shootings that had occurred. It made him sick to think of it. And now, a little more than a month later, he might have to make the call again.

"Millie," he called, "please get Rafael in here right away."

"OK, Colonel," she responded.

A few minutes later, Rafael appeared at his door.

"You wanted to see me, Bill?"

"Yes, Rafee. This is like deja vu, don't you think? Sit down, will you." He picked up his wooden dowel pointer and snapped the tip on the big tracking chart on his wall. He said, "Look at Cleo's path! So far, it's almost identical to Bart's. It's unbelievable how similar they are."

"Now, Bill, let's not jump to any conclusions yet. Bart turned and Cleo might too. So far, she's stayed in the ocean. She spared my homeland - she must have some feelings."

"Forget about her feelings; I want to know her travel plans! Look at these tracks. There's something vaguely familiar looking here. I felt it with Bart, and I feel it again, but I just can't put my finger on it."

"I don't recognize anything there," said Rafael.

"There's a pattern here, I know it. Rafee, I want you to have the folks in your section do a computer graphics analysis of this storm track. Compare it with all the hurricanes that we have in our data base. See if you can find anything similar in the past."

"That's a lot of work, Bill, especially now. My people are tired. They've been working overtime for two days now."

"I know," said Phillips, "but there's something here. I can feel it."

"How about if I..." began Munoz.

"Wait," interrupted Phillips, "something's coming in on the printer." He walked over to the machine and stood there. He gnawed the knuckle of his left forefinger while the machine slowly and reluctantly let go of its message. He scanned it and a smile started to crack his unshaven jaw. "Here, look at this," he said, handing the sheet to Rafael.

Rafael's features crinkled. "I told you this might happen!" Rafael walked over to the chart. With the grease pencil, he marked the latest reported position - longitude - 71.5, latitude - 25.0. Cleopatra had turned north!

Phillips rubbed the back of his neck. He sipped his coffee. He felt a sense of relief. Not one of complete safety, of course, not yet. But it was definitely one of relief. Once they turned north in this area, they rarely turned back.

"Rafee, this is good news. It gives us some breathing room, at least. But I still want your section to do that comparative analysis. I want to see it tomorrow morning. I know it's late, I know they've been working hard, but I still want it by morning."

After Rafael left, Phillips looked around. The small cot under the window looked particularly uninviting. He decided to go home. It would be nice to sleep in his own bed tonight. He was looking forward to his first good night's sleep in several days.

* * *

Coral Gables, July 29

Phillips was awakened by a ringing. Still groggy, he groped for his alarm clock. He couldn't see the button, but he knew where it was. He pressed it. Something was wrong; the ringing didn't stop. Then he realized it was the phone.

"H'lo," he answered with his eyes closed.

"Bill, sorry to wake you." At the sound of the voice, Phillips came fully awake at once.

"Rafee, what is it?"

"You had better come to the office."

"Why? What's happened?"

"It's Cleo - she's turned again - back to the west."

Forty-five minutes later, Phillips walked into the office; he glared at the tracking chart. The grease pencil trail told him half the story. Cleopatra had stayed on her northern track until she reached 25.1 north latitude. Then, she had turned directly west. Her new position was 72.8 degrees west and 25.2 degrees north.

He turned to Rafael for confirmation. Rafael's normally very well groomed appearance was long gone.

"You look like hell, Rafe," he said. "Tell me what happened."

"Cleo stayed put until about midnight. I was here helping my people with that computer analysis you wanted. When the midnight report came in, I didn't want to wake you, so we waited until the 2:00 am report.

"I had to call you then, Bill. Something happened to her tonight; she's picked up a lot more energy somehow. Winds are up to 210 mph, the pressure's down to 26.1 inches, and she's moving due west at 18 mph!"

"Oh, God!" Bill put a clenched fist to his mouth.

Rafael continued wearily. "Our computer projections show a 60% chance of landfall between Marathon Key and West Palm Beach sometime within the next 24 to 36 hours."

Just then a young lady walked up to the door. She, too, looked worn out from the night's work. "Rafael, I think I might have found something," she said.

Rafael turned and saw who it was. He said, "Come in, Melissa." By way of explanation he said to Bill, "Melissa has been working on that comparative analysis you wanted." Then, looking back at her, he said. "Tell us what you found, please."

"Well, I was going back year by year, like you said. I was overlaying the storm tracks from past hurricanes with Cleo's and trying to find a match. I got back to 1947, and I found it."

"Well, show us, dammit," snapped Phillips.

Rafael shot Phillips a hard glance, then said "Melissa, can you interface your computer to Bill's here so we can project it onto the big chart?"

"Yes, I think so."

Melissa walked over to Phillips' computer, which had been on 24 hours a day, all week. She punched the keys rapidly. In no more than 90 seconds she had locked into her machine down the hall, and had accessed the database she needed. "Can you get the lights, Rafael? Watch this," she said.

She turned on the projector. The bare tracking chart from Phillips' twelve inch computer screen leaped onto the six foot wall chart. Next, she adjusted the projector a bit until the longitude and latitude tic marks lined up. Finally, she projected a storm position, a thick black circle with cross hairs in it, on the wall chart.

She started talking. "This was Storm No. 6 in 1947. This is her position on September 12, 1947. Now watch what happens as we roll through the next seven days."

Phillips gasped as he watched the replay of a 1947 hurricane as it closely traced the grease pencil markings that now chronicled Cleo's movements in 2023. "My God," he said, "it even stopped to turn north where Cleo did!"

Melissa ran the projection to Cleo's last plotted position, then stopped it. She said, "From here on, there will be two tracks: the solid black line is the 1947 storm, the dashed line is our computer projection of Cleo."

She started the computer again. The 1947 storm came ashore just below West Palm Beach, crossed south Florida dipping a little south and curved up into Louisiana, well to the west of New Orleans. Cleo's projection line was actually a band that got wider the further out it went.

Melissa explained, "With our new program, we plot the path of highest probability as a dashed line, and the software will give a zone or band of uncertainty around it as dotted lines. We can set the band width as a percentage of certainty. I've set it at 75% certain - any higher and the band gets uselessly wide. I know that sounds like a contradiction, but the truth is that the more certain you want to be that Cleo will stay within the band that you plot, the wider you have to make the band. Also, as you can see, the band always widens out as you go further into the future. Nevertheless, it gives us a reasonable tool for forecasting."

Bill Phillips looked at the areas between the two dotted lines. An area from Coral Gables to Fort Lauderdale was sliced out of the east coast of Florida; on the west coast, the slice widened to include the southwestern corner of the Everglades National Park on the south, and Ft. Myers on the north. Looking past Florida, Cleo was forecast to move into the Gulf of Mexico and then turn northwest. She might landfall again anywhere from Mobile, Alabama, to Galveston, Texas.

"Thank you, Melissa," said Phillips, somberly. "I need a few minutes alone now. Rafee, you better go home and get some sleep. I'm going to need you tomorrow...uh, later today. Take the official car, so you can get through when you come back."

As Rafael turned to go, Phillips changed his mind. "No, wait a minute. Can you sleep down the hall? Traffic will be a nightmare a few hours from now." After he left, Phillips sat at his desk and stared at the wall chart for a full minute. He re-read the last three satellite reports. He looked back at the 1947 storm, and that cemented his decision. Phillips was going to order another evacuation.

He opened his top drawer of emergency phone numbers and dialed the home number of Carlos Alvarez, head of Civil Defense for greater Miami. With 36-48 hours to landfall, that left at most 24-30 hours for evacuation. Twenty-four to thirty hours; Alvarez was not going to like this one bit. He could just hear Alvarez screaming at him now, questioning if this was another false alarm. Reason told him that another false alarm would be a blessing. But, in a perverse way, he almost hoped that Cleo would come straight on in.

No, Alvarez was not going to like this. And neither would millions of other poor souls.

* * *

South Florida, Tuesday, July 30

The news of the evacuation order reached most people as they were waking up. So now instead of the morning routine of dressing for work and jumping in the car, or getting the children ready for school and to the bus stop on time, people throughout the Greater Miami area were faced with a frightening departure from the routine. And because of the false alarm a few weeks earlier, arguments raged throughout the city. One such argument was going on in the Jones' home.

"Al, don't be such a stubborn fool! You heard the bulletin. You need to evacuate!"

"Don't you yell at me like that! You're going to go into that power plant of yours. I can do what I damn well please. That other hurricane turned and this one might too."

"That other storm was a baby compared with this one, Al! Use your head, for God's sake. If this one landfalls here, Miami Beach will cease to exist!"

176

"Now, you're the one not using her head. No storm could do that. You're being melodramatic."

"Al, please listen to me. Winds are over 200 miles per hour and the eye is twenty miles across. This is a monster hurricane!"

Al continued to sit at the table drinking his coffee. The TV was on and giving evacuation instructions. Deb had never felt so frustrated. Finally, she gave up.

"Al," she said softly, "I have to go now. They need me at the plant."

He gave her a sour look, but said nothing.

She came over and hugged him tight around the neck. "I love you. Please take care of yourself," she said simply. She picked her car keys off the hook on the kitchen wall, and walked out the door.

The evacuation was not going well. Not enough people were responding quickly enough. What made things worse was that it was turning out to be a beautiful morning. The sun was shining brightly. A strong breeze, but nothing more than a strong breeze, was coming in from the northeast. To veterans and newcomers alike, there appeared to be no threat at all.

A number of people of course hadn't gotten the word, and were already on the road going to work. The worst thing was the heavy truck traffic. The interstate truckers who had been driving all night and were just arriving with their loads were streaming into Miami and adding to the confusion in the streets. The schools had closed, but many businesses were still open. The good weather and the 'business as usual' attitude were frustrating emergency personnel who were trying to get people to move out.

Carlos Alvarez was especially frustrated because he knew that they had less than twelve hours to move out before the winds picked up and the rains started.

"We need to stop any more traffic coming in, and we need to do it now!" said Alvarez.

Raul Sanchez, Chief of the Metro police force, was calmer than Alvarez. "Carlos, take it easy. Have you seen the latest bulletin from the Center? Cleo has stalled again. It might decide to go away like the last one."

"I have talked with Phillips myself. He doesn't think so. He says we should use this extra time like a gift from God to get the people out of the way. We must move swiftly."

"All my spare officers are already patrolling the Beach areas and using their car loudspeakers to warn people."

"But we need to do more. We are letting more and more people into the city; we must stop that at once."

"OK, OK. I will talk with Ft. Lauderdale about closing I-95 southbound. That will stop any more incoming trucks and cars. Then if we need the extra lanes, we can make the whole thing one way north all the way up to West Palm Beach."

* * *

Coral Gables, Wednesday, July 31

At noon on July 31, Bill Phillips got the strangest report on a hurricane he had ever received. The reconnaissance plane that had flown into the eye had radio'd back the astounding data - sustained winds of 240 mph and a barometric pressure of 25.4 inches of mercury, the lowest ever recorded! But then came the strange part. The pilot had flown into the eye - a huge one - and in that calm sunny region, had decided to fly down closer to the surface of the water. He had reported seeing the sea foaming and bubbling like he had never seen before. He also said that he thought he heard a loud 'popping' noise.

Phillips still pondered that. How he had heard anything over the plane's engine noise? It must have been enormously loud, more like explosions than popping.

The pilot had reported that he saw a great amount of foaming and frothing on the sea, not the usual calm water associated with the eye of a hurricane. He said it was like the sea was boiling. The next words from the pilot's report still haunted Phillips: 'with the sea foaming like this and with this popping sound, I feel like I'm inside the neck of a giant Coke bottle when the top is popped.'

The pilot had then reported engine sputtering – almost like it was starved for air – and had taken the plane up and away. As soon as they had retreated away from the surface, the engines had come back to full power and the plane had made it back to base.

Phillips thought about the report another minute, then mentally shrugged. I don't have time to sit and theorize about this popping noise, he thought. The wind and the pressure, now those are reality. He fed the data into his desktop computer, and watched with dismay as it displayed the results on the screen. "Good grief!" Phillips said out loud when he saw the numbers, "What's happened?"

At the last report, Cleo had stalled over the Gulf Stream and had moved north a bit. But now it seemed that she had magnified her energy even more. And now she was accelerating again. Coming off the Gulf Stream like a giant stone from a slingshot. A giant stone aimed right at Miami.

* * *

Miami, Thursday afternoon, August 1

Deborah Jones was watching the bulletins continuously. Her stress level seemed to be rising in direct proportion to the reported wind speeds near the eye of the storm. Her own plant's anemometer was already showing winds at 46 knots and gusty. With her in her office was Earl Wilson.

"Have we secured all loose objects?"

"Yes, ma'am." There's not a thing left out there that can fly around."

"Can we put any extra bracing on anything?"

"Deb, stop worrying. This plant was designed to take it. It can withstand an earthquake and a hurricane at the same time. We'll make it through."

"I guess you're right," she said. "It's just that I feel the responsibility so much. If we go down, Miami loses one third of all its electricity, just like that." She tried to snap her fingers, but only a soft 'flub' sound came out. "We've got to keep operating."

"We will, Deb, we will," said Earl.

Meanwhile, Hurricane Cleopatra continued to bear down on Miami like a freight train. At four o'clock that afternoon, while the eye of Cleo was still two hundred miles offshore, the rains started. By six o'clock, the winds were blowing hard and the sky was dark with driving rain. By now, reality had sunk in for most people in the Greater Miami area. The roads were clogged with people trying to move inland. At the intersection of NW 2nd avenue and NW 62nd street, a pick-up truck had just collided with a small foreign car. It was a low speed collision, and fortunately no one was hurt, yet.

Two burly men jumped out of the pick-up and started running through the gusty rain towards the small car. The white-haired retired gentleman and his wife, already nervous about the minor accident, began shaking with fear.

"Out of the way, Pops!" yelled one man.

The old man locked his door. The driver of the pick-up saw this and flew into a rage.

"Get this piece of shit out of here!" he screamed. He started to beat on the roof of the car with his fists.

"James, please drive away," his wife said, crying.

"I'm trying, Ellen, I'm trying," moaned James. His car engine was flooded. He turned the key again and again, but the car just wouldn't start. He looked out the window, all he saw was the big chest and stomach of the man drumming on their car. Then the pounding on the roof increased; the other man had joined in. The noise was deafening. "For God's sake, leave us alone!" James screamed.

Suddenly, the pounding stopped and the car started to rock. Both men were on Ellen's side; they were trying to tip them over. "Please, stop!" James begged. The car started to tip, then rolled over. His wife crashed into him, pinning the old man against the door. The men ran back to their pick-up and drove around the car, trying to make their way to the interstate.

* * *

Miami, Thursday night, August 1

Mary Taylor peeked outside at the darkness. The wind was making a horrific noise and the rain was belting her wooden storm shutters. She looked back into the well-lit house. It looked so cozy, so safe.

"Did you get candles?" she asked.

"Yes, Mary, I've got everything we need."

She walked over to where Joe sat on the couch. She sat down beside him. "I'm so glad you came over here this morning," she said. I'd be so worried about you over there on the beach."

"You should still be worried," said Rosenthal. "They just said that wind near the center is up to 290 mph. They don't know how big the storm surge is going to be, but they're saying it will be much worse than when Hugo hit Charleston all those years ago."

He shook his head as he continued to speak. "I sure wish you had gone north with me on Monday. Then we wouldn't be in this situation."

"Oh, we'll get through it. This house has been here for sixty years. It's seen a lot of hurricanes. But thank you for taking the time last week to stock up on provisions. You know, maybe I'd better fill the bathtub with water."

* * *

Miami, Thursday night, August 1

The darkness of the night was compounded by the darkness of the falling rain. From Crandon Park on the south, to Surfside on the north end of Miami Beach, the onslaught of high winds pushed the water six feet above normal high tide. The torrential rains poured onto the saturated ground, filling all the street drains. The water had nowhere to go. Most roads were now underwater, effectively stopping any remaining traffic. Many yards were filling up and rising water had already entered several homes. Salt water was running through the lobbies of some of the fanciest hotels on the Beach.

On the island of Miami Beach there were only a few hundred people left. Most of the rest had escaped earlier and had found their ways to the various emergency shelters across Biscayne Bay in Miami. The ones that hadn't made it out now put the finishing touches on the barricades of their doors and windows, and hoped for the best.

One of those families was Michael and Theresa Armstrong and their two little girls. They didn't own a car, and hadn't been able to get to a bus in time. Michelle was asleep, but Suzie, the older daughter, was still awake.

"Mommy, there's water coming in under the front door," she called from the front foyer.

"What?" Michael, who had been watching television in the den, came running out. He saw a dribble of water seeping into their foyer. He reached for the door knob.

"Don't open it!" cried Theresa.

"We must be getting some rain in under the weather stripping. I just want to see how bad it is," he said.

Michael turned the knob and was flung backwards by the door swinging wide. Salt water, ten inches deep on their front porch, poured into the living room. The wind howled in through the door. It blew down all the lamps and blew all the pictures off the walls. Theresa screamed, and grabbed Suzie.

Michael staggered back to the door, fighting the gale, and managed to force it closed, but only after the water was six inches deep in the living room. "My God," he panted, and looked at Theresa, his fear reflected equally in her eyes. Without speaking, they sloshed towards Michelle's bedroom so they could all be together.

* * *

Miami, Friday morning, August 2

It was 1:22 and the Eagle Point power plant emergency management team was huddled in the operating command post. This bunker was the safest place to be; its steel reinforced concrete walls had been built to withstand a direct hit with a conventional high explosive bomb. Even those thick walls, however, couldn't hold back the awful noise of the wind.

"How long can we stand this," cried Jones, trying to make herself heard above the shrieking wind.

"All monitored systems are still OK," yelled back Wilson.

"What's the wind?" Jones gestured to the shift superintendent who was standing at the instrument panel, behind and to the right of the chief operator.

"Two hundred and eighty knots," he yelled back.

Doug Johnson, assistant plant manager, stood closer to Jones. He had been transferred in only last month from headquarters. A rising young star, he had been sent to Eagle Point to be trained by the veteran, Jones. During the past thirty days, he had been arrogant and abrasive. Now, management's golden boy was just plain scared.

He shouted into her ear. "Deborah, we've got to shut down! The plant can't take this much longer. We need to 'safe' the reactor."

"No!" she shouted back. "The emergency crews in the city need our electricity output! The hospitals, the police stations, even the traffic lights are tied into us. We must stay on-line. Eagle Point was designed to take this kind of pounding."

Suddenly a tremendous gust of wind came along and the anemometer was torn away. The shift superintendent looked over at Jones and yelled, "Now, we're flying blind." A small dribble of water started in from the roof where the anemometer had been connected.

A claxon horn started blaring; alarm lights lit up all over the control panel. "Ms. Jones, we've got excess vibration in the outboard bearing of the main turbine!" The chief operator started punching up other key indicators. "I've got to slow the rotation or she'll go to pieces."

Earl Wilson walked over to stand next to Deborah Jones. He cupped his hands around his mouth and leaned close to her ear. "Deb, we've got to scram the reactor. If the turbine comes apart in this wind, or if we lose cooling water, we'll be spreading nuclear wastes all over Miami!"

Jones felt a bitter taste in her mouth. She didn't say anything, but she knew he was right. Her stomach tightened. She felt like she was deserting an old friend in his most urgent hour of need.

"Deb!" repeated Wilson. All eyes were on her.

Jones looked over at the shift superintendent. His mouth was set in a grim line as he nodded his agreement. She walked closer to the chief operator. In spite of the wind, she spoke softly. But, despite that, everyone in the control room heard her next words. "Shut down the reactor, Chief. Take us out of the grid." Moments later, throughout Miami, the lights blinked out, all at once.

* * *

Coral Gables, Friday morning, August 2

Bill Phillips wasn't worried about providing storm warnings anymore. He was worried about surviving. It was now August 2, a little after 3:00 a.m., and he had been up almost 24 hours. All power was gone except for the emergency back-up batteries they used to run their critical instruments and their communications equipment. But the communications equipment was no longer functioning. The big dish had blown away an hour ago.

The wind was a continuous shriek now. The howling was unbelievably loud. He could barely hear Rafael when he yelled across the room to him. He could just make him out by the glow of the instrument panel on his wall.

"What?" yelled back Phillips. He walked over towards Rafael who was standing in the doorway.

Just then something enormous hit the outside wall. The heavy concrete wall cracked, and the window glass smashed despite the sheet steel storm shutters covering it. Phillips was blown to the floor by the surge of wind and rain coming through the gaping hole. He got to his knees, and turned to look back at where he had been sitting, moments before. By the dim glow in his office, he could see a large branch of a huge oak tree jutting through the window like a spear. And like a spear, it had pierced his chair, pinning it to the opposite wall.

"Looks like I owe you one, Rafee," he yelled.

Rafael nodded grimly. He yelled back, "I came to get you away from these damn instruments and to the shelter. Everyone else is there."

Bill Phillips staggered to his feet. He took one last look at his office and then turned to follow Rafael down the hall to what was perhaps the safest place in all Miami right now.

* * *

Miami, Friday morning, August 2

Water was coming in under all the doors. It was pitch dark except for the flashlights each of them held. Mary and Joe huddled on the living room couch, their feet up, out of the water. The wind was howling, but they didn't really want to talk anyway. They sat and held each other and waited.

* * *

Miami Beach, Friday morning, August 2

The storm surge arrived along with high tide about 7:00 in the morning. The surge was enormous, in part because it was high tide, in part because of the wind driven water, but also because the ocean level itself was 8 feet above normal due to the extremely low pressure in the eye! Michael and Theresa Garrett heard it coming. They were in their back bedroom, standing on their bed, which had gotten water logged and had sunk an hour ago. They were each holding a girl; Michael had Suzie, and Theresa had Michelle. The parents were up to their waists in the swirling salt water, in total darkness. The girls were crying, but their cries couldn't be heard above the wind. Then, above the piercing shriek of the wind, they heard the rumble and roar of the wave. They didn't know what it was, but they sensed that their night of ordeal was coming to an end.

The wave was unlike anything ever seen before. Those survivors in the upper floors of some of the big hotels, the hotels that were anchored deep in the coral rock, later told the media that is was like a tsunami. The wave towered 35 feet above the ground level, and it came like a battering ram at over twenty miles per hour, slamming into buildings, crushing houses, and rolling cars like toys.

In Apartment 304 of the Ocean View Condominiums there had been quite a party going on, at least until the power had gone out. With the loud music no longer blaring, the "hurricane party" participants had had nothing else to do except to listen to the banshee screaming of the wind and the pounding of the surf. Hours of listening to that intense, unrelenting wind and the rain beating on the sliding glass doors of the condo had driven away any trace of the earlier 'to hell with the hurricane' mood of the party. Even the early drunks were now sober. All the young people there were trapped and they knew it. But, with the optimism of youth, most still believed they would make it. The condo building was strong, and, after all, they were on the third floor.

The fifteen or so people who had decided to ignore the evacuation order and party through the hurricane were all now huddled as far back as they could get from the sliding glass doors that made up the entire front wall of the condo. They no longer cared to watch the surf pound over the puny sea wall and run up into the building lobby two floors below them. They felt some small degree of security having drawn the drapes, but it wasn't much. They could still feel the apartment "flexing" with the wind as each new gust bore down on the glass wall in front of them.

Then they heard it - a roaring above the shrieking. The surging tidal wave of Hurricane Cleopatra sounded exactly like a dozen freight trains approaching at high speed.

The sliding glass doors that had held out so long before the wind were blasted away by the force of the monster wave. In Apartment 304, as in all the other ocean view apartments on the first, second, and third floors, the wave tore through the glass doors, and swept into the room. The stereo, the TV, the coffee table, the chairs, and the sleeper sofa were picked up and carried at high velocity towards the back of the room as a giant fluid battering ram.

The wave and its debris also picked up the people and then slammed them and everything else into the front wall of the apartment, creating a huge hole where the door and window had been. Those unfortunate party-goers who were not killed instantly, were carried out into the night by the killer wave. They all died minutes to hours later from the battering of floating debris or simply from drowning in the dark swirling waters.

For three thousand feet in each direction, up and down the beach, the best built hotels and condos shuddered but held under the impact of the wave. However, in all of them, without exception, the first three floors were gutted. Many of the smaller buildings simply imploded as the towering wave crashed into them.

The huge storm surge destroyed, in a few minutes, the many magnificent buildings that humans had built over the previous one hundred years. Ironically, the wall of condominiums and hotels that lined Miami Beach helped break the unified force of the wave. Miami Beach hotels were the breakwater and first line of defense for Miami.

* * *

Miami, Friday morning, August 2

By the time the wave had crossed Miami Beach and Biscayne Bay, it was down to only 18 feet above sea level, and was more spread out. Once it hit the mainland, and started rolling inland, it lost most of its killing power. However, it was still strong enough to knock down the many doors of the University of Miami's basketball arena. The arena quickly filled with water; all 1,950 people who had taken shelter inside drowned.

When the wave hit Mary Taylor's home, almost a mile inland from the edge of Biscayne Bay, there was little force left. But the force was enough, as the wave rolled over the top of the house, to strip the wind-weakened roof from the walls. Mary screamed and clung tighter to Joe. They were washed towards the kitchen. Mary hooked the bottom of a kitchen cupboard with her foot and somehow held on.

She shouted at Joe to hang on, and he tried. But the wind and the waves were too strong. Joe was washed out of the house. By the white foaming of the waves, Mary saw him go, floating up and over the wall that had been the back of the house. She screamed once for him to come back. Then Mary let go of her foothold to follow him.

At 9:30 in the morning, the howling wind suddenly stopped, and the sun shone strongly on a devastated Miami. People began to emerge like ants, crawling from beneath the rubble, stumbling from inside those houses still intact. After that awful night, they all just wanted to see the light of day again.

These unfortunate people did not have to die; but die they did. They had never bothered to learn about the eye of a hurricane.

Thousands and thousands of people were out in their yards, or outside shelters when, at 10:20 a.m., the wind sprang back to life from the southwest. The enormous eye of the hurricane had taken a full fifty minutes to pass over Miami. Now, there was no long build-up of wind, no warning period. Now, suddenly, there was only the reality of the intense winds near the center of the largest, fiercest hurricane ever recorded.

Thousands of people were caught out of doors and unprotected. Many were blown off the ground and tossed about by the wind until they were slammed into a nearby building. Many more were killed by small ordinary objects, objects that had become deadly missiles in that fearsome wind. Now Cleopatra would exact an even higher toll from the citizens of Miami.

Many hours of torment later, after Cleo had moved on to terrorize the west coast of Florida, the survivors in Miami came out from their hiding. The few who could still function started to try to help one another as they waited for emergency relief. The big questions for the relief agencies were: who was left to give relief, and how in the world could they even begin to deal with 2.5 million homeless people, many of them injured, many of them elderly, and all of them in a state of shock.

Meanwhile, Cleopatra had hardly been slowed up. The flat open Everglades did nothing to impede her progress. She steamrolled across the bottom tip of Florida making a beeline for Marco Island, the fancy resort community south of Naples. There was little loss of life at Marco. Most of the people living there were wealthy and had heeded the storm warnings, evacuating early. However, property damage was another story. After Cleo rolled over Marco Island, there was literally only a third of it left. Fully two-thirds of the low-lying sand island was sucked out into the Gulf of Mexico and dispersed over a thousand square miles. Cleo headed west into the Gulf to rest a bit before beginning her assault on the soft underbelly of the United States. New Orleans...or Houston...or Mobile, it didn't matter – all were equally unprepared for massive Cleo.

CHAPTER 34

New Orleans, August 3

Zack woke up feeling like a kid on Christmas day. His first thought was 'the big day is here at last!' After the long months of planning and worry, after the weeks of frustration at the wrong turns and delays, after these last few unbelievably hectic days of frenzied last minute work, today was finally here. Today was the day that Zachary Taylor would present his Ross Ice Shelf demonstration to the world. Saturday, August 3, 2023, would be a day to be remembered in New Orleans.

Zack quickly gulped down his usual bowl of cereal with sliced banana. He wanted to get to the stadium early, just to make sure nothing had gone wrong since yesterday. He grabbed his clipboard with his final checklist. As he exited the front door, he noticed the morning paper rolled up by his door. He kicked it inside to read later. It slid to a stop next to yesterday's rolled up and unread paper.

As Zack drove quickly towards Tulane Stadium, he glanced at the clouds gathering in the south. They were moving fast across the sky, from east to west. He willed the rain to hold off one more day. He had been very lucky these last two weeks, with no rain to foil their last minute construction tasks, putting in the final details on the ice shelf simulator.

In fact, the good weather had been essential to finishing the project at all. During the first two weeks of July, there had been a lot of rain, and it had seemed impossible to finish. But with these last two weeks of sunshine, and with Zack frantically driving the contractors and himself to the edge, they had managed to finish everything just yesterday.

Zack was physically and mentally drained - he hadn't slept more than four hours a night for the past ten days. He had lost touch with everything except for the project. He was totally focused on that. He had no idea what he would do after today, but by God, today was going to be magnificent. He pulled into the parking lot at 7:30 am, four-and-a-half hours ahead of the scheduled start of the demonstration, and immediately went to work.

* * *

Cleopatra poured into the air space above the warm waters of the Gulf of Mexico. Her circulation patterns grew more pronounced, her winds renewed some of the energy that she had expended while demolishing the southern tip of Florida. The clouds of the enormous hurricane filled the entire Gulf, yet no one knew just exactly where she was headed next. Officials in cities throughout the Gulf Coast huddled in their contingency plan meeting rooms, but for many people in those cities it was business as usual on this Saturday morning.

* * *

Where had the time gone!? Zack glared at his watch, as if it was to blame: 11:40; he was supposed to have been in the press box ten minutes ago. He took one more look at the switch settings on the electronic controllers mounted on the master panel on the field, then began the long climb up to the box.

Zack looked around as he climbed. The stadium was pretty empty - he guessed about 4,000 people. He was disappointed; he had hoped for a better turn out. Maybe it was the weather, he thought, and glanced at the skies again. The clouds were closer together now and darker. They did not look good. If only the rains would stay away for a few more hours!

In the box at last, Zack saw Jeff Mitchell, looking relieved to see him come in the door. Zack also noticed Buck Mullens talking with a distinguished looking man, a man Zack thought he recognized. About the same time, Mullens saw Taylor.

"Zack," called Mullens, "come over and meet someone." Taylor walked towards them. "Zack," said Mullens, "this is Senator Lane Stillwater, our guest speaker."

"Pleased to meet you Senator," said Zack, still puffing from his long climb. "I believe I've met you before, at ...."

"Likewise, son," interrupted Stillwater. "I understand you're the Greenhouse expert down here."

"Yes, I guess you could say..."

Stillwater interrupted him again. "Well maybe you can tell me if this hurricane is a result of Greenhouse."

Taylor looked at him blankly. "What hurricane is that, Senator?"

Stillwater laughed nervously, "You must be the original absent-minded professor all right! Hurricane Cleo - the one that's sitting down there five hundred miles south of us right now, that hurricane!"

Zack was genuinely confused. "How'd it get there? Last time I saw the news it was north of Puerto Rico and drifting further north."

"You been in outer space this last week, Professor? Cleo just flattened Miami and tore across south Florida. Now it's in the Gulf trying to decide where to go next. Those clouds racing across the sky up there ought to tell you something!"

Zack shook his head, and grinned sheepishly. "I didn't have any idea - I've been so absorbed in my work." Then his mind suddenly made the connection; his grin disappeared instantly. "Did you say it hit Miami?"

"Sure did - and 'hit' is a kind word. It flat tore Miami apart."

"Oh, Lord, my mother lives in Miami!"

"I'm sorry to hear that," interjected Mullens. "Let's hope she got out of there in time. Listen, I hate to sound so impersonal, but hadn't we better get started? The Senator's aide has been in touch with the National Weather Service and they think that Cleo may have started to move north! They say we've only got 24 to 36 hours before the weather forces the airport to close down. The Senator and I have a private jet to Washington waiting for us, so we'll be leaving just as soon as the show's over. You're welcome to come with us."

Zack's head was spinning; too much information was coming in at once. "Uh, thanks, but I don't think so. I've got some things I have to do here. But you're right - we need to get started." Zack walked to the control booth technician and asked him if everything was ready. The technician nodded and handed him the microphone. "Whenever you're ready, Doc," he said.

Taylor took the microphone, glanced at Jeff, and began speaking. In the stands, Jacqueline Jordan jumped when Taylor's voice boomed out over the loudspeaker system. She had come to this event in order to ... what? She really didn't know why she had hung around this last month. At first, she had hoped that Zack would call her. After she had heard his message on her machine, she had been encouraged, but had decided to wait and see if he would take some initiative and call her again. Then, as she realized that he was not going to call, she had started thinking about moving from the city. But she really didn't know where she wanted to go. And, in a way, she felt that the project was partially hers also, so she had decided to stay and see this demonstration. Jacqueline sighed and adjusted her sunglasses as she turned her attention to the miniature version of the U.S. East Coast and Gulf Coast down there on the football field.

High above the field, in the shadows of the upper deck, sat a man with binoculars pressed to his face. He sat alone on the opposite side of the field from the crowd, who had all been directed to one side of the stadium. He focused his attention not on the field, but on the crowd. He appeared to be looking for someone in particular.

Suddenly his slow methodical scan of the crowd stopped, he adjusted the focus slightly, and his lips curled back in a triumphant smile. His search was over; he had found her. An ugly sound emanated from his mouth..... *Tsssccht.*

The speeches were over at last. In the press box, high above the field, Zack took the microphone from Stillwater, and began his explanation of the events they were about to see. He concluded by saying, "Now, remember, the flooding that we are about to portray would result if ALL the supported ice shelves in Antarctica, not just the Ross Shelf, were to break free and slide into the ocean." He glanced at Jeff in silent acknowledgement of his concession to truth.

"In actual time, once this process gets started, it could take anywhere from a few weeks to a few years. However, the consequences would be economically incomprehensible in either case. Now let us watch the process in fast motion."

He pressed a button and the electronic controllers took over. Soft music started from the loudspeakers, and the electronic video scoreboard became a giant screen TV with scenes of a peaceful looking fishing village. Zack's voice, in a pre-recorded voice-over, began talking about the ice shelves and how the warming of the earth was weakening the links that held them in place.

On the far end of the field, the large white steel and plaster 'ice shelf' began to send up billows of white smoke. Dramatic license thought Zack, as he watched the spectacle unfold. After a two minutes of smoking, the 'shelf' began to 'crack apart' at the designated points. Pre-positioned cameras zoomed in on the shelf as the front edge scraped against the 'ground' and began to slide down the tilted ramp and into the water. The narrative continued as the background music built in volume and in tempo. The slow slide of the shelf accelerated as small hidden jets underneath the shelf sprayed their lubricating oil onto the ramp. Suddenly, the last of the elastic linkages snapped, and the whole thing rapidly slid headlong into the water.

The waters of the 'Atlantic Ocean' and 'Gulf of Mexico,' which had been dyed an inky blue and to which a wetting agent had been added, quickly sought a new equilibrium level above the lowest levels of the white molded plastic model of the United States coastline. In less than a minute, the blue stain had covered the bottom half of the state of Florida, much of southern Louisiana, and parts of Mississippi, Alabama, and coastal Texas, and had crept miles inland along all the major rivers in the Eastern Seaboard. Various densely populated coastal cities, that had been marked in bright yellow, in New York, New Jersey, Massachusetts, Delaware, Rhode Island, and Virginia, were now an ugly green, the result of the yellow showing through a thin layer of blue.

While the water undulated on the miniature United States below, the scoreboard video showed actual newsreel footage from various floods from around the world. The loudspeakers played a Wagnerian opera, interspersed with terse commentary, and with people screaming. The impact of the multi-media assault on the human senses was everything that Zack had hoped it would be. He felt a triumph that it had worked, and a great sense of relief that it was over. The news media duly recorded the scene below for later replay on the networks.

The aftermath of the event was anticlimactic to the extreme. Stillwater, Mullens, and the other Washington politicians, anxious to depart New Orleans, left immediately. The news media technicians, began packing their equipment at once, getting ready for their next assignment. Even the audience hurried away, hastened along by the first few drops of rain that miraculously had stayed away during the actual demonstration, but that now were beginning to fall. Zack, watching the hasty departures, wondered if he had done all this in vain. Unable to answer the question, and not knowing what else to do, he too turned to go.

"Well, Dr. Taylor, it worked!" Jeff looked as excited as Zack had ever seen him.

"It sure did, Jeff. Thanks in large part to your excellent help these past months."

"Thank you for letting me participate. It was great fun! Do you want to come over to our apartment and celebrate?"

"No thanks, Jeff, maybe tomorrow or the next day. Right now all I want to do is go home. I've got to make a phone call, and then I need to get some sleep."

"OK, no problem. But I doubt we can do it tomorrow or the day after. If that hurricane comes north, it'll catch us full force in a couple of days. Hope you're prepared for a blow."

"Oh, yes, the hurricane. I haven't done much to prepare. Let's hope it goes west." Zack allowed himself a tight-lipped grin. He and Jeff got in the elevator together and rode down to the ground level. They shook hands and then turned in separate directions to go to their cars.

Zack ran through the big but widely spaced drops and made it to his car relatively dry. Driving home was difficult because of the heavy traffic and the increasingly hard rain. He turned on the car radio and listened to the latest news of Cleo. The look on his face became grimmer and grimmer as he listened to the reports of the damage done to Miami and South Florida.

Back in his apartment, Zack walked straight to the phone and tried to dial his mother's number. He heard only a computerized voice telling him that all circuits were busy, and to please try the number later. He placed his phone on automatic redial and opened the refrigerator to look for something to eat. He was tired, but he was hungry too. The phone rang as he was chewing on a left-over piece of fried chicken. He rushed to pick it up, his mouth still half-full.

"H'llomph," he said, trying to swallow the remaining food in his mouth.

"What number are you trying to dial, sir?" Zack was disappointed that it wasn't his mother, but was glad that at least this was a real person, not a computerized voice.

Zack related the number, and waited while the operator tried to connect. A moment later, she was back on the line. "I'm sorry sir, all our trunk lines into the Miami area are temporarily out of service."

"You mean there's no way I can get a call in there or that someone can call out?"

"That's right, sir. I'm sorry."

Zack hung up. He didn't know what to do next. He was so tired, but he felt like he should be doing something. He picked up the newspaper from the floor and unrolled it. From the pictures and the stories on the front page, he began to realize that Cleo was no ordinary hurricane. Would it strike here? At least, New Orleans was a little bit inland. And, he thought sleepily, his apartment was on the high point in the City. Well he still had time, and he had to have some sleep if he was to do anything to battle the storm later. He recalled reading an old spy novel where the hero occasionally reminded himself that sleep was a weapon too. In a daze, Zack walked into his bedroom and collapsed on the bed.

* * *

Cleopatra had grown more fearsome during her brief stay in the Gulf. Now that she was ready to roll again, she took off like a sprinter out of the blocks. Her heading was due north.

The battered Hurricane Center in Coral Gables was useless now, so all official forecasts were coming out of Washington. The Washington office was staffed mostly with bureaucrats, so they in turn depended on data and analysis from the National Climatic Data Center in Asheville, North Carolina. However, NCDC did not have the same level of expertise with Hurricanes as the National Hurricane Center, and they were further hampered by the failing GOES satellite. Consequently, their forecasts were not as good. They had estimated New Orleans had 36 to 48 hours of usable time for evacuation, but they were wrong, very wrong. In fact, New Orleans had only 20 hours until the eyewall would arrive, and far less time until strong winds and heavy rains would start and put a stop to the evacuation.

The evacuation process broke down quickly in New Orleans for several reasons. First, there really was no coherent plan for such a rapid and complete evacuation. Second, the rain began falling heavily many hours before the winds reached gale speeds. Third, the big drainage pumps were in disrepair and the streets flooded early in many parts of the City. The fourth and most important reason, however, was the panic. People became like animals, fighting and clawing to be the ones to escape the low-lying trap they perceived they were in. The law and order needed for a safe and effective evacuation disappeared as soon as people panicked.

On one street, as on many others in the city, a mob had gathered. Most of the people in this particular crowd were black, the usual residents of this particular neighborhood. Some were watching while others were looting a TV and appliance store.

A short, balding white man was walking by on the other side of the street, trying to avoid being noticed. He had almost succeeded when two black men, barely out of their teens, saw him and started running in his direction. No one else joined them; the others were more interested in getting a new TV. The two young black men yelled at the one old white man, and splashing their way across the street, came up on the sidewalk about 20 feet behind him and ran towards him.

The man, who had neither increased nor decreased his pace, now stopped and turned to face his would-be attackers. Calmly, he reached underneath his coat and withdrew a 9 mm automatic pistol. The two youths saw the gun and tried to slow their momentum. Before they could come to a full stop, however, each had received a bullet in the heart. They fell to the wet sidewalk, dead, six feet in front of the stocky bald man.

The shooter calmly surveyed the crowd across the street.

Tsssccht.

Seeing no one else interested in him, J. R. Hunter replaced his gun and turned back in his original direction. Grim-faced, he plodded on through the blowing rain towards the Uptown area and Jacqueline Jordan.

* * *

Zack was awakened by the ringing of his phone. It was dark and the wind was blowing strongly outside. He had no idea of what time it was. The phone rang insistently. Groggily he rolled over in the bed to answer it.

"Hello," he mumbled.

"Zack boy!" Gator's voice boomed loud into Zack's ear. "Be you ready for Big Mama?"

"Gator! Where are you?" Zack glanced over at the clock on his dresser - 6:42. Was that a.m. or p.m.? Zack tried to collect his thoughts.

"I'm right here where I told you I'd be! At the marina! Now, you bring yourself down here an' get me. We don't have much time before that big wind, she come."

"Yes! I'll be down soon - stay put!"

"I ain't goin' nowhere!"

Zack felt for his keys in his pocket as he raced to the door. He got drenched as he ran through the blowing rain to his car. He stood ankle deep in the parking lot trying to unlock his car door when he suddenly dropped his keys. "No!" he yelled, and fell to his hands and knees to look for them in the inches-deep water. Luckily, his key chain was heavy, and he found them quickly. He opened the door and jumped in.

The car ride to the marina was a nightmare. Time and again Zack passed smaller cars that were already bogged down in the water. Fortunately, most of the traffic was going the other way, away from the lake. Several times he had to drive up on the neutral ground to get around deep pools of water and stalled cars. At one intersection, a six car pile-up blocked most of the path. One opening was available, so Zack started for it.

Just then, through the rain, Zack could just make out a large, chrome covered pick-up truck coming from the opposite direction, heading for the same opening. Zack braked his Cherokee just in time to let the big pick-up come barreling through. Zack then gunned the engine and drove through the gap. The water lapped the doors of his Jeep but he kept going. He drove on through the wind and rain towards the marina.

As chance would have it, the big fancy pick-up that had nearly run into Zack was driven by Steve Resnick. After hours of indecision, Resnick had decided to flee his home in Lakeview. Molly had wanted to stay, so he had abandoned her to try to make it out of the City. He felt relatively safe high up in the seat of his truck, and he showed no mercy for any other driver on the road. Resnick was driving away from Lake Pontchartrain on West End Boulevard, trying to make it to the elevated portion of Interstate 10. As he approached Harrison Avenue, he saw that his way was hopelessly blocked by a tangle of cars. He cut across the neutral ground and into someone's front yard, then turned west to try to get to Veteran's Highway.

Hurricane Cleopatra, even thought she was still far out in the Gulf, was heading towards land just to the east of New Orleans, so the winds in the city were coming in hard from the northeast. That wind direction was extremely unfortunate for the city because Lake Pontchartrain sits directly north of New Orleans. The wind was blowing so hard that the sea water in Lake Pontchartrain was being scooped, as if by a giant hand, out of the lake and into the shallow bowl of the city. Not only was water falling in buckets from the sky, it was over-topping the levees in wave after wave. New Orleans was filling up!

The dense rain sliced across Resnick's windshield from right to left, rendering his windshield wipers useless. Resnick could barely see twenty feet in front of him, but still he drove on as fast as he dared. He got to Veteran's Highway and started up the bridge to cross the 17th Street Canal. A huge gust of wind caught his big high truck broadside, and the truck slid sideways on the wet bridge. Before he knew what had happened, Resnick found himself and his truck floating in the swirling waters of the canal.

Resnick didn't panic. He still had faith in his big water-tight truck. He was being carried along with the fast current. He knew his escape from the City was no longer possible, but he figured he would get out and force his way into someone's home when his truck lodged against something stable. He reached over and touched the shotgun lying on the seat next to him while he waited for the truck to make contact with something.

A loud, high-pitched whining noise imposed itself on Resnick's ears. For the first time tonight, Resnick felt the cold touch of fear. When he finally saw the big pump up ahead, he got a view of it that few people have ever experienced. Pump No. 3 at Pumping Station No. 6 was the largest drainage pump in the world. And Resnick was staring at its whirling steel impellers as he was being carried straight into its huge 14-foot-diameter maw. Right now, the pump was complaining with a high-pitched wail as it strained to empty the flooded canal. The pump's steel blades whirled like a huge food processor. Each second, it sucked in thousands of gallons of water, along with everything else that happened to be there in the water.

Mercifully for Steve Resnick, he didn't have long to contemplate his fate. He screamed in terror as his once-mighty truck was sucked head first into the massive pump. The heavy iron impellers, being flung around the inside circumference of the pump at 1200 revolutions per minute contained an enormous amount of kinetic energy. The pick-up truck contained a significant amount of steel. When the two met, there were no winners. The huge pump ground to a halt, but not before the truck and everything inside it had been shredded into little pieces.

Zack pulled up in an elevated parking area overlooking the marina. The wind was furious here next to the lake. Below him, the marina itself appeared as a scene from a watery hell. Boats were being battered and tossed by the combined energy of the wind and the wild waves that were being forced from the main body of the lake into the tiny harbor. The water level was already up over the docks, and the seaside refueling station was on fire. He leaped out of his car and desperately looked around for Gator.

As Zack looked towards the east, he saw an amazing sight. The winds of these outer bands were still fierce, and were starting to blow huge sheets of water over the top of the seawall. Coming in from the north-northeast, the wind now seemed intent on emptying Lake Pontchartrain into the City of New Orleans!

Then Zack spotted Gator about two hundred yards away. He appeared to be standing on a piece of the dock that had torn away and was floating down the street. Zack raced to his car and jumped in, intent on driving closer. As he drove down the access road, the remnants of a huge wave came flooding up the paved way. It caught the Jeep and spun it around, leaving it about twenty feet away on a grassy slope. Zack tried to restart the vehicle but the engine was drowned. He jumped out and yelled futilely at Gator. Then he started to run/wade in his direction.

Gator saw Zack splashing towards him. Zack was getting weary and had salt water in his eyes, and therefore had to blink twice before he could believe what he saw next.

Gator swung the piece of dock around and started towards him at high speed! Then Zack realized - Gator was in his airboat!

Zack scrambled aboard, then fairly shouted at Gator, "Did you come all this way on this thing?!"

Gator grinned and replied, "You see any other damn t'ing?" Then he added unnecessarily, "We best be gettin' away from this here place!"

Zack pointed and said "My car's dead! We're stuck!"

Gator revved the powerful engine on his boat. "Oh no we ain't! Hold on!"

With the wind at their backs, the boat literally flew down the flooded street. It was a scene Zack would never forget as they sped down the water-filled streets of New Orleans, dodging stalled cars, and often bumping up over curbs and other high spots that were covered by only a thin layer of water. They were headed in the general direction of Zack's apartment. Then something clicked in Zack's mind.

"Hold on, Gator!" screamed Zack to make himself heard above the combined noise of the engine and the wind.

Gator throttled back and the noise lessened.

"We've got to go into town!"

"What for? We ain't got much time at all before Big Mama get here; she really be comin' fast now."

"We've got to get Jacqueline! I just realized that I love her!"

"Fine time to be fallin' in love - that what I say!" Gator shook his head and a big smile cracked his face. "But better late than never, that what I say too! Here, you drive; I'm goin' be the lookout." They switched places and Gator picked up his shotgun.

"What do you need that for?" yelled Zack as he throttled up and turned the boat towards Uptown.

"For peoples like dem, what wants to take my boat!" Gator pointed to a group of men that had been wading towards them, but who were now being left behind. One man had a pistol and fired a frustrated shot at them as they sped away. Zack shuddered and didn't say anything. He knew Gator was right. And there might well be more incidents when they got further into the City, closer to Jacqueline's home. As he drove on in the wind and rain, Zack prayed that Jacqueline would be there.

* * *

At that very moment, Jacqueline was indeed home. She had barely made it back to her house before the flooding streets had stopped any more travel in the Uptown section of the city. She had driven fast and furiously to beat the rain, and now had a cozy fire going, giving her both heat and light.

Despite the loss of electricity, she was not overly worried. There were many buildings around her and they were serving to break the wind. She felt she could ride out the storm, but now she had a new concern. Her house was built up on blocks, well above ground level, but the water was rising very rapidly outside. Even in the worst rains of the past few months, the water had never been up over the top of her front porch steps before. Now she noticed a trickle of water seeping in under the front door.

Jacqueline came out of the bathroom with two towels in her hands, and headed for the front door, intent on stopping the leak. Suddenly, the door burst open, and Jacqueline screamed in fright. But it wasn't the surprise of the door flying open that frightened her. There, in the doorway, with water streaming off him, stood J. R. Hunter.

"What's the matter, Jackie, surprised to see me?" J. R. came in quickly and closed the door behind him, never taking his eyes off Jacqueline.

"What...What are you doing here?!" said Jacqueline when she got her breath back.

"I was at the big demonstration, too. Afterwards, I followed you part of the way but my car couldn't keep up with yours. You know, Jackie, you shouldn't speed like that. You could have an accident." J.R.'s tone was mocking.

"Anyway, shortly after I lost you, my car got flooded out in one of the damn holes in the streets of this damn city. I knew your address, and I was within range so I just hiked the rest of the way. Not very nice of you to make me walk on a day like this, Jackie."

Hunter moved over closer to the fire. "Now, I'm all wet and cold. I don't suppose you have any dry clothes here for me to borrow, do you?" Hunter smiled evilly. "No, I guess not," he continued. "You're not the kind to give me the shirt off your back." He threw back his head and laughed.

*   *   *

Zack hugged the wheel of the boat as he fairly flew down Canal Boulevard, the major thoroughfare from Lake Pontchartrain into the heart of the City. The wind was still mostly at their backs, and the street was completely covered with water. He found he could navigate by staying between the speed limit signs, the street light poles, and other objects that indicated the edge of the road. The only challenge was avoiding the abandoned cars that littered the road. The water in the streets was deeper now, but still the airboat occasionally slid roughly over something. Each time, Zack hoped that it was only the top of a submerged foreign car, or some other inanimate object.

With every passing minute, the winds grew more intense. After Zack turned left onto Canal Street, the wind blew from his left and channeled in between the taller buildings. It swirled out at them in unexpected places. Zack fought the wind constantly, all the while looking out for submerged cars. He knew he should slow down, but something inside him urged him to keep going at high speed.

* * *

Jacqueline shuddered at the sound of Hunter's laughter; she sensed that J.R. had snapped. Her warm and cozy home of a few minutes ago had ceased to exist; danger was now present in the room like a rattlesnake. Jacqueline considered her options, which appeared to be few. She decided that she had to try to keep J.R. talking.

"Why did you come here?" she ventured.

"I had to see it for myself - the big demonstration that was supposed to change the world. And I came to finish some business." Hunter laughed again, loud and harsh.

Listening to his laugh, Jacqueline <u>knew</u>. She was now positive that Hunter was crazy. The question was, what would he try to do next? It was an eerie, frightening feeling, with J.R. inside and the gale howling outside. Jacqueline shuddered again. The old house was beginning to shake now, under the constant tearing of the wind. Boards creaked, and in an apartment upstairs, a shutter started to bang. She forced her mind back to J.R.; she had to keep him talking until she could find some advantage for herself.

"What kind of business, J.R. - something to do with me?"

"Maybe that too," sneered J.R. "But I was talking about your friend, the Professor."

"So you <u>were</u> the one behind that beating!"

"Yes! And I did it to teach <u>you</u> a lesson, Jackie. I wanted to show you that I was still in control!"

Jacqueline felt anger growing inside of her, anger that she was not able to control. Her voice was shaking as she said, "You... you despicable little man! You're evil through and through. I don't know how I didn't see that before!"

"You were easy to fool, Jackie. You were blinded by your love for your Daddy's memory. I tricked you just as I tricked your father!"

Jacqueline stopped, totally confused by J.R.'s statement.

"But I thought he saved your life in Afghanistan?"

"Ha! My life was never in danger. I spotted that ambush in time, and got into good cover. I could see everything as it happened. Your father thought he had led his men into a trap. He thought it was all his fault. It wasn't though, it was just a freak accident - a one-in-a-million chance encounter of two forces in the mountains.

"He was wounded and the Taliban left him for dead. Later, he and I were the only ones to make it out of there. The trauma was too much for him. His memory of the incident was fuzzy, so I clarified it for him. My version, of course. I fed him false information. I made him believe that he had made a tragic mistake, a mistake that cost the lives of the men in his squad. I let him believe that he had run and gotten shot; then I dragged him with me. Of course, I swore I'd never turn him in. From then on, I owned your father."

"You bastard! You let him live with that guilt for years! He always believed you were covering up for him; that's why he felt he owed you. No wonder he never liked you!"

"I know that! No one ever liked me; I got cheated out of my promotion to Colonel and shoved out of the Army. But I landed on my feet. People respect me, now; no, even better, they fear me.

Yes, Jackie, your father hated me, but he feared me. He was afraid that I would tell the world about him. I owned your father, and from time to time he served me well. Just as you've done. But now, it looks as though that may be over. Pity."

J.R.'s sneer was maddening to Jacqueline. "Get out!" she screamed. "I don't care if you die in this hurricane, get out of here this instant!"

J.R. grew quiet, almost serene as he looked at Jacqueline. As he grew quiet, his old habit of sucking air came back.

Tssscht.

"Not so fast, you long-legged bitch," he said with almost surreal calmness. "Now that you won't work for me anymore, I'm going to do something I've been wanting to do for years."

Tssscht.

"We're going to have some fun, you and I, before we part company." J.R. licked his lips, and smiled. "Take off your blouse," he said.

"You slime. You'll have to kill me first!"

"That can be arranged," he said coldly as he pulled his gun from beneath his coat. "Now, get into the bedroom. Move!" he barked. "If you please me, I may let you live."

Jacqueline looked around desperately for something to use as a weapon. But she couldn't do anything while he had that gun trained on her. She walked slowly into her bedroom, noticing that there was now an inch of water on the floor. The flickering light of the fire in the living room cast dim, moving shadows on the walls. Once inside, she turned quickly to face him before he could grab her from behind. Her eyes darted left and right, trying to find something she could use as a weapon. They rested momentarily on the heavy silver frame around her father's picture.

"J.R., be reasonable, don't do this!" she said as she edged towards her dresser.

Hunter's face was no longer calm. He fairly shouted at her "Take off your blouse!"

"What if I refuse?" said Jacqueline, desperately trying to stall him a few moments longer. She judged the distance to the dresser, then the distance to J.R. Too far, she thought, still too far!

"Then you die! Now do it!" His eyes widened until Jacqueline thought they would pop out of his head. The hand holding the gun started to tremble. Jacqueline held her breath as she awaited the explosion of the gun.

The noise of a horrendous crash filled the room. A heavy redwood lawn chair had just been blown through the French doors and into the room. By reflex, Hunter swung his arm and eyes towards the shattered remains of the doors. Jacqueline saw her chance and took it.

With all the force she could muster, she delivered a mighty kick to Hunter's forearm. The gun went flying. Jacqueline slashed her open hand at J.R.'s throat but he had reacted quickly and partially dodged the blow. Jacqueline's hand caught the side of his neck rather than the front of his throat. Jacqueline moved to hit him again, but she slipped on the wet floor.

J.R. had been knocked off balance by the blow to his neck, and had the further disadvantage of disorientation in the darkened room. He lashed out with his foot in Jacqueline's direction, but missed. He slipped and staggered backwards.

Jacqueline regained her balance first. While J.R. was still staggering, Jacqueline kicked him hard in the stomach. J.R.'s eyes glazed over, but he remained standing.

Jacqueline spun around as she had done so many times, oh so many times, in practice, years ago, swinging her leg around with a round-house kick aimed at the side of his head. The kick landed on target, and Hunter fell back under the force of it, hitting the back of his head against the computer desk as he fell. He lay there not moving.

Jacqueline stood there for an agonizing minute, not knowing what to do. Then, she heard....could she believe her ears? She heard her name being called from outside!

She ran to the living room and peered out the window. She couldn't believe her eyes! There was Zachary outside in a boat. Another man was with him, they were trying to get the boat up close to the porch. She opened the door and rushed out into the storm. She got drenched immediately and was almost blown off the porch. But Zack had made it to the porch. Holding onto a pillar with his left arm, he grabbed her with his right and pulled her close.

"I love you!" he shouted, grinning from ear to ear. "I love you too," she shouted back, "now let's get out of here!"

Gator held the boat close to the porch, as steady as he could against the gusting wind. Once Zack and Jacqueline had scrambled aboard, Gator shouted at Zack. "The wind, she be too big! We ain't goin' be makin' it back to your place!"

Zack looked at the trees whipping in the wind and knew Gator was right. They had made it down here only because they had been going mostly with the wind; they could never make any headway going straight into this gale. He had an idea. He shouted back to Gator, "Head over to Canal Street! We've got to find a tall building!"

Normally, it was a short car ride from Jacqueline's to Canal Street. But this was anything but a normal situation. The airboat pitched and rolled like a car on a roller coaster as Gator fought to keep the boat upright. For every hundred yards of forward progress, the boat slid fifty yards across the water or backwards. The winds were fierce and growing fiercer; and the eye of Cleo wasn't even close yet.

As they struggled past the Superdome, they saw many hundreds, maybe thousands of people on the steps leading to the entrances. The doors were locked and the rising water had turned the dome into an island. And the island was rapidly shrinking. The people nearest the doors were beating on them trying to force them open, but the heavy doors were not budging. Every minute that passed, a few more people on the lowest steps were washed away.

They got to Canal Street near LaSalle, when Zack yelled, "Over there!" He pointed to the First National Bank of Commerce, a seven-story building. The water had risen to the second floor, and some of the windows on the north side were already gone. Gator gunned the engine and the boat inched its way forward against the wind.

The wind seemed to step up in intensity; their boat was being blown backwards again! Gator turned the wheel and headed sideways, angling away from the building.

"What are you doing?!" screamed Jacqueline, but her words were blown away by the wind.

Suddenly, they were on the south side of the building, on the lee side of the wind. All at once the wind seemingly disappeared. Gator turned back and held the boat in the building's wind shadow, as he approached it from the back.

There was still a problem. There were no entrances on the second floor. Then Zack had an idea. He reached down and grabbed the shotgun. "Get closer!" he commanded Gator. Zack raised the gun to his shoulder and fired straight ahead at the plate glass window of a second floor conference room. The window shattered into a million pieces, and Gator drove the airboat straight into the opening. They crashed into the big conference table, and were thrown into the foot-deep waters.

Zack grabbed Jacqueline's hand and hollered at Gator to follow. He led them towards the stairwell and they climbed another half-flight up. Exhausted, the three of them collapsed in the quiet dry area of the stairwell landing, safe, at least for now.

* * *

At that same moment, the waters weren't nearly as deep at the King's home, which was on higher ground. The streets had been flooded early, but their house was on a particularly high lot, and had stayed dry until about two hours ago. The water had finally found its way into their house, and now was rising fast. The Dean and his wife were sitting on the dining room table, huddling in the dark, and holding each other in silence. Soon they felt the cold water lap over the edge of the table. They got up on their knees so they wouldn't have to sit in the water.

"June!" he yelled to make himself heard above the shrieking of the wind. "June, if the house fills up, we'll be trapped against the ceiling and we'll drown. We're going to have to get out. We've got to make it to our oak trees! They'll stand against this wind - I'm sure of it!"

June merely nodded, too frightened to speak. The water continued to rise quickly, being fed by the massive sheets being swept out of Lake Pontchartrain over the seawall and into the city. Soon King and his wife were standing bent over on the table, with their heads touching the ceiling, and with water up to their waists.

"Let's go!" shouted Alan. "We can't wait any longer!" They stepped off the table and swam to the back door which had long before been forced open. Treading water, and holding on to the roof gutter, they slipped along the back wall of the house, protected by the house from the tearing wind. They got to the corner of the house, but the wind was too strong to go any further. King knew it was only ten feet to the nearest tree, and he knew that safety lay in its branches, now within easy reach of the surface of the water. But how could they get there?

"I want to go back inside," cried June. Almost as she said it, part of the roof was torn away. "No good," King yelled back. Then he had an idea. "Under the water," he yelled. "The wind won't get us if we swim underwater to the trees. Can you do it?" June shook her head violently.

Alan thought for a moment, then yelled to his wife. "I'll get a rope!"

Turning back, he felt his way along the wall to the back door to the garage. He swam inside and felt for the coil of rope he kept hanging from the wall. It was still there!

King swam back outside, and tied one end of the rope to the wrought iron burglar bars on his back window. Then he made his way back to his wife who was still clinging to the gutter on the wind-sheltered side of the house. He yelled, "I'm going to swim over and tie one end of this rope to the tree. Then you can come over holding on to the rope."

"No! Alan, don't do it! It's too dangerous!"

"I must - it's our only chance!"

King inhaled a big lungful of air. Taking the free end of the rope in his teeth, he pushed himself down into the black water and kicked off in the direction of the trees. He had been right about the wind - he could swim underneath the water; but it was impossible to see anything. He kicked madly and felt all around in front of him as he went. By a miracle, he bumped into the trunk of the nearest oak tree. He hugged the tree and circled the rope around it. He ran two loops around his left arm and wrist. Only then did he kick upward towards air.

Gasping for air at the surface, he sensed victory. He completed the knot, and tugged on the rope to make sure that it was secure. He turned to yell for June. Again and again he called for her, but he neither heard a response nor felt any pressure on the slack rope. He was exhausted, but he ducked back under the water and followed the rope back to the relative shelter of the house.

June was gone. He searched madly throughout the back porch area, and even went back into the house partway. But she was nowhere to be found. He had no choice but to go back to the tree. Again he ducked under the dark waters, and followed the rope back to the sturdy oak. By this time, the water was high enough that he didn't even have to reach up to grab the first big branch. He swung his leg up on the branch and rested for a while.

The water was still rising; King decided to move a little higher into the branches. He placed his foot on the branch below and inched his body up along the trunk. He looked up and could dimly see two thick branches above him, one to his left and one to his right. He decided on the right side, and reached up to catch hold of it.

All the decisions that King had made that night had been good ones. All the decisions that took thought or planning or brave action on his part had been right. The one decision that was random chance, the one that took no thought at all, the one to choose the right-side branch - that decision turned out to be drastically wrong. On the top of the right-side branch was a large water moccasin, also seeking shelter in the tree. When King looped his right arm around the branch and pulled his head up, he was met by the fangs of the poisonous snake. He was struck once in the face and then again in the neck. King fell back into the waters and was swept away.

* * *

Thousands of people lost their lives that night, and there was enormous property damage in New Orleans caused by Hurricane Cleo. But perhaps the one thing that etched Cleopatra's name into the history books for all time was what she did to the Mississippi River.

It is still uncertain how it happened, perhaps it was the huge winds, maybe it was the extraordinarily high tides, or even the intense rains. Probably it was some combination of them all, as Cleo slid along the coast from the east towards New Orleans. Soon, she pushed directly against the flow of the Mississippi.

Whatever the reason, the result was astonishing. The full force of massive Cleopatra met the full force of the mighty Mississippi, and Cleopatra won. The huge storm acted like a giant plug, and held back the flow of the mighty river for several hours. Unable to flow out into the Gulf of Mexico through its normal channel, the river began rising in its banks. From New Orleans all the way back to Baton Rouge, the Mississippi River rose unbelievably fast.

Years ago, the Corps of Engineers had planned against flooding in New Orleans because of the Mississippi River. They built the river dikes in the city high - nearly 25 feet. And they planned for an alternate route for the river. Near Baton Rouge, the Mississippi takes another of its thousands of twists and comes very close to an ancient course that it once ran, the present-day Atchafalaya River.

The planned emergency exit for a flood-swollen Mississippi River is the Corps of Engineers' Atchafalaya Spillway. The plan is for the flood control operators to slowly drain off excess water coming down the Mississippi from the north. The flood waters would be drained out through the Atchafalya, keeping the water levels in the southern-most stretch of the Mississippi below the critical point. But, of course, the plan never envisioned the mighty river backing up.

The Atchafalya Spillway worked - it worked too well. Once the Mississippi River was blocked in her normal channel, it didn't take long at all for her to find her way to the ancient course. The river flowed into the Atchafalya with a vengeance, carving a new course that went around, over and through the spillway. So good was this new course that the River forgot all about her old path. So in a matter of a few hours, all the thousands of oil tankers, barges, tugs and other boats that regularly ply the Mississippi every day between Baton Rouge and New Orleans, were left lying in the mud on the river bottom. The mightiest river in America now emptied America's heartland into the Gulf some hundred and twenty miles to the west of New Orleans.

CHAPTER 35

Zack woke up feeling stiff and sore all over. Every muscle in his body ached, his head hurt, his throat felt raw and hoarse. With effort, he sat up on the hard concrete floor. At first he wondered where he was, but then he remembered.

He glanced around in the dim light provided by the battery-powered emergency exit sign one-half flight above him. He checked and saw that Gator and Jacqueline were still sleeping. What a night it had been! For hours they had been kept awake by the howling wind, its abominable noise being pierced occasionally by the crash of another window being shattered in the bank building. Finally, somehow, they had succumbed to their exhaustion, and drifted off to sleep.

He was still just sitting there on the floor when Zack noticed the silence. The terrible wailing of the wind of last night was gone, replaced by a deathly stillness. There was no traffic noise from outside, no office noise from inside, not even the hum of the air conditioner. Zack got up quietly, wanting to see the daylight. He started down the stairs, but his way was blocked by water before he could get to the second floor exit landing. He climbed back to where the others were still sleeping.

Some noise that he made roused Jacqueline. She moaned softly as she rolled over from her side to her back. Zack watched in the semi-darkness as she slowly went through the waking process. Her hair was wet and tangled, her face was dirty, her clothes were damp and wrinkled. Zack didn't see those things; he only saw Jacqueline.

"Hi," he said quietly. "Glad to see you this morning."

"Hi, yourself," she answered sleepily. Then her eyes widened, and she said, "I must look a mess!"

"You look great," he smiled. "Just great. Did I mention that I love you?"

She smiled - that fabulous smile that Zack knew so well. "Yes," she said softly, "I believe you did." She stood up gingerly, and moved closer to Zack. They embraced, and stood there for a long minute in each other's arms, just hugging.

"Harrumph." Gator had awakened, and was letting them know that fact.

"Morning, Gator," said Zack, reluctantly releasing Jacqueline. "Sleep well?"

"I done better," Gator admitted. "This be your lady fren', I presume?"

"Yes, this is Jacqueline. Let me introduce you to each other."

After the formalities were over, Zack said, "Let's find a window so we can see what that hurricane did to us." They climbed up a half-flight to the third floor exit landing. They pulled open the door, and stepped out into what used to be the commercial loan department. Sunlight flooded into the room, making them squint their eyes as they entered from the stairwell.

The office was in a shambles. The big plate glass window on the northeast side, facing Canal Street, had shattered during the night, and the wind and driven rain had played havoc inside the room. Broken glass was strewn everywhere - on the floor, on the desks that were still upright, on everything. Most of the chairs were jumbled into a pile against the wall opposite the big window, having been blown there when the wind had violated the office. Zack led the way as they carefully picked their way over to the ragged opening in the wall where the window had been.

Each of the three had known that the damages would be great, but each was unprepared for what they saw down below them. The city was still grossly flooded; water levels were up to the second stories of most buildings. Many houses were unroofed, and every commercial building in sight had almost all of their windows missing. Pieces of wood, small trees, furniture - debris of all kinds floated in the still water.

But the worst thing of all, the thing that none of them had prepared for, was the sight of the dead bodies. Literally hundreds of human bodies were floating in the ugly brown waters directly below them. Many more bodies could be seen in the distance up and down Canal Street. Jacqueline turned her head away from the gruesome sight.

"My God!" she whispered.

Zack continued to stare at the scene below him. "I think I'm going to be sick," he said, as he felt his stomach turn.

"No you ain't," said Gator, roughly. "We got work to do."

Zack looked at him strangely. "You don't really think we can do anything to help those people down there?"

"Don't be a fool, boy. Nobody can help those folks - they're dead. We got to help ourselfs."

In spite of her distress, Jacqueline smiled slightly when she heard Gator call Zack 'boy.' She turned back towards Zack and said, "Gator's right. We need to prepare ourselves. From the looks of things down there, we might have to get by on our own for some time before any rescuers get to us!"

Gator spoke again. "She be right. There ain't goin' to be no food an' no water in this city for the nex' week or two. We mus' find some of dem supply now, if'n there be anyt'ing left to find."

Zack tore his eyes away from the scene below. Looking at Gator, he said, "You're right, of course. We'll need food, water and a place to stay. If we could get to a grocery store, even if it's still underwater, we might be able to get in and find some bottled water and some canned food. But how...?"

"I think my airboat be workin' yet - that be how!" Then Gator grinned, and said, "An' don't be worry 'bout openin' dem cans." He unbuckled the top strap on the knife holder on his belt and pulled out his foot-long alligator hunting knife. "This here knife be the bes' can opener you ever seen!"

Zack laughed, and said, "Alright, Gator, let's go. With you here, I think we might just make it! Jacqueline, you stay and search through the top floors of this building. See if you can find a dry place for us to stay, and anything that might be useful. This may be our home for the next few days!"

CHAPTER 36

Cairo, September

Halfway around the world, the problem was not too much water, but the severe lack of it. Anwar Abdelal, president of a country with one of the oldest civilizations on earth, was almost ready to declare war on his neighbors because of the lack of water. He was ready to make his final decision today. But he had to explore one last option. That was why he had called his old friend, Gamel Haddad, in to see him.

"Gamel, come in, please. Have you got an answer for me?" Abdelal wasted no time on preliminaries today.

"Thank you, Anwar," said the Minister of Irrigation. He sat down slowly and carefully, so as not to aggravate his weak back. "Yes, I have an answer for you. But first, let me say a few things.

"I evaluated the American proposal as you asked. I must say that their idea is a good one. And how typically American - such an enormous project! To build a massive aqueduct, and divert two billion gallons per day of water from the Zaire River into the upper stretches of the White Nile!

It is indeed an enormous project. It would have to cross 300 miles of jungle plus a mountain range! But yes, it could be done. They have done it in California and in several other places in the United States."

"But what about here, for us? How long will it take?" interrupted Abdelal, impatient for his answer.

"Ah, yes. How long will it take? And the more important question: Can Egypt survive that long?" He paused momentarily, his eyes sweeping the presidential suite. Then he looked directly at his long-time friend.

Even before Haddad spoke, President Abdelal knew what the answer would be.

"No, Anwar, we cannot. Even if those rich Americans can buy the water rights, and even if they can get the approvals from Sudan quickly, the construction will still take four years. And we cannot hold out that long. We just cannot."

Abdelal didn't try to argue, persuade, or convince. He didn't even ask a single question. The finality he saw in Haddad's eyes told him that no other answer was possible. With a heavy sigh, he said simply, "Thank you, my friend." He sat back in his chair and looked out the window at the dry earth outside. He said nothing more, waiting for Haddad to leave.

Haddad spoke again. "What I don't understand is why the Americans would be willing to do something this expensive this quickly. Usually, they would try to get the United Nations to contribute." He looked hard at Abdelal. "Anwar, what is going on here?"

"It is nothing, Gamel. Do not concern yourself."

Gamel stared at Anwar until their eyes met. Then Haddad knew. "So," he said softly, "it is war. When?"

Abdelal nodded ever so slightly. Then he said, "It will be soon - very soon. Not a word, Gamel, not a word! General Bani-Sadr tells me that surprise is everything."

* * *

New Orleans, September

The recovery was going very slowly in New Orleans. Efforts by the Red Cross were severely hampered by lack of funds and manpower. Resources were being shared with not only Miami but also all the states north of Louisiana that had tasted some of Cleo's fury before she finally wore herself out in Minnesota. Not only had she inflicted her damages directly - her winds had ripped apart houses in Mississippi; her rains had flooded entire communities in Arkansas - but also she had also spawned more than seven hundred small but deadly tornadoes. Like random arrows from a madman's bow, these tornadoes had spread misery throughout the heartland of America.

In addition, unusual weather throughout the nation continued to disrupt the normal flow of food, supplies, and medicine long after Hurricane Cleo died away. Intense thunderstorms in the Northeast caused unexpected and severe flooding, while intense heat and drought in the West and Southwest continued to parch the land. After the long days and months of searing summer heat and stagnating air, finally some breezes stirred in southern California. But when the breezes grew into fierce winds, dust storms were created that defied description.

Some of the older residents - those who had moved west after WW II - recalled the stories their grandparents told of the dust bowl, when the skies were filled with rich black top-soil that should have been on the ground, and you didn't see the sun for days.

Then, on September 8, the worst chain-reaction highway accident in California's history happened. It all began when a car traveling at 70 mph ran into a wall of black dust, kicked up by a sudden wind storm. The wind driven dirt created conditions of zero visibility with essentially no advance warning. Startled, unable to see fifteen feet in front of him, and afraid of running into something, the driver of the car braked hard. He was rear-ended by a van carrying a family of five, then both of them were hammered by an 18-wheeler. Before it was all over, a 178-car pile-up resulted that closed Interstate Highway 5 for two solid days. The smoke from the burning cars added to the black dust for a short while, and the carbon dioxide from the fires added a tiny amount more to the atmospheric burden of that particular gas.

All over the country, it was as if the weather consciously tried to torment human beings and thwart their efforts in every way possible.

In New Orleans, once electricity was restored to the big pumps, the water was drained from the city, and initial efforts were focused on handling the dead bodies. Over 9,700 corpses were found, giving New Orleans the dubious distinction - in the category of natural disasters - of being the second-hardest hit U.S. city in history. From the San Francisco earthquake of 1906, to the Port of Galveston explosion and fire of 1954, to Hurricane Hugo's rampage through Charleston in 1989, New Orleans had vaulted into second place. First place was occupied by a newcomer also - the worst natural disaster to strike any U.S. city had happened only two days earlier in Miami. Both first and second place belonged to Cleopatra - the first of the great Greenhouse hurricanes of the twenty-first century.

The Army, the Reserves, and the National Guard were pressed into service to help remove the bodies that littered the streets of New Orleans. The U.S. Public Health Service, concerned about disease, declared a state of emergency, and took control of disposal of the dead. Due to lack of space in local cemeteries, and the high ground water levels in surrounding lands, burial was impossible, so the Health Service ordered all the bodies cremated.

A new twelve-inch trunk line was run from the main Texaco natural gas pipeline to a huge funeral crematorium oven that had been hastily constructed some forty miles north of the city. The gas flames burned continuously for a month, consuming the waterlogged flesh methodically and completely. Ironically, even with the best pollution controls available, this fire sent more carbon dioxide into the air, adding to the ever-accelerating Greenhouse Effect.

The insurance industry, years earlier, had calculated that Hurricanes Harvey, Irma and Marie had caused property damage worth more than 250 billion dollars in 2017. Now, insurance estimators were already talking in terms of 500 billion to 1 trillion dollars for Hurricane Cleo. Even while the United States wrestled with the staggering costs in terms of dollars, a huge storm in the Indian Ocean, Typhoon Pete, swept into the Bay of Bengal and slammed into eastern India and western Bangladesh, killing more than 150,000 people in Calcutta alone.

C. David Cooper

CHAPTER 37

Caracas, October

The Council of Seven had reassembled for the second time in one year, an event that had occurred only once before - in 1945, the year that the U.S. exploded two atomic bombs over Japan. The debate was raging.

"I tell you - the situation is critical!" Emilio, the climate expert, had the floor. "In the past eight to ten weeks, Hurricane Cleo, Typhoon Pete, and the others have accelerated the Effect by eight to ten years!"

"How is that possible?" asked Mugombo.

"Did you read about that 'popping' noise that was reported by the pilot who flew into the eye of Cleo? Do you know what that was?" When Mugombo shook his head, Emilio looked around at the others. "Do any of you know?"

No one answered, so Emilio continued. "I'll tell you. It was dissolved carbon dioxide being released spontaneously out of the ocean under the extremely low pressure eye of the storm. Just like in a gigantic can of soda when the pressure is released suddenly, the gas bubbles out immediately.

"We all know that the oceans contain much more CO_2 than the atmosphere. The oceans have always been an important regulator of atmospheric carbon dioxide. But Hurricane Cleo was so powerful, and the barometric pressure in the eye was so low, that it changed the equilibrium condition. Huge amounts of carbon dioxide were released from solution in the ocean water. Sucked right out of the sea and into the air!"

"So that explains why that plane lost power when it flew down into the eye," interrupted Mugombo. "The engines couldn't get enough oxygen, there was so much carbon dioxide at that point!"

"Right!" exclaimed Emilio. "And that's how both Cleo and Pete got so extraordinarily powerful. Their furious winds were supercharged by CO_2 pumping! And, worst of all, with respect to climate in the long run, since they were over water

212

a long time, hundreds of millions of tons of carbon dioxide were shunted into the air, increasing the atmospheric concentration noticeably in just a few short weeks."

Ricardo snorted and appeared ready to say something but changed his mind. He merely continued to scowl at Emilio.

Simon asked to be recognized. He stood up and Emilio sat down. "Speaking of the oceans, I have some good news to report. We have always known that the oceans are a very important sink for carbon dioxide; that is why we have been focusing so much of our resources in that area."

"Too much if you ask me!" interrupted Ricardo.

Simon appeared flustered, but after a moment, he continued to speak. "Specifically, we have been funding research efforts at several universities to improve the overall efficiency of the oceans for absorbing carbon dioxide. One of 'our' graduate students is at Harvard right now, and has helped create the breakthrough that everyone has been hoping for.

"Researchers at Harvard, as well as at many other universities, have been experimenting with genetic engineering of bacteria for many years. But in the last three years, Dr. Rachel Feinstein has been searching for a way to cross a bacteria with an ocean-habitat algae. The purpose would be to create an organism that can absorb carbon dioxide at a much faster rate than ever before.

"We have funded her efforts from the start. Last year, one of our own, Rwanda, volunteered to go up to Boston to work with her. Can you imagine living in that kind of cold! Rwanda is a very dedicated young man. Anyway, from his latest reports, it sounds like they have achieved success. Of course, the new organism must go through several years of testing before it gets governmental approval for release."

"We may not have several more years!" It was Aranxta, whose specialty was world politics. As she stood, Ricardo reluctantly took his chair. He had wanted to talk more about the new bacteria. Aranxta was a powerful speaker, though, and she commanded the group's attention at the moment.

"Egypt has invaded the Sudan," she said bluntly. "Libya has declared war on Egypt, and it looks as if Ethiopia and Saudi Arabia will send aid to Sudan. Israel has announced its support for Egypt, and of course Syria and Iraq have made threatening statements towards Israel."

Aranxta paused to catch her breath. She looked around the room at the grave faces, all reflecting her own serious look. "Of course, you all know the consequences of a major war in the Mid-East, and the risks of it escalating. If the U.S. and Russia get involved, it could be the nuclear trigger that sets off the Conflagration on this planet."

Several of the others gasped at the mention of the Conflagration. A hush fell on the group. Ricardo broke the silence. With the irreverence of youth, he said, "You know, I've heard about this myth ever since I was a child, but in all honesty, I must tell you, that I find it most difficult to believe!"

Marguerite was shocked. "How dare you question that?! Our history is clear and without doubt! We are descended from those who witnessed the Conflagration with their own eyes!"

"What history?" Ricardo's tone was mocking, his eyes a little wild as he challenged Marguerite. "All I know is some folk tales passed to me from my parents who heard them from their parents and so on. That we came from an advanced civilization on Venus. That we had to flee our home two thousand years ago, when the Greenhouse Effect on that planet got out of control. That the entire planet caught fire, burning all living things, and converting all organic matter to carbon dioxide! Oh, come on! Who can believe these stories?"

Marguerite was furious. "How did you ever get elected to this Council?" she fairly screamed across the table. "Have you no respect? Have you not studied the ancient lore?"

Ricardo shot back. "I am not a blind believer like you. Those old stories are just that – stories, and nothing more! No one knows if there is any truth in them. What I do know is that this Council is a powerful group. I know that we have great wealth and influence in many countries. And I also know that under your leadership, the Council's great wealth has diminished rapidly. I've done some checking, Marguerite; you've been squandering our wealth at an unbelievable pace in this mad quest of yours – trying to prevent the problem that is not a problem." Ricardo looked around the table; at least two heads nodded approval.

Marguerite bristled, but with effort, calmed herself. She glanced at the faces around the table. She knew she had at least two faithful supporters, but what of the others? If it came to a vote today, how would they go?

She looked back at Ricardo, and spoke to him - but also to the swing votes that she hoped to win. "The money is of little importance in the face of the possible consequences! You must remember, the technology of our ancestors was much like that of present-day earth. Our scientists were able to give us some warning, but the political leaders failed to listen - they were too involved with the conflict between nations to worry about the fate of our world. A small group of dedicated people worked very hard. They were lucky to be able to construct a few ships, and escape to Earth, just weeks before the Conflagration."

Marguerite was becoming absorbed in the re-telling of the ancient story. She hoped that some in the room would remember the teachings and be moved by hearing it again.

"Our ancestors came here from Venus almost exactly two thousand years ago. They escaped with little, but they brought with them the knowledge of this terrible global catastrophe, and how quickly it can happen!

"A world war broke out on our home planet! It was the spark that ignited the whole world. Once the big fires started, with Greenhouse trapping the excess heat, the process couldn't be stopped. For twelve weeks, our ancestors here on Earth watched helplessly as Venus lit up the night sky with the flames of the Conflagration. People on Earth thought it was a bright star, but our ancestors knew that they were witnessing the end of our civilization, indeed the end of our planet!

"Twelve weeks - what a short time it took to destroy a planet! The evidence is there, if you will only open your eyes and see it! What about the many stories of the Star of Bethlehem?"

"Again, only stories!" Ricardo's tone was mocking, but his eyes were hard. He had made up his mind to challenge Marguerite, and he would not be swayed. "Who would believe us if we told people that we are descended from immigrants from Venus? What real proof is there? You can't even count on DNA. Even if I believed you, which I do not, over the centuries our people would have intermarried with people from Earth, and now we would be as human as they are!"

Marguerite now had her emotions under control; she would not let Ricardo's tone or words get to her. She said, "I see it is useless talking with you. Nevertheless, with you or without you, this Council will do what it can to prevent the same thing from happening to Earth. Our ancestors brought little with them, but one thing that they did bring was great resolve. We carry that determination to this day. The Conflagration must never happen again! That is our legacy and our mission!" Several Council members nodded their heads.

"Wait!" exclaimed Ricardo. Suddenly, he felt his position weakening. "Wait - we must vote. You are Leader of this Council, not its Emperor! I call for a vote of confidence."

* * *

Amsterdam, October

Peter Haarhuis bit at a piece of skin near one of his fingernails. 'Nasty habit,' he thought as he looked down at the shred of skin. He brought his finger back up towards his mouth and continued to nibble at the loose flesh. 'What more do they want of me? What did I do wrong in my last few years?'

He was sitting in the outer office of Hans Broecker, president of his former company. Peter had, of course, seen and read everything the news media reported about Hurricane Abigail and the damages she had inflicted on the new dike project, as well as the damages to older dikes. Despite heavy economic losses, though, the country had been spared major loss of life.

215

That was the good news. The bad news was that his former company had suffered severe financial losses, and was being held liable by the government for alleged sub-standard construction. Haarhuis nibbled away at his finger, wondering if they were somehow going to try to blame him.

At last the door opened. Haarhuis couldn't believe his bad luck! There was Nils Lindgeren coming out of Broecker's office. Oddly, though, Lindgeren just gave him a quick, bitter look, then walked by without saying a word. Then Broecker appeared at the doorway and beckoned to Haarhuis, summoning him into the office.

"Peter, please come in and sit down. So good of you to come on such short notice."

Broecker's big smile and friendly tone threw Haarhuis off balance a bit. He was still apprehensive, so he kept his voice neutral when he replied. "Thank you," he said as he seated himself in one of the luxurious leather chairs. "It is quite all right; my schedule is rather open nowadays."

Broecker's smile faded. "Ah, yes, a very regrettable incident. You have my sincerest apologies. And rest assured, that man you just saw leaving, who was responsible for almost driving away..." Here Broecker's big smile returned, "...our best dike engineer, you with such an outstanding record of service to the company. Please be assured that Mr. Lindgeren is no longer employed with this company."

"It was a grave injustice to force you to resign like that." Broecker shook his head almost as if he didn't believe that it could have actually happened. "Believe me, it was done without my knowledge. The company would never dispute your talents or judgement. When I heard about it ... after I got the full story ... I immediately took measures.

"I do hope that you can forget about that unpleasantness. It certainly was not what the company wanted to do. In fact, the reason I asked you to come in today is to say that I am happy to offer you a complete re-instatement to your former position, with full benefits. Including your pension rights, of course. I hope you will accept."

Haarhuis was stunned. He had never expected this. He sat speechless, just staring at Broecker. Finally, Broecker became uncomfortable, and said, "Well, Peter, what do you say? You really aren't ready to retire yet, now are you? The company can still use your engineering talents. We have quite a re-building job in front of us, you know."

Haarhuis was thrilled by the offer, but also he was no fool. He recognized his bargaining position. He said slowly and deliberately, "I have some conditions."

Broecker hesitated, but said "Just name them."

"First, I must be in charge of the entire project, and I will report only to you." Broecker nodded his acceptance.

"Second, I must be allowed to build the dikes as strong as I feel necessary, without regard to profit margins." Broecker appeared ready to object, but thought better of it.

216

He remained silent waiting to see what else Haarhuis would demand. Peter paused for a moment, thinking. Then he said, "And third, I want that young engineer, Henry, as my assistant. I think he may have some potential, and I would like to try to develop it. That is all."

Broecker's eyebrows arched. "You haven't mentioned anything about salary. I would have thought that you would press me on that point."

Haarhuis said simply, "I have faith that you will treat me fairly."

Broecker smiled ruefully. He knew he had no choice, and he suspected that Haarhuis knew it too. But he said only, "Of course! Shall I show you to your new, larger office? We need to get you back to work immediately." They stood up and walked out to the reception area. They started past the executive conference room. Peter stopped.

"Please - before we get started - just give me a minute in there. Do you mind?"

Broecker looked puzzled, but said, "No, I don't mind."

Haarhuis turned to his left and walked into the big room. Slowly, he looked to his right, and then to his left. He turned back to this right and began to stroll quietly around the perimeter of the room. For several minutes, he gazed silently at the drawings and photographs of his past engineering projects. They were all still here, hanging in their rightful places. Slowly, a great smile grew on his face, matching the warm feeling that grew inside him. Peter Haarhuis was back home.

CHAPTER 38

Washington, D.C., November

A desperate meeting was in progress in one of the large conference rooms in the Capitol Building. The Secretary of the Interior, the Secretary of the Environment, the Undersecretary of Commerce, the Assistant to the Presidential Chief of Staff, and eight Congressional leaders, including Senator Lane Stillwater, surrounded one end of a long oval conference table. Various 'experts' and staffers huddled at the other end of the table, each trying to keep their presentations short and factual, yet each trying to put a 'spin' on his or her statement to make his or her department look good. The 'important' decision makers verbally jostled for position at their end, sniping at each other along party lines.

The whole scene disgusted Zack who was sitting in a chair along the back wall, along with other invited guests. He had been invited by Stillwater who had been pressured to do so by Mullens. But once Zack had arrived, he had been virtually ignored by Stillwater and the rest. Finally, Zack could stand it no longer. Leaping to his feet, he fairly shouted out his first statement of the meeting. "You people all remind me of Nero! You're fiddling while the earth is burning!"

It wasn't quite the opening statement that he had planned when he had worked on his speech these last few days. Nothing even remotely resembling it could be found anywhere in his prepared notes. However, it was certainly effective at quieting the room and getting everyone's attention. Now that all eyes were on him, Zack felt that he had to say something intelligent, something professional. But his mind was clouded with anger and frustration; he couldn't think of anything clever to say.

"Don't tell me," someone on the staffers' end of the table called out. "You're one of those who want to save the planet, right?!" A few people in that end of the room laughed nervously.

Taylor's fighting spirit was roused by the jab at him. "What you don't realize," retorted Zack, "is that the planet will survive. The earth will keep on spinning through space, providing a home to those species who can survive in the new climate conditions. Only we might not like our new home very much!" As he spoke, his nervousness disappeared, and he began to feel more comfortable.

Someone else said, "Do you claim to know for sure what it's going to be like?"

"No one can claim that, and you know it! No, I can't predict the future, but I have done enough climate modeling to know that we are fast approaching a major tipping point in our climate. A tipping point is when climates can shift dramatically – changes that might normally take centuries, can happen in just a few month or years! There could be massive and sudden changes in our atmospheric weather patterns, and in the ocean conveyor belt currents. And, dammit, most of you know that too! What about this unbelievable heat wave that's been gripping Washington for a week now? What about Hurricane Cleo two months ago? What about Hurricane Hank that just smashed into Mexico?

"Deep down inside, most of you <u>know</u> that our climate is changing. But you all are hiding behind your belief, or hope actually, that the really big changes are going to happen fifty or a hundred years from now. You think what's happening this year is just a fluke, an unusual whim of the weather. So you wait, hoping you won't have to be the ones to make the hard decisions. But I ask you, if you people won't take any responsible action, who will?!"

Zack paused for a breath, but nobody said a word. His dynamic style, his arm waving and gesturing, his animated voice had them all in his spell.

"And I want to tell you that you're wrong about the time scale! The time for action is now. If we wait any longer, there won't be any time left. There are too many positive feedback loops that are on the verge of being triggered. We need to take steps to reverse Greenhouse now, before it's too late!"

"Professor!" Stillwater injected himself into the silence. "As you may know, I've called these positive feedback loops by their more common name 'vicious cycles.' Can you give us some examples? And while you're at it, son, tell us exactly why it's so urgent to do something now."

Zack felt a surge of energy; Stillwater was giving him his opening! Maybe the Senator was just showboating, but Zack took advantage of the opportunity.

"OK, Senator. Here are a few examples. As temperatures rise, carbon dioxide becomes less soluble in ocean water and more CO_2 comes out of the water and stays in the air. This speeds up the warming even more. In a warmer world, there is more release of methane from ocean sediments; it bubbles up through the water and into the air. Methane is a major greenhouse gas. Another enhancement.

"Polar latitudes will warm more rapidly than the equatorial regions. Ice reflects sunlight energy, but when it melts it exposes open water which is darker than ice. This will increase absorption of solar energy. Again this feeds on itself and causes even more warming. Northern Boreal forests will die back significantly in a warmer world, releasing a lot of stored carbon. As the permafrost melts, methane trapped in the frozen organic matter will be released, <u>again</u> accelerating Greenhouse. Are these enough examples for you?"

The Undersecretary for Commerce spoke up. "Is this why you say we've got to act now?"

"Yes! These vicious cycles, once they get started, are like the proverbial runaway freight train. They're almost impossible to stop."

"What do you suggest we do?"

"We must immediately reduce our use of all fossil fuels by fifty percent. We must start scrubbing carbon dioxide from all power plants. We..."

"Whoa!" The Undersecretary of Commerce interrupted. "That's preposterous! It would send our country into financial ruin to do those things. We can't act unilaterally. The rest of the world won't follow."

The Undersecretary stood up to emphasize his words. "A perfect example is Russia. President Zupin recently announced that they believe the Greenhouse theory is a United States conspiracy to hurt their Siberian wheat farmers. Zupin says he believes that further study is needed, and that they are willing to contribute ten million rubles towards an international study.

"It's a political smokescreen, of course, but the point is that the U.S. economy just can't afford to take the kind of industrial cuts you're suggesting while the rest of the world doesn't. We've got to go slowly on this."

"No, sir, we do not!" Zack fairly shouted back. He hadn't retaken his seat, so he was able to wrest control of the audience back from the man at the other end of the room. "That's the one thing we must not do! The rest of the world has been ready for years to follow our lead. And I'm not talking just U.S. economy - I'm talking survival of life as we know it. Greenhouse killed my father nineteen years ago, and it killed my mother two months ago in Miami. It will kill millions more before we get it under control - if we can still do it!"

Zack had their attention again. Unconsciously, he shifted back from passion towards reason and logic once more.

"There's one more thing I didn't mention about the vicious cycles. Recent evidence has shown beyond doubt that the thinning of the ozone layer has decreased the plankton population in the ocean."

It seemed such an odd shift from the topic at hand that the room became silent again. Zack sensed he had only a few more minutes to sway the group if he could.

"It is an ironic twist, indeed, but as temperatures rise, the chemical reactions involved in the depletion of the ozone layer occur at a faster rate, thus letting more ultraviolet light reach the earth's surface. More ultraviolet light striking the top layer of the ocean kills a higher percentage of phytoplankton, which are at the base of the entire marine food chain. But, <u>and this is the important thing from a greenhouse</u>

perspective, fewer phytoplankton means a reduction in their very major global contribution to soaking up carbon dioxide."

"Speaking of phytoplankton, have you heard about the work of Dr. Feinstein at Harvard?" The question came from a tall black woman, who had been sitting in the back along the same wall as Zack. It was Marguerite, the leader of the powerful, but as yet undisclosed, Council of Seven. She was a striking-looking woman, who despite the heat wave, was dressed in a wool suit, and she seemed to command the attention of everyone when she spoke.

Zack stepped forward and turned towards his right to be able to see her better, and then answered, "Yes, I've read some of her work in the technical journals. She's been experimenting with genetically modifying algae and plankton; trying to get them to absorb carbon dioxide faster and more efficiently."

Marguerite replied, "I think you might be very interested in what I have learned about her most recent experiments. But first, let me just say that it sounds like, from what you were saying a few minutes ago, that you have concluded that the planet is on the verge of drastic alterations in climate. Is that right?"

For some reason he could not explain, Zack felt compelled to answer her with minimal interruption. He did so with a nod.

"I am in complete agreement with your conclusion," Marguerite continued. "However, the steps you just mentioned are slow as well as economically painful. I think we need a more drastic solution than what you have proposed. And we need it now, not five or ten years from now. This is where Dr. Feinstein's research comes into play.

"Dr. Feinstein very recently has discovered a way to genetically combine algal cells into a certain type of marine bacterium. This new organism has the ability to absorb carbon dioxide from ocean water, and gram for gram, it does so orders-of-magnitude faster than any existing plant on earth. And, finally, it reproduces at geometric rates. And, of course, as it removes CO_2 from ocean water, the ocean can then absorb and remove more CO_2 from the atmosphere.

"But, most importantly...," Marguerite paused for effect and let her steady gaze sweep the room. Then she finished her sentence, "...it also absorbs calcium from sea water. Then during respiration, it biochemically combines that calcium with the carbon dioxide. It excretes calcium carbonate as a waste product."

Zack's jaw literally dropped open. He was immediately struck with the wonderful potential of her words. "Is this organism viable now?" he asked, excitedly.

The woman nodded and was about to continue speaking, but was cut off by a fat man with glasses and a salt and pepper goatee. He was sitting more than half way down the table, but not quite to the end.

"That organism has been quarantined," he said matter-of-factly. "Dr. Feinstein's research was conducted without proper government oversight, and the

Food and Drug Administration, Division of Genetic Engineering, has seized all of Dr. Feinstein's experimental bacterial colonies along with all of her laboratory notes."

"What!?" exclaimed Marguerite. "How can you do such a thing? That organism might be the only thing that can save us, we've gone so far into the Greenhouse."

Zack broke in. His voice reflected his feeling of incredulity. "On what authority can you seize university research projects?! Is this America or is this Russia?"

The fat man flushed. "Our agency has all the legal authority it needs. We need to be certain that any new micro-organism is safe before it is released into the environment. The consequences of this particular one could be devastating. Think, man! It absorbs carbon dioxide and calcifies it! What if it grew out of control and absorbed too much CO_2, depleting the atmosphere?!"

Just then Senator Stillwater interjected himself into the conversation. "For the benefit of those of us who are less technical than you experts, can somebody please explain what it is that these micro-orgasms, uh, these micro-gonisms, uh, these critters do, exactly."

Zack turned to face the man who might become the next President. He said, "Senator, if I understand correctly, these genetically modified critters are a cross between algae and bacteria, and they will ingest carbon dioxide and excrete calcium carbonate, thus removing the carbon from the atmosphere and putting it into solid form, which deposits on the ocean floor."

James Cooper, who was seated slightly behind and to the right of the Senator, leaned over and whispered into Stillwater's ear. The Senator looked surprised at first, but then a wide grin grew on his face.

His face positively glowed when he finally understood what was being said. He looked at Zack and said, "You mean to tell me that these bugs will eat carbon dioxide gas and poop rocks?! And those rocks just fall to the bottom of the ocean?"

Despite the seriousness of the situation, Zack smiled at the Senator's choice of words, then said, "You got it, Senator. And if these bugs can grow fast enough, maybe they can provide a quick and inexpensive temporary solution to Greenhouse while we modify our industry and get our carbon emissions under control."

The fat man from FDA spoke again. "As I said, our agency has seized the organisms. We will not allow this kind of unknown life form loose into the world's oceans, simply because a madcap professor and a few small groups feel threatened by some unusual weather patterns. As we all know, there is still no valid scientific proof that the so-called Greenhouse Effect will do all these drastic things you people say."

Stillwater answered. "Spoken like a true lackey of the Administration, Charlie. Now, 'fess up. We want to see your records. We need to know what you're doing with those bugs."

The man named Charlie sniffed, and stood up from the table. "I'm sorry, Senator Stillwater, he said. "I can't release that information."

"What do you mean, you can't?" roared Stillwater. He was now standing also, his eyes ablaze with anger. Zack had to admit he looked an imposing figure. "I'm a U.S. Senator and I demand that you tell me!"

Charlie smiled tightly, his goatee pointing obscenely towards Stillwater. "Well, Senator, I'm sure you're aware of the Ecosystem Protection Act of 2021. Under the provisions of that act, our Agency has sole authority to deal with new, genetically altered life forms that we judge to be potentially dangerous to ecosystems. And we have ruled that this organism poses a great risk to ocean ecosystems. We will not even consider releasing it until we have thoroughly researched it ourselves, even if that means several years of study. And we will not reveal where we are keeping it!"

With that, the fat bureaucrat turned and walked out of the room. The meeting virtually exploded into a dozen different conversations. Stillwater, pale with anger, leaned over to Cooper. Marguerite had disappeared along with several others who had followed Charlie out of the room.

"Shit!" Zack said to no one in particular. He got up and left, feeling angry and frustrated.

CHAPTER 39

Zack exited the Capitol Building near the top of the long steps on the House side, and looked directly across the lawn to the Library of Congress. Even though he was in the shadow of the Capitol, the heat of the breezeless afternoon struck him as he left the air conditioned building. Taylor glanced at his watch. After five o'clock, he thought, and still this hot! And in November! Unbelievable!

From the top of the steps, Taylor looked to his right and spotted Jacqueline waiting for him, sitting on a bench in the shade of the trees lining Independence Avenue. He started down the steps, angling towards her. Jacqueline stood up when she saw Zack walking towards her.

It had been only a short walk under the glaring sun, but by the time Taylor got there, he already felt the first drop of sweat roll down his side from under his arm. As soon as he reached Jacqueline, he peeled off his sports jacket, saying, "Whew, it must be 100 degrees today!" The horns of the taxi cabs in the street behind Jacqueline seemed to echo Zack's annoyance.

Jacqueline nodded, acknowledging the intense heat wave, at the same time wiping her forehead with a damp Kleenex. "Well, how did it go?" she asked. But even as she asked the question, she could read the bitterness on his face.

"Just about like you said it would," Zack replied. "I can't believe these people are so myopic! Can't they see what's happening right under their noses?"

Zack then proceeded to tell Jacqueline everything that had transpired in the meeting. He ended with, "If only we could get our hands on that modified bacteria. I'd throw it in the ocean myself! Then it could start reproducing and spreading out. If they really reproduce as fast as people say, we might be able to stop the Greenhouse before it's too late!"

Jacqueline stared at him. "You can't mean that!" she said. "What about the possible side effects? Nobody knows what that stuff could do to the environment."

"Nobody knows what's going to happen to the environment in the next few years anyway! Letting those bugs loose might be the best thing we could do." Zack paused a moment and listened to his own words. When he spoke again, his tone was a bit more subdued. "You're probably right - I couldn't just release them like that. But we need those microorganisms <u>now</u>, not three or four or ten years from now. I'd damn well make sure that scientists all over the world got a sample right away, so research would move quickly.

"Jacqueline, we just don't have the luxury of time anymore. My Dad had a favorite saying: 'Do something, even if it's wrong!' He had no patience with bureaucrats. I'm a little more laid back than Dad was, but sometimes I feel the same way. We need to do something!"

"You – laid back?" said Jacqueline, allowing herself to smile at the thought.

In spite of his frustration, Zack had to smile too. "Yes, in fact, I am very mellow compared with him," he said, calming down. He reached over and took her hand in his. With her free hand, she reached up and touched his cheek. "You had to know him," he said simply.

"I'm sorry I missed him," said Jacqueline, "but I'm looking forward to knowing you for a long time."

They both were quiet for a moment, then Jacqueline said slowly, "Maybe we <u>can</u> get our hands on those bacteria. Tell me again what Charlie said. Try to remember his exact words. Maybe he gave us a hint as to where they're keeping it."

"I don't remember his exact words. But I know he said something about quarantine, and about researching it themselves, even if it meant years of study."

Jacqueline looked pensive. "I wonder...."

"What?"

"He said 'years of study' - I wonder. That might mean that they've got it at their research lab in Bethesda. That's less than ten miles from here as the crow flies. It would be a good secure spot. And the cover is good - they're always doing some kind of biomedical research there."

"Great - let's get up there right away!"

"Hold on! We can't just go up there, knock on the door and say 'May I borrow some of that dangerous new bacteria you've got,' now can we? I mean, even if we <u>knew</u> it was there, which we don't, we'd still need a plan."

"Yeah, you're right. OK, let's go back to the hotel and get out of this heat so we can think straight."

They walked towards the street, and started angling towards a taxi that was parked at the curb a little ways down the street. Before they had gotten half-way to the curb, one of the multitudes of cab drivers who were constantly cruising the city had spotted them. He swerved across two lanes of traffic and pulled up next to the curb, blocking the line of taxis behind him. Horns blared and voices shouted, but he ignored them, and jumped out to open the door for Zack and Jacqueline.

"Taxi, please?" he inquired. He smiled, revealing extraordinarily white teeth. His swarthy look and straight black hair indicated a middle-eastern heritage, which put him into the majority, at least as far as Washington taxicab drivers went.

Zack shook his head in disbelief at the driver's actions, then he looked to his left towards the cab first in line. Through the windshield, Zack saw the driver's lips moving in a silent, angry curse. But the gray-haired fellow wasn't getting out of his cab.

Zack shook his head again, and despite the young man's protests, headed back to the legally parked cab. The older driver at first seemed surprised as Zack walked up. But he recovered quickly, "Taxi, sir?" "Yes," replied Zack, "To the State Plaza Hotel; 19th and F Street."

"Yes sir! And thanks for refusing that crazy kid up there." The driver got out quickly to open the door for Zack and Jacqueline. After they were inside, the driver slammed their door closed, then jumped back into his seat. He was not as old as Zack had first thought. He took off into the traffic, barely bothering to check his mirrors.

The driver had a reassuring look about him. His gray hair was combed back and not parted. He had a receding hairline, which accentuated his dark bushy eyebrows. He was stocky, but not fat. His hands were thick, and he had a lot of hair on his muscular forearms and the backs of his hands. As soon as they were in the traffic stream, the driver began talking.

"What about this heat, my friends? Is this strange or what? Seventeen years I've been driving this hack, and I never had to run my air-conditioner so much this late in the year. I feel like the entire city of Washington is sitting in a big frying pan, you know what I mean? Yeah, that's what the newspapers have been calling the city this year - the big frying pan. And somebody just keeps turning up the heat. I was in the Navy for almost seven years before I came here, so I been around, you know. And I tell you, we sure got some strange weather happening."

The teacher in Zack couldn't help but respond. "You know, this heat is a result of a stalled high pressure area, which has developed into a subsidence inversion over the city. The inversion has created a layer of superheated air about 1,500 feet up. It traps the heat and the air pollution of Washington, and keeps it all down here near the ground. But actually, the cause of all this extra heat to begin with is the Greenhouse Effect."

"Yeah, I believe in that Greenhouse Effect, I really do," said the driver. "I been reading up on it - ever since Martha died three years ago during the summer of '21." His voice sounded a bitter note. "Martha was my wife – got hitched right out of the Navy; we were married 23 years. She died of heat stroke. Can you beat that? Heat stroke - and her still a young woman. The frying pan killed her." His voice trailed off.

Zack said softly, "I'm sorry - I lost my father in the heat wave of '05, in Miami," but couldn't think of anything further to say. The noises of the traffic intruded into the cab as the three occupants were quiet, but the interior silence didn't last.

"I get to do a lot of reading while I'm waiting for fares," the driver said, shaking off his momentary bitterness. "Do you know that the Greenhouse Effect is accelerating? I just read that in the Post yesterday morning, and I believe it, too. They were having some sort of Senate hearings on it this afternoon on the Hill."

Zack responded, "I agree with that part about it accelerating. In fact, I was at those hearings today. And I have to tell you, I was very disappointed. Many of our government leaders still don't seem to want to do anything to stop Greenhouse."

Just then they pulled up to a red light. The cab driver turned around and peered at Zack. He said, "Hey, I know you! You're that professor - the one who was on that TV special about the Ice Shelf. You're...um...you're...."

"Zack Taylor," said Zack, extending his hand. "Pleased to meet you."

"Likewise. My name's Sanders, Norman Sanders."

Zack turned towards Jacqueline, saying, "And this is Jacqueline Jordan, my fiancé."

"Pleased to meet you Miss. So, professor, you came up here for those hearings. And you say that they're not listening to you? Well, that don't surprise me none. That sounds just like bureaucrats and politicians. The government don't want to help people no more. All our tax dollars, and we get no help from them at all!"

The light turned green and Norman resumed driving. For the remainder of the short drive, the three of them exchanged views on the Greenhouse Effect and on the Government's lack of effectiveness in dealing with such a long-range problem. Sanders pulled up at the State Plaza Hotel; Zack and Jacqueline got out, and Zack leaned in to pay the fare.

"Listen, Professor," said Norman earnestly, "if you need to get anywhere while you're in town, anywhere at all, you just give me a call." Norman handed him a card with his cell number printed on it. "Anywhere, anytime," he emphasized. "With just me at home now, you can call anytime."

Zack and Jacqueline walked up the ramp and into the lobby. Jacqueline, always observant, spotted the difference right away and stopped; Zack, oblivious as usual to his surroundings, continued walking towards the elevator.

"This isn't our hotel," said Jacqueline.

Confused, Zack asked "What do you mean? The sign outside says State Plaza."

"This is not the same lobby that we came into last night," said Jacqueline emphatically.

"That's crazy," said Zack, looking around. "It looks the same to me!"

"It's not the same," Jacqueline repeated. "That Chinese desk over there..." She pointed. "... was an old English drop-leaf table last night. And there's something about those steps that's different."

"Look, just come over here and we'll ask at the front desk." He took her by the upper arm to steer her towards the lady behind the counter. Jacqueline gently but firmly took his hand from her arm, and smiled at him. "I can walk by myself, thank you," she said easily.

Zack, still confused by the allegation of the wrong hotel, now was not sure if they were having an argument or not. He walked briskly over to the counter. He took out some of his feelings on the clerk. "Is this, or is this not, the State Plaza Hotel?" he demanded in a gruff voice.

"Yes, sir, it is," responded the slightly bewildered desk clerk.

"You see," Zack said smugly, looking at Jacqueline.

The desk clerk cleared her throat. "Excuse me, sir," she said. Zack looked back at her. "Sir, this is the E Street lobby."

Now it was Zack's turn to look bewildered. The clerk continued, "We have two entrances and two lobbies. The other one is on F Street. They look almost identical."

Jacqueline laughed and said, "I knew it was different! Norman must have dropped us at the E street entrance." Looking at Zack, she said, "I believe you owe me an apology, mister." Her friendly tone and half-smile told Zack that she really wasn't angry. And, he realized, she had been right. He began to see the humor in the situation.

Zack hemmed and hawed for a few moments, but finally he said, "Alright, I admit it. You're more observant than I am. You were right and I was wrong." He laughed, adding "Again." Jacqueline joined him in his laughter, and gave him a hug.

"OK, OK, don't overdo it. It's not that big a deal," she said. "Let's go up to our room; I have an idea."

A big grin appeared on Zack's face. He lowered his voice and whispered in her ear, "I have some ideas, too."

"That's not what I was talking about!" said Jacqueline. "And you know it!" She released Zack, and stepped back, holding him at arm's length.

Zack's face became more serious, and he said, "I know, I was just teasing. We've got work to do."

* * *

It was after 10:00 at night. The room smelled of coffee and half-eaten egg-salad sandwiches. Jacqueline sat in front of Zack's laptop computer, which at that minute was hooked into his cell phone through bluetooth. Zack stood behind her. They had been trying to break into the master computer at Bethesda for almost three hours now.

Jacqueline leaned back in the chair and sighed audibly. Zack massaged the small muscles at the back of her neck and above her shoulder blades. "Mmmm, that feels good," she said, leaning back further. "But still no luck here. Their security system is a good one - almost too good. It makes me think that this might be the right place."

"Let me have another turn," said Zack.

"OK, just let me try this last set of words." Jacqueline leaned over to check their list of key words. A long page of lined-through words stared back at her. She punched in a new string of words, using up the last few on the page, then gave the command to the computer to try all possible combinations of letters. The hard drive whirred. Suddenly, the computer beeped.

"Bingo!" yelled Zack.

"This looks good, really good," said Jacqueline, excitement creeping into her voice. Her fingers flew across the keyboard, accessing file after file. Finally, she found what she had been looking for. "Here it is! Here's the file on the bacteria!" she exclaimed.

"All Right!! Then it is there - it's really there?" Hope permeated Zack's voice. For the first time in over two hours, he felt encouraged.

"Yes. It's there! And it's a good thing we found out about this tonight! Here's a notation to get the bacteria ready for transport first thing in the morning - 8:00 am. It appears that the Senator has made some demands that FDA doesn't want to meet. They've decided that the Bethesda lab might be too obvious a place for them to keep it."

Zack broke in, "They were right about that!"

Jacqueline nodded and continued talking. "They're going to remove the samples to a safe storage house, but it doesn't say where."

"That settles it. We've got to act tonight!" said Zack. "Listen, I have an idea. They're going to move it tomorrow morning, right? So why don't we be the ones to move it? I mean, it's perfect - we show up before the real transport team; they hand it over to us and we're out of there before anyone's the wiser."

Jacqueline looked at him admiringly. "You know, that's a great idea. It's simple and direct - it has an element of truth, and it has the surprise factor. We get there in the early hours, tell them the time change is for the sake of increased security. They just might fall for it."

Zack said, "If we act like we know what we're doing, that will carry the bluff to a certain extent. But we'll need some good identities, and we must have some papers and credentials."

"And the pass codes," added Jacqueline. She punched a few more keys. A smile grew on her face as she watched the screen produce the desired results. She said, "All right here, Zachary. All right here. Just hook up your pocket laser printer, and we've got us a couple of identification cards on the way!"

* * *

At four a.m. they called Norman at his home. In a few minutes they walked down to wait. Each carried a small rolled up bundle of clothes and supplies that Zack had purchased a few hours earlier. The bundles contained white lab coats, a stethoscope, badge holders with their fake i.d. cards, a clipboard, and various pens and pencils. It doesn't take much to disguise yourself as a medical researcher, Zack had realized as he had made the purchases.

In addition, Zack carried his portable computer case. It was empty now except for some rolled up underwear and tee shirts. This was to protect the vials of bacteria from breaking during transit. The front desk clerk gave them a curious look as they walked through the lobby, but didn't say anything to them. Zack saw the taxi as it pulled up outside.

They walked quickly to Norman's cab and hopped in. Sanders greeted them with a question. "Good morning Professor - morning Miss. I didn't think you'd be calling me again so soon. What are doing out at this time of night?"

Zack hesitated. Jacqueline had warned him against giving away too much information. But he sensed that Sanders had to be told all about their plans; his cooperation and assistance were going to be vital to their success. Besides, he had a good feeling about Norman.

Taylor looked over at Jacqueline; she shook her head slightly. Zack looked back at Norman, who was still turned around watching him. Then Zack made his decision; he said, "We're out to save the earth, tonight, Norman. I hope you're ready to hear a wild tale as we drive! Head towards Bethesda Medical Research Lab."

While they drove on in the darkness, Zack related his involvement with Greenhouse. He sketched out their plan to Sanders, and why it was so important to succeed. Jacqueline, once she saw that Zack was going to tell it all, joined him in relating the story, and filled in some of the missing details to try to ensure Sanders' willingness to cooperate.

But it turned out that Jacqueline's worries were groundless; Sanders was clearly excited about helping. "I've often wondered what an ordinary guy like me could do about something like the Greenhouse Effect. I've prayed for a chance to make up for Martha being taken from me! Now I've got my shot. You bet I'll help. At least we'll be doing something active about this while all those stuffed shirts in Congress continue to sit on their butts."

As they talked, Zack and Jacqueline put on their white coats and clipped on their ID badges. As envisioned, Norman's part of the operation was simple - but vitally important. He was to drive almost up to the entrance, but not close enough to be easily seen from the doors. He was to wait for them while he and Jacqueline went in to get the samples. As soon as they were out the door, he was to pick them up and drive off before anyone could react. If anyone followed, Norman was to lose them in the maze of Washington streets.

When Taylor came to the part about losing any would-be pursuers, Norman rubbed his hands together and said, "That'll be a pleasure, Professor, a pure pleasure!"

Before they knew it, they were pulling up to the main gate at Bethesda. Taylor glanced at his watch - 4:45 am. A sleepy-looking uniformed gate guard stopped them. Zack showed his papers. The guard looked at the papers, and checked his clipboard. "You guys are early; you weren't supposed to get here until 6:00."

'Six o'clock!' thought Zack, they must have decided to come earlier, too! He explained to the guard that they had been worried about secrecy, so they decided to get an earlier start and to not use an official looking car. "We decided that we wanted to blend in, and what could be more anonymous than a D.C. taxi?" Zack smiled confidently at the guard, who nodded and said, "Yeah, that sounds like a good idea to me, too," then waved them through.

* * *

Zack and Jacqueline were having trouble finding the right lab. They had stopped at the main entrance to the hospital, and had gotten rather sketchy directions. They were now walking through the labyrinth of hallways towards the Bethesda Biomedical Research Lab. The halls were mostly deserted, but each time they met the occasional nurse or resident or technician, Zack's stomach churned inside him. He felt that even the walls were watching him.

They made several wrong turns, and didn't want to attract any extra attention by stopping people to ask for directions, so it took them almost twenty minutes to find the research wing of the huge building. As they walked up to the guard at the door, Zack glanced down at his watch - 5:10 already!

This guard was the first person who really looked at their identification papers; the lady at the main reception area had just given them a cursory glance, and no one else had asked for them. Zack held his breath, but the guard merely passed them back to Zack and Jacqueline. He seemed more interested in looking at Jacqueline in person than at her picture. At last, he picked up the phone and called the lab technician inside.

The lab tech came out the door. She was a young, mousy-looking girl who seemed to take an instant dislike to Jacqueline, and by association, to Zack. She complained,

"You're early; I haven't finished preparing the samples for transport. You're going to have to wait!"

Zack smiled the friendliest smile he good muster and said, "Please hurry. Part of our plan is to get on the roads before the morning rush hour traffic." Mouse-girl gave him a sour look and disappeared back into the room.

Zack and Jacqueline could do nothing but wait. The minutes passed like hours. 'Come on!' Zack screamed in his mind. Finally, the lab technician returned with the bacteria. Two 500-milliliter flasks were packaged tightly in a sturdy Styrofoam container. "You're going to have to sign for these samples," whined the technician. She meticulously read the sign-out sheet procedures. "Let me see," she said slowly and deliberately, "do I sign on this line or do you?"

Zack glanced at his watch again - damn! It was 5:30; where was the time going? Finally, the papers signed, he was handed the bacteria. His face calm, but his heart pounding, Zack retraced his steps back towards the waiting door. Jacqueline was at his side talking with him in a soothing voice. At one point he wanted to turn left, but she steered him to the right. The halls seemed to go on forever. 'Come on!' his brain shouted.

Finally they were back at the entrance. They walked quickly, but not too quickly, towards the door. Now they were at the door, now outside. Norman was not here!

Taylor couldn't believe it! Where was Norman? Zack felt the panic creeping into his brain; he looked wildly left and right, but didn't see anything. He looked at his watch - 5:45, less than fifteen minutes to go before the real transport team was scheduled to arrive! What could he do now?

Then, all of a sudden, the cab screeched to a stop right in front of them. Norman leaned over and said through the window "Sorry - they made me pull around out of the ambulance driveway. Come on, get in; let's go."

It was 5:50 when they approached the gate. Simultaneously, an official looking van was just pulling up from the other direction, coming into Bethesda. The gate guard had to decide who to deal with first. Norman blew his horn impatiently, as only experienced cabdrivers can do. The guard looked back and forth once more. Recognizing the cab and its important occupants, the guard opened the gate and let them through. He then turned his attention to the two men in the white government van. Norman drove through quickly, but not too fast, and then they were on the public highway. Safe!

Back at the gate, the guard felt his face getting hotter. The driver of the van was yelling something at him, but he couldn't seem to understand the words. He continued to stare at the paperwork - it looked official. But then so had the other forms! He was so confused. He held the papers up side by side - why couldn't he spot the fraud? He looked back at the driver of the van. The man's mouth was moving but the guard still couldn't make out the words. What should he do?

The right rear passenger door opened, and a uniformed Marine stepped out. He strode confidently around the front of the van to the gate house. It took only forty-five seconds for the Marine Sergeant to figure out that someone else had come in before them for the bacteria, and that they had just left in a taxi! Less than five seconds after that, the Marine was sprinting back to the van. Then the van squealed around the glass and concrete outpost in a desperate U-turn and roared off in pursuit of the imposters.

The cab was less than two minutes into its escape when the big siren at the main gate of Bethesda Medical Research Center wailed its howling protest. Zack, Jacqueline and Norman all heard it simultaneously. "Oh shit!" muttered Zack. Jacqueline reached over to hold Zack's hand.

"Now comes the fun part!" said Norman, as he pressed his foot to the floor.

Shortly after the van had roared off, the guard had switched on the siren because he didn't know what else to do. He delayed calling the police, because he was worried that it would reflect poorly on his own organization. That delay proved to be of vital importance to the three fugitives.

The cab took off like a shot. In his rear view mirror, Norman could see the distant headlights of the van. "We got company," he said tersely, "better buckle up."

The two cars were flying down State Road 355 back towards Washington. Fortunately, or unfortunately, traffic was still pretty light on the road. It was fortunate because Sanders could get up a good rate of speed, but it was unfortunate because there were few other cars in which to lose his pursuers.

Sanders was doing 80 mph as he approached Dorset Ave, when he had an idea. "Hold on," he yelled. He braked hard and skidded around the corner, turning east on Dorset. He was less than a mile from Chevy Chase Circle where he could connect with Highway 185. Zack wrenched his head around to look behind them. The van screeched around the turn and accelerated after them; it was gaining. In the early morning light, Zack could barely make out the front passenger. However, Zack could see that he was wearing a white coat and was talking into a radio or a phone.

Sanders careened around the Circle and headed south on Connecticut Ave. The traffic was getting heavier, but he was using his horn freely and maneuvering around cars expertly. He was able to keep his speed up around 50 mph. The driver of the van was unable to match Sanders driving ability, and started to drop back.

As soon as they passed the National Zoo, Sanders turned left onto Calvert Street and crossed the Duke Ellington Bridge. He took a quick right just after the bridge and got onto 19th Street. He slowed down, merging with other traffic. He turned left onto Wyoming Ave, then right again on 18th Street. The light at the next intersection was red, and he slowed to a stop, behind one taxi and beside another.

"We made it!" he said, turning his head to smile as his passengers. "We're invisible now!"

Zack sighed his relief and said, "Thank you, Norman." Jacqueline added "You were wonderful!"

"It was nothing, don't mention it. It was fun! But now, where to? What are you going to do with that stuff?"

A very good question, thought Zack. He really hadn't decided. He would like to distribute a number of sub-samples so various researchers could study it. But how? That would be a tough problem. Zack knew he was tired; this was one decision he needed to sleep on.

"Let's go back to the State Plaza; I need some time to think. I have to decide the best way to distribute this to researchers around the world. I believe that's the right thing to do."

"I think you're right, Professor. OK - State Plaza Hotel."

Sanders turned right onto G Street, which is one-way going west, in order to come back up on F Street to the hotel. As soon as they were on G Street, Norman said, "Something doesn't feel right about this."

Jacqueline grew wary instantly. "About what, Norman?" she asked, thinking he might be having a change of heart. After all, he had just helped them steal vital government property.

"About the traffic. It's usually much heavier in here by now. Something's definitely not right here." Then Norman spotted a thin man standing by a dark sedan. As they drove past, the thin man leaned over and said something to another man seated in the car. "I know that guy! He's an undercover cop. I bet they've set a trap at your hotel!"

"A trap?" said Zack, astonished at the thought. "How could they know?"

Jacqueline said, "The people at Bethesda might have recognized our pictures, and found out where we were staying. Or they might have traced last night's computer tap to our room. Either way, we're caught!"

"Not yet," said Norman. He made a sudden U-turn, much to the surprise and annoyance of the other drivers on the one-way road. But, more importantly, Norman's move surprised the thin man who was still standing by the dark sedan. Horns blared as the few cars facing the cab swerved out of the way. One car ran up on the sidewalk, narrowly missing two young women, and crashing into a storefront. The cop shouted at the cab as it roared by them, going in the opposite direction.

Almost immediately, they heard a siren from somewhere behind them. "Professor, I think you're going to have to make that decision pretty quick, now," yelled Norman as soon as he made it back to 19th Street, and turned right. He was now heading south, towards the National Mall.

It didn't take Zack long to make up his mind. Perhaps, unconsciously, he had been thinking of this all along. It's amazingly simple, he thought, after deciding.

"Head for water, Norman! Get me to the nearest body of water; that's all I ask!"

Sanders gunned his engine and laid on his horn. He went as fast as he could down 19th. He could hear the police cars behind him now. He turned left on Virginia Avenue, right by the Department of the Interior Museum. When he got to Constitution Avenue, he saw the police blockade to his left. The Washington monument gleamed in the early morning sunlight, tantalizingly close, but blocked from them as surely as by a solid wall.

"Damn!" he yelled, "I was headed for the Tidal Basin, but they've cut us off." He wrenched the wheel hard to the right and sped west on Constitution Avenue.

They all saw the blockade in front of them at 21st Street at the same time. Ironically, it was set up just in front of the building that housed the National Academy of Science and Engineering.

"Damn again!!" yelled Norman.

"We're caught for sure now," said Jacqueline. She looked over at Zack.

"We're not finished yet," hollered Norman. He slowed his cab a bit, looking for something on his left. He saw his opportunity and swerved hard to the left, cutting across three lanes, headed for a park. The cab bumped over a low section in the curb, and up onto the grass of the Garden area of the National Mall. They bounced along the lawn headed directly for the Lincoln Memorial.

Norman shot a quick glance over his shoulder. He laughed as he said, "Good thing I just bought some new shocks for this baby!"

Zack saw the reflecting pool in front of the Lincoln Memorial. He shouted, "Norman - it can't be this pond! It's got to be open water; it's got to connect to the ocean!"

Norman set his jaw even tighter. "You professors do make it tough sometimes." Then he laughed. "OK, Doc, I'll get you to the River!"

They heard a helicopter above them. Through a loudspeaker, they heard a voice commanding them to stop. Norman ignored it. By now he had made it across the grass and was bouncing towards the pedestrian circle around the Lincoln Memorial. It was still too early for tourists, so they had a clear opening to the paved circle. Norman accelerated and jumped the old cab over the fairly high curb. Its tires thumped hard onto the pavement, squealing their protest.

"Damn, there go those new shocks!" grinned Sanders.

They zoomed around the traffic circle at the Lincoln Memorial, and up towards Arlington Memorial Bridge. When they got to the top of the rise, they saw the police cars coming up the other side, blocking any escape that way. "Get ready, Doc," yelled Norman. He squealed to a stop about a third of the way across the bridge.

Zack ripped off the tape around the Styrofoam case. "Hold these!" he said to Jacqueline, handing her the two flasks. He flung open the door, and leaped out. Then he reached back inside for the samples of bacteria. Jacqueline was one step ahead of him and had removed the stoppers.

At least eight policemen were running towards Zack from the other side. The voice in the helicopter boomed out, "Stop where you are! Put your hands over your head!" Zack glanced behind him; a patrol car was careening up the bridge.

Feeling as if he was doing everything in slow motion, Taylor ran around the front of the cab, towards the side of the bridge. He reached the side just as a police car screeched to a halt fifteen feet behind them. A man in a white coat jumped out. "Don't do it!" he screamed.

Zack looked down into the greenish-brown waters of the Potomac River. He looked back at the man in the white coat; he looked over at Norman and Jacqueline. Everyone seemed frozen in time and space.

Zack hurled the un-stoppered flasks as far out into the air as he could. He watched as they described a graceful arc down to the water. They landed in the river, one breaking on impact, and mixing its contents instantly with all the other microscopic life abounding in the surface waters of the Potomac. The other flask, unbroken, floated upright for a short while, then tipped, filled with water, and sank out of sight.

"Go forth and multiply," said Taylor softly.

"My God, what have you done?" whispered the man in the white coat, as he joined Zack by the edge. Jacqueline and Norman came over as well. Zack put his arm around Jacqueline's shoulder. She, in turn, put both arms around his waist, and pressed her head to his chest.

"The ocean has been battered so much," said Jacqueline tenderly. "Now, if these tiny creatures can stay alive until the river carries them out there, the ocean can start to heal."

Zack looked down at Jacqueline's upturned face. She understood perfectly. God, he loved her. Would he ever see her again? Was it worth this kind of sacrifice? He didn't know if his throwing these microbes into the river would make any difference to the onslaught of Greenhouse. He just knew that he had had to try.

"What have you done?" repeated the man from Bethesda, as the police closed in.

Quietly, Taylor replied, "Taken us out of the frying pan, I hope."

"I just hope you haven't thrown us into the fire," came the curt reply. The FDA official stood apart as the police converged on the group.

CHAPTER 40

Washington, D.C., December

Zack sat in his small apartment in Washington D.C. and pondered what to fix himself for lunch. Disgusting, he thought! Out of jail for only three days, and already he was reduced to being worried about lunch. He stood in front of the refrigerator door and looked inside for inspiration. Just as he was about to give up and microwave a frozen burrito, he heard a key being inserted into the front door lock, and Jacqueline let herself in.

"Hi!" he said cheerily.

"Hi, yourself," she replied. "Brought you something," she said playfully, holding her hands behind her back.

Zack put his arms around her, only half-trying to find out what she was holding. He kissed her lightly on the lips.

"No sir," she said, pulling back. "Right now, it's lunch time." She held out the Taco Bell bag.

"Great," Zack said, "I was just going to have some Mexican."

In just a few minutes, they were both sitting at the kitchen table. "You know what I still can't figure..." said Jacqueline. "...is how come we were released from jail so quickly?"

"I've been thinking about that too," said Zack. "The only thing that makes sense is that the Senator used his influence. He might just be the next President, you know." Just then, Zack cocked his head. "Did you hear that?" he asked.

"Hear what?" Jacqueline replied.

Zack listened for it again but didn't hear anything. "Nothing, only..."

"What?" asked Jacqueline, her eyes sparkling.

Zack replied, "I thought I heard an animal outside, but I guess I was wrong. Anyway, I'm convinced that the Senator used his influence. I think he knows we did the right thing."

"Speaking of that," said Jacqueline, "I heard on the news this morning, that some French scientists have already found traces of the organisms in the Channel."

"I know! It's really exciting; they're thriving. Maybe these bacteria will be able to halt Greenhouse. Who knows, in a few years...."

Zack stopped and turned his head in the direction of the door. "I heard it again. Didn't you hear that? There's something out there."

Jacqueline's eyes shined with suppressed excitement. "Yes, I believe you're right. Why don't you go see?"

Zack walked quickly to the door. He hesitated, his hand on the knob and looked back at Jacqueline, who was watching him intently but hadn't gotten up from her chair. Then he heard it again. Close to the door, he didn't mistake the sound this time. He pulled the door open and there right by the door, was a small wire cage, with a bright red bow on top. Inside the cage was a beautiful German Shepherd puppy. Zack bent down to the puppy and it began wagging its little tail furiously. He felt his voice grow husky and his eyes grow moist as he turned to look at Jacqueline, who by now had joined him at the door.

"I thought you might like an early Christmas present," she said simply.

Zack couldn't find the right words, couldn't find any words. He knew his voice wouldn't have let him speak them even if he knew what to say. He simply embraced Jacqueline in his arms and held her for eternity. A small yelp brought him back. With a quick motion, he scooped up the puppy, and the next thing he knew, he and Jacqueline were lying on the floor with the puppy romping on top of them.

AFTERWORD

Dear Reader,

I hope you enjoyed reading *Out of the Frying Pan*. As you now know, the first half of the book is informative and filled with facts about Global Climate Change, while the second half is imaginative and fanciful. I chose not to put any data tables or graphs in the book because I felt it would interrupt the flow of the story, but if you want to see some of the graphs that Zack mentions during his lectures, here they are along with some links so you can explore these topics in more depth if you wish.

End of Chapter 2 & start of Chapter 4, human population exponential growth curve:

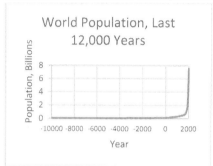

Population Growth over 12,000 Years

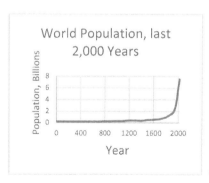

Over 2,000 years, growth still is explosive

There are many similar-looking graphs available online; it is probably best for you to just search: "human population growth curve"

Chapter 4; Temperature Anomaly & CO_2 correlation for the previous 420,000 years
(note: these graphs are a a few years out of date; CO_2 concentration first surpassed
400 ppm in 2013)

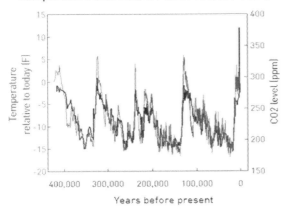

Temperature and CO2 for Last 400,000 Years

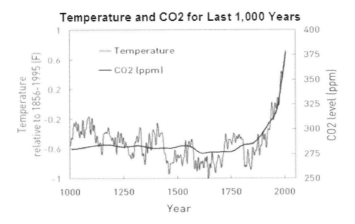

Temperature and CO2 for Last 1,000 Years

Source of the above figures is:
http://blogs.edf.org/climate411/2007/06/29/human__cause-3/

Chapter 4; Growth in CO_2 concentration in our atmosphere from 1958 to present (also known as a Keeling curve). Note the saw-tooth nature of this curve – due to the different rates of plant growth and CO_2 uptake during the seasons of each year.

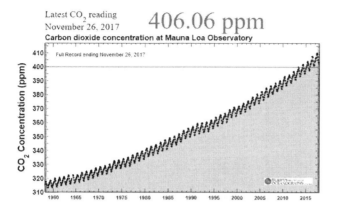

The above figure comes from: https://scripps.ucsd.edu/programs/keelingcurve/wp-content/plugins/sio-bluemoon/graphs/mlo_full_record.pdf

Chapter 20, Greenhouse gas emissions in the United States:

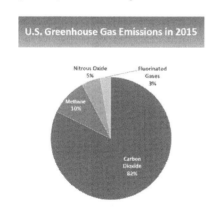

The above figure comes from: https://www.epa.gov/ghgemissions/overview-greenhouse-gases

Chapter 20. Side-by-side photos of glaciers.

People say that a picture is worth 1,000 words. Take a look at these two photographs of the Muir Glacier located in southeastern Alaska taken from the same spot, but 63 years apart.

(a) 1941 photo of Muir Glacier, Alaska   (b) 2004 photo taken from same spot

Source of above photos is Climate Science Special Report; Fourth National Climate Assessment   Available online from: https://science2017.globalchange.gov/

Here is another side-by-side comparison, from Glacier National Park, Montana, 92 years apart.

Figure 2. Shepard Glacier, Glacier National Park, MT, 1913 and 2005

1913   2005

SOURCE: U.S. Geological Survey Repeat Photography Project, http://nrmsc.uegs.gov/repeatphoto.

Author's Note

I wrote the first draft of this book in 1991 (unfortunately, never published). Way back in 1991, based on what scientists were saying then about the possible weather effects of Global Climate Change (GCC), I predicted a massive hurricane (Cleopatra) that turned out to be eerily similar to Katrina (2005). The devastating hurricanes of 2017 – Harvey, Irma, and Marie, and the drought and fires in California and other western states prompted me to go back and clean up the book and publish it. The book is filled with factual information, but is presented as a fast-moving fictional tale that will keep you reading, and leave you wanting to know more about GCC, and hopefully wanting to do something about it.

In the last few decades, thousands of reputable scientists have become convinced that the inevitable result will be an overall warming of the earth. A few degrees increase in the average temperature of the earth may not sound like much, but a one degree increase in temperature represents an enormous increase of the total energy content of the atmosphere and oceans. It is already showing up as disruptions in the earth's weather (extreme temperatures, droughts, storms, rainfall patterns), severe damage to ecosystems, a rising sea level, and unusual weather events that are happening more often.

In the 1980s and 1990s, discussions of the greenhouse effect moved from the scientific arena to the political. Governments studied the problem, but did not take steps to solve it. Why not? Simply because any significant action steps would hurt industries or even entire economies in the short run, while the benefits are long term. Pressure by lobbyists and certain politicians prevented any effective action by governments. Only if enough people suffer actual damages, and if it can be proved that the greenhouse effect is responsible, will action be taken.

In the early years of this century, progress was being made to prove GCC was occurring. The Intergovernmental Panel on Climate Change (IPCC) was publishing good science from researchers around the world that reported evidence of the effects of climate change, and linked those effects to excessive emissions of greenhouse gasses. But then in 2009, a computer hack of some emails between people working within the IPCC appeared to show that some individuals were biased in their outlook and actions, and that revelation (dubbed "Climategate") tainted the results and conclusions of the IPCC. Even though thousands of scientists from many countries, after reviewing the emails, maintained that the science was sound and the conclusions were still correct, many people lost faith in the IPCC. A huge political uproar took place, and politicians (especially one U.S. Senator who was a long-time climate change denier) made political "hay" over this event. The Senate blocked the U.S. from signing any climate treaties, so the Obama administration tried to accomplish emissions reduction through the EPA regulatory process. During the Trump administration, actions were taken to reverse those regulations.

I am convinced that the IPCC was and still is correct. The earth is experiencing rapid warming and climate change. The fundamental science behind this heat retention in by these gases is correct. The anecdotal evidence of extreme weather is overwhelming. Consider hurricanes Katrina (2005), Sandy (2012), Harvey (2017), Irma (2017) and Maria (2017). Consider the 2011 super outbreak of tornados that roared through Alabama, Mississippi, Arkansas, Georgia, Tennessee, and Virginia. Consider the extreme drought in Texas (2010-2013). Consider the extreme drought in California (2012-2016), followed by extreme flooding in many parts of the state (early 2017), followed by huge destructive fires in the (again dry) Napa and Sonoma Valley regions (October 2017), and then the huge fires in the Los Angeles area fueled by the vicious dry Santa Ana winds (December 2017). All that excess energy that is building in our atmosphere and our oceans has to be released somehow.

In November of 2017, the United States government issued a massive climate science report that stated that climate change was real, and that humans were causing it. This, of course, contradicts the statements of the President, and other high government officials, but the report was issued nevertheless because it was backed up by sound, credible, climate science and many, many real-world observations. In that same year, as reported in numerous newspapers, public opinion shifted toward the belief that the scientists were right – that GCC was occurring, and that humans were causing it.

Nevertheless, it is extremely hard to prove such a thing beyond a shadow of a doubt. By the time we get irrefutable evidence, it may be too late to solve the problem. Our world is massive and change takes time. I liken our current situation to the Titanic when it spotted the iceberg and tried to change course; but since the ship was so big, it could not make the turn in time.

Our children and grandchildren must live with the world we are creating, and they may not like it very much. Way back in 1983, the U.S. Environmental Protection Agency said as much in a report to Congress. Two of the adaptive strategies EPA suggested was (1) building dikes around our major coastal cities or (2) abandoning them! I quote from the conclusions of that report:

> Based on the evidence marshalled to date, some warming of the lower atmosphere...from...greenhouse gases seems inevitable. The only questions remaining are how large the temperature rise will be and how fast it will occur. These questions are critical.

> ...our findings call for an expeditious response. A 2°C increase in temperature by (or perhaps well before) the middle of the next century

leaves us only a few decades to plan for and cope with a change in habitability in many geographic regions. Changes by the end of the 21st century could be catastrophic taken in context of today's world.

...it is extremely unlikely that substantial actions to reduce CO_2 emissions would be taken unilaterally. Adaptive strategies undertaken by individual countries appear to be a better bet.

Many authors have declared that two of the most likely outcomes of GCC are longer and more frequent droughts in the U.S. farm belt, and more severe and more frequent hurricanes in the Atlantic and Gulf coastal states. But I guess we should just get used to the idea. After all, the U.S. government long ago told us to "undertake adaptive strategies," that is to start preparing now to live in a hotter (and likely more hostile) world.

I believe that people want to do something to help slow down or stop GCC. It is impossible to do so without world-wide cooperation, but fortunately many countries around the world are starting to take steps, even without U.S. leadership. Many U.S. states and cities are taking actions on their own. But until we can convince our national leaders to take firm actions, and until we show the world that we are serious, we are letting precious time slip away from us.

The old expression, "think globally, act locally" still applies. Individuals can make a difference. First and foremost, conserve energy. Every kilowatt-hour (kwh) of electricity you don't use at home saves the burning of three kwh worth of fossil fuel in a power plant. Buy LED energy-saving light bulbs, turn off lights when you leave a room, set your thermostat higher in summer and lower in winter. Carpool or use a bike or take the bus. Buy a hybrid car or an electric car. Support wind, solar, and even nuclear power. And keep pushing your elected officials to do more to cut greenhouse gas emissions and embrace renewable energy!

C. David Cooper, December 21, 2017

Made in the USA
Lexington, KY
02 January 2018